EVA DOLAN

Eva Dolan is an Essex-based copywriter and intermittently successful poker player. *After You Die* is the third book in her critically acclaimed DI Zigic and DS Ferreira series, the first of which, *Long Way Home*, was published in 2014 and the follow-up, *Tell No Tales*, in 2015.

ALSO BY EVA DOLAN

Long Way Home

Tell No Tales

EVA DOLAN

After You Die

VINTAGE

1 3 5 7 9 10 8 6 4 2

Vintage
20 Vauxhall Bridge Road,
London SW1V 2SA

Vintage is part of the Penguin Random House
group of companies whose addresses can be found at
global.penguinrandomhouse.com

First published in Vintage in 2016
First published in Great Britain in 2016 by Harvill Secker

A CIP catalogue record for this book is available from the British Library

ISBN 9781784701765

Printed and bound by Clays Ltd, St Ives plc

Penguin Random House is committed to a sustainable future
for our business, our readers and our planet. This book is made
from Forest Stewardship Council® certified paper.

Prologue

'I'm not scared.'

Nathan repeated it under his breath as he walked, focused on the words, using them to block out all the worse ones buzzing around in his head. The loud and terrifying ones which wouldn't leave him, the begging and pleading and swearing.

He heard the scream, the sound of her body falling to the floor.

'I'm not scared.'

A car passed him in a surge of engine roar and aggressive bass, moving so fast that its slipstream tugged at his clothes. He looked up from his feet, watched it disappear as the road dipped, brake lights blinking.

It would be easy to walk out in front of the next vehicle that came. Wait for one of the big lorries that thundered along this road, heading down to the A1. He'd seen it happen on TV. A bang and everything went black.

'I'm not scared.'

But he was. Too scared to do that, even though he knew it would mean an end to the voices and the danger. Even though everyone would be safe if he was gone.

Nathan kept walking along the hard shoulder, the grass bank rising steeply to the left, as high as a house, blocking out the final flare of the evening sun, casting a shadow deep enough to raise goosebumps on his bare arms and hide the bloodstains on his camo-print trainers.

A car slowed as it approached him and he tensed but kept moving, fighting the urge to turn, knowing not to make eye contact with the driver. If he did that there would be no escaping. They'd see what was wrong with him and then he'd never get away.

The window opened as the car drew up next to him, something rattling under the bonnet, and a woman's voice asked:

'Are you alright?'

He sneaked a glance out of the corner of his eye; a small red car, an old woman, grey-haired and posh-looking, with a fluffy white dog on the passenger seat.

'Does your mother know you're out?' she asked.

The scream again, in his head.

'I'm on me way home,' he said.

It was a stupid lie. There were no houses here. Nothing but the road cutting between the steep and tangled banks, then the service station on the side of the A1 and the industrial estate beyond that.

'You shouldn't be out here on your own at this time of night,' she said. 'It isn't safe for a boy your age.'

'I'm okay.'

'Why don't I take you home?' she said. 'I'm sure your mother must be worried sick about you.'

He shook his head, felt his throat tightening, closing up around the words he barely managed to force out. 'I live there.'

'Where?'

He pointed across the road towards a gated farm track, still avoiding her eyes. 'Down there.'

'Alright. Well, be careful crossing the road, they drive like maniacs along here.'

She pulled away, but slowly and he realised she wasn't going to leave while he was walking along the hard shoulder. She was probably already taking her mobile out, thinking about calling the police, telling them about the boy out walking alone in the middle of nowhere on a Saturday evening. Children didn't do that here.

Nathan ran across the road, towards the metal gate, and when he saw it was padlocked climbed over it, scratching his arm on a branch from the hedge. There was a farmhouse ahead of him, barns and tractors, barking dogs.

He began to walk towards it, slow, shuffling steps, and when he'd walked far enough turned and double-backed, peeped around the hedge to check that the woman had gone.

He waited, hands shaking, for a few long minutes, in case she double-backed as well, and when he couldn't wait any longer climbed over the gate again and started on towards the service station.

There was just enough light from the setting sun to make out where he was going – no street lights here – and he felt safer in the gloom, his tear-stained face and the blood on his trainers hidden.

'I'm not scared.'

He tried not to think. He knew he couldn't let the fear overwhelm him again.

The service station spread out in front of him, lit up bright and cheerful, people everywhere, coming out of the fast-food places and the hotel, couples and families, men and women on their way home. They would be like the lady in the car, asking questions, wanting to help him. The wrong kind of help.

Nathan made his way to the petrol station, skirting the main forecourt, and headed to the area where the lorries filled up, looking for one heading in the direction he needed to go. There were a few parked up for the night nearby and he thought it would be easy to cut a slit in the fabric side of one and slip inside, curl up and wait for morning.

Most of them had foreign writing on them, foreign number plates. He hadn't planned for that. One was from Birmingham, a bakery. Not where he wanted to go but on the way.

As he turned the knife handle around in his pocket, willing himself to make the cut, a heavy hand came down on his shoulder and he flinched away, just managed to stop himself bringing the knife out.

'What you doin', son?' The man was smiling and when Nathan didn't answer, he cocked his head. 'You speak English?'

'Yeah.'

'Thought you was a stowaway or something.'

'No.'

'What you doing hanging around here then? Waiting for your dad?'

'I need a lift.'

The man looked him up and down and Nathan's fingers tightened around the knife in his pocket, the perforated steel sticky against his skin. 'Bit young to be hitch-hiking, aren't you?'

'I'm sixteen,' Nathan said, adding five years on, praying the man would believe him.

He nodded. 'And not from round this way, I reckon?'

'No.'

The man pressed his key fob and the bakery lorry's lights flashed as the doors unlocked. 'You running away from home?'

'I'm trying to get home,' Nathan said.

'Where's that?'

'Manchester.'

'You don't sound Manc.'

'I am.'

The man sighed as he opened the driver's-side door, paused with one foot on the step. 'Alright then, young'un. Let's get you home before you get yourself in trouble.'

Nathan walked around the lorry and found the passenger's-side door open already, the man leaning across the seat, holding out his hand.

'You get up alright on your own?'

Nathan hauled himself up and into the cab, smelling the bread in the back, but something else too, sharp and sour.

They'd been driving for a few minutes before the man spoke.

'You're not really sixteen, are you?'

'I am.'

'I'd say you're more like eleven or twelve.'

Nathan gripped the hand rest. 'I'm small for me age.'

'Don't worry, son, I'm not going to tell anyone.' The man laughed and something about the sound put a cold lump in Nathan's stomach. 'It'll be our little secret.'

Through the grimy window he watched fields smear by, the tops of houses gone in seconds, the village he'd left falling away behind them, so quickly that he wanted to shout for the man to stop, turn around, take him home. But it wasn't his home, never had been and never could be. Not now.

'I'm not scared.'

SUNDAY

I

'I'm not sure now,' Anna said, standing in the doorway of the box room, one hand cupped under the bump showing through her tunic. 'It's very pink.'

Zigic stopped painting and stepped back from the wall, the ghosts of four darker shades still visible through the first coat of paint he'd put on, ragged patches half a metre square.

'You liked it an hour ago,' he said.

'The light was different then.'

He suppressed a sigh of irritation.

They'd spent most of Saturday looking at colour charts, Anna placing them against the Cath Kidston fabric she'd already picked out for the curtains and the very specific ivory of the new cot he didn't want to put together yet, sure they were tempting fate by getting the nursery ready when she was only six months gone. He told her to choose whatever colour she wanted, he was just the muscle, and after an exhaustive decision-making process they arrived at this one – Middleton Pink.

'It didn't look this bright in the tin,' she said.

'Paint always dries lighter.'

'The first coat's dry.' She touched her hand to the wall, showed him her palm. 'Look, completely dry.'

Zigic dropped the sheepskin roller into the tray, spattering paint across the dust sheets which still bore traces of the emulsion they'd used to decorate the nursery for Stefan in their old house. Five years ago now and seeing the spots and arcs of sky blue he felt a plunging sadness about how quickly the time had passed. He could still remember the red checked shirt Anna wore, knotted above her cumbersome stomach as she knelt down to do the skirting boards, Milan 'helping' her with a tiny brush. Didn't remember the decor choices being such a nightmare then.

This was different though.

This was the little girl Anna had always wanted.

'Do you want to change it?' he asked.

She made a non-committal murmur, eyes moving around the room.

'I don't mind redoing it,' he said. 'But let's decide now while it's early enough to go out and buy something else, okay? I might not have another weekend off in a while.'

Anna grimaced. 'I'm just not sure.'

'Think about it for a minute.' He kissed her cheek as he walked past, heading for the door. 'I'm going to have a beer. This manual labour stuff is harder than it looks.'

Downstairs the boys were playing on their Wii, the curtains in the living room drawn against the late sunshine battering the back of the house. They leapt about, on and off the sofa, flinging their arms around wildly, raising more racket than should have been possible for two small children, although most of it was coming from Stefan, who was providing his own sound effects every time he struck a ball.

Zigic closed the door on them and went into the kitchen.

A chicken was simmering in a pot on the hob, the smell of salty, herby stock filling the room, ready for the risotto Anna would make later. It was too hot for it really. Too hot to eat anything. Definitely too hot to be painting a small, south-facing room where even with the window wide open there was no cooling breeze.

The weather had been stifling for weeks, still and relentlessly sunny, a combination which seemed to bring out the worst in people. Encouraged reckless driving and frayed tempers, started people drinking earlier and kept them at it till later at night. Like their colleagues in CID, the Hate Crimes department had experienced a spike in activity as the summer drew on into early September; more senseless violence, more harassment. A recent influx of Roma into Peterborough had sparked a series of scuffles on the streets around New England, the rest of the residents forgetting their old rivalries to turn on the newcomers as one.

Thankfully the situation was settling down though. They'd charged three of the most vocal instigators with a range of offences which would see them serve a few months in prison, enough to stop the momentum from building any further, he hoped.

Zigic took a bottle of Peroni from the fridge and snapped the top off, stood in the open door letting the chill blast him while he drank, wondering if having a second and putting himself over the drink-driving limit might save him from another expedition to B&Q. Knowing it probably wouldn't he closed the fridge again, smiled automatically at the photo of his new daughter pinned to the door with a heart-shaped magnet.

His child. Curled up. Sleeping. Waiting.

Two weeks ago he'd ducked out of work to take Anna to the hospital, sat holding her hand while the nurse explained what they were looking at, an image he had seen twice before but which still provoked a sense of awe.

When the nurse asked if they wanted to know the sex of the baby Anna said:

'I already know. It's a girl.'

As if she'd managed to will it. The nurse smiled, took it in her stride, well used to the fervent certainty of expectant mothers, Zigic guessed.

Anna came into the kitchen as he was opening another Peroni.

'I can't decide,' she said. 'Maybe we should get the second coat on and look at it again.'

'"We" should do that?'

'I'll make it worth your while.' She took his beer from him, held the bottle a few inches from her parted lips but didn't drink. 'What do you say?'

'Is that why the plumber didn't charge a call-out fee when the boiler broke down?'

She swore at him, laughing, and handed back his beer. 'Come on, Dushan, you'll be finished in an hour, then you don't have to do anything else up there for months.'

He flicked an eyebrow at her.

'Okay, weeks.'

'I'll remember you said that.'

An hour later he was still at it, the room close and fumy, the sounds of his neighbours' lazy Sunday afternoons wafting in through the open window, along with the smell of meat charring on a barbecue and freshly mown grass.

Three walls down, just the long blank one left to do and his arm was aching, the muscles across the back of his neck and shoulders tight. He stopped for a moment to stretch and looked at the squares of darker pink still stubbornly showing through the second coat of paint. He should have blanked them out before he started but thought he'd get away with it, despite the advice of the man in B&Q: 'Fail to prepare – prepare to fail.'

He abandoned the roller and started painting a strip of wall just above the taped-off skirting board, his right thigh complaining every time he shuffled forward to reach the next section. A gnawing pain centred on the spot where a two-inch carpenter's nail had been driven deep into the muscle, courtesy of a bomb vest strapped to a neo-Nazi ex-police-constable who'd decided he wouldn't be taken alive.

Seven months on, it was an old injury. That's how he thought of it, trying to contain the incident, and every physio he'd seen, as well as his GP and an acupuncturist, had all told him it was perfectly healed now, but still it twinged. Part of him believed it was psychological, a little stab of guilt for his failure to anticipate Christian Palmer's homicidal intentions, for failing to contain him, and mostly for failing to protect Ferreira.

The surgeon who treated her had removed three dozen tacks and nails from the backs of her legs, a payload which would have hit him full on, abdomen and groin, if her reflexes hadn't been so sharp. He imagined the pain he felt now multiplied thirty-six times and the guilt jabbed at him again.

She'd been off work for four months afterwards, fell out of contact with them all, holed up at home being nursed by her mother, an enforced absence he knew her well enough to realise must have been almost unbearable; went through several operations to treat damaged ligaments, extensive rehabilitation and weekly visits to a police-approved psychiatrist which had recently ended with him giving her a clean bill of health, freeing her from the desk where she'd been stationed across the summer on light duties.

Zigic was far from convinced that she was ready for a return to the front line.

As her senior officer he'd read the psychiatrist's report, saw her recovery develop in fits and starts, the usual process of anger and denial, the desire for revenge she would never get followed by a 'cathartic outburst' which was marked as a significant turning point.

Exactly what the man wanted from Ferreira.

Reading about the 'comfort she'd found in her faith' sealed it for Zigic. She was desperate to get back to work and had sold the psychiatrist a line. Given him just enough resistance to make the final, tearful acceptance of her situation seem real.

She hadn't accepted it. Wasn't ready. Wasn't *better*.

Superficially she was the same Mel who walked into the burnt-out shell of the Polish Ex-Servicemen's Club back in February, all mouth and unshakable instinct, but she was putting on a show for them. He saw the expression on her face when she thought no one was looking, the new hardness in her eyes.

Outside, a lawnmower started up and he inched forward into the corner of the box room, painting the final half-metre of wall above the skirting board, biting down on the pain in his thigh as he moved. At the last brushstroke he collapsed back onto the dust sheets, his hand coming down in the paint tray.

He swore loudly and wiped his palm clean on a rag.

Anna called his name from the hallway.

'I'm fine,' he shouted back. 'Just a spill.'

Her feet came up the stairs, slow and careful, and he was righting himself when she appeared in the doorway holding out his phone.

'Mel, for you.' She drew back her hand as he moved to take his mobile from her. 'If you arranged this to get out of decorating . . .'

She smiled but there was no humour in it. They both knew what phone calls on Sunday afternoons meant.

2

Ferreira sat on the bonnet of her car, parked at the mouth of a gated farm track opposite what remained of the house. It was one half of a pair of semi-detached cottages owned by the estate, like dozens of other properties around Elton village. 'Cottages' was too pretty a word, suggested stone walls and leaded windows and thatched roofs. These were ugly, squat houses, concrete tiled and shabby, with small single garages to the side and short front gardens, set at the northern edge of the village, cut off from their nearest neighbours by a cobble-walled village hall advertising the previous day's antiques fair.

At least the house which remained was.

Twelve hours earlier, just after 1 a.m, its neighbour had been ripped open by a gas explosion which blew out its rear and side walls, sending debris flying into the field behind, leaving the facade precariously standing and badly cracked, the metal windows forced open by the blast, twisted in their frames, shattered glass sparkling in the parched front lawn and across the road, which was still closed to traffic.

Fire investigators were inside now, making the reinforcements necessary for them to search the site. The early thinking was a slow build-up of gas from the hob, which hadn't been turned off fully. No immediate signs of foul play but they were keeping an open mind. Too many 'accidents' looked that way to begin with and the absence of the owner was a cause for suspicion.

The attached house – the one Ferreira had visited late last year – was cordoned off behind police tape. An entirely separate crime scene.

The pathologist had given her his preliminary thoughts to pass on to Zigic, all very straightforward, he said, then went home to enjoy the last few hours of his weekend, promising he would make a slot for them tomorrow afternoon – *Not that I expect to find anything interesting*.

Absently she reached down to scratch her calf. The scars didn't itch any more. This was something different. Something she didn't even want to think about. The doctor had warned her that there was other material in her legs which they hadn't been able to reach. Assured her not to worry, it would migrate to the surface eventually, then he could deal with it.

She wished everything that irritated her could be cut out so easily.

Zigic's car turned onto the Oundle road and he honked his horn at her before pulling into the car park of the village hall, where most of the other police vehicles were. Earlier there had been a few onlookers too, but they had moved on quickly, once they realised no one was going to give them the gossip they were so desperate to hear.

It said a lot about the place that a gas explosion and a police presence had provoked so little interest. Not one of those close-knit, incestuous English villages, Ferreira thought. It was too affluent, full of commuters who probably didn't know their neighbours' names or care if they lived or died.

Problematic from an investigative perspective but she could understand the appeal. After suffering months stuck in her parents' pub, enjoying a dubious celebrity among the Portuguese community they served, constantly questioned about what had happened and how she felt and whether she would return to work, anonymity seemed like a luxury worth paying Elton's overinflated property prices for.

She met Zigic at the cordon. He'd put on something approaching work clothes, jeans and dark shirt, but there were flecks of light pink paint in his hair and she noticed more of it dried on his forearm and hand when he gestured towards the ruptured house.

'At least that one's not ours.'

'You might wish it was when you see what we've got.'

He stopped at the chaos in the driveway, chunks of masonry lying here and there, pieces of plasterboard covered in scorched patches of patterned wallpaper.

'I'm guessing it's pretty messy in there,' he said.

Ferreira followed his gaze to the exposed interior, the staircase and chimney stack basically intact, everything else churned up, ripped up and mangled, as if a tornado had dropped down through the roof and spun the house around. That wasn't their concern.

The hole punched through the dividing wall into the neighbouring kitchen was.

'Wait until you see it from the other side,' she said.

'How bad?'

'The fire was put out fast,' Ferreira said. 'So there's that to be thankful for. We could have lost everything.'

'Where's the owner?'

'Don't know yet. Away, somewhere.'

'We need to find them. First priority.' He slowed as they passed a corroded blue skip parked in front of the house, a few off-cuts of plasterboard sitting on top, brick rubble underneath. 'What's this about?'

'Our house has got the builders in,' Ferreira said. 'They're converting the garage and linking it up.'

Zigic went along the driveway ahead of her, peered in through the window newly cut into the brickwork. She'd done the same, found a bare room divided from the main part of the house with thick plastic sheeting hung like a curtain.

They went back to the scientific support van, pulled on bodysuits and foot protectors before they could go inside. The scene was already contaminated, had been entered previously by the attending fire crew, anxious to evacuate the occupants, then the uniformed officers they called to deal with what they discovered, but the rules had to be followed.

Zigic paused at the door.

'Are you okay?'

'I've been in already,' Ferreira said, ignoring what he was getting at; her first case back on full duties and it was an explosion, the scorched odour lingering, the memories she would deny it provoked if he pushed her. 'I'm fine.'

He opened the door and immediately recoiled from the smell, gathered himself before he went in, Ferreira following, breathing through her mouth, shallow breaths, trying not to take too much smoky air into her lungs.

Dawn Prentice's body was laid out in the middle of the kitchen where she'd fallen, one leg folded under her, arms flung wide; bloated from lying undiscovered in the relentless summer heat, skin blistered and discoloured, but the stab wounds in her chest still clearly visible.

The pool of blood around her was long set, muted by the coating of debris. Dried smears either side of her body suggested her attacker had stood or kneeled astride her hips, struggling to keep their footing on the slick floor. Hopefully slipping and putting out a hand to stop them falling.

There was no sign of that though. Areas of interest were marked out, colour coded and numbered, but nothing that looked like usable prints.

Zigic took one small step towards the body.

'Don't come any closer,' Kate Jenkins said, from behind her face mask. 'We've had enough big, clumsy feet in here already.'

She straightened up from bagging Dawn's left hand, preserving what, if anything, was under her fingernails.

'How bad is it?' he asked.

'Worse than it looks. If you can believe that.' She gestured to the blood, a few inches away from Zigic's feet. 'The grunts weren't careful when they came in, we've got partials, police-issue boots, fire-issue.'

'And the good news?'

Jenkins pulled her mask down to her chin, frustration written clear on her face. 'Thin on the ground, I'm afraid.'

'Murder weapon?'

'No sign of it,' she said. 'But there are a couple of knives missing from the block. Might be in with the washing-up – she wasn't exactly a domestic goddess.' She stopped him as he went to speak. 'It's my next job.'

Ferreira looked at the sink, full of water, a few plates and wooden handles poking up through the surface. The worktop beside it was scattered with crockery and she imagined the moment the explosion jabbed through the wall, sending a pile of dirty dishes flying, how they would have splintered, slivers of cheap whiteware shooting in all directions.

Her calf started to itch again and she fought the urge to reach down and scratch it.

'Mel, time of death?' Zigic asked, his tone suggesting it wasn't the first time he'd said it.

'No less than forty-eight hours,' she said quickly. 'He wouldn't commit to anything more precise before the PM.'

She filled him in on the basics from the pathologist; ten distinct wounds to the chest – frenzied – some quite shallow, the angles varied, one to the throat, a direct hit on her windpipe, just a nick but enough to kill her. Defence wounds on her hands but they hadn't slowed down her killer.

'Any signs of forced entry?'

'Fire crew found the back door closed but unlocked. After they'd kicked the front door in. So she either let them in or they had a key.'

'Or she kept the back door unlocked.'

'Not very security-conscious of her.'

'Not everyone thinks like a copper.'

Zigic didn't look up from the body, brows knitted together above his mask. 'Is there a boyfriend?'

'Dawn didn't mention one when I talked to her,' Ferreira said.

'What about the daughter?'

'I seriously doubt it.'

As she spoke the floor overhead creaked and all eyes followed the noise.

'You need to change before you go up,' Jenkins told them.

They went out onto the driveway again, sucked down lungfuls of fresh air. In the rear garden two more suited figures were making a fingertip search of the grass, a challenging job when there was so much rubbish out there from the neighbouring house and the building work in progress.

Ferreira stripped out of her suit and pulled on another one, aware of Zigic watching her, something he was doing more often now that she'd returned to work.

'How far did you get with this?' he asked, as they headed for the front door, taking a clean route back into the house.

'I did a preliminary interview. She didn't have any idea who was responsible. There was no real evidence we could use.'

'You told her to start a log, though?'

'Yeah. I made a couple of follow-up calls but she seemed to lose interest in the whole thing.'

Zigic nodded at the PC stationed on the long, shallow ramp which led up to the front door and he let them inside.

'That's common with harassment. They want you to come in and fix the problem straight away, then when they find out you can't they get dejected.'

'It was minor stuff,' Ferreira said, thinking back to the conversation, how unaffected Dawn Prentice was, more irritated than scared. 'There was nothing to suggest it would escalate to this.'

Zigic paused at the bottom of the burgundy-carpeted stairs. 'It isn't your fault, Mel. These cases are unpredictable.'

'Yeah, I know that, thanks.'

She went up ahead of him, pushing away the annoyance, eyes on the family photos hung on the wall, ones going back to before Holly's birth, people who must have been Dawn's parents and grandparents, bleached images, old Polaroids in frames the wrong shape for them, beach holidays and birthday parties, Holly growing up in her school photos as the stairs rose, until she hit her early teens and they stopped abruptly, the last one hanging above the stairlift Dawn had used to move her severely disabled daughter.

On the landing the crime-scene photographer was packing away his equipment, wiping each piece with a soft cloth before it went back into the case, and he looked up briefly as they approached, inched over so they could squeeze around him.

'Don't touch anything in there. We're not done yet.'

This room was exactly as Ferreira remembered it. Undisturbed by the blast. Nothing but the dust floating in the air to suggest what had happened. An ordinary teenage girl's bedroom, painted sunflower yellow, posters on the walls and a desk with a closed laptop on it. Unremarkable except for the wheelchair in the corner and the hospital bed with raised bars which was tucked under the window, placed so Holly could see the sky and feel the sun on her skin as she lay, unable to move, hour after hour, day after day.

She was still there, propped up in a sitting position, a tiny, half-wasted figure in light cotton pyjamas covered with soaring birds. Her hands were in her lap, a purple iPod by her fingertips, earphones still in place. Holly had a limited range of movement after the accident, couldn't raise her arms, just use her hands enough to manipulate whatever devices Dawn gave her.

Zigic stood over her, one fist pressed to his mouth.

'She hasn't been dead as long as her mother.'

'No,' Ferreira said. 'Twelve hours, not much more.'

'Because of the gas leak?'

'He doesn't think so. Again – wouldn't commit. But he thinks it'll turn out to be natural causes.'

'This isn't natural,' Zigic said.

Neither of them spoke for a few minutes, as he worked through the implications and Ferreira waited, knowing he was picturing the same sequence of events she'd worked through as she waited for the pathologist to arrive.

'There's no sign of violence,' he said. 'Could she talk?'

'Yes.'

'So she could have raised the alarm?'

'If there was anyone to hear her, yes.'

Ferreira looked at the iPod, one of the few connections Holly had to her old life, and wished it was a phone in her hand, or her laptop, something that would have allowed her to call for help.

Instead she'd been forced to lie there, alone, scared, wondering where her mother was, why the house was so quiet, wondering what the smell rising up from the kitchen was.

Did she think Dawn had abandoned her?

Or did she hear everything? Know exactly what had happened and realise that she was absolutely alone and helpless?

'How did she get like this?' Zigic asked quietly.

'Rock-climbing accident. Holly's rope wasn't tied off properly, she fell, broke her back. Her spinal cord was completely severed. That was about two years ago.'

He moved away from the bed, eyes pinkish above his mask, and went over to a pine shelving unit where Holly's trophies were lined up. Cups for cross-country running and windsurfing, junior championships, county-level competitions. Medals for netball and hockey. In the team photographs she was always front and centre, dark hair pulled into a high ponytail, smiling triumphantly, a short but powerfully built young woman; a natural athlete.

Two years' incapacitation had whittled her away to a pale and shrunken version of herself.

'Was she having physio?'

'Yeah, once a week. Dawn said it was helping.'

'How did she seem?' Zigic asked. 'Holly? Was she coping?'

Ferreira shrugged. She'd barely spoken to her at the time. Came up and poked her head around the door, felt a clenching discomfort when she saw the drip and the catheter, said 'hello' and all but bolted out of the room again.

It was a moment of selfishness she hated herself for now.

If she'd put aside her awkwardness and actually talked to the girl would things have gone differently? It was easy to dismiss Dawn's complaints because she didn't seem bothered by what was happening. Would Holly's version of events have been more compelling? Stirred Ferreira's sympathies enough to drive the investigation on?

A scenes-of-crime officer was hovering in the doorway, waiting for them to take the hint and leave.

They took it.

3

Zigic waited at the bar while Ferreira went out into the Black Horse's beer garden, a ten-pound note clutched in his hand, listening absent-mindedly to the conversations going on around him; two couples, already drunk, talking about a shared holiday, a small group of middle-aged men at a nearby table discussing some football match. Quieter, underneath the carefree chatter, he caught a woman regaling her lunch companion with the moment she heard an almighty bang and thought a plane had come down in the village.

He turned slightly, saw her sitting in the front window, head bent close to another woman who might have been her mother, white haired and frail, but neatly put together, paying scant attention to the story as she picked at her cheesecake.

Right now it was just a shocking accident with no fatalities, but the uniforms arrived while he and Ferreira were in the house and he deployed them in three teams to canvass the village, wanting to make an early start on the door-to-door, catch people while they were at home, no excuses not to take the necessary few minutes to answer questions.

Within the hour news would start to filter out. Two deaths. Unthinkably brutal. Here, of all places.

When Ferreira first gave him the address on the phone he thought he'd misheard her. It was so far away from their usual territory, socially if not geographically, the last place he expected to find a hate-crime report filed from. And it was a naive assumption for a detective, he knew that, but Elton seemed too comfortable and moneyed to be a breeding ground for aggressive prejudice.

Perhaps that was why Ferreira hadn't pursued it.

'What're you having?' The barmaid waited with her hands on her hips.

He ordered two Cokes, wanting something more astringent to wash the taste of the crime scene off his tongue but aware that the day wasn't over yet, even if the constraints on overtime meant the real work wouldn't begin until tomorrow morning.

'Did you see?' she asked, nodding away to the north end of the village. 'That explosion? Crazy. My mate reckoned he heard it all the way over in Oundle. That'll be five-twenty.'

'You know who lives there?' Zigic asked, handing her the tenner.

'Yeah.'

She took her time scooping his change out of the till and dropped it into his palm already looking for her next customer, only to find there wasn't one.

'They weren't home when it happened,' Zigic said. He showed her his warrant card and it softened her expression but not very much. 'We need to talk to them, let them know the situation so they can make arrangements.'

'Was it an accident?'

'We believe so.'

She still looked dubious but she slipped her mobile from the pocket of her black tabard. 'Luke – he did our website when we had the refit.'

'Surname?'

'Gibson.' She gave Zigic the number and he keyed it into his phone. 'He's a nice guy. He wouldn't have done something like that on purpose.'

Zigic thanked her for her help and went out through the bustling dining room into the beer garden, a north-facing terrace bordered by a high stone wall and wallowing in shadows deep enough to have driven the afternoon trade inside. Ferreira had claimed the table furthest from the door and he was glad they wouldn't have an audience for their conversation.

'Is there anything in that?' she asked, as he put down her drink.

'No, thought we'd be better keeping clear heads.'

'It's going to take way more than a shot of rum to drive that lot out of my head.'

He sipped his Coke, resisted the urge to ask if she was okay. A year ago it would have been a flippant comment, now he was looking for a buried cry for help in it.

'Holly must have heard everything,' Ferreira said. 'Can you imagine what that must have felt like? She would have heard her mother getting murdered, then she had to lay there knowing she couldn't do anything about it. For days.'

'Didn't Dawn have people coming in to help with her?'

'A nurse, yeah. Not sure if she came in every day though.'

'Still, we're talking, what, two days with nobody visiting the house or coming to check up on them.'

'She seemed isolated when I talked to her. It was just a feeling I got, but living like that, having to be a twenty-four/seven carer . . . people stop visiting, I guess. They don't want to keep listening to the same old complaints, do they?' Ferreira started rolling a cigarette, one butt already in the ashtray. 'I don't know how she coped with it.'

'You look after your kids, no matter what,' Zigic said. 'That's the deal when you have them.'

Ferreira kept shredding tobacco, more than she needed. 'Yeah, but you're signing up for eighteen years, maybe a couple more, not the whole of their life.'

She didn't understand and she probably never would.

'What about the father?'

'They're separated. Divorce was in progress when I spoke to her.'

'Acrimonious?'

'Not according to her.'

'You think he might have been behind the harassment?'

She sealed her cigarette. 'He lives in the village, so he's near enough to make a nuisance of himself if he wants to. Dawn didn't accuse him, though, and most dumped women are pretty quick to put the finger on their ex.'

'He definitely did the leaving?'

'Oh, yeah, Dawn was very clear on that.' She lit up. 'He had a total breakdown when Holly got injured, fucked up his business, went completely off the rails. Dawn reckoned it must have been going on for a while before that, though. The other woman took him in. She owns that boarding kennel down near the green.'

Zigic knew the place. It was less than five minutes' walk from Dawn's home, straight through the centre of the village. Not a good route to take if you were covered in blood but the street lights in Elton were few and far between and by early evening the place was silent.

They didn't have a time of death yet but he saw this as a crime committed under the cover of darkness, couldn't imagine it going down any other way. Not when it had remained unreported for days.

'Tell me about the harassment,' he said.

She leaned forward in the black rattan chair, hunched against eavesdroppers who weren't there. 'It started soon after Holly was moved home from hospital. Very minor stuff. Nuisance factor more than anything else – silent phone calls, bit of vandalism in the garden. Dawn ignored that – it's a nice area but you've got stupid kids here just like everywhere else.'

'Then what?'

'She got a modified people carrier to take Holly out in. It was on the drive for a day before the tyres were slashed.' Ferreira frowned. 'Someone sprayed the word "cripple" across the side of it. Which is why it got sent up to us, of course.'

They'd dealt with a few cases centred on prejudice against the disabled but nothing which had gone this far before. Taunts and threats, occasional broken windows.

Nobody could see Holly as a danger, though, surely.

'Did Dawn have any idea who might've been responsible?'

'No. She said she thought it could be someone pissed off because she was getting more support from the council than them.' Ferreira shrugged. 'I don't know, it sounded unlikely to me, but I suppose that kind of thing bothers some people. Say their benefits have got cut – bedroom tax kicking in, something like that – and there's her being given a brand-new Espace, getting a load of building work done. A sense of entitlement makes people do some pretty shitty things.'

He considered it for a moment. 'This shitty, though?'

'It feels personal, doesn't it?'

'I think so.'

Ferreira slapped her palm on the tabletop. 'I should have pushed her more. She just seemed so *comfortable* about it all. She said she only called to get a crime number for the car insurance, then I turned up and it was like she was really reaching for things to complain about because I'm sitting there with my notebook out and she didn't want to look like a time waster.'

'What about the follow-up calls?' he asked.

'She didn't want to talk. I tried three or four times but whenever I rang she insisted she was really busy with Holly. I didn't question it, she was obviously under pressure looking after her on her own.'

'She must have said something.'

A man came out of the pub, shouting into his mobile as he fumbled a packet of cigarettes from his shirt pocket with his free hand. He moved away to the other end of the terrace but Zigic saw that he kept watching them as he laughed and swore in a polished accent which didn't sound entirely natural.

'I honestly wondered if she was making it up to get her husband's attention.'

He snapped back to Ferreira. 'You know how rare that is?'

'Of course I know! And I know you're never supposed to think it, but her whole attitude was out of step with someone who's being harassed. She wasn't scared, she wasn't even angry – how can you not be angry?'

'Not everyone has it as their default response.'

Ferreira stubbed out her cigarette. 'You didn't see her.'

'No, I didn't, so I'm relying on your impressions now.'

'She wasn't taking it seriously. That's my impression. She was a knackered, sad woman – with plenty to be pissed off about in life and a lot to deal with, but whatever hassle she was getting didn't seem to be impacting on her.'

'Until now.'

'You're assuming it's all part of the same thing,' she said, a little defensively. 'Dawn had a life beyond caring for her daughter.'

'I thought you reckoned she was isolated.'

Ferreira scowled at him, annoyed at being caught out. 'You know as well as I do, dead woman, first port of call we should be looking for the boyfriend.'

Zigic drained his Coke. 'Or talking to the ex.'

4

Nene House was separated from the village by a hundred yards of dusty and rutted farm track, almost far enough away to stop the insistent barking of their canine residents floating across the grass fields and up to the neighbouring cottages, but not quite.

It was a rambling old place, surrounded by tin-roofed dairy sheds and tumbledown stables, a twin-gabled sprawl, half of it painted white with a sagging pantile roof, the rest stone built and recently re-thatched. It made for a disconcerting first impression, a sense of disjointedness which was only increased by the sight of the breeze-block kennels; the newest, most solid-looking buildings on the site.

As they approached the front door a woman emerged from the side of the house, heavy footed in her wellingtons, a shovel slung over her shoulder. A quintessential farmer's wife, blonde hair tied back from a scrubbed-clean and weathered face, small eyes in a permanent squint against the elements.

'Hi, I'm Sally, are you dropping off?' Her smile died when she noticed Zigic's warrant card. 'What's happened?'

'Mrs –'

'Ms Lange.'

'Ms Lange, I'm afraid there's been an incident,' Zigic said. 'A very serious one, with Dawn and Holly.'

She dropped the shovel. 'Are they okay?'

'I'm sorry, no, they were both killed.'

Her hands went to her face, blue eyes widening above her grubby fingertips and Zigic thought he caught the briefest, merest, hint of pleasure in them.

'I've got to tell Warren.'

She ran off towards the kennels, shouting his name, and Zigic saw a man look up from where he was squatting to scratch a spaniel's belly. He straightened and the dog got up too, followed him as he rushed towards the gate, into the yard.

'Sally, what is it?'

She blurted out the news and he crumpled back against the fence, opened and closed his mouth a couple of times but didn't speak. He didn't look capable of forming words, face slack, hand at his head. Sally stood close to him, rubbing his shoulders and whispering in his ear, words Zigic couldn't hear and which didn't seem to be helping.

Eventually she slipped an arm around his middle and drew him into the house, one faltering step at a time.

Again they followed, Ferreira throwing Zigic a questioning look across her shoulder: *Are we buying this routine?*

He wasn't sure yet.

The kitchen was large but gloomy, all dark wood units and heavy oak beams blackened by age and generations of cooking grease, a room which should have been homely but somehow wasn't, dominated by a pine table big enough to seat twelve.

Sally coaxed Warren into a chair and he immediately buried his face in his hands, while she sat next to him, her fingers curled tight around his arm.

Zigic let the silence develop, aware of how uncomfortable Sally was becoming, sitting with her eyes lowered but stealing glances at them through her lashes, shifting incrementally closer to Warren, shielding him.

Around them the house ticked and creaked and Zigic thought of its previous inhabitants laying their dead out on the kitchen table, all the bad news and trauma this room had witnessed. Hundreds of years of it soaked into the stone walls.

Finally the quiet got too much for Sally.

'Was it a car accident?'

'No,' Zigic said, watching them closely. 'Dawn was murdered.'

'What about Holly?'

'At present it looks likely to be natural causes.'

Warren shook his head, tears coming freely. 'This isn't real. This is mad.'

Zigic apologised, the words just as useless as they always were, too small, too commonplace to address the obliterating scale of a parent's grief. Warren doubled over and let out a deep, wailing cry that tugged Sally from her seat.

She went to him but he shrugged her off so forcefully that she stumbled into the Aga's drying rail. By the time she'd righted herself he was out of the door, moving at a sprint.

Zigic took her by the arm and steered her back to her chair, gesturing for Ferreira to go after him.

'Where's she going?' Sally tried to stand again but Zigic held a firm hand on her shoulder. 'He needs to be alone.'

'She'll be gentle.'

Sally looked unconvinced. Worried what he was going to say without her there to stop him. Did she think he was capable of murdering his estranged wife and daughter?

When he was sure she wouldn't bolt for the door he sat down again, watching her nibble at a ragged fingernail.

'He'll never get over this,' she said. 'He's only just started to deal with Holly's accident. He blamed himself. Stupidly. He was a serious climber and Holly always wanted to do what her dad did . . .' She shook herself out of it suddenly. 'Can I make you a cup of tea?'

'Thanks.'

Sally busied herself filling a black cast-iron kettle and set it on the range, talking about Holly's sporting exploits, how proud Warren was of her, how close they were. And Zigic didn't doubt the truth of it, but he heard a slight edge coming into her voice, something like bitterness, and he wondered if she'd been envious of their relationship.

'It must have been very difficult for Warren.'

Sally leaned against the range, hands tight around the rail. 'She wasn't the same girl any more. All the light went out of her.'

'Were you and her close?'

'I liked her.'

Not what he'd asked but it said plenty.

'It would have been different if she wasn't . . . how she was.' Sally grimaced. 'We never really had a chance to get to know each other. Dawn wouldn't let her come here, I couldn't go there. Obviously.'

'Dawn was protective of her?'

Sally laughed, a short, humourless snort. 'No. Not how you mean.'

'How then?'

'They were in the middle of a divorce and Dawn was dragging it out.' She plucked a tea towel from the drying rail and folded it up, clutched it to her chest. 'All Warren cared about was Holly, and Dawn knew that, so she used her against him. She could have come here. She could have moved in if she wanted to. We've got the space. I'd have been delighted to have her.'

It sounded rehearsed. Something she'd said to Warren a hundred times without meaning a word of it.

'But Dawn insisted this wasn't a "fit environment" and Warren was scared of challenging her because divorce courts always side with the mother. He knew how easy it would be for her to block access altogether.'

The kettle began to whistle and she whipped it off the heat, carried it over to a stretch of worktop under the kitchen window to fill up their cups, taking the opportunity to check the scene out there.

'Sounds like Dawn was pushing the pair of you,' he said.

Sally turned on him. 'Warren didn't kill her. She was being difficult but she had her own problems and Warren was fully aware of that. If anything, he felt sorry for her. We both did.' Sally plucked the teabags out of the water with her fingers, added them to a little pile of used ones on the draining board.

'These problems Dawn was having . . .'

'Vandalism, that kind of thing,' Sally said. Another quick look back through the window. 'Elton's a lovely village but there are some idiots of course and idiots tend to pick on the vulnerable.'

'Did Dawn talk about it much?'

'Well, not to me, obviously, but Warren knew about it. He encouraged her to call the police and get it down on record.' She straightened. 'Do you think that's who killed her?'

'It's very early for us to start making assumptions,' Zigic said. 'But we're looking into the possibility.'

The kitchen door opened with a bang and a gangly teenage boy walked in, headed straight to the fridge in the corner without looking up from his mobile, one white ear bud plugged in, the other trailing loose over his shoulder.

Sally followed him with her eyes, frowning at his lack of manners or maybe the slogan on his T-shirt, *The idiots are winning*.

'Benjamin, I think you should sit down.'

He popped the top of his Coke can, gave Zigic the barest glance. 'I'm good, thanks.'

'This is very serious.'

He didn't move. Didn't speak.

Zigic recognised the stance from his own teenage years. The boy had obviously done *something* wrong, now he was trying to figure out which bad thing they knew about and how much they knew and whether he could blame someone else.

'Sweetheart, there's something I've got to tell you,' Sally said. 'It's about Holly and Dawn.'

The boy relaxed visibly. 'Yeah, I saw, the house next door blew up. Fuck, you're not going to ask them to move in here, are you?'

'No.' Sally put her mug down but didn't make any further move towards him. 'They've been killed.'

‘Shit.’

‘Murdered,’ Zigic said.

‘Fuck.’

Sally frowned at him. ‘There’s no need for that sort of language.’

He shrugged, attention on Zigic now, curious rather than shocked, and Zigic wondered if his lack of emotional response was the usual adolescent attempt at worldliness or something darker.

‘Were they raped?’

‘Benjamin!’ Sally turned to Zigic and apologised. Back to her son. ‘What a disgusting thing to say.’

He held his hand up. ‘I was only asking. Jesus. It’s what happens, isn’t it? That’s why women usually get killed.’

Zigic stood slowly and walked over to the boy, seeing him fight the growing discomfort which backed him into the fridge door. He was used to saying what he wanted, Zigic guessed, weathering no worse punishment than his mother’s scandalised disappointment.

Up close he was definitely a boy, rather than a young man, fourteen or fifteen. Bad skin and sugar-stained teeth, glasses smeared with greasy fingerprints. The kind of boy who girls weren’t interested in, who started hating them for it young.

‘How old are you, Benjamin?’

‘Sixteen,’ he said, struggling to meet Zigic’s gaze.

‘The same as Holly. Did you go to the same school?’

He nodded.

‘Friends?’

‘We were in the same class.’

‘So, you weren’t friends then.’

‘We were. Sort of.’

Zigic nodded, let the boy see his contempt. ‘And when your sort-of-friend dies the first thing that comes to mind is whether she was raped.’

Sally was at his elbow now, one hand on her son's shoulder. 'Benjamin, I think you should apologise to the inspector. It was a very crass thing to say, wasn't it?'

'You don't have to apologise,' Zigic said, giving him a thin smile. 'There's nothing we appreciate more in a murder investigation than an honest response from potential suspects.'

He left the boy babbling apologies and denials, Sally telling him that she was ashamed to call him her son, that he treated everything like a game and this was serious.

Zigic didn't believe he was a credible suspect, not for a heartbeat – he was just another budding misogynist, devoid of empathy – but he'd wanted to shake some of the arrogance out of the boy.

He scanned the yard for Warren and Ferreira, saw no sign of them. Checked his phone, nothing from Jenkins yet but Anna had messaged him: *The paint looks fine now it's dry x*.

As he pocketed his phone Ferreira emerged from one of the breeze-block kennels, brushing down the back of her jeans, doing all the talking while Warren followed her, nodding along.

He'd stopped crying but his eyes were bloodshot and sunken, cheeks hollowed under his greying beard. Zigic could see Holly in him, though, the same athletic build, same long face and strong nose.

Ferreira left him with the dog and fell in step with Zigic as he started away from the house, along the farm track back towards the village, their feet kicking up puffs of dust. The sun was dropping, cutting low across the fields, throwing long shadows ahead of them.

'Did you get anything out of him?' Zigic asked.

'He was pretty honest about his feelings towards Dawn – the divorce was getting nasty, she wanted money, he insists he doesn't have any.'

'They look well enough off,' Zigic said.

'It's Sally's money. Dawn thought she should be getting maintenance, though.'

'From where?'

'Sally. Warren's living with her – off her, really – so Dawn considered that his income.' Ferreira slowed to roll a cigarette as she walked. 'It was never going to happen. So, annoying for them but no reason to murder her. And he'd hardly leave Holly to die like that, would he?'

He considered it as they crossed the lane, a couple of kids on skateboards cutting in front of them. Sally was too careful, the boy too cold and Zigic never trusted anyone who ran from bad news like Warren had. Not when murder was involved. It was the easiest way to avoid questioning, grab a few vital minutes to gather yourself and prepare a response.

After her six months away from work he didn't trust Ferreira's instincts as far as he usually would either.

'I'm not ruling him out.'

5

It started as a joke on her pretensions – Julia's Atelier – but now that's how she thought of the uninspiring double garage with the whitewashed walls and the concrete floor. Matthew bought her a little hand-painted sign that they hung on the door, a curly script, black on dove grey. Very Parisian, hinting at the beautiful things she made inside; the neglected old wardrobes and bureaux she'd scouted out among the classified ads and local auctions, pieces from house clearances nobody else wanted.

She lovingly fixed them up, filling and sanding, burning off ill-advised colour choices, recreating them as chic armoires in Farrow and Ball tones, adding crystal handles and pretty lining paper.

The last piece she'd finished was a reproduction dressing table painted celadon green and touched with gold here and there. She'd sold it last week and now it was waiting for the buyer to come and collect. In her home but no longer really hers.

There wouldn't be any more projects for a fair while now. Not with the baby due in a few months.

Her atelier had lost its magic, the lovely sense of potential which drew her in every morning, eager to see how the day before's finishes had dried or to try some clever new combination which had occurred to her just as she nodded off.

Now, when she walked in she saw a mess of abandoned pieces sitting sadly in the weak evening light, a simple elm plate rack which needed stripping, a bergère screen to be re-caned. On the workbench under the window, a Victorian nursing chair she'd stripped of its grubby velvet, the shapes already traced onto tissue-thin paper, ready for her to transfer them onto a blush-coloured linen. Reupholstery was out of the question, too much dust in the disintegrating hessian linings, too many spores in the horsehair.

She hadn't waited this long to get pregnant only to jeopardise the baby's health with sawdust or paint-stripper fumes or microscopic fibres from wadding.

She was forty-two years old, nature was already against them.

Julia stood at the workbench, her fingers straying to the pattern she'd cut, the paper crinkling as she folded the pieces and slipped them away into the drawer. She straightened her rulers and the sliver of chalk she used to mark up, retrieved a pencil which had fallen to the floor and put it back in the pot on the windowsill, an earthenware jar she'd found buried in the garden soon after they moved in. Its glaze was cracked and crazed but she still loved it.

People were too quick to throw things away for the slightest damage.

The tears welled suddenly, and hunched over the workbench she let them come, trying not to make a sound, aware that Caitlin was doing her homework in the kitchen next door.

She was supposed to be providing the girl with a safe, stable environment, not adding fresh misery to the complex baggage Caitlin carried around.

She was also supposed to be doing the same thing for Nathan, but he was gone, missing since Saturday afternoon. She would never forgive herself if anything happened to him. He was so young for his age, eleven going on eight, and so small. Completely defenceless against the kind of people who would prey on him out there.

For the hundredth time she imagined him bundled into the back of a van, tape over his mouth, hands and feet tied. She'd been doing this job long enough to know all of the terrible, inhuman things that could happen to young children. She'd cared for the survivors, seen the physical and psychological scars which never completely healed, tried to help them the only way she knew how, with patience and kindness.

Twenty-four hours ago he left the house and nobody had seen him since.

Now it was out of her hands and all she could do was try and hold herself together for the sake of her baby, keep things as normal as possible for Caitlin, and wait for the phone call telling her Nathan had been found.

Part of her was still capable of hope – he'd taken off before and found his way home safely – but as the hours drew on with no word, that optimistic part of her was shrinking.

In the kitchen the phone began to ring.

'Caitlin, would you answer that, please?'

They weren't allowed to tell Caitlin anything about Nathan's situation and that was another source of guilt for Julia.

Even though he'd only been here for a couple of months Caitlin was attached to him and now she was suffering much worse than any of them expected. She knew better than anyone what danger he was in and all their bland reassurances were doing nothing to soothe her.

She knocked tentatively on the door of Julia's workroom. She'd been told before she didn't need to do that but still she did, conditioned by the harsh regimes of former foster carers.

'Come in, lovey.'

Caitlin lingered in the open doorway, one foot on top of the other, holding the phone to her chest. She had tears in her eyes, her bottom lip ominously trembling.

'What is it?' Julia rushed over to her. 'Is it Nathan? Have they found him?'

'No.' She held the phone out, said, voice breaking, 'It's Dawn. She's dead.'

Julia felt her knees threatening to give but Caitlin caught her and helped her to the kitchen table. Taking the phone she heard

Sally's voice, borderline hysterical on the other end, telling her about a gas explosion and Dawn being murdered and Holly dead too, all of it coming out in a torrent, no gap for Julia to speak.

'They think Warren killed her,' Sally said. 'I just know they do.'

Julia wrapped her hand around the phone. 'Caitlin, go and tell Matthew what's happened.'

She waited until she was alone before she spoke again, using the firm tone which always worked with Sally.

'Calm down. You're not helping anything like this.'

'He's furious, he won't talk to me,' she said, almost wailing. 'Why won't he talk to me about this, Jules?'

'Listen to me . . . he's just lost his daughter, he's distraught. Let him absorb this. That's something we all need to do right now.'

'I know,' Sally said. She stopped to take a noisy gulp of what would almost definitely be red wine. 'You're right, of course you are. God, though, it's insane. Can you believe this? I mean, Dawn, yes, she was a grown woman but what could Holly possibly have done to deserve that?'

Julia closed her eyes, wishing she could end the call.

'Do you think it's that builder she's had in?' Sally asked, excitement coming into her voice, as if they were picking apart some thriller she'd chosen for their book club rather than accusing a man of murdering her boyfriend's soon-to-be-ex-wife and daughter. 'I saw him in the shop a couple of weeks ago, he looks a complete animal. Attractive enough but you wouldn't get away with saying no to him.'

'When did it happen?' Julia asked. 'Do the police know?'

'I don't know, they wouldn't tell us anything. We don't even know how they died.' Another mouthful at her end. 'The detective in charge went ballistic when Ben asked if they'd been raped, so – oh, I can't even bear to think about it.'

Matthew came in from the garden, propped the hoe against the wall and went to wash his hands in the utility room, followed by

Caitlin, who was asking him if she should call Nathan's mobile and tell him about the murders.

'Best not to upset him,' Matthew said gently, then told her to go and watch some television.

Sally was running through her suspects list, every man in the village virtually. Tactfully she left Matthew out but Julia didn't trust her to make the same omission when she was talking to the police.

'It must be the neighbour, though,' she said, almost regretfully, as if she'd solved the case too soon. 'They get murdered just as he *happens* to have a gas leak. He was trying to cover up the evidence, obviously.'

Matthew gestured for her to end the call and she nodded, waiting for an opening which wasn't coming. He paced away from the table, to the window and back again, long impatient strides, one hand clamped to his forehead, fingers twitching in his receding hair.

'Sally – look, I've got to go. Caitlin is in a real mess here, I need to sort her out.'

'Oh, okay. Yes, sorry, I shouldn't have just blurted it out to her like that, should I? Didn't think. God, that's me all over, isn't it?'

'I'll call you later,' Julia said and cut her off before she could protest.

Matthew took the phone from her and replaced it in the dock by the message board. His movements very deliberate but she could still see the slight tremor in his hand. He pulled out the chair closest to her, sat down, their knees touching.

'We need to tell the police about Nathan.'

Julia pushed away from him. 'What? My best friend's just been murdered and that's your first thought?'

'She wasn't your best friend,' Matthew said, giving her a pointed look. 'She might have been once but we both know better so don't pretend you're cut up about it.'

'What about Holly? Am I allowed to be upset for her?'

He leaned back in the chair, eyes closed, as if the full force of it had hit him finally. He liked Holly, she knew that. She was smart and Matthew had always respected and admired intelligence above everything else.

'She had so much potential,' he said. 'She could have done anything she wanted.'

'She was a lovely girl.'

'God, what a waste of life.' His took off his glasses and rubbed his eyes and when he slipped the heavy black frames on again there was a new resolve hardening his face. 'Holly's at peace now, anyway. That's something, I suppose.'

'It's not much,' Julia said.

Matthew patted her on the thigh. 'I think we both need a drink.'

She sat silently while he made two gin and tonics in the antique French tumblers she'd bought from a little shop in Stamford. Today she needed it in a highball glass, too much bad news for a single measure.

She wasn't allowed that, though. Just the smallest splash to taste. Barely a teaspoonful.

'We can't tell anyone about Nathan,' she said, striking first. 'We agreed.'

'That was before.'

'Before?' she asked, incredulous. 'This has got nothing to do with him.'

'You don't know that.' Matthew placed his own drink on the table. 'He was round there all the time, we've got no idea what was going on between them.'

Julia scowled at him. 'You read his case file, there's no suggestion that he's dangerous or violent. My God, Matthew, do you think I wouldn't see it if he was?'

He picked his G&T up, took a long mouthful. 'You always find the best in people.'

'That's usually considered a good thing.'

'It is, but it's a weakness too because you end up ignoring the bad that's in them.' She knew what he was thinking. They didn't discuss *the incident* any more, it had been picked over enough already and she'd admitted he was right. Her reward was never to have it mentioned again.

She told herself to stay calm.

'Even if we wanted to tell the police you know we can't.'

'We have to,' he said, taking her hand, his skin cold and wet from the glass. 'There's a reason Nathan ran away this weekend – of all the times he could have done it – and if it's because of Holly and Dawn's murders we owe it to them to come forward.'

Julia shook her head. She wouldn't let him do this.

'We're supposed to be protecting him. I won't do it.'

'Someone's going to tell them eventually,' he said. 'How will it look when the police find out we've been hiding this from them?'

He was right but she wouldn't be bullied. Not by him and not by the police. She knew Nathan was a good, kind boy and she'd promised to look after him. She'd failed him once, she wouldn't do it again.

'No, Matthew.' She pulled her hand free and stood up. 'We are not going to talk to the police. We made promises and we're going to honour them and if you go bchind my back on this, I'll never forgive you.'

6

Sunday evening was diehards-only time in the gym and Ferreira saw the same old faces sweating on the static bikes, grunting through another five reps on the machines as Lite FM blared across the open-plan space. She nodded to a couple of people as she tucked her ear buds in, making for the bank of treadmills pushed up close to the windows overlooking the car park and the industrial estate beyond it, pleased to see the one she wanted was free.

She stepped up and chose a programme that would take her across a series of demanding hills at a speed she was still struggling to maintain, wanting to stretch herself tonight, test the progress she knew she was making, despite the dire predictions of the NHS-approved physio she'd stopped going to almost two months earlier. He didn't know what she was made of, was too used to advising people wallowing in self-pity.

Instead she listened to her body and it said go on, go harder, fuck that pain, like some half-insane personal trainer who wanted to see her wrecked and on her knees. She'd been there; dropped weak legged off the treadmill and dragged herself into the changing rooms, every step an impossible agony, cried while she hid in a shower cubicle, desperate for one of the prescription painkillers she'd been told to take three times a day.

She didn't even collect them from the pharmacy, sure they would drag her down faster, shield her from the damage so she wouldn't have to face the uphill battle of healing.

It was easy to give in. It was what losers did. Christian Palmer would love to think of her defeated and addicted, given the lifetime of suffering he'd blown himself up to escape.

Thinking of him made her calf itch again but she ignored it, focused on her breathing and the rhythm of her feet hitting the belt.

The police psychiatrist was obsessed with Palmer. No matter what they discussed and how she tried to move the conversation on he always came back to Palmer and how she felt about him. She was supposed to learn to understand him, accept his actions and ultimately find it in her heart to forgive him. Because he was troubled or sick, not in complete control of himself when he thumbed that detonator.

She knew better, remembered his words: 'I'm glad you're here, Mel.' The venom in them. He'd felt no remorse for his actions and went out content in the belief that he was taking her and Zigic with him.

It was one of the last things she did remember from that day.

After that all she had were snatches, odd words and images, but nothing coherent, no sense of how it all unfolded.

Ferreira glanced at the treadmill's console, twenty minutes done, another twenty to go and the big climbs were coming up. She felt her thighs beginning to ache, muscles burning. The ligament behind her right knee, the one which took the most damage, was complaining but not loud enough for her to listen to it. She thumbed the volume up on her iPod, kept going.

On the television set bolted to the wall beside her she saw the local news starting and turned away from it, focused on her reflection in the window, the sky darkening now, lights popping on across the car park. They would be leading with the story, no real details to report, just two bodies found in Elton, victims not yet named.

Zigic wanted her to handle the official identification tomorrow. They could have sent a family-liaison officer but he was dubious about Warren and decided it was important for her to be there, use the opportunity to study his reaction to his daughter's corpse.

His love for the girl was obvious but Ferreira knew it didn't rule him out as her killer. Especially when you factored in the violent manner of Dawn's death.

Except there had been no animosity which could spark off such a brutal attack. Not that Ferreira had seen. When she'd spoken to Dawn, at that initial interview last year, she gave the impression that everything was fine between them and when Ferreira suggested he might be responsible for the harassment Dawn shot the idea down instantly. He was too dedicated to Holly to do anything that might upset her.

Was there something more to it, though?

Warren had abandoned Dawn with their disabled daughter, putting the full burden of care on her. She should have been raging and instead she defended him, insisted he was a good father and good man.

Maybe she saw his relationship with Sally as a temporary aberration, something she was going to let him work out of his system before returning to his family, writing it off as just another element of the breakdown which hit him after Holly's accident.

Ferreira couldn't understand it but she knew there were women capable of patiently waiting for a cheating partner to come back to them, apologetic and re-dedicated. The kind of passive-aggressive women who delighted in the martyrdom of their quiet forbearance.

Warren and Sally made no sense as a couple. He was younger than her, handsome even through his wailing grief and shabbiness, no hiding the good bones in his face and the lean body. She was an almost matronly woman with a grating personality and a teenage son – hardly a catch. Especially placed next to Dawn who had been pretty in that petite and girlish way most men seemed to love.

Had Warren and Dawn still been close? Closer than they should have been?

Warren wouldn't be the first separated man to cheat on his girlfriend with his wife.

The treadmill began to level out, the belt slowing to a fast walk and then finally a full stop and Ferreira's attention returned to the room as she stepped down.

She wiped the sweat off her face and took a long drink of water, looking at what was left of the early-evening crowd; a couple of women on the bikes, another sitting on a power plate by the door, two men grunting among the free weights, their bodies grotesquely pumped and glowing under the lights. A boxercise class was emptying out of the studio at the back of the gym, lots of high fives as the wannabe pugilists made for the juice bar and the changing rooms, veins still flooded with adrenalin.

In another hour or two they'd be back at home, wine and ready meals and something soporific on the television, softening them up for another Monday morning.

Ferreira went into the studio to tape her fists.

The room was close and high smelling, sweat and liniment, the scent of all that suppressed rage and frustration punched out during the previous forty-five minutes, strong enough to give her a contact high if she'd needed it. But she didn't.

There was a knot of fury permanently lodged somewhere behind her solar plexus, throbbing dully, pulsing harder every time Christian Palmer entered her mind, insinuating his way in during an absent moment or suddenly breaking through her thoughts, prompted by the sight of a nail head or a short blond haircut, or, more commonly, a police uniform.

She hadn't told her therapist about that. If he knew how many times she'd almost lashed out at some PC since returning to work he'd have never signed her off for full duties.

In her darker moments she imagined digging up Christian Palmer's corpse and battering it until his skull or her knuckles broke, but it was a thin and unrewarding fantasy because there was nothing left of him, just the lumps of flesh and odd bone fragments scraped off the walls of that cellar his wife had had cremated.

She'd even been denied the pleasure of spitting on his grave.

'Fourth time this week, you're keen.'

Ferreira tucked the end of the bandage into the gap behind her fingers, looked up to see one of the personal trainers watching her. His name tag said *Aaron* and he suited it, a wiry, tan-skinned bloke with a severe undercut and full-sleeve tattoos writhing up both arms.

'Fifth, actually.'

He smiled. 'You want to take a go on the pads this time? Most people won't stand still while you knock them about.'

Ferreira shrugged. 'If you're happy to risk it.'

He grabbed a set of black and grey pads, shoved his hands into them, smiling at her again, small white teeth, sharp and back slanting. 'Tell you what, if you can catch me I'll buy you a drink.'

She gave him the once-over as they squared up, being blatant about it, and he played up to the appraisal, showed her an Ali shuffle, quick on his feet, ducking and weaving.

'How about this,' she said. 'If you can stop me, I buy you a drink?'

'You're on.'

He took a wide stance, leading with his right foot, braced for the first few straight shots she threw at him, peppering the pads as he held them high, covering his face. He taunted her from behind them – 'Come on, girlie, you got better than that!' – shuffling forward, forcing her to give ground. She landed a quick jab, no power in it, and he swung at her, a wide arcing path which disturbed the air above her head and left his right side open. Ferreira poked at the gap but he skipped away from her.

'You really want me to buy you that drink,' he said, grinning at her, guard lowered.

'Seems like you're working harder than I am.'

'Worried about my pretty face, aren't I?'

'Bit late for that.'

Aaron showed her his chin but she let it hang there, went for the pads; hook, jab, jab. As she moved in close he covered up his face, tucked his elbows into his ribs and rode out the body shots she threw at him, taking them all on the arms. She was finding a rhythm now and it was different from working the bag, more challenging and more satisfying. No room for Christian Palmer in her head as she studied the way Aaron moved.

They danced around on the mats, their grunts and hard-slapped impacts the only noise in the room, the closed door reducing the music from the gym to nothing more than a bassline.

'You're throwing from the shoulder,' he said.

She brought the next shot up from her toes, aiming for the pad protecting his midsection, and at the last moment he drew it away, letting her fist crunch into his abs.

'Shit.' He winced. 'You got me. Looks like I'm buying.'

Ferreira shook her head, smiling despite herself. 'I'll meet you downstairs.'

In the changing rooms she stripped out of her sweaty gear, thinking of what a cheesy come-on it had been. He was decent looking, though, had a good body; she didn't need him to be original too.

She showered quickly, the hot water making the scars on her legs prickle. As she dried off in the cubicle her hand kept returning to the odd little lump under the skin of her right calf. She knew what needed to be done but not here or now and definitely not tonight.

A couple of middle-aged women had come in while she was showering and they shouted to each other across the room as they pulled sweats on over their shorts and T-shirts, too bashful to strip off but confident enough to rip apart someone they'd been working out near.

As Ferreira walked past them the conversation cut dead. She could feel their eyes on her, knew the look they were sharing because she'd seen it so many times before in here.

'What happened to your legs, love?'

She turned and fixed the woman with a hard stare. 'Excuse me?'

'Your legs? What on earth have you done to them?'

The woman's friend said her name, very quietly, but she wasn't giving up.

'Accident, was it?'

'No, not an accident.' Ferreira forced herself to smile. 'Just bad luck. Like your face.'

She dropped her towel and started to get dressed as the women sniped on in an undertone. A minute later they were gone and Ferreira let out the breath she'd been holding, sank onto the slatted wooden bench, and swore into her hands.

Christ, being pitied by someone who looked like that bitch.

She thought of Aaron waiting for her downstairs. They both knew what was going to happen tonight, all the talk of a 'drink' just a bullshit nicety, the real communication already done. But what was he going to think when he saw her naked?

Maybe she could distract him from her scars, move in fast, take control.

A bloke like him wouldn't go for it, though. He was the full-contact type, she could see it on him and that's what she wanted, a properly comprehensive fuck after months of self-conscious and unsatisfying quickies where she'd been too obsessed about hiding the damage to fully let herself go.

There would be no hiding anything from him.

Her hand strayed to her right calf again, stroking the hard nugget under her skin. She pinched it between her fingertips and the sensation of it, moving there, made her stomach turn.

She imagined Aaron running his hand up her leg, the frown on his face as he stopped, wondering what the hell that was.

It shouldn't matter, she kept telling herself, as she pulled on her jeans and T-shirt, slipped her feet into her Converses and threw the dirty kit into her holdall.

Who was he to judge her? After what she'd been through.

But he would. Because she was flawed now and women weren't allowed to be.

She went down the stairs into the reception area, saw him stand as she approached the cafe, a wide smile spreading across his face, a promising hint of greed in his eyes which almost changed her mind.

'Where d'you fancy then?' he asked. 'Draper's Arms?'

'Sorry, I can't.' She held up her phone. 'Work called.'

'On a Sunday night?'

'I'm a copper, we don't get to say no.'

He nodded, looking around them, awkward suddenly.

'Another time, then?'

'Sure,' she said, knowing there wouldn't be.

MONDAY

7

Zigic woke to the sound of a dog barking, high yelps coming from the floor near the foot of the bed, the sound of a paw scratching insistently at the rug. Sleep fuddled, he kicked off the thin, summer sheets and hauled his heavy head from the pillow.

Since Stefan had worked out how to open the back door their neighbours' dog kept mysteriously finding its way into the house and he didn't relish the prospect of taking it home again at this time of morning, making the same apology they were all getting tired of. The little mongrel was good-tempered at least, which was more than you could say for its owners.

'I'll deal with this, will I?' he said to Anna, who smiled at him and rolled over towards the wall.

He got up, only one eye fully open. 'Come on, Lucky. Come here, boy.'

The yelps became a growl and as his eyes adjusted to the thin light seeping in around the blackout blinds he saw Stefan crouched alone under the window, furiously scraping at the rug as if he was trying to dig his way out of the room through it.

'Stop that,' Zigic snapped.

Stefan cocked his head, starting to pant with his tongue stuck out.

'What are you doing?'

'Just take him back to bed,' Anna said. 'You know there's no point trying to reason with him when he's acting like this.'

Zigic picked him up and threw him over his shoulder, Stefan whimpering and pawing at his back as he carried him out through the hall into the bedroom he shared with Milan. The star-shaped nightlight in there was glowing softly in the corner, beams falling across the mess of scattered toys.

'Is it time to get up?' Milan asked, knuckling his eyes.

'No, go back to sleep.'

Zigic put Stefan in bed. Immediately he was up again, turning a circle before settling down at the centre of the mattress, still playing his game of make-believe.

'Alright, sleep, both of you,' he said. 'You've got school in a couple of hours.'

He pulled the door closed behind him and went downstairs into the kitchen, started a pot of espresso on the stove, fully awake now, mind already turning towards the coming day; the tasks waiting for him and the rest of the team, the challenge of unpacking the background to Holly and Dawn's murders.

More than anything he wanted to see Ferreira's original report.

The sparse information on the harassment was worrying him. It was possible that Dawn only reported it in order to satisfy her insurers and push forward the claim for damage against her vandalised car, but he didn't believe it was that simple.

Before the establishment of Hate Crimes he'd done an eighteen-month stint in Anti-Harassment, working alongside a put-upon but determined detective sergeant who managed a caseload running into the high three figures and rarely saw the perpetrators spend any time in prison. It was a dispiriting period in his career, more akin to social work than policing, doling out sympathy to the victims of stalking cases that had been running for years, offering advice about how to minimise the disturbance to their lives and stay as safe as possible when they had no expectation of being completely free and at ease ever again.

The coffee bubbled up into the top of the pot and he took it off the heat, poured a double measure, one eye on the clock, thinking about going for a quick run. His arms were aching from the day before's painting and he realised he wasn't in the mood to go tramping around fields and woodland this morning.

He switched the television on and ate his breakfast at the kitchen table while the news played in the background; Iraq leading, then Ukraine, an unexpected by-election victory in the north-east for the English Patriot Party. A Labour stronghold falling.

By rights they should have imploded after Richard Shotton stood down in February, but like most noxious substances they were persistent, and within hours of his resignation one of his deputies had stepped into the breach. The scandal around Shotton did less harm to the party's reputation than anyone expected. They ran effective damage limitation in the run-up to the general election, distanced themselves quickly and completely enough to maintain the momentum Shotton had been building and went on to capture six seats. Seven now.

Zigic switched the TV off and went to get ready for work.

The road was quiet on the way in, pre-rush hour, pre-school run, and he made Thorpe Wood station in ten minutes, finding the car park almost empty but Ferreira's Golf already slotted into a space near the main doors.

She was alone in the office, seated at her desk with a coffee and a half-eaten panini, going through a small black notebook he recognised as Dawn's harassment log. The search team had delivered it, along with Dawn and Holly's laptops, early yesterday evening, just as Zigic was preparing to leave.

'You're in early,' he said.

'I wanted to have a look at this before we got started.'

He sat down opposite her at DC Wahlia's desk. 'Did you find anything interesting?'

'Not really. She hardly logged anything after I spoke to her. So it was either very sporadic or she wasn't seriously intending to pursue the issue. See what you think.' Ferreira tossed the book to him and went back to her breakfast.

Zigic had read a lot of these logs during that eighteen months working in Anti-Harassment and what surprised him about them was the inevitable frequency of the incidents; most victims barely went a day without something bad happening, as their stalkers sought to keep them constantly on edge.

Looking through the half-dozen pages Dawn had filled he saw no pattern, no escalation. There were instances of damage to her garden, silent phone calls, hoax calls on a couple of occasions which resulted in unwanted pizza deliveries and taxis arriving at her house. Petty stuff, annoying but impersonal, in no way related to Holly's disability.

If it wasn't for how her car had been vandalised this case would have gone to Anti-Harassment rather than Hate Crimes.

'It's thin,' he said.

'And across a very short time period. I make it about six weeks.'

'When exactly did you first go there?'

Ferreira nodded towards his office. 'I put the original report on your desk.'

He found a slim file sitting waiting for him, brought it back to the main office.

Dawn had reported the vandalism on 4 December last year, called the non-emergency number and was finally put through to Hate Crimes, to Ferreira who went out to the house the following day for an initial interview. All the relevant details were there, a statement from Dawn which was short and to the point, no emotion in it, photographs of the silver people carrier she'd taken delivery of a few days before, its slashed tyres sitting on their rims and its driver's-side doors spray painted in black, the word 'CRIPPLE' in block capitals almost a foot tall.

'No witnesses?' he asked.

'I tried the neighbour but he wasn't at home. Dawn said he worked away a lot and wasn't there the night it happened.'

'Definitely an overnight thing?'

'Yeah, that's what she said.' Ferreira put down her panini. 'They're out of the way, edge of the village. No witnesses except the neighbour, potentially. And maybe someone driving by. I could hardly put out a call for a petty vandalism, could I?'

'What about Neighbourhood Watch?'

Ferreira swivelled in her chair, fist balling. 'I didn't speak to them. We were in the middle of a major case at the time, I shouldn't even have been dealing with it.'

Zigic looked back at her without speaking, waited for some of the heat to drain out of her face.

The last thing she'd written in the file was 'Follow-up call' and a date. Before that, notes of three other calls which Dawn had terminated. He could fully understand how she'd let it slip; whoever shouted loudest got the attention and Dawn had gone silent.

'This isn't my fault,' Ferreira said, voice even but he could see she was working at it. 'Nobody could have anticipated an act of petty fucking vandalism blowing up into a double murder.'

'I didn't say it was your fault.'

'Like you're not thinking it.'

Zigic leaned forward across the desk. 'Mel, if I thought you'd missed something I'd tell you. In no uncertain terms.'

She slumped where she sat, threw her head back and let out a long, slow breath before she straightened up again, started to roll a cigarette. 'I think we need to talk to the builder today, he's been at the house for a while by the looks of it. If anyone's been hanging around he'll have seen them.'

'He's got access,' Zigic said, thinking of the new extension which linked the kitchen to the garage conversion. 'And there's a fair chance he'll have a key, since it isn't finished yet. Do we know who he is?'

'I got his details from the sign outside the house,' Ferreira said, holding the unlit cigarette between her fingers as she pulled her keyboard towards her. 'Company name, Oundle phone number. Hold on, I'll see if I can find him.'

Zigic got up from Wahlia's desk and went over to the murder board which had been started yesterday afternoon. They were running two other major investigations, both stalled with little prospect of new movement. He was grateful this had come at a quiet period for them, sensed that it was going to suck up man hours. Last night he'd spoken to Riggott about expanding the team, made clear the emotive nature of the case and the attention it would invariably draw down on them, but he didn't hold out much hope for support.

CID was undermanned, the recently arrived DI Sawyer off after a car accident, a detective constable on suspension following the disappearance of evidence from a murder scene, Grieves taking leave for stress. Not that he would have tolerated her back in Hate Crimes.

An internal investigation had cleared her of colluding with Christian Palmer but she'd returned to a hostile environment she was ill-equipped to withstand and hadn't lasted a month back at the station before she cracked. Word was Riggott had come down hard on her, frequently and very publically showing his contempt, and where the DCS led the rest followed.

It was exactly what Zigic had wished on her – exile – but he took little pleasure in knowing she was suffering it now. He'd rather she'd kept her mouth shut when Palmer started nosing into their investigation and continued to be the hard-working and diligent copper he'd been coming to regard as a worthwhile part of his team.

'He's got a website,' Ferreira said. 'Looks like the business is based out of a yard on the edge of town.'

Zigic continued to stare at the board where Dawn and Holly's photographs, taken from the house, were stuck up. Holly in her school uniform, fresh faced and smiling slightly, her hair worn long with a blunt fringe. It was the kind of image which the press liked and potential witnesses felt tugging at them when the time came to speak up. Nothing like the girl she'd been for the last two years of her life.

Dawn was smiling in her photo too, deeply but without conviction, her eyes heavily kohled, pixie-cut, peroxide-blonde hair giving her a punky vibe. She didn't look old enough to be Holly's mother, skin unlined and dewy, but maybe that was cosmetic. Zigic never could tell.

There was little else on the board so far.

No murder weapon. That was a worry.

Jenkins's team had turned the house and garden inside out looking for the knife that killed Dawn and found nothing. Two missing from the wooden block, both needed finding. The next step would be an organised search of the surrounding fields and roadsides. Assuming he could get Riggott to agree to it.

'Gary Westman,' Ferreira said. 'Westman & Sons General Builders Limited. Excellent reviews on Rated Tradesmen dot com. Thirty-eight years old, couple of speeding tickets, couple of instances of drink-driving and he did two years back in his early twenties for possession.'

'Of what?'

'Class B drugs.'

Ferreira turned her chair over to him while she went to light up, swearing as the window refused to open without a fight, the metal frame swollen from the heat.

Zigic scanned Westman's record, rereading what Ferreira had already told him before returning to the mugshot. It was too old to draw any conclusions from and his form suggested nothing more than a reckless streak.

'We'll talk to him this morning,' Zigic said. 'Get it out of the way. What time are the post-mortems scheduled?'

'Ten-thirty start.'

'You'd better sort out the identification for this morning then. I'll talk to Westman.'

She flicked ash out of the window. 'You could send Bobby.'

'No, I need him here. Whoever Riggott gives us won't be as effective. It'll probably be Parr, you know he's always surplus to requirements downstairs.'

'We always get the rejects.'

Zigic smiled. 'Doesn't say much for the rest of us, does it?'

Fifteen minutes later Parr walked into Hate Crimes, grey suit jacket thrown over his shoulder, shirtsleeves turned back to his elbows and a bright orange tie neatly knotted. With his light tan and gelled hair he looked like the manager of a mobile-phone shop, clean-shaven but somehow sleazy.

'The boss reckons you needed reinforcements,' he said, standing with his hands spread to his sides. 'Double murder, yeah?'

Zigic led him over to the board and brought him up to speed, explained that he'd be managing a mobile incident unit in Elton, marshalling the second round of door-to-door and making contact with local Neighbourhood Watch. They discussed the best place to site the van and settled on the village green, wanting visibility even if it meant they'd attract the odd passing ghoul.

Parr seemed more focused than usual, asked plenty of questions, made some decent suggestions. Zigic wondered if hed judged him too harshly before, mistaken the stress and sleeplessness of new fatherhood for incompetence and disinterest. He wasn't ready to write that impression off completely but he felt better about having Parr involved now.

Wahlia arrived as they were finishing up, trailing a handful of uniforms, two of them new faces to Zigic, recent recruits he'd have to remember to split up and pair with older heads. The PCs scattered around the room, taking up positions at the empty desks nearest the murder board, all eyes focused on the photos of the victims.

Zigic clapped his hands together, silencing the murmuring voices. 'Okay, ladies and gents, this is a bad one.'

8

Accompanying family members to identify their dead was the worst part of the job. Even more awkward and painful than the dreaded house calls to inform of a loss. This was where it got real. No more hopeful denials, no more fantasies of clerical errors or innocent mix-ups. After this morning Warren Prentice would have an image of his daughter's corpse in his head and nothing would completely clear it away until the day he died.

And Dawn, of course. Objectively that was the more disturbing sight – she'd been dead longer, decay had set in – but something told Ferreira it wasn't going to bother him quite so much.

She'd asked Warren to meet her in the cafe at City Hospital, suggested he brought someone along for moral support. Most people were in no condition to drive home afterwards.

Inside, she found him seated alone at a corner table, hunched over with his chin resting on his fists. He didn't stir as she approached, stared straight through her with pink-rimmed eyes, the knuckle of one thumb caught between his teeth, as if inflicting some small physical pain on himself could wipe out the all-consuming emotional one that he was suffering.

He snapped out of it when she reached the table.

'Is it time?'

'We can wait for a while if you prefer,' Ferreira said.

'Sitting here isn't going to change anything, is it?'

'I'm sorry. I wish there was another way we could do this.' She glanced around them; a few more people were dotted about, all lost in their own thoughts. 'Where's Sally? I think we should wait for her.'

'I wanted to do this on my own.' He took a deep breath. 'I can deal with this.'

Like you dealt with Holly's accident, Ferreira thought. Strange how only Sally could see him through that grief but he didn't want her support during the darkest moments of this one. She thought of how he shrugged her away yesterday at the house, ran full pelt from the comfort she was offering.

'If you're ready then . . .'

They went down to a small anteroom, saturated with the exhaustion and fear and grief of all the people who had waited in it before, and Ferreira settled Warren on the sofa before she went into the mortuary.

The assistant was waiting for her, no sign of the pathologist yet.

'Dawn and Holly Prentice, we're here for the ID.'

The assistant ducked into his office and consulted the computer. 'Coming in or staying out?'

'He's not up to coming in,' she said. 'We need to do this quickly, I'm not sure how much longer he's going to keep it together for.'

'Quick as I can then.'

In the side room Warren was on his feet, pacing back and forth with his hands wrapped around the back of his neck. Gently she sat him down again and they waited for a couple of interminable minutes with the sound of the steel drawers opening and closing audible through the wall. More than two, suggesting the assistant wasn't as on the ball as he'd seemed. It had happened before, the wrong body brought up on screen.

But not today.

A low, monotone voice came through the speakers, giving them warning, then a white sheet filled the screen and Warren let out a keening groan that he managed to stifle as disembodied hands entered the shot, lifting the sheet away to reveal the bloated and ruined remains of Dawn's face.

Warren lurched where he sat but held it together. 'It's her. That's Dawn.'

Ferreira patted his shoulder, told him he was doing great, the words feeling stupid and inappropriate but she didn't have any better ones and if she did she would have saved them for the next part of the process.

The screen went blue again and he was praying under his breath and cursing – God, Fate, Dawn, all of them equally to blame for bringing him here to this moment.

Then there she was, Holly, almost peaceful looking as the sheet was drawn back.

Warren moaned, rocking where he sat, unable to tear his eyes away from his daughter's face. 'My beautiful girl.'

The emotion clenched his limbs and tightened the muscles in his face and he kept staring at the screen long after the image was gone. Ferreira inched away from him as subtly as she could, gave him space and herself space too, feeling bruised by being in such close proximity to his grief.

'She didn't deserve this.'

Five minutes passed, with the dim sounds of the mortuary coming through the wall, footsteps on the tiled floor, the distant rattling of instruments as the pathologist's assistant prepared for his arrival, humming thoughtlessly, some tune Ferreira half recognised and Warren didn't seem to hear.

Finally he snapped back to reality. 'I need to get out of here.'

The hospital was busier as they reached the reception area where people were milling about, into the newsagents and the cafeteria, a woman's voice filling the space as she talked in an exaggerated tone to the young man she was pushing around in a wheelchair.

Outside, Warren didn't pause, just kept walking as if Ferreira wasn't there, head down, keys already in his hand. He stepped off the pavement straight in front of a taxi pulling away from the drop-off point and didn't even pause.

Ferreira stopped and waved the taxi on before following him.

Warren was already half in his battered old Range Rover by the time she caught up with him. He had one leg tangled in the seat belt which hung loose outside the open door and his mounting frustration at it prompted an outburst which drew disapproving looks from a nearby couple.

She couldn't let him drive out of here in that state, blurry eyed and emotionally shattered; anything could happen and she didn't want another Prentice family tragedy on her conscience.

'I think you should take a couple of minutes,' she said. 'Just get yourself together, okay?'

'I'm perfectly safe.'

'No, Warren, you're not.' He moved to close the door but she had hold of the frame. 'You're shaking. Come on, don't force me to be a policewoman about this.'

Warren glared at her. 'I can't believe you're wasting your time ordering me around when you should be out there looking for whoever killed Holly.'

'There's a team setting up in the village right now. We're going to get whoever was responsible. But I need to be sure you're okay before I let you go.'

His head dropped again and he withdrew his hand from the door.

Ferreira reached out and took the keys from him. 'I'll get us a drink.'

She went back into the cafeteria and waited in line behind a man who hacked his lungs up all over the display of sandwiches and wraps. He paid with a pile of change and the woman at the till only realised it wasn't enough money when he was already gone. She rolled her eyes at Ferreira and took her order.

Warren was sitting with the door open when she returned to the car and she was thinking how much calmer he looked a split second before she caught the scent of skunk on the air, sweet but diesel tinged. He reached over to let her in, took his coffee from her.

'You're not going to be a policewoman about this too, are you?' he asked, gesturing at her with the joint.

'Whatever you need to do.'

He took a deep drag and held it down for a few seconds. 'I stopped smoking years ago, hadn't even had a cigarette since I left uni. Then Holly had her accident . . . you think alcohol's going to do the job but it doesn't.'

Ferreira rolled one of her own – unadulterated – and cracked the window before she lit up, needing a through wind to drive the scent of Warren's green out of her hair and clothes. If she went back to the station reeking of it there would be questions.

For a while they talked about Holly, Ferreira doing no more than prompting, Warren relaxing as he smoked but she could see it was only a temporary fix. Occasionally a bolt of anger would shoot through his narcotic neutrality; at the instructor who hadn't checked Holly's ropes properly, the surgeon who should have done more. Not at Dawn though.

'I should have made more of an effort with her,' he said. 'I should have helped Dawn out more but I didn't know what to do. And she wouldn't ask. She was always so bloody stubborn.'

'Was she getting any help?' Ferreira asked.

'She had a nurse come once a day. She handled the medication, that stuff.'

Ferreira wondered why the nurse hadn't raised the alarm and made a mental note to follow up on that.

'Dawn seemed quite isolated when I spoke to her.'

'She was.' Warren frowned. 'You'd be amazed how quickly people abandon you when things get tough.'

'She must have kept in touch with some of her friends?'

'Julia and her stayed close.' He crushed the butt of his joint in the ashtray between their chairs. 'But Julia isn't like the rest of them. She's used to dealing with other people's problems. She lives for it.'

'Nosy, you mean?'

'Let's just say she's a good listener.' He took the lid off his coffee and swallowed a mouthful of bad cappuccino. 'If anyone knows what was going on in Dawn's life, it's Julia.'

'Like who she's been seeing lately?'

'There'll be someone,' Warren said, no judgement in his tone. 'Dawn was always a very – um – physical woman, you know? She needed someone.'

'You've no idea who?'

'It's not the kind of thing you ask your estranged wife.' He looked down into his coffee. 'Especially not when you walked out on her.'

'But there was Holly to consider,' Ferreira pointed out. 'If Dawn was having a relationship, surely you'd want to know who was in the house with your daughter.'

'Dawn wasn't stupid,' he said. 'She'd never put Holly in danger.'

He started to roll another joint and Ferreira stopped him.

'One of them and I can let you drive home. Two – we'll be here a while.'

He slipped the foil wrap back into his tobacco pouch and tucked the bundle away. Whatever was already in his system was beginning to clear and a morose expression darkened his face.

'Do you know how Hol died?' he asked.

'Not yet. We'll have more information tomorrow, but there were no signs of violence. It looks like she might have died from complications in her condition.'

'Neglect, you mean? Dawn was dead and she couldn't look after her, so she died?'

'As far as we're concerned it's still a murder investigation. Whoever killed Dawn left Holly to die.' Ferreira glanced at the dashboard clock; the post-mortem would be starting soon and she needed to get back to the office. 'Can you think of anyone who might have wanted to do this?'

He shook his head, turned away from her.

'If Dawn didn't have many visitors we're looking at a limited range of possibilities. Who's in that range?'

'I don't know,' he said. 'Me, I suppose, Julia definitely, maybe Matthew – that's her husband.'

Warren drew the car door shut, suddenly ready to leave, done with the conversation. But Ferreira still had his keys in her pocket.

'Who else?'

He hesitated. 'She's got a builder in at the moment.'

'We know about him.'

'Can I have my keys back, please?'

Ferreira took them out, held them in her closed fist. 'Either it's the green or you're just not very good at hiding what you're thinking, but I can see that you know who I need to talk to.'

'It's nothing.' He reached for the keys and she pulled her hand away.

'Then tell me.'

'Julia has a couple of kids living with her at the moment. A boy and a girl – she's a foster carer, so God knows what kind of shit they're capable of.'

'And?'

'I've seen them at the house a few times.'

'Is that all?'

He shot her a hard look but didn't reply.

It was a big conclusion to draw from such a small thing, Ferreira thought, and she didn't like the way he'd immediately jumped on them as a threat when they were probably victims of circumstance themselves.

'They made you uncomfortable,' she said. 'Why?'

'The boy.' Warren's fingers closed around the steering wheel, white-knuckle tight. 'Nathan. The last time I went to visit Hol he was in her bedroom.'

'Doing what?'

'Just standing there,' Warren said. 'Looking at her.'

9

Nathan woke with a start and instinctively lashed out, his fists finding nothing but air and darkness and then, just a few inches away from his shoulders, solid wood. He stifled a scream and rubbed his throbbing knuckles, telling himself not to panic.

Just breathe. Think.

He tried the exercise Julia had taught him, running the alphabet backwards in his head as he took deep, slow breaths, picturing each letter in the gloom, making it solid and real in front of him, always blue. That was the calmest colour, she'd told him. Clear skies and calm seas and cornflowers.

He saw it differently. The bright blue of Everton's home strip, the number 3 his mum bought him, Leighton Baines.

There was blood on the top.

Blood on the walls and the floor. In her hair, on his hands.

Nathan felt his heart pounding behind his ribs, felt himself losing control again. He made the floating letters green; the safest colour. He couldn't think of anything bad that was green.

Slowly his eyes adjusted and he realised he was in a wardrobe. Saw the dimensions coming out of the shadows around him, a big wardrobe, with a chrome rail above his head, empty except for a couple of wire hangers. The floor of it was carpeted and he whined quietly to himself when he realised it was wet. He tugged his combats away from his groin, the damp fabric sticking to his skin.

It was the nightmare.

The man in the lorry with the tobacco breath and the yellow teeth. The knife . . .

Nathan scrambled in his pockets, turned them inside out, panic tightening his skull. The knife was gone and it wasn't a nightmare.

He fell out of the wardrobe into an empty room, blinking against the sunlight flooding in through the bare window. The sight of the patterned carpet and papered wall triggered a surge of memory that was almost too much for him to control.

Everything was jumbled up in his head, Dawn and Holly and his mum and his brother and that man, the one who seemed nice but wasn't, who said he'd take him home but didn't. Nathan tried to put the memories in order, deal with them how Julia told him to, push away the things that hadn't happened and focus on what he needed to know right now.

He walked around the empty room – moving helped – dragging his fingertips over the bumpy patterned wall, watching his feet until he noticed the blood on his trainers. The man told him to sleep for a bit but he only pretended to.

When he reached the bedroom door he stopped. Scared suddenly.

Who else was in the house?

There was no furniture here but not everyone had loads of furniture.

He pressed his ear to the door and listened for a long time. No sounds of life. Nothing but his own breathing and heartbeat and the gurgling of his stomach.

It was too late to be scared.

Slowly he opened the door and explored the rest of the upstairs. Two more bedrooms, both of them empty, and then the bathroom. No toilet roll or towels. The open window brought back something more. An image there and gone in a second. He caught hold of it, focused.

He saw himself walking, late at night, shivering and crying but trying to hide it because he knew that nobody would help him. Crying got you hit. That was what he knew for sure. He saw himself on a street of lit houses like the ones he'd left back home and he heard his brother's voice in his head telling him he needed to get inside.

But what was he going to do, knock on a random door and ask for a bed?

His brother had a better plan. He always knew how to get round problems like this.

Nathan walked until he found a house without its lights on and a board outside saying 'To-Let'. They'd broken into houses like that before. Not the ones 'For Sale'. The people would still be in them sometimes. These were the ones you wanted. You could go in them and smoke and drink and nobody would stop you.

He found the side gate locked but managed to climb over it. That was where he scraped his hand.

The back garden was dark and it scared him but he saw an upstairs window left open. Not easy to get to. Not without his brother to give him a boost, but he climbed onto the roof of the old outhouse and made it to the window, dragged himself up and inside.

He'd landed in the bath. That was where the bruise on his arm came from.

Then there was the other window.

The one so far off the ground that Nathan didn't think he could drop down without breaking his ankles. But the door was locked and the man was talking and through the windscreen of the lorry he could see the police station, all the cars outside and the big vans and two men in uniforms standing on the street.

The drop didn't look as scary as the man did, telling him they had to go inside. That the police would call his mum and dad and they'd come to take him home.

Nathan picked at his combats again. They were dark blue but you could see the wet on them. Too obvious to go outside in. He looked around the bedrooms again, checking in the fitted wardrobes, finding them all empty.

Downstairs the rooms were just the same. Nothing in any of them.

Bare cupboards in the kitchen, but through the window he could see into the neighbours' garden. There was washing out on the line, lots of it, mainly kids' clothes.

Last night he'd tried the back door and found it locked and now he searched the drawers for a key, the cupboard under the sink and the corners of the empty room. Nowhere to hide anything and nothing to find.

He climbed up onto the worktop, feeling the draining board wobble under his foot, and reached for the window over the sink. The paint was flaking and the catch was old but he managed to open it with a hard shove, then jumped out into a flower bed full of weeds.

For a few minutes he didn't move. You had to listen and watch, be sure no one knew you were there. The end of the garden had a high wall along it, a factory or something, with no windows for nosy neighbours to see him from. That was lucky.

Nathan crossed the grass and pressed his eye to a hole in the fence. The kids there had a trampoline and a paddling pool, loads of toys chucked about. It was a tidy garden, though, like Julia and Matthew's, with a vegetable plot down the far end. They'd probably be the same kind of people. They'd help him if he asked because people like that did. But then they'd ask him things and he wouldn't be able to answer.

It made him feel better about stealing from them, knowing they wouldn't mind.

Up and over the fence and into the garden, quick as he could, keeping an eye on the kitchen window just in case the woman was at home. He snatched pairs of shorts and T-shirts off the line, took a man's hoodie that would be too big but there was nothing else warm.

Back over the fence, back into the house. He changed into the clean clothes in the hallway, went and got his mobile from where he'd left it on the wardrobe floor.

He turned it on. The battery was still full. Twenty missed calls and messages – Julia, Caitlin, the woman he was supposed to call Rachel.

Nathan ignored all that and went to the map, saw a little red pin drop down to show him where he was. Grantham.

He pinched the screen until the map zoomed out enough for him to work out how far he was from home. It looked like a tiny journey. An hour or two and maybe it would be if he knew how to steal a car. His brother never let him do that, though. Said he was still too young and how was he going to drive anywhere when he couldn't reach the pedals?

The little red pin was close to the centre of Grantham. Close to the train station.

He needed money and food. He could get both there. People didn't pay attention, too many bags and running late. That was how he'd get home.

As he stared at the map, trying to memorise the names of the roads, his phone rang – Rachel.

He started to shake, feeling as if she could see him through the camera. She saw everything, knew things she wasn't supposed to.

Finally she gave up and he forced himself not to think about her, went back to the map and tried to make the street names go into his head.

The phone pinged. A new message from Rachel flashed up across the top of the screen.

Don't move. We're coming to get you.

IO

Westman & Sons General Builders was a more significant outfit than Zigic was expecting, sitting on an acre of prime market-town real estate with a new Waitrose on one boundary and playing fields on another, water meadows separating the yard from the Leicester Road. A few slow, ginger cows ambled around under the morning sun, a lone, bold heifer coming close to the perimeter fence where an old stone trough was full of rainwater.

The yard was crammed with reclaimed building materials, piled so high they'd give even the most lax health-and-safety inspector an instant coronary; packs of soft red bricks, chipped and dusted with mortar, precarious towers of local limestone, odd chunks littering the ground around them, roof tiles lined up and interleaved, worn slates and pantiles, lengths of old railings and dozens of different chimney pots.

Anna would been in her element here, Zigic thought. Finding things for him to clean up.

He spotted a white-haired man with stooped posture unloading a set of pine doors from the back of a pickup truck, adding them to the selection ranked up in an open-fronted shed. He moved slowly but lifted each door easily, his squat physique toughened by a lifetime of heavy work.

'Is Gary about?' Zigic asked.

'In the office.' The man gestured towards the main building, a corrugated-metal barn with its sliding door wide open and a mangy tabby cat sunning itself on the threshold.

Inside, the temperature was a few degrees colder than out in the sun, the space double height and echoing, lit by hanging fluorescent strips running along the vaguely defined aisles. There were hundreds of internal doors in racks, sash windows and ancient sanitary ware crusted with dirt and limescale and rust, elaborate fireplaces made of cast iron and wood and four different types of marble, too big for modern houses and too gaudy for modern tastes. Everything smelling of dust and damp.

Zigic found Gary Westman in a partitioned cubbyhole, standing with his big fists planted on his hips as he talked to a woman on speakerphone, quoting her prices she didn't sound very happy with.

'If you can find someone else to do it cheaper, then go for it,' Westman said. 'But don't expect me to come and put their work right when they balls it up.'

He cut the woman off, smiled at Zigic.

'They'll spend ten grand on an oven but ask six to build the room they want to put it in and you're a rip-off merchant.'

Westman looked much the same as in his mugshot, a few pounds heavier, a few lines on his square face, but the reckless twenty-something in white sportswear was now pushing forty, respectable enough in his designer jeans and polo shirt, biceps straining at the pink aertex. If he wanted women with ten-grand ovens to use his services he needed to show them the right kind of package.

'Anyway,' he said. 'What can I do for you?'

Zigic introduced himself and Westman nodded immediately.

'Dawn, yeah? Mate of mine called this morning, said she'd been killed. Holly too, he said. I said, that can't be right. Not in fucking Elton.'

'I'm afraid it's true,' Zigic said, seeing the bemusement slacken his face. 'I need to talk to everyone you had working at Dawn's house. There's a chance they might have important information.'

'Yeah, course.' He took his phone out, got the right unlock code on the second attempt. 'I've been over there a bit. Me and Deano. Dean Carter. You want his number?'

'And the address.'

Westman read them out and Zigic noted them down.

'Seems like managing this place is a full-time job. Do you usually go out on site?'

'Dad manages the yard. He's getting on a bit. Should have retired years back by rights but there's no stopping the old fella. He's convinced he'll drop down dead the minute he quits.'

'Still, not your usual kind of project,' Zigic said.

'We can't afford to turn down the small ones. They're bread and butter, you know. Only so many people round here want bricks at twelve hundred pound a thousand and reclaimed Jacobean staircases.' He shrugged his big shoulders. 'And it's on the estate, anyway. They like to deal with companies they know.'

'Who was paying for it?'

'The council. House is owned by the estate but Dawn applied for a grant to convert the garage and it came in.' The phone on the desk began to ring and he glanced at it for a split second before returning his attention to Zigic, eyes widening. 'Don't tell me that's how they got in. I'll fucking kill Deano if he left the place unlocked.'

'Does he do that often?'

'Kid's not got the sense he was born with.'

'When was he last there?' Zigic asked, itching to call in the man's name and check his record.

'Now hold on,' Westman said, hands going up. 'He's a bit dense but he's soft as shit.'

'I'm sure you're right, but we need to establish how the killer got into the house and if Dean left the door open it changes things for us. So, when was he last there?'

Westman calmed down slightly, but the nerves were still buzzing behind his eyes. 'Thursday morning. Both of us were there till dockey – elevenish – then we went on to another job in Yarwell.'

'Was Dawn at home when you left?'

He nodded. 'She didn't go out much. She was always there when we were.'

'So, why would you think Dean left the door unlocked?'

Westman didn't answer, glanced at his feet.

'Presumably you didn't leave without telling Dawn,' Zigic said. 'The extension is attached to the kitchen, it's all very open. Did you tell her you were going?'

'Yes.' Still looking at his feet.

'And did she see you out?'

'She saw me out,' he said, finally meeting Zigic's gaze. 'Alright? You know what I'm saying now?'

He did, but he wanted to hear the full explanation, see how Westman talked about Dawn, what emotions his recollection of that morning would provoke.

'Clarify it for me.'

Westman sat down in a wobbly leatherette chair at his desk, elbows on his knees, right hand cupping his left, hiding the thick platinum wedding band Zigic had already noticed.

'Me and Deano stopped by early to get a couple of hours in. The plasterboard was due to be delivered this week and I wanted him to go clear all our stuff out so the dry liners could make a quick start. The job's been dragging on, fucking delays with the bricks and the windows not right.'

Too much detail, Zigic thought. Off topic. He was hiding something.

'So I left Deano to get on and I went in to see Dawn.' He gave Zigic a pointed look, willing that to be enough. 'I don't know how long he was working but he was already in the van when I left, so I didn't bother checking the back door. I was a bit – well – shagged out.'

'How long have you been involved with Dawn?'

'We weren't involved,' he said. 'It was just sex. I went there to price up and we got on okay, it just happened. You know how women are with builders.'

'Married builders.'

'What are you, the fucking morality police?' Westman snapped.

'Does your wife know about this?'

'She knows what I'm like and she doesn't care.'

'Would she say that if I asked her?'

Westman pressed his fist harder into his cupped hand. 'This hasn't got anything to do with what happened to Dawn. It was just a casual thing, we weren't hurting anyone. She had a lot on her plate looking after Holly, you know, she needed someone to make her feel good now and again.'

'Maybe you weren't the only one paying her attention,' Zigic said. 'Did she mention other men?'

'We didn't do much talking.'

'Did you know she was being harassed?'

'Like I said, we never talked much.' Westman frowned. 'Couple of weeks back, though, me and Deano went over to cut the new window in, and there was some bloke parked up over the road watching the house. Proper eyeballing it. I didn't think too much of it, but Dawn wouldn't open up when I knocked and I knew she was in there.'

'What happened then?'

'We got started. We could get in round the back but I like to give folks a courtesy knock – just good manners, isn't it?'

Zigic nodded. 'Did you see Dawn that day?'

'Yeah.' He turned his ring around on his finger. 'Hour or so later she came out with tea and bacon butties.'

'And the bloke in the car?'

'Long gone.' He leaned back in his chair. 'Dawn was upset. Really upset, she'd been crying, but she was pretending to be fine. She wasn't like that normally. Pissed off, sad, yeah, but not like that.'

'Did you ask her what was wrong?'

'I should have,' he said. 'I didn't think anything of it until now though.'

A woman in a disintegrating waxed coat came to the edge of Westman's office, trailing a terrier on a long lead, and asked where the wood burners were. He directed her to the furthest corner of the building and when she lingered, assured her he'd be with her in a few minutes.

'This man,' Zigic said. 'What did he look like?'

He huffed out a fast breath. 'I dunno. I didn't really have a good look at him. Bald. Old.'

'Was he wearing a suit? A uniform maybe?'

'No.'

'What about the car? Make? Colour?'

'Burgundy. Might have been a Passat. That sort of size. Oldish.'

'Registration? Even a partial would help.'

'Sorry.'

It could be nothing, Zigic thought. Was almost definitely nothing. People pulled off the road for all sorts of reasons. Mostly innocent and even if they were up to no good it would be a leap to assume it had anything to do with Dawn.

'I need you to come to Thorpe Wood and make a formal statement, Mr Westman.'

'What, now?'

'Yes,' Zigic said. 'I'm sure you realise that this is a very important matter and the more information we can get and verify, the better chance we have of catching whoever was responsible.'

He nodded, but the panic was clear on his face. He'd been in police stations before, maybe he thought they hadn't checked his record yet and walking into one again, of his own free will, was a risk best avoided. As if he had another option.

Zigic gave him a card. 'You can drive in yourself or I can have somebody come and collect you if that's easier.'

'No, I'll drive.' He looked down at the card. 'I want to help.'

A few minutes later, sitting in his car parked at the kerb opposite the entrance of the yard, waiting for Ferreira to answer her phone, Zigic saw Westman leave in his pickup truck and wondered if he'd have an alibi ready when he was asked for it.

11

Dawn Prentice's house was still wrapped in police tape when Ferreira drove past, but a few of her neighbours had made the short walk to the edge of the village since the news broke and a small collection of bouquets now sat at the gateway.

She stopped the car, threw it into reverse and got out to look at them, found the usual bland messages of condolence and regret and wondered how many of those people had been to the house in recent months, if any of them had given Dawn and Holly a moment's thought when they were still alive and in need of real emotional support. She took out her phone and carefully photographed the little shrine, ensuring the names were in shot, curious whether any of the women – and they were all women – would come forward in the next couple of days.

The neighbouring house cracked and creaked, its blasted shell settling as it continued to cool, occasional distant thuds as something inside fell. The debris remained on the driveway and in the front garden but the road was clear, everything that had scattered brushed up into a mound just off the pavement, waiting for the owner to return and begin the fight with his insurance company.

If he returned. No word yet and no reply to the messages they'd left on his phone.

She got back into her car and drove to the village green, where the mobile incident unit was set up, an ugly white brick of a vehicle which the cottages around seemed to be shuttered against, gates closed, blinds drawn.

Zigic was already there, standing in the doorway talking to Parr.

'Julia Campbell,' he said, coming down the steps, leaving Parr to his work. 'She's been here this morning, wanting information about Dawn and Holly.'

'What did they tell her?'

'She already knew some of it. Sally's been gossiping.'

'Maybe that's why Warren didn't bring her to the ID with him.'

'Cracks appearing so soon?' Zigic asked, smiling humourlessly.

'Widening, I'd say.'

'Interesting that the new woman and the best friend are so close.'

Ferreira nodded. 'She's picked her side.'

Julia Campbell's house was a minute's walk from the green, tucked away down a narrow lane barely one car wide, behind the village chapel; a long and low stone cottage with a thatched roof and a wooden porch almost completely covered in glossy ivy. Tiny windows looked out across the road, the view from them partially blocked by metal planters running wild and full of tumbling purple flowers.

It was so different from the places they usually found themselves. No sheets tacked up across the windows, no broken bottles in the garden or foreign voices whispering from inside, scared and suspicious, and Ferreira realised it was the nicest house they'd been to since moving into Hate Crimes. So idyllic she found herself wondering how anything bad could happen here. You'd have to go looking for trouble, she thought.

Zigic knocked on the front door and it was answered instantly by a heavily pregnant woman with a lot of curly brown hair and a haunted expression, dressed in a Breton tunic, skinny legged in tight white jeans.

Julia Campbell was all fizzing nerves and excessive good manners. She shook their hands, her gold bangles jangling, and drew them inside, through a claustrophobic hallway, cluttered with painted furniture and too many clashing rugs, into the sunlit kitchen at the back of the house. Another room holding twice as much stuff as it was designed for. She offered them tea and put a plateful of home-made biscuits on the table as they sat down, busied herself with the kettle and cups.

Ferreira watched her while Zigic went through the formalities, answering her questions about the murder, being more evasive than usual. Quickly he moved onto her pregnancy and when was it due and did she know what she was having, talking about his own baby that was on the way – a girl, much to his wife's delight. Ferreira wasn't sure if he was trying to create a connection with Julia or if he just wanted to talk about it. You couldn't fake that glowing pride.

Julia looked too old to be pregnant, she thought. Forty, at least, and washed out despite the flawless yummy-mummy uniform and the swipe of geranium-pink lipstick.

Warren said she lived for other people's problems and Ferreira could easily imagine Dawn and Sally and however many other women were in Julia's circle, sitting here of a morning, drinking tea and eating her home-made biscuits while they poured out their traumas.

Ferreira didn't trust people like that. They took while they appeared to be giving, were nothing but gossips who paid for their information in baked goods and murmurs of sympathy.

'How long have you known Dawn?' Zigic asked.

'Oh, years. Since her and Warren moved into the village.' Julia sat down, pushed a white ceramic pot across the table. 'There's sugar if you want it. Um, it must be ten or eleven years now. They bought a lovely big house on Back Lane but when Holly had her accident things got slightly tight with Warren and his business and they lost the house.'

'Did Dawn have many friends in the village?'

'I'm not sure how much she saw of them any more.'

'What about boyfriends?' Ferreira asked.

'I wouldn't call them boyfriends,' she said sadly. 'Dawn desperately needed a boyfriend, a stable one, someone who'd look after her. But most men aren't prepared to take on a woman with kids, let alone a kid like Holly.' She glanced away from them. 'Warren was a marvellous father before the accident, absolutely dedicated to her, but look, even he left when the going got tough.'

'These non-boyfriends,' Ferreira said. 'What did she tell you about them?'

'She found them online. I didn't think it was a very good idea and I told her so. I mean, getting involved with someone you don't know like that. Letting them come into your home . . . Holly was there, she was a vulnerable girl. God knows who those men were.' The hard line of her mouth set slightly firmer. 'It was so selfish of her.'

Easy for you to say, Ferreira thought. Nice house, settled marriage, baby on the way. She wondered how long Julia would last as a single mother with a disabled child before she went looking for some not entirely safe fun to remind herself she was alive.

'Why didn't Dawn find a babysitter?' Zigic asked. 'She had friends still. She had you.'

Julia's fingers strayed to her necklace. 'I did go around and look after Holly when she asked me to. Once a week or so. I never minded spending time with Holly, she was a lovely girl. No trouble.'

'But you said Dawn had men at her house,' Ferreira said. 'Why did she do that when she could have asked you to help out?'

'I'm not sure.'

It sounded like a lie. A slight hesitance in her tone, the way her eyes dipped. Ferreira wondered if Julia's friendship with Sally had trumped the one she had with Dawn. Some people would always make you choose.

'Do you think one of them was responsible?' Julia asked, looking to Zigic for her answer. 'Please tell me Holly wasn't . . . wasn't *hurt*?'

'We're still waiting for the results of the autopsy,' he said.

Julia pressed her hand to her mouth and blinked away the brimming tears. 'She's at peace now. I suppose we should try and take some comfort in that.'

Zigic nodded, agreeing even though he looked slightly disturbed by the idea.

They had discussed the possibility of a mercy killing during the morning briefing, a flippant suggestion from Parr, provoked solely by Holly's condition, which was swiftly disregarded. Holly had suffered a prolonged and isolated death, trapped in a house with her mother's corpse. By no measure could that be considered merciful.

'When was the last time you saw Dawn and Holly?' Zigic asked.

'Sunday. Not yesterday, last Sunday. I dropped by for a couple of minutes to give her some jam, we've had a glut of plums this year.'

'Did Nathan go with you?'

Julia blinked rapidly. 'Sorry?'

'It's a simple question,' Ferreira said.

'No, I don't think he did.' Julia reached for a biscuit and bit it in half, avoiding looking at either of them. 'Why do you ask?'

'We understand Nathan was a regular visitor.'

'Dawn was very kind to him,' Julia said. 'And Caitlin. She really was very good with children. It's a shame she didn't have more.'

'And what about Holly?' Zigic asked. 'How did Nathan get on with her?'

Julia brushed a few biscuit crumbs off the polka-dot tablecloth. 'He made an effort with her. He's very young for his age but he understands what she's been through. It wasn't easy to talk to Holly.'

'She could communicate perfectly well, I understand,' Zigic said.

'Yes, she could talk but she'd become very introverted over the last six months.' Julia put the rest of the biscuit in her mouth. 'She just didn't want to talk very often. What can you say to someone in her situation?'

'Maybe Nathan can tell us,' Zigic said. 'What school does he attend?'

Julia looked between them quickly. 'He doesn't go to school.'

'Why?'

'He has, um, a very particular and challenging combination of educational needs.'

Zigic straightened in his seat. 'Which are best handled by him not going to school?'

'It's a complicated situation.' Julia got up from the table and went to the sink, threw her tea into it and washed the cup, bracelets jangling furiously.

Ferreira glanced at Zigic, saw his attention fixed on Julia's back.

'Are you home schooling him?'

'Yes. Something like that.'

'We'd like to speak to him, Mrs Campbell.' Julia turned around but didn't move from the sink. 'Now, please.'

'This has got nothing to do with Nathan.' Her voice was low and hard and suddenly it was as if they were dealing with another woman altogether. 'I won't let you upset him.'

'I don't think you understand what's happening here,' Zigic said. 'Two people – friends of yours – have been killed. Nathan might have seen something that can help us catch this monster.'

'He doesn't know anything.'

'Then he can tell us that himself.'

Zigic nodded at Ferreira and she got up, making for the kitchen door. The house was small, he wouldn't take much finding and Julia could complain about their tactics later if she wanted to. Right now talking to the boy was what mattered.

Julia moved to block her path.

'Wait.' She put her hands up. There were tears in her eyes again and Ferreira saw how hard she was fighting to stay calm. 'He's not here.'

'Where is he?' Ferreira asked.

'He ran away. Saturday afternoon. We haven't seen him since.' The tears came then and they looked genuine. 'He's such a sweet boy, he's not capable of surviving out there on his own.'

Zigic took her by the arm but she shrugged him off, returned to the table and gently lowered herself into her chair, one hand cupping her bump. Ferreira nodded towards the door but he shook his head.

She thought of the doctor's initial assessment at the crime scene. If he was right Dawn was murdered two days before Nathan went missing.

'Have you reported it?' Zigic asked.

'Of course I have.'

'Who's the officer you're dealing with?'

A shutter came down behind Julia's eyes. 'I'm not allowed to discuss this. I've signed agreements. Confidentiality agreements.'

'Don't you want to find Nathan?' Zigic asked, sitting down near her, trying the gentle approach. 'You realise he might have seen something that scared him. It's probably why he ran.'

'I can't,' Julia stammered. 'I'm sorry but I can't help you.'

Ferreira walked over to her, leaned on the table, into her face. 'What's Nathan done?'

'Nothing.'

'If you've signed confidentiality agreements he's done something serious.'

'No,' Julia snapped. 'He needs to be somewhere safe. That's why he's here. I'm supposed to keep him safe.'

She broke down and Ferreira walked out of the kitchen, leaving Zigic to mop up the spilled emotions; be the good guy.

Upstairs she went through the master bedroom; four-poster bed, black beams and white linen and an ancient-looking rocking horse with a maniacal face. Then a girl's room done out in predictable pink and frills, impermanent and impersonal despite the little touches Julia had added to make it appear homely. There were no photographs, very few clothes. Ferreira wondered how long the foster daughter had been there and how long before she moved on, whether it would be to a better life.

Nathan's room was the smallest in the house, a single bed pushed against the wall, a pine wardrobe and sea-green walls. They didn't have a warrant but they could get one if she found anything.

Ferreira looked in all the obvious places, then the less obvious ones. There was nowhere to hide anything significant in the box room and what she saw suggested the boy owned very little. A few changes of clothes, a few comic books. No laptop or phone, but he'd probably taken that with him when he ran.

She noticed the lock on the bedroom window and when she tried to open it found she couldn't. No sign of a key anywhere. Going back to the girl's room she encountered the same arrangement. The locks looked new, didn't fit with the style of the windows or the impression Julia had given them of herself and her family.

As she headed back down the stairs she could hear them talking still in the kitchen, Julia's voice rising into a shout occasionally, then more crying, impotent wailing. Zigic held steady, laying on the compassion. Ferreira let herself out of the cottage and smoked a cigarette while she waited for him to get what they wanted or give up the cause.

They needed to talk to the girl. Away from Julia, if it was possible.

Those locks on the windows . . . why were they necessary? To keep the kids in or somebody out?

A few minutes later Zigic emerged from the Hobbit-sized door, slammed it behind him.

'She's passing on my number to Nathan's case officer,' he said.

'And who's that?'

'She won't say.'

Ferreira eyed the bedroom window again. 'There's something very wrong about all this.'

12

Julia retreated to her workshop until the tears dried up and her heart stopped hammering. She sat in an old armchair she'd rescued from a skip outside a house in Oundle, taking deep breaths scented with pipe smoke and old perfume, the smell of its horsehair stuffing which was poking through a rip in the desiccated brocade.

She held the phone between her hands, wanting to dial but not quite ready to face the conversation they would have.

This time yesterday she didn't think the situation could get any worse. Nathan gone, out there, God knows where, facing more dangers than an innocent eleven-year-old boy could even imagine. But the universe could throw endless new sufferings at you. She knew that, she'd seen the evidence even if she'd never felt the effects on herself.

In a few hours Nathan had gone from vulnerable runaway to, what, a murder suspect?

DI Zigic had tried to play the concerned detective, pretended he needed Nathan as a potential witness, but she knew he was lying, assuming she was naive about how the police operated. She understood their ways better than he could know.

As he badgered and cajoled her she thought back to the days before Nathan ran away. Had he been quieter, more introverted? She didn't think so. He wasn't a particularly communicative child – no surprise given his situation – but if he'd seen something that disturbed him he would have told her. He wasn't strong enough psychologically to hide it.

The idea of him hurting Dawn and Holly was ludicrous. She wanted to tell DI Zigic that, explain how close they'd become in the months Nathan had been living here, the time he spent sitting with Holly or gardening with Dawn. She was always happy to take him and Caitlin in when there was nobody else to look after them for a few hours. Secretly Julia wondered if it was because she missed the normal mother-and-child interaction she didn't have with Holly any more. If that was why she loved having them with her.

Not that she could tell Zigic anything about it. If he knew Nathan came and went there as he liked he'd become their main suspect. Assuming he wasn't already.

This wasn't helping.

Obsessing over things she couldn't affect, looking for any reason to delay the inevitable.

Julia dialled the number she had committed to memory and waited for Rachel to answer.

'What is it, Julia? We're a bit busy here.'

'The police have just left my house.'

Rachel swore, loudly. 'Did you call them? I told you specifically not to involve the locals.'

'It wasn't like that,' Julia said, her throat tightening. Rachel intimidated her at the best of times. 'A friend of mine's been murdered, her and her daughter, they—'

'What's this got to do with Nathan?'

'The police want to talk to him, they think he might have seen something.'

A door slammed shut at the other end and Rachel's footsteps moved fast across a hard surface. Julia could see the expression on her face, barely suppressed fury, the determined gait full of aggression.

'What did you tell them, Julia?'

'Nothing, I didn't say anything. Somebody must have seen him there and mentioned it.'

'Seen him when?'

'I don't know. Nathan did visit the house—'

'We talked about that, didn't we? I told you to minimise contact between him and outsiders. You know it's not safe.'

'But they're friends of mine,' Julia said, feeling the tears threatening to spill again. 'They were nice people. Nathan liked them.'

'Yeah, well, now they're dead and he's missing and you've got the local plod in your fucking house.' Rachel let out a snarl of frustration. 'Did you tell them about me?'

'I had to.'

'Did you give them my name?'

'No, I said I'd ask you to get in touch with them, I thought that would be for the best.'

Rachel sighed and remained silent for a few seconds. When she spoke again she sounded calmer. 'Do they know why Nathan's with you?'

'No, of course not.' Julia stood up and walked to the work table overlooking the garden, focused on a sparrow bathing in the dust. 'Are you going to speak to them?'

'Yeah, this needs straightening out before they post a public appeal or something stupid like that.' Rachel asked for Zigic's details and as she took the number down Julia felt some of the weight lift from her shoulders. 'Did this DI Zigic ask you where Nathan was when the murders happened?'

'Yes, I told him Nathan was here with us.'

'Good,' Rachel said. 'Okay. And where was he really?'

Julia ran her fingertips along a gouge in the work table's surface. She saw the tool which made it, held in a small fist, heard the despairing roar as the awl struck the wood.

'He was here,' she said. 'The whole time.'

'Julia, I need you to be honest with me.' Rachel turned on her other voice, the one she used with Nathan, softer and higher, the one she probably used with her own kids. And people she thought were stupid enough to trust her. 'If there's any chance Nathan's involved I need to know about it now. Not when Zigic throws it at me. So, where was he?'

Julia bowed her head. 'I think he was here. I'm sure he was. But Zigic asked me where he was from Thursday afternoon until he went missing on Saturday. It's two days, he might have slipped out.'

'We're paying you a lot of money to make sure he doesn't "slip out",' Rachel said. 'What were you thinking?'

'Matthew was here, he was looking after Nathan. I'm sure he didn't let him out on his own.'

'Is that what he says?'

'I . . .' She felt bile rise in her throat, swallowed it down. 'He'd tell me if something happened.'

She could feel the wheels turning in Rachel's head. Trying to decide whether she should smooth this over or bring her full wrath down on Matthew. Julia prayed she didn't do that. He was ready to turn Nathan over already and once he'd made a decision there was no moving him.

'I'll deal with this,' Rachel said finally.

'What about Nathan? Is there any news? Do you know where he is?'

Footsteps again, Rachel preparing to end the call. 'We've had a positive sighting in Grantham.'

Julia dropped onto the stool. 'Oh, thank God he's safe.'

'He isn't safe,' Rachel said. 'Not by a long way.'

She ended the call, leaving Julia staring at the phone, smiling with relief. Part of her wanted to jump in the car and drive up to Grantham right away. It was a ninety-minute journey and a small city, she felt as if she could find him if she looked hard enough.

Rachel had it under control, though.

Nathan could be home within hours, tired and scared, but she knew how to soothe him. She'd make the sausage pasta he liked and chocolate cake for dessert, covered in frosting an inch deep and studded with Maltesers. She wouldn't be angry with him, not even once the relief had passed.

Julia went into the kitchen, flipped the kettle on and cleared away the remnants of her visit from the police. The woman hadn't touched her tea, neither of them ate the biscuits. She cursed herself for welcoming them into her home so warmly. But it was what you did when you were a good person, you helped the police.

The kettle came to a boil and she didn't hear the footsteps crunching down the gravel at the side of the house. Didn't realise there was someone in her garden until Warren banged on the back door. He was wild eyed and dishevelled, his T-shirt on inside out and when Julia opened the door he lurched inside as if he was drunk.

Immediately she regretted letting him in.

'Where is he?' Warren said.

'Who?'

'You know who, that delinquent you let loose on my fucking daughter!'

'Nathan isn't here and he isn't a delinquent.' Julia backed away from him, got the table between them. 'Warren, I wanted to call you, I'm so sorry about Dawn and Holly.'

He wasn't listening to her. He stood with his head cocked, trying to gauge where in the house Nathan was. For the first time since he'd run away Julia was glad he wasn't there. Warren looked capable of ripping him apart.

'Please, Warren, I think you should go home—'

'Not until I've talked to him.'

'He isn't here,' Julia said, trying to stay calm. 'And he didn't hurt Holly. Or Dawn. He isn't that kind of boy, honestly. He's very sweet.'

Warren sneered at her. 'I know what kind of boys you look after, Julia, so don't give me that rubbish.'

She felt her face flush and Warren moved in on her.

'Sweet, is he? Like that kid you had a couple of years ago, the one who cut up Mrs Arthur's sheep.' Julia backed away and he followed her. 'I seem to remember you screaming his innocence until you found a bag of ears stuffed in your airing cupboard.'

His nose was inches away from hers.

'Stop it! Just shut up about that.'

Warren smiled as if she'd capitulated and walked out of the kitchen, into the hallway, shouting Nathan's name. She sat down, hands stroking her stomach, trying to ignore his heavy footsteps and raging voice. She told herself he was mad with grief, he didn't know what he was saying, but all she could think about was the meaty smell as she'd opened the carrier bag and the split second of blissful ignorance before she realised what she was looking at.

But Nathan wasn't like that.

He wasn't.

13

'We need to know who this boy is,' Zigic said, standing at the murder board where Nathan's name now sat in the Persons of Interest column, underneath Gary Westman, the builder who'd been having an affair with Dawn, and the labourer who worked for him.

'If Julia's protecting his identity it's because he's done something major,' Ferreira said. 'This isn't a regular foster-care placement, she's too evasive for that.'

'So what's the other option?'

'Well, the kids' bedroom windows were locked, that's pretty unusual, I think. You'd only do it if you were worried about them absconding.'

'Which he has.'

Ferreira nodded. 'Or because someone's going to come looking for them.'

'Like who?'

'Depends who he is,' she said. 'His parents maybe, if he's been taken off them and they're not happy about it.'

Zigic moved to the timeline of the murders they were working on, still very little information on it but the post-mortems would be finished soon and a preliminary report was due from forensics this afternoon. He added a spur at the time of Nathan's disappearance; twenty-four hours before the bodies were discovered, roughly forty-eight after Dawn was murdered. It was a long delay if he was responsible or a witness, but until they had a concrete time of death from the pathologist Zigic would keep an open mind.

There was one other mark on there already. The point on Thursday morning when Westman left the house; the last-known person to see her alive.

Riggott had sent up another detective constable to help them out for a few days and she was with Westman now, taking his official statement and getting an alibi. They would request a DNA sample for elimination purposes, but if he decided to refuse and force them to step up proceedings that could be dealt with. It would give them time to check out his alibi too.

Julia's comments about Dawn's sex life suggested they'd be asking for a lot of DNA samples in the coming days. Assuming they could locate the men she'd been involved with. They were still waiting on the tech department to access her phone and laptop records before that particular task could start.

It was highly possible their killer would be hidden somewhere on Dawn's contact list, partially screened behind a dating-site username. The ferocity of the attack suggested a man with a temper, one who'd been spurned or mocked and had lashed out. Statistically it was the most likely explanation.

But how did Holly's death fit into that scenario?

Did whoever killed Dawn simply not know Holly was in the house?

Behind him Wahlia and Ferreira were still speculating on Nathan's potential identity and the reasons for Julia's stoic refusal to discuss the matter, running through ever more sensational possibilities; unhinged parents looking to get him back, witness protection, a new identity necessitated by him committing a high-profile murder.

'Why else wouldn't she give you his surname?' Wahlia asked.

'We should be able to find that out,' Zigic said.

'Do you want me to call social services? I know a woman down there, she'll have access to the Campbells' records.'

'Yeah, try her now.'

Zigic waited while he dialled, looking at the space on the board where the murder weapon should have been. He took out his phone and checked the next few days' weather forecast, rain due by the end of the week. If they were going to search the surrounding area it would have to be soon, but he wanted a better idea of where it might be before suggesting such an expensive operation to Riggott.

And for that he needed a concrete suspect.

Wahlia left a message on the answerphone and hung up. 'She's probably out on a call. I'll stay on her.'

The computer in Zigic's office chimed as an email came in and he found the preliminary report from forensics, flagged as urgent, waiting in his inbox. He set it to print out – needing to see everything in front of him on paper, the only way he could remember and process it fully – and went to get a fresh cup of coffee.

Ferreira already had the report open on screen, running through it so fast he was sure she couldn't be taking it in properly.

'Have you seen this?'

'Not yet,' he said, going to collect the sheets of paper from the printer. 'Hold on a minute.'

'There's blood on the banister and the treads.'

Zigic grabbed a seat at an empty desk, knowing that if he didn't they'd end up shouting at each other across the office. He scanned through the part she was looking at, a couple of pages in.

'No clear footprints,' he said. 'How is that possible? There was blood all over the kitchen, they must have tracked it right through the house.'

'Jenkins reckons somebody tried to clean up afterwards.'

Zigic skipped ahead to where she was. Jenkins's notes described finding flecks of white cotton on the treads of the stairs, smears up the banister, destroying any fingerprints laid down on the painted wood. The bloodstained towels used for the job dumped in the linen basket. She'd retrieved a few strands of hair from them. It was a start.

'They didn't panic,' he said. 'Doing all that would have taken time.'

He imagined a figure moving through the house, slow and methodical, checking every surface, calmy removing themself from the scene. Who behaved like that after committing such a violent crime? What kind of person could hold it together, think ahead, be logical, see the crime scene the way a copper would and anticipate their actions well enough to frustrate the coming forensics officers?

The efficiency of it disturbed him more than the violence of Dawn Prentice's murder.

Or, rather, the understanding that one person could switch so quickly between the two mindsets. It suggested they wouldn't make mistakes further down the line. No drunken slips to a family member, no guilt gnawing away at them.

'Whoever did this was confident they wouldn't be discovered in the act.' Ferreira leaned away from the screen. 'Suggests they were familiar with Dawn's routine, don't you think?'

'We need to know when her home help was due in,' Zigic said. 'Where are we with that?'

'Waiting for a call back,' Wahlia told him. 'She was using a small independent health-care company. They don't seem very organised.'

Or concerned, Zigic thought. Five days since Dawn was last seen alive, shouldn't Holly's nurse have visited during that period? He didn't know much about how home help worked but he was sure that somebody in Holly's condition would have been visited more than once a week. Meaning the nurse would have gone to the house, seen the mess next door and the crime-scene tape, but not come forward.

'Chase them up, Bobby.'

'I only called them an hour ago.'

'Call again.'

Zigic went back to the beginning of the report and read it through properly, finding that the contamination of the site was even more serious than it looked. The kitchen was so heavily covered in debris that any future prosecution would be open to difficult questions about where each particular piece of evidence originated. And, just as Jenkins warned, the emergency services had managed to wipe out or obscure most of the useful footprints on the bloody kitchen floor.

There was no sign of the murder weapon. The whole kitchen had been searched, every available knife taken and examined, but none bore traces of blood or matched the dimensions of the wounds on Dawn's body. None fitted the two empty slots in the knife block either – one six-inch blade missing, the most likely weapon, but a smaller five-inch one was gone too and the lack of explanation for that bothered him.

The rest of the house had remained more or less clean, the worst of the blast damage restricted to the kitchen and the living room – photographs of that showed an old-fashioned carpet and wallpaper, a new modular sofa which matched neither and the remains of a bookshelf toppled by the force of the explosion. No signs of blood in the room and if it had seen any violence there was no way of telling.

'Holly's room was clean,' Ferreira said. 'No blood traces, no signs of disturbance.'

Zigic looked up from the file. 'Was her bedroom door closed or open?'

'Open when I got there.'

'But before that?' Zigic asked. 'Did the uniforms go in there?'

'Fire crew was first in the house, they were looking for people to evacuate . . . I get you. Hold on, I've got the bloke's number, I'll find out.'

Zigic drank the rest of his coffee as he went through the file again, wanting everything fixed in his head. Ferreira was waiting on hold, impatiently turning her lighter around between her fingers and tapping it on the desk.

He got up and went to the gents, took a detour to the technical department to check where they were with Dawn's phone and laptop and found the offices deserted. The tail end of the lunch hour, they'd be back soon at least. He realised he hadn't eaten yet either but didn't fancy whatever was in the vending machines or the canteen and couldn't be bothered driving out to pick something up.

Ferreira was finishing her call when he returned to the office, thanking the man on the other end, checking one last time that he was absolutely and definitely sure what he'd seen.

'Closed,' she said, as she put the phone down. 'His mate found Dawn, he went upstairs to check the bedrooms – this was the middle of the night, of course – Holly's door was definitely closed. He saw her, assumed she was still alive, but couldn't move. Then when he went to pick her up . . . she was cold.'

'Okay.' Zigic went over to the board again. 'So, we've got no blood traces in Holly's room and nothing suspicious on the door handle and the door's closed when emergency services arrive.'

'Did the killer even know she was in the house then?' Ferreira asked. 'If it was some bloke who was there for Dawn it's possible he wouldn't have known Holly existed.'

'But they went upstairs to use the bathroom. They took the time to wipe down the stairs. You do all that but don't check the other rooms?'

'And risk being seen by someone?' Ferreira asked. 'No. Look, if nobody's come to see what the hell you're doing. If they haven't heard the commotion and got involved, you wouldn't automatically go looking to get yourself witnessed.'

Zigic stared at Holly's photograph, thinking of her hearing feet coming up the stairs, water running in the bathroom. Was she used to that? Hearing Dawn's temporary boyfriends in the house?

'The other explanation is they knew Holly was there and that she couldn't do anything about it,' Ferreira said. 'So they just left her alone.'

'To die?'

Ferreira nodded. 'This is fucking sickening. Christ, if they did know she was there, and they knew what kind of state she was in – that's worse than what they did to Dawn.'

'And it's not murder,' Zigic said bitterly. 'When we find this bastard, we're not even going to be able to charge him over her death.'

'Manslaughter?'

'Does that feel like enough to you?'

She walked away, over to the window where she'd left a half-smoked cigarette sitting on the sill. 'Maybe the autopsy will turn something up.'

'You saw her,' Zigic said. 'She wasn't murdered.'

Not in a way the law would regard as murder. Manslaughter maybe. Neglect most likely. It would all hinge on whether they, and the CPS, could prove that the killer knew Holly was in the house and too severely incapacitated to survive without her mother's care. Westman knew that. Warren knew it too – but Zigic seriously doubted that he'd let Holly suffer.

Nathan? The boy was a void still. Until they could get some kind of handle on his history and personality it was impossible to even guess at what he might do.

Wahlia's phone rang and he snatched it up, mouthed 'social services' at Zigic when he looked over.

It was a quick conversation, minimal input from Wahlia's end after he told the woman what he needed and assured her it would be off the record. A promise he couldn't actually keep. Two minutes later it was over and he shook his head at Zigic.

'They've got no record of a boy being lodged with the Campbells.'

'She must be mistaken,' Zigic said. 'He might be there under another name.'

'No boy of any name.' Wahlia was still frowning at the phone. 'They've got the girl, Caitlin Johnson. She's been with them just over two years. But no boy.'

‘Maybe he’s been brought in from out of the area,’ Ferreira suggested.

‘No, she’d have a record of him. The different regions have to liaise.’ Zigic stared at Nathan’s name in the Persons of Interest column, the letters almost pulsing. ‘If he’s been deliberately kept off the official database it’s because he’s high risk. Question is – who to?’

14

Mr Talbot – Caitlin's head of year – didn't look much like a teacher. Or nothing like the teachers Ferreira remembered from school. He was young and smartly suited, hair well barbered, wearing a light stubble over a deep tan. Middle management, she would have guessed, if she'd seen him on the street. Financial sector, something in law perhaps. Mid-level now, but ambitious and capable enough to move up quickly.

She guessed that was what heads of years were, though. Aspiring top-level management, temporarily holding an unwanted but necessary teaching position. He looked like someone who thought in buzzwords and bullshit concepts.

'I'm surprised Caitlin's in today,' Ferreira said. 'What with everything that's going on.'

Talbot shifted his weight in the leather chair, eyes flicking away to his computer screen for a split second. Ferreira would have laid money Caitlin Johnson was barely on his radar half an hour ago. He'd boned up before she arrived, now he was going to play the conscientious *loco parentis*.

'The staff have been made aware of the situation,' he said, smoothing one manicured hand down his purple silk tie. 'In the barest terms, of course. Mrs Campbell and I thought it would be best for Caitlin to come in. Maintain her routine.'

'And how's that going?'

'Caitlin's no trouble,' he said. 'Her teachers are all very happy with how she's progressed since she enrolled her. We've got high hopes for her GCSEs and beyond.'

'That must be unusual. Considering her background.'

'Most children thrive with stability.' He smiled, something queasily earnest in the look he gave her. 'She has a dedicated learning support assistant too. Mrs Fraser, you'll meet her in a moment.'

'If Caitlin's a good student why does she need an LSA?'

Talbot paused, hand straying to his tie once again. 'Mrs Fraser was assigned to help Caitlin with more social issues. She's quite a self-contained girl, which is only natural given her – well – experience. We'd like to see her come out of her shell a little more.'

A soft hand tapped on his office door and Talbot told them to come in, standing to make the introductions. Ferreira stood too, as a middle-aged woman in jeans and Fair Isle jumper entered the room, trailed by what Ferreira first took to be a teenage boy.

Caitlin was tall for her age and heavily built, in black uniform trousers and a sweatshirt two sizes too large. Everything about her appearance was designed to camouflage her femininity. She wore no make-up and her brown hair was severely cut, very short and razored underneath, her fringe hiding half of her face. The only girlie touch was a pair of silver-and-topaz studs in her ears.

She was a girl who didn't want to be noticed, Ferreira thought, and wondered what in her previous life had led her to believe that was the safest option. If she didn't know Caitlin was in care she might not have considered the underlying reasons but now she guessed at a history of abuse, too much history for a thirteen-year-old to deal with.

Her look was a shield against the kind of perverts and predators she'd encountered already but Ferreira knew it would never work. Not completely. Because men like that would see through it, see that she was already damaged and know they could damage her more.

'Caitlin, I'm Mel.' She stuck her hand out and the girl shook it warily, giving her the briefest second of eye contact from behind her fringe. 'I'm investigating Dawn and Holly's deaths.'

Caitlin looked at Mrs Fraser, who squeezed her arm and smiled encouragingly.

'Why don't we all sit down,' Talbot suggested. He gestured towards a grey fabric sofa and two armchairs, arranged around a low coffee table, and they took their places, Caitlin sitting close to Mrs Fraser on the sofa, Ferreira and Talbot taking the chairs.

'Has Julia told you what happened?' Ferreira asked.

Caitlin nodded. 'Dawn was murdered. She thinks it was one of her boyfriends.'

'And what do you think?'

'Dawn wasn't stupid. She wouldn't let herself get bullied by a bloke.'

Mrs Fraser started to say something and Ferreira cut her off with a look.

'Some blokes do what they want, though,' she said. 'It wouldn't matter how smart or strong Dawn was.'

Caitlin shrank slightly where she sat.

Change tack, Ferreira thought, quick.

'Did you go round to Dawn's house very often?'

'Sometimes.'

'You must have known Holly before she had her accident.' Caitlin nodded again, still closed off, eyes averted. 'What was she like?'

'Nice. Really sporty.'

'Were you two friends?'

'I don't like sport.' She blinked but didn't brush her hair away. 'Me and Dawn were friends. When Holly and her dad went off for the weekend doing stuff me and Julia went round to see Dawn. She was funny. You could talk to her.'

'About what?'

Caitlin drew her hands up into the cuffs of her sweatshirt. Another uncomfortable topic.

'Anything.'

Mrs Fraser was watching Caitlin very carefully and Ferreira noticed how she mirrored every expression that crossed the girl's face. Either she was deeply empathic or a natural mimic, a skill which would be useful for dealing with vulnerable kids, good for earning their trust, making them believe you genuinely cared.

'How about Nathan?' she asked. 'How did he get on with Dawn?'

Caitlin folded her arms over her middle. 'Why do you wanna know?'

'We need to talk to everyone who was close to Dawn and Holly to see if they might know anything. If they saw anyone hanging around the house.' Ferreira tried to dip into her eye line but the girl was staring at her lap. 'Holly's dad mentioned that Nathan and her were friendly. Is that right?'

'Yeah. I suppose so.' Inside the cuff of her sweatshirt her fingers were nervously working at something. 'He used to go up and sit with her.'

'And do what?'

'Talk. I don't know.' Her fingers kept twitching. 'What else would he be doing up there?'

Mrs Fraser reached out and closed her hand around Caitlin's, told her in a soft voice not to be scared. 'Just tell the lady what you saw, Lin.'

'I didn't see anything,' she snapped. 'Nathan's a little kid, what do you think he was doing? What, you think he was fiddling with her or something?'

'Nobody's saying that,' Mrs Fraser said gently.

Caitlin wasn't listening, though. She was looking at Ferreira, a challenging stare shooting through the shards of her fringe, daring her to voice a contradiction.

Ferreira had her full attention now.

'Why do you think Nathan ran away from home?'

'I don't know.'

'Did he tell you why he's in care?'

'He's there for the same reason I am. Because nobody wants him.'

'Is that what he told you?'

'He won't talk about it,' she said. 'He doesn't like talking to anyone. Except Julia.'

'And Holly?'

'He wouldn't hurt her,' Caitlin said, a surprising vehemence in her tone. As if she was defending her own blood. 'You don't know him. You think everyone's shit. Just because we're in care it doesn't mean we're shit.'

Ferreira forced herself to sit back, wait, let the girl's words fade slightly before she went on. She didn't know how to deal with children, always thought it best to treat them just the same as adults because it's what she would have wanted at that age. She reminded herself that Caitlin was grieving and worried about Nathan. She obviously needed to be at home and Ferreira wondered why Julia sent her in to school today.

Mrs Fraser took a packet of tissues out of her bag and handed one to Caitlin. She wadded it up tight in her fist.

'No one cares about us,' she said, chin tucked down into her chest.

'Julia cares.'

'Yeah, right.' Caitlin started to shred the tissue into her lap. 'If she cares why isn't she on the telly trying to get Nathan back?'

Ferreira didn't have an answer. Or not one she was going to share.

'That's how you find missing people, isn't it?' Caitlin asked. 'You go on the news. You use Twitter and that.'

'I'm sure the officer in charge will involve the media when he thinks the time's right.'

'She.'

'What?'

'Rachel. It's a woman looking for him.'

Ferreira tried to think of a Rachel serving on the local force. There were none she knew of in plain clothes and it was unlikely a uniform would be involved in any major capacity.

'Is this your family-liaison officer?'

'She's a detective,' Caitlin said.

'What's her surname?'

Caitlin cocked her head. 'Shouldn't you know that? You're looking for Nathan, you should talk to her.'

'We should,' Ferreira conceded. 'But she's not been in contact. I guess because she's working so hard on getting him home right now.' Caitlin looked unconvinced. 'When was the last time you saw her?'

'Saturday night. She came to the house.'

'This is when Nathan ran off?' Caitlin nodded. 'And Julia called nine-nine-nine?'

'No. She called Rachel. Rachel looks after Nathan. She's supposed to make sure he doesn't get in t—' Caitlin stopped herself.

'Trouble?'

Quick blinking, brain whirring. 'Doesn't get into danger.'

'Why does Nathan need a detective to look after him?' Ferreira asked, an uncomfortable sensation spreading across the back of her neck. 'What's he done?'

Caitlin brushed the flecks of tissue off her thighs, onto Talbot's pristine blue carpet. Delaying answering, trying to dredge up a lie or a denial.

She was convinced the girl knew much more about Nathan than she was letting on but getting it out of her would be tough. Especially once Julia became involved, which she was entitled to do as her legal guardian.

'Caitlin,' Ferreira said. 'You know it isn't normal for Nathan to have a detective looking out for him, don't you?'

She stiffened. 'This isn't anything to do with you.'

'Yes, it is. Because your friend Dawn has been murdered and Holly's dead and now Nathan's run off.' Ferreira straightened up.

'All in a matter of a couple of days. You're a smart girl, how do you think that looks for him?'

'He didn't do it,' she said, a flush rising on her face.

'I think you're probably right,' Ferreira told her. 'I think Nathan saw something or someone and he got scared. That's why he ran away.'

'I've been calling him,' Caitlin said. 'I've messaged him. He won't answer.'

'Can you give me his number, please?'

Caitlin brought out her phone and Ferreira saw how few numbers Caitlin had in her contacts as she scrolled down to Nathan's. Two years at the school but she obviously hadn't settled as well as Talbot's notes suggested; kids were too sharp and too cruel and any hint of difference or suffering was just an invitation to strike harder. Being ignored by her classmates was probably the least bad outcome.

'Are you going to find him?' Caitlin asked.

Ferreira smiled as warmly as she could. 'We're going to try.'

15

The post-mortem report arrived while Zigic was trying to make a dent in the mountain of paperwork covering his desk and he opened it, grateful for the distraction, even one as grim as this.

Dawn had died, as expected, from multiple stab wounds, impossible to tell which was the killing blow but most likely the small nick across her windpipe. The pathologist noted the ferocity of the attack, the force necessary to drive a blade clean through to her back – a blade at least six inches long, he suggested, which meant their murder weapon was probably one of the missing knives from the wooden block in her kitchen.

She would have died within minutes, choking on her own blood. Estimated time of death, Thursday evening between six and midnight.

Holly hadn't been so lucky. She'd hung on until Saturday evening before suffering a massive stroke brought on from the build-up of toxins in her system. A death which could have been avoided if only someone had been there to empty her catheter.

He put the report down to answer his mobile, a caller-withheld number on the display and a woman's voice on the other end.

'We need to talk.'

'Who is this?'

'If you need to ask that you shouldn't be a DI.'

'I'm an idiot,' Zigic said. 'Humour me.'

'I'm Nathan's guardian angel.' There was engine noise at her end, expensively insulated. 'The lay-by at Norman's Cross, meet me there in fifteen minutes.'

'Come into the station.'

'It's Norman's Cross or nothing,' she said, and killed the call.

Zigic made the meeting point in under ten minutes, wanting to get there first and gather as much information about his shadowy contact as he could. He'd debated taking someone else along with him, just to see how she'd react, but decided against it. Ferreira was still out of the office, everyone else fully occupied.

He felt uncomfortable about this meeting taking place off the record, just the two of them present, knowing that anything he got from Nathan's mysterious guardian would become legally debatable because of the circumstances. No decent copper carried on like this.

She'd picked a suitably cloak-and-dagger spot for it. The lay-by was on one of the main roads into the city centre, just off the A1, which he could hear roaring as he climbed out of the car, engine noise driven in on a stiffening wind that carried an autumnal edge. There were no houses nearby and the passing traffic moved quickly, drivers still set at motorway pace, but the fast-food van parked up tight to the hedgerow was doing a brisk trade, enough to warrant the presence of a couple of chrome cafe tables, both taken, with more people eating in their vehicles, radios playing, doors open. No women, though.

Zigic bought a Coke and drank it sitting on the bonnet of his car, looking across the road to an empty grass field bordered with trees just beginning to turn. It was the site of a Napoleonic prisoner-of-war camp, the first purpose-built one in the world, and had housed thousands of captured soldiers and 'enemy aliens' in varying degrees of luxury according to their means. The wooden barracks were long gone, only the agent's house and the stables remained, substantial white-painted buildings which looked grander than their origins and somehow retained a besieged air, standing in this stagnant hinterland between the motorway and the suburbs.

The old stable block was an art gallery now, selling paintings and small sculptures by local artists, and for a moment he assumed the woman walking along the path must have come from there. But it wasn't a place you walked to or from and he doubted she was heading back into Peterborough from the Premier Inn on the side of the road either, although she was dressed like a cleaner who'd just come off shift, in jeans and a loose cotton shirt, open over a white vest.

She was careful, he realised. Paranoid even. Had parked along the road somewhere so he couldn't identify her from the number plate on her car.

It didn't bode well.

She waited impatiently for a gap to appear in the traffic and finally managed to get across the road when a delivery van pulling out of the lay-by blocked off one lane, the driver waving her across. She put a hand up to him and strode over to Zigic, her finger already jabbing the air.

'You need to back off,' she said.

'And you need to tell me who the hell you are.'

Across her shoulder Zigic noticed a young man climb out of his parked vehicle, watching to see how this went and if he needed to intervene. The woman followed his gaze and, as she turned, the young man asked if she was okay.

'Fine, thanks. No worries.' She glared at Zigic. 'We're not talking here.'

With a sharp nod of the head she started across the tangled verge, stomping through wind-blown branches and barbed blackberry crawlers, expecting him to follow her over the thigh-high mesh fence and onto the gated service road beyond. Zigic swore at her retreating back, knowing he was ceding ground and the best thing to do was get in his car and drive away, but there was something amiss in the Campbells' household and she was the only person who could explain it to him.

Assuming he could persuade her to.

Her attitude suggested he was more likely to end up in the water-filled knothole she was leading him towards, moving as if she was magnetised.

He ran around these old clay pits occasionally and he always felt the sheer scale of the man-made lakes tugging at him as he got closer, an elemental and unfathomable compulsion. It was a blasted terrain, studded with piles of building rubble and fly-tipped household waste, only the hardiest plants able to find nourishment, breaking through the patches of tarmac and grey gravel paths. The gunmetal water sparkled as the low afternoon sun hit its rippling surface, but he knew how deep the pit was, how cold and dark its depths went.

'Rachel,' she said, when he reached her.

'Rachel what?'

She braced her foot against a chunk of concrete spiked with rusted reinforcing bars. 'That's as much as you get.'

'It's not enough,' Zigic said. 'Are you police?'

'What else would I be?'

'You're not acting like it.'

'This is a delicate situation and I can't tell you any more than what I'm going to.' The wind whipped her long blonde hair across her face and she brushed it away behind her ear. 'My superior officer will be in touch with your DCS. Riggott, isn't it? He'll square what we're doing.'

'And what is that, exactly?'

'I can't tell you.'

'Because it's delicate,' Zigic said, fighting the rising annoyance. 'I've got a murdered woman and a dead child and there's every chance Nathan can help me find who's responsible. I need to talk to him.'

'He's gone.'

'I know that. And I want to know where he is.'

She looked over the shimmering lake. 'We're working on it.'

Across the lunar-like scrub a volley of shots rang out and she flinched, cocked her head to try and read their position, assess the threat level. They'd come from a shooting club a few hundred yards to the south, the light pop of .22 handguns discharging into paper targets, but the peculiarities of the landscape bent the sound so they seemed much closer.

'What's Nathan done?' Zigic asked.

'You don't need to know that.'

'Social services have got no record of him being placed with the Campbells – why is that?'

'It's not your concern,' she said, turning on him. 'You need to stay the fuck out of this.'

She was losing it, Zigic thought. She'd been given a job and she'd failed to see it through and now there would be pressure mounting, more than she could cope with, and until Nathan was found it was only going to get worse. Offering to help wouldn't soften her, he realised, although it was his first instinct.

Which only left one option.

'There's strong evidence that Nathan was present at the murder scene,' he said. 'Forensic evidence. I can't ignore that and I won't have my investigation limited by your inability to track this kid down.'

She crossed her arms, fists bunched tight. 'What evidence?'

'You don't need to know that,' Zigic said, taking a small pleasure in throwing her words back at her. 'It's enough to arrest him. Especially when we consider his . . . unusual relationship with the dead girl and the fact that he's run away.'

'Nathan isn't a murderer,' Rachel said fiercely.

'I've only got your word for it and frankly, the way you're behaving, I'm inclined to trust the evidence more.'

'He's a good boy.'

'Why's he in protective custody then?'

'It isn't what you think,' she said. 'If I could tell you the background to this I would, but I can't. It's a highly complex, highly dangerous situation, and Nathan's safety is my primary concern right now.' She gave him a meaningful look. 'We're not the only people trying to find him.'

'You don't seem to be trying very hard,' Zigic said. 'Why didn't you alert us?'

She just shook her head.

'Where are you even from?' Zigic asked, exasperated. He waited but she didn't answer. 'Right, you can't tell me that either.'

Her accent was Estuary but he knew better than to believe it meant anything. Even if she'd started out around London it didn't mean that she was based there now or that Nathan's case, whatever that might be, was tied to the city. Especially as he was clearly meant to be kept hidden away out here on the edge of the Fens. The more he thought about it the more likely it seemed that Nathan was a recently released offender and the only ones who warranted such an intense degree of protection were those with high-profile crimes inextricably linked to the names they could no longer use.

'You realise there's nothing to stop me going public with this,' he said. 'My case, my suspect, I can have his face on every major media outlet within the hour.'

She stepped up to him, toe to toe. Six inches shorter but swollen with aggression. 'I will have your fucking job.'

'I'm prepared to risk it.'

'You've got no idea what's at stake here.'

'Not if you won't explain it to me,' Zigic said. 'And until you're prepared to do that I'm going to pursue Nathan however I think best.'

She backed down slightly, half a step, creating some breathing space. The anger was still there though and she glanced towards the lake for a second, teeth bared, as if she was seriously considering making a move on him.

Suddenly Zigic felt stupid for meeting her here, off the record and the radar, no witnesses to their conversation. She could do or say anything and it would be his word against hers. She was furious and desperate, a combustible mix he needed to get away from.

He started back towards the car, feet crunching over the gravel, more popping gunshots rolling around the basin as he made the slight rise from the banks of the knothole, feet skidding on loose stones.

'If Nathan's face goes public he'll be dead within hours.'

Zigic stopped.

'Do you want that on your conscience?'

She was a few feet away from him, holding out a slip of paper folded between her fingertips. 'This is my number.'

He didn't take it.

'I'm not trying to stop you talking to Nathan,' she said. 'When I find him you can talk to him. I promise you that. Whatever you need to ask him, I'll make sure he cooperates.' She gestured with the paper. 'Please.'

Zigic took it from her and tucked it into his pocket. 'What if you don't find him?'

'We know where he's heading,' she said. 'I just hope to God we can pick him up before he gets there.'

They walked through the scrub and climbed back over the fence into the lay-by which was still full of vehicles but different ones from those he'd seen before. Zigic's Coke was sitting on the bonnet of his car where he'd left it, sun-warmed now and undrinkable and he threw it into the nearby bin.

'I'll keep you updated,' Rachel said, by way of a goodbye, and strode off across the road, heading back towards wherever she'd hidden her car.

For a moment he debated following her – something about the story didn't ring true, the evasions and threats she'd pulled out of the air – but as he snapped his seat belt into place his phone buzzed, a message from Riggott: *My office ASAP*.

16

Riggott's secretary looked up from her computer as Zigic approached the office.

'You'll have to wait, he's in with someone at the moment.'

It was about as pointless a statement as anyone had ever made, with an unbroken stream of machine-gun ranting blasting through the closed door. Whoever was on the receiving end of the boss's ire had wisely decided to stay silent. It was the best option with Riggott whether you were right or wrong. But especially if you were right.

The DCS suffered from too much pent-up aggression, that was the problem. At heart he was still a detective, made for crushing suspects' stories in the interview rooms. Zigic had sat next to him through countless hours of probing and cajoling, violent threats and seductive promises all delivered with impeccable credibility. Management gave him limited scope to flex his skills and only one audience for them.

The office door opened and a red-faced detective constable hurried out, chased by a single vehement curse.

Riggott poked his head around the door, pointed at Zigic.

'You're up, big man.'

A fan whirred in the corner of the room, rustling the papers scattered across Riggott's desk, and as it turned it blew a chocolate wrapper onto the floor. He worked in chaos and Zigic wondered if it was another symptom of his reluctant removal from the fray, a way of keeping things intriguingly complex for himself.

Riggott gathered the file he'd been looking at and dropped it on top of the pile of ones just like it in his out tray. Whatever transgression the office's previous victim had committed would be in there and now Riggott was done with that.

He waved for Zigic to sit down and produced an e-cigarette from his shirt pocket.

'I've just had a very interesting phone call about you.' He took a short puff. 'And I can tell you, I don't appreciate being left stammering like a fucking tube because one of my officers has left me out of the loop.'

'It was a fast-moving situation—'

'Fast-moving my hairy left one,' Riggott said. 'We have these amazing devices now called smartphones. You don't even have to talk, you can just tap in a message and it comes straight to me. Something like . . . I'm poking my nose into bigger shit than I can deal with. Help!'

'I didn't have a chance,' he said and kept talking despite Riggott's rolling his eyes. 'This copper – Rachel – she made the call before I even knew she existed. She's a piece of work.'

'She knows her business, you mean.'

'She's uncooperative, unprofessional, and I'm pretty sure she's hiding something of significant importance to my case. Now she's used whatever pull she's got to have you tell me to back down. Am I about right?'

'What d'you reckon she's on with hiding then?' Riggott asked.

Zigic explained about Nathan, the mystery over his identity and the claims by Holly's father of a potential threat from him – exaggerating slightly but he needed Riggott firmly onside. Told him the boy had run away and nobody had bothered to report it.

He saw that he was getting through to the DCS, piquing the detective inside the superintendent.

'So, you're thinking this wee feral's a wrong'un?'

'I'm struggling to see another reason for all the secrecy,' Zigic said. 'She's desperate to keep his face out of the press. That suggests to me that he's highly recognisable. Not many eleven-year-old boys are.'

'No, just the sort who drown toddlers in paddling pools and set fire to their nanas.' He took a thoughtful pull on his cigarette, exhaled vapour. 'How strong a suspect you reckon he is?'

Zigic shrugged. 'Until we know more about the kid it's tough to say. Maybe he's just a witness. He saw something that scared him so he ran. It's a brutal crime for a child to carry out.'

'You're thinking like a father,' Riggott said. 'We both know what eleven-year-old boys can do when their wiring's not right. DNA at the scene?'

'Hairs in bloodstained towels in the bathroom. Our killer cleaned up before they left the house.'

'Nothing at the locus?'

'It was too badly contaminated.'

'And the family's covering for him, aye?'

Zigic nodded. 'The foster mother won't cooperate. She's hiding behind some confidentiality agreement they had her sign. I don't know if we can compel her?'

'Word on this has come from mighty high up,' Riggott said gravely. 'Now, you know me, I'm never one to worry about stamping on toes and I wouldn't expect you to put this Rachel woman's case before yours, but you're going to cooperate with her. No sneaking about, no leaks. Not if you want to keep your job.'

It wasn't an idle threat, then. She'd come at him with real clout.

'Did they tell you anything about him?'

Riggott shook his head and Zigic could see how much that annoyed him. A crime on his patch and he couldn't intervene, hadn't even been given the professional courtesy of an explanation.

'Other suspects?' he asked.

'Nothing concrete yet,' Zigic said. 'I'm hoping we can get something more from the nurse. She'd have been there, seen more of the comings and goings maybe. But the girl died from natural causes brought on by neglect, so it's an odd combination of circumstances.' He explained them briefly and Riggott nodded along. 'It looks like we can rule out the estranged husband. He wouldn't have left Holly to die. That rules out anyone close to them, I think. If they had an issue with Dawn alone, why punish Holly too?'

Riggott's mouth twitched. 'Catch yourself on, son. The nurse should've arrived the next morning, I take it – anyone familiar with their routine would expect Holly to be found the next day. Don't go ruling people out on that basis.'

He was right, Zigic realised. It was a gamble on the part of the killer but not much of one.

'What else?'

'We're looking into Dawn's love life,' Zigic said. 'Still waiting on the tech department to go through her contacts but several sources say she was hooking up with random guys at her house.'

'Dangerous behaviour to be undertaking, that.'

'Potentially, yeah.'

'Sure, there's no potentially about it. Carry on like that long enough you'll find a thug.' Riggott sighed. 'Ann Summers on every high street, fucking dildos in the chemists, and these women still go putting themselves under any bastard with an Internet connection and a hard-on.'

'Maybe it wasn't just about the sex,' Zigic suggested. 'She was lonely. She was struggling. Maybe she needed the company as much as anything else.'

Riggott waved his words away. 'Don't be soft, Ziggy. You've got a puritan's view of women, you know that?'

He wasn't going to sit there and argue sexual politics with his boss, as much as he disagreed. Fact was, Riggott knew far more about random hook-ups and one-night stands than he did, if the station rumour mill was to be believed.

'How's the disability angle looking?' Riggott asked.

'She wasn't taking it seriously,' Zigic said, happy to be back on firm ground. 'Her harassment log is virtually non-existent, no suspects, no witnesses. Right now I've got serious reservations about the extent of it in general, let alone as a potential motive.'

'Give it another couple of days, then. If anything turns up, you stick with it, if not I'm having it back in CID.'

When we've done all the hard graft, Zigic thought.

'Don't gimme that face,' Riggott said. 'You know how this works.'

'I don't want to rule the harassment out prematurely. It isn't always an obvious crime. Not these days. If we can find whoever vandalised her car that would be a good start, rule them in or out.'

'It's minor.'

'But it's indicative of a prejudiced and aggressive mindset,' Zigic said, voice firm. 'And it was over a year ago. Who's to say they haven't escalated during that period? They slashed her tyres, they're obviously knife-happy.'

'That's a mighty big stretch, Ziggy.'

'I need time to look into it.'

Riggott's eyebrows lifted. 'You've had nigh on a year.'

'It wasn't a priority then,' Zigic said through gritted teeth.

'End of the week.' Riggott pointed with his e-cigarette. 'Missing kid or no missing kid, you need to bring me progress.'

Zigic went back up to Hate Crimes, trying to put the meeting with Rachel out of his mind, the pistol shots and black water and the sight of that gun holstered on her hip as the rising wind snapped at her shirt. There was no point wasting his time speculating on what Nathan had done or who she was trying to protect him from. Until he could actually sit down and speak to the boy he might as well not even exist. It was all up to her now.

Work had temporarily halted in the office but evidence of the day's industry was there on the desks, hidden under drinks and plastic cartons from a severely belated lunch break. Wahlia was eating a sandwich with one hand, his mobile phone in the other. An unopened salad was sitting on Ferreira's desk while she stabbed buttons on the printer and swore at the paper tray. Behind her DC Colleen Murray was tucking into a chocolate pudding and she met Zigic's eye as he came in, vaguely guilty looking, as if she'd been caught skiving off.

She was one of the least likely skivers in the building. A careful, sceptical woman, who'd come into the police after a long stint in the RAF. She'd retired out at forty, divorced at forty-one, retrained while she raised two teenagers single-handed and now they were both away at university her job absorbed her totally. She was the kind of copper who'd happily work until midnight and sleep at her desk, be ready to go again at seven a.m.

Useful as that was to her senior officers, Zigic didn't think it was very healthy for her. She looked five years older than she was, twenty pounds heavier than she should be, and it was a rare morning that she didn't carry the scent of the previous night's drinking on her.

'I'm going to talk to Dean Carter's girlfriend in a minute,' she said.

The labourer; Zigic had almost forgotten about him, too many other possibilities crowding in. He was glad of Colleen's diligence.

'Did Carter's friends come through for him?' She nodded. 'What about Westman? Does his alibi hold?'

'Yes, sir. But I don't know how much credence you'd want to give his wife.'

'Does the wife suspect anything?' he asked.

'My feeling is she's resigned to him having affairs. I didn't have to spell it out to her, sir. She caught on right away.' Colleen dropped her half-eaten pudding into the bin. 'Once a woman's decided her security's more important than fidelity there's very little you can do to lean on her.'

Zigic went and poured himself a coffee. 'Where does she say they were?'

'At home getting ready, then a romantic dinner. That swanky pub in Fotheringhay.'

'Check with them,' he said. 'Just to be on the safe side. The price that place is, Westman must have been apologising for something.'

'He was fucking Dawn a few hours before,' Ferreira said. 'That must have been worth three courses and a bottle of prosecco.'

She let out a triumphant laugh as the printer whirred into life and stood with her fingers poised above the tray, waiting for it to spit out the paper, her whole body screaming anticipation. Zigic sugared his coffee and rattled around in the biscuit tin, found nothing substantial enough to see him through the late-afternoon slump.

'There's a salad on your desk,' Ferreira said, glancing over her shoulder. 'Chicken and couscous. It was all they had left.'

He went and fetched it, took a couple of forkfuls but was too eager to see what she was so excited about to sit and eat it at his desk. When he came up behind her she was tacking a photograph to the murder board.

'Where did you get that?'

'Caitlin. She had it on her phone.'

'And she just gave you it?'

'I persuaded her it'd help get him home.'

Nathan. A full-face shot, taken in Julia's kitchen as he sat at the painted wooden table with the red-spotted oilcloth cover, a slice of heavy chocolate cake on a plate in front of him, the rest of it, still bearing multicoloured candles, just to the left.

He was young for his age, cherubic looking, with freckled cheeks and bright, green eyes under thin, auburn brows. His hair was dark brown, though, far too dark for the rest of his colouring.

'They've dyed his hair,' he said.

'Yep. Trying to change his appearance. What does that tell you?'

Zigic took the picture down and gestured for her to follow him back into the office, closed the door behind her.

'What?' she said. 'Do you know who he is?'

'No, but we can't do anything with this photo.'

'Why the hell not? We need to find him, our best chance is putting this out there.'

Zigic told her to sit down and she flopped into the chair like a grumpy teenager, kept her annoyance on show as he explained about the meeting with Rachel, the threat which had come through Riggott and which they couldn't ignore.

'And what if he saw something completely vital to our investigation?' she asked. 'We're losing valuable time. We need to talk to him.'

'We'll get a chance,' he said, hoping it was true. 'But for now he's off the table. And if we don't find something to suggest this is a hate crime very soon it's going to be kicked over to CID. So we need to focus on that for the time being.'

She held her hands up. 'Fine.'

'Did you get anything else out of Caitlin?'

'Eventually, yeah. She didn't want to admit it but I got the impression something was going on between Dawn and Matthew Campbell.'

'She said that?'

'Not explicitly but when I asked about how friendly they were she said Matthew isn't allowed around there any more. I asked why, she wouldn't answer. I pressed her and she clammed up.'

'Doesn't want to rock the boat at home?'

'Or implicate either of her foster parents,' Ferreira said. 'She's in a decent place, the school are happy with her. I'd try to preserve my security in her position, wouldn't you?'

'Up to a point, yeah.'

'I was going to talk to him at work.' She smiled. 'They hate that, always puts them on the back foot, right?'

'Where does he work?'

'Girls' school in town. And apparently he stays late a lot.'

'Handy, that.'

Wahlia's face appeared at the glass panel of the office door and Zigic told him to come in.

'What is it, Bobby?'

'The neighbour's surfaced.'

17

Luke Gibson was a short, wiry guy, sporty looking in tropical board shorts and T-shirt, a shark's tooth strung on a leather thong necklace. Mid-thirties maybe but his skin was deeply creased and weather-beaten from spending a lot of time outdoors. It fitted with his claim of being away in the Peak District for a few days' cycling with friends.

He'd blurted that out as they entered the interview room. Nervous, and perhaps a little claustrophobic Ferreira wondered, seeing how his eyes strayed to the thin, high windows which gave only the slimmest sight of blue, and how reluctant he was to sit down at her invitation.

As she explained the process he nodded jerkily. Agreed to everything, stated his name and told them he was happy to help. More than happy to cooperate.

'Why did it take you three days to come forward?' Zigic asked.

'The boys have a strict no-phone policy,' Gibson said. 'Part of the fun, you know, we get away from work. Return to nature. I only turned it on this morning because I was expecting an important email about a job. There were dozens of calls and messages about the house, I couldn't believe it.'

'You've the seen the damage?' Ferreira asked.

'I should have come here first, I know that. But I thought it was a wind-up.' His cheeks flushed through his tan. 'That bloody cooker, I've been on at the landlord about it for months.'

'You'll have records of your complaints?'

'Of course. You have to keep full records when you're renting, you get ripped off something chronic otherwise.' Then it struck him. 'Wait a minute, you don't think I left the gas on deliberately?'

Neither of them answered.

'Why would I do that?' he asked, looking between them, eyes wide with panic. 'I wouldn't. Not deliberately. Why would I?'

'Dawn was murdered,' Zigic said. 'Holly's dead. And the explosion from your house has contaminated the crime scene.'

Gibson's face went slack and he stammered through the same denials again. More panicked than guilty Ferreira thought, but he'd had plenty of time to prepare himself for this moment and maybe he'd decided dumb incredulity was the best option.

'I can't believe this.' His fist closed around the tooth on his necklace. 'I would never do anything to hurt anyone. Let alone Dawn and Holly. They were lovely people. I can't believe anyone would want to hurt either of them.'

'How well did you know Dawn?' Ferreira asked.

'I moved in about eighteen months ago, she was welcoming, a good neighbour. I didn't know anyone here so it was nice to have someone friendly next door.'

'So you were close?'

He caught the insinuation, gave her a withering look. 'I'm gay. And before you ask, I've got records of that too, Detective.'

Zigic asked where he was on Thursday.

'I left here just after eight in the morning. We'd arranged to meet at a pub in Matlock for lunch and a few beers before we went on to the cottage. The owners wouldn't let us take it until four so we had lunch at a pub in the village, then we checked in to the cottage, went out for a ride in the evening. Back to the pub until chucking-out time.' He shrugged. 'I don't know what else to tell you.'

'There are people who can corroborate this?' Zigic asked.

Gibson nodded. 'My friends, yes. And the landlady. I put down a deposit online and paid her the balance when we checked in. With my card. I've got the receipt somewhere.'

He lifted a leather messenger bag onto the table, pulled out a couple of cycling magazines and a thick paperback with a cracked spine, his iPad snug in a suede case, before coming up with his wallet. 'There. See.'

Zigic checked the receipt, made a note of the cottage's name and handed it back to him. 'So, you left just after eight on Thursday morning. Did you see anyone hanging around Dawn's house at that point?'

'No,' he said. 'I was in a rush.'

'What about otherwise?' Ferreira asked. 'People hanging around? Hawkers? Anyone who seemed out of place?'

He shook his head. 'I'm not the right person to ask.'

'You live next door and you work from home. You must have seen something.'

'I spend eight hours a day staring at my computer screen. I don't have the time or the inclination to monitor my neighbours' lives.'

'You design websites, is that right?'

'Among other things,' he said. 'Online brand development, platform building, reputation management. Whatever I can do on a computer that pays the bills.' He gave her a self-deprecating smile. 'I set up Holly's blog for her.'

'Holly had a blog?' Zigic asked. 'What was she using it for?'

'She wanted somewhere she could chart her recovery, talk about what was going on with her. It was a way to stay in touch with the world, I suppose.'

Ferreira thought of her visit to the house, Holly sitting up in bed, laptop open on a pillow across her thighs. She tried to remember what was on the screen but it was so long ago and she'd ducked out of there so quickly.

'Do you want to see it?' he asked.

'We do,' Zigic said.

'I don't know if it'll help.' Gibson opened his iPad case, swiped and tapped a few times then slid the screen across the table to her, the blog's header dominating, a beach under blue skies, the typeface like letters scratched in the sand. 'Hol on Wheels – that was her idea. She had a very dark sense of humour.'

Zigic gave it a cursory glance before passing it over to Ferreira and she spent a minute scanning it as they talked, longer than she meant to but this was her first real contact with the dead girl. She found herself pulled in by Holly's voice as she scrolled down through the posts, lots of them short and sharp, the usual teenage obsessions with music and films peppered with keen observations and funny asides, but as she went further back, through the summer and spring, she found links to blogs about assisted suicide and dignity in death, impassioned calls for change to the right-to-die legislation.

Zigic was pressing Gibson about his daily routine, where in the house his office was, did the computer face a window, surely he had a good view of the driveway from there?

When there was a lull Ferreira chipped in:

'Have you read these posts, Luke?'

'Yes, I keep an eye on it. She got hacked a few months ago and I had to get in there and fix the problem for her.'

'Hacked by who?' Zigic asked.

'One of those cyber-terrorist groups,' he said. 'It wasn't a personal attack. They took down thousands of sites in a few hours. Loads of people were affected.'

Ferreira jumped back to the last blog post Holly had written. Two days before she died, a piece about the portrayal of disabled people on television. It was too long to read in detail just then but her eye was drawn to the comments at the bottom. Five of them. Three had profile photos and names attached, people thanking her for such a thoughtful post, wishing her well.

The other two were anonymous and dripping with bile.

'"Who wants to look at a fucking spazz like you on TV,"' she said read. '"You crippled bitch, I hope you die in your own shit."'

Gibson groaned. 'I thought we'd sorted that out.'

'What do you mean? Was she getting hassle?'

'Everyone gets hassle online. You put your head above the parapet, have an opinion, be politically engaged – hell, just be female – and the trolls come out.'

'How long has this been going on?'

'Since the beginning.'

'And you didn't think to report it?'

He looked stunned. 'Report some mean comments on a blog? You'd have charged us with wasting police time.'

'It's a hate crime.' Ferreira's hands came down flat on either side of the iPad. 'Did you know Dawn was being harassed?' He shook his head. 'We've had a file open since her car was vandalised last December. They sprayed "Cripple" on the side of it.'

'I didn't know about that other stuff,' Gibson said quickly. 'Dawn didn't mention anything about it. Neither did Holly. If I'd had any idea this had moved into real life, I'd have insisted she made an official complaint.'

He was panicking and Ferreira realised she'd snapped at him with no good reason, just because he was the person in front of her to take it. She smoothed her hand over her hair, forced herself to stay silent for a few seconds, seeing the black spray paint on the side of Dawn's people carrier again, how thickly it was laid on, thinking about the anger in the finger holding down the nozzle.

'Luke, this is very important,' she said. 'Did Holly have any idea who was behind these comments?'

'I didn't talk to her about it. I didn't think I needed to. She grew up with this online stuff, she knew to be careful. I told her to fix her security settings so the spam filter would block anonymous comments but for some reason she didn't.'

‘Was she worried about it?’

He slumped in his seat, fists pressed together on the table, one thumb rubbing the knuckle of the other. ‘I don’t know. I think she would’ve said something if she was. But you have to understand, Holly was fearless. You must know about the accident – do you think a girl who climbs a sheer rock face is going to buckle because some piece of shit leaves a nasty message on her blog?’

‘Did you know her before the accident?’ Ferreira asked.

‘No. I moved in a few weeks before she came home from hospital. I didn’t really know either of them then. But you only have to look at how she dealt with it to see she was made of stern stuff. I couldn’t have kept going like that, paralysed, could you?’

‘She sounds like an amazing girl,’ Ferreira said, not wanting to answer him, not even in her head.

‘She was and she deserved better than this.’ He sighed deeply. ‘I should have said something to Dawn about it.’

‘Wouldn’t Holly have told her?’

‘Your guess is as good as mine,’ Gibson said. ‘But surely if she did, Dawn would have told you about it. You were dealing with the harassment. Why wouldn’t she have mentioned it?’

It was exactly what Ferreira was wondering. All of those follow-up calls she’d made when Dawn couldn’t wait to put the phone down, all of those missed opportunities and one word could have stopped this. Dawn didn’t know. It was the only explanation.

‘Were they close?’ she asked. ‘Dawn and Holly?’

There was a minute pause before he answered and she read the complex expressions which ticked across his face before he spoke: guilt, reluctance, embarrassment.

‘What kind of question’s that?’

‘A very important one.’

His fingers twitched inside his cupped palm.

She could see the knowledge he wanted to share, as clear as if the words were written on his parted lips, fighting against the hard-wired, constantly reinforced belief that you should never speak ill of the dead.

'When I first moved in Holly was much more outgoing. I mean, she actually went *out*. Only once or twice a week but Dawn would put her in the car and they went places. This day centre or something, shopping even. But that all stopped at the end of last year.'

'Why?'

'I don't know.' His brow furrowed. 'Dawn was still having people around – she invited me over a few times – but Holly never came down for any of it.'

'What people?' Ferreira asked.

'Dawn's friends. Julia and Matthew from the village, their kids. Some other women she knew.'

'Matthew and Dawn, how close were they?'

'Were they having an affair, do you mean?'

Ferreira nodded, seeing that the idea didn't shock him, was maybe something he'd asked himself already and was now considering more deeply, new significance brought to the question by Dawn's murder.

His mouth twisted before he spoke, another weighing-up. 'Look, sometimes I heard bedroom noise from Dawn's side but I couldn't tell you who was making it. She didn't scream his name or anything. Not that I heard.'

'Did you ever see him go round there?" Ferreira asked. 'On his own?'

Gibson nodded. 'He stopped by pretty often actually. I figured he was going in to see Holly, him being a teacher. She wasn't back at school yet. I don't think she wanted to go back, to be honest.'

'How often are we talking?'

'Once a week maybe. Early evening. I suppose he was stopping on his way home from work. I haven't seen him for few months, though.'

For someone who insisted he barely noticed his neighbour's movements he seemed to have seen plenty.

'What about Holly's dad?' Zigic asked. 'Was he a regular visitor?'

'Not lately.'

'When did you last see him?'

'A few weeks ago, I guess.' Gibson rubbed his bare arm, fine hairs rising across his skin. 'He might have been back since but I didn't see him. They – it sounded like they were arguing.'

Zigic cocked his head. 'What about?'

'I heard Dawn shout something about him going around there but that's all I know.' Gibson shrank in his chair, discomfort growing. 'I wondered if she was annoyed with him not seeing Holly very often. Holly was depressed, anyone could see that. I suppose maybe Dawn needed him to be more involved. It was a lot to deal with at her age.' He shifted where he sat. 'I mentioned it to Dawn . . .'

'And she wasn't happy about that?'

'I wasn't rude. I just asked if there was anything I could do. She flew for me. I mean, she went ballistic. I don't have kids, who am I to question her parenting. That kind of thing.' He looked uncomfortable just relating it. 'That's the last time I talked to her.'

18

The school where Matthew Campbell taught was a short drive from Thorpe Wood station, set among large houses all gated and watched over by security cameras. It was hidden away at the bottom of a long, tree-lined driveway which took them past caged tennis courts and sports fields bigger than any other school in the city could boast.

'How the other seven per cent learn, hey?' Ferreira said, as she pulled into a space outside the main building.

Zigic murmured agreement, thinking it best not to mention that this was one of the schools Anna was eyeing up for their daughter. Another conversation he was trying to avoid having, another set of numbers to be crunched. The fees were exorbitant but she was confident her mother would contribute. Meaning the deal was already done. Grandma Jacqueline thought it was important to educate girls properly. Not well. Just properly. Like she'd been.

There were a few other vehicles in the parking area, teachers' cars, not parents', judging by the makes and number plates. Almost five now and the students were long gone, except for a few boarders sitting out under a cypress tree with their books across their knees, too much laughter for them to be working.

It was a beautiful setting. Zigic imagined his daughter growing up in this environment and wondered if it would spoil her, decided it might but he wouldn't mind that, not when he considered the alternative.

Then he thought of Milan and Stefan and how they'd never have this advantage and felt a stab of annoyance for Anna's mother, using her money to divide his children.

Ferreira walked on ahead of him, towards the grand old Victorian house which served as the main building. She stopped a maintenance man carrying a stepladder and asked where they could find Matthew Campbell.

The man gestured away towards a converted coach house and they followed his directions, accompanied by the decreasing scales of someone practising clarinet in a nearby music room, no bum notes, but no fluidity either.

'What does he teach?' Zigic asked.

'What they all teach here – baseless superiority and oppressing the masses.'

Zigic smiled. 'You old commie.'

'Come the revolution . . .'

'You'll be standing at the barricade protecting them from those masses,' he said. 'You already are.'

Her turn to smile. 'And *I'm* the communist.'

There were two classrooms in the coach house, whitewashed and wooden floored, smaller than the rooms Zigic had been taught in, containing enough desks for a dozen pupils at most, but they were cavernous spaces, open to the eaves. One was empty, the other not and Matthew Campbell looked up from a stack of marking as they entered.

'Can I help you?'

Zigic made the introductions and Matthew's irritation gave way to discomfort. He shifted in his seat, put down the pen he was holding and picked it up again, saw his fingers tighten around it and put it aside once more.

He was a nondescript sort of man, lean and pale, greying brown hair receding from a hangdog face dominated by heavy-framed black glasses. He wore a shadow of stubble that probably hadn't been there when he arrived for work in the morning and sideburns too extravagant for his age.

As they settled on the desks in front of him he straightened the green knit tie which had been hanging loose at his neck, but forgot the unfastened collar button. Neither of them spoke. He looked between them, wet his lips.

'You're here about Nathan.'

'No,' Zigic said, before Ferreira could reply. 'We'd like to talk to you about Dawn and Holly.'

'But Nathan's run away,' he said. 'Don't you think that might be significant?'

'We're more interested in your relationship with them.'

'Dawn and my wife were very good friends.'

'What about you and Dawn?' Ferreira asked, the desk creaking as she crossed her legs. 'Very good friends too?'

Matthew aimed a vaguely disgusted look at her. 'What are you insinuating?'

'It's a perfectly reasonable question.'

'We were friends. Men and women can have platonic relationships, you know?'

Zigic was expecting him to get defensive but not so quickly. If he was trying to look innocent he'd done a bad job of it. But he seemed the nervy type and most teachers Zigic had come across hated having their authority or probity questioned, especially by adults they couldn't shout down or put in detention. Maybe Ferreira was a little bit too similar to the girls he taught as well; too much cheek by half.

He'd let her take this.

'When did you last see Dawn?' she asked.

'I can't remember the exact date. It was weeks ago. Perhaps longer.'

'That doesn't sound very friendly. Did you have a falling out?'

'I've been busy.'

'Over the summer holidays? What were you busy with?'

'Teachers work during the holidays,' he said grimly. 'This is a boarding school, you may have noticed. We have fifteen girls who don't go home for the summer. Somebody has to keep them out of trouble.'

'Sounds more like they were keeping you out of trouble.' There was a teasing note in Ferreira's voice and Matthew Campbell bristled at it, jaw tensing. 'Before this . . . busy-ness of yours, you were a regular visitor to the house.'

He relaxed slightly, against Zigic's expectations.

'Dawn was concerned about Holly falling behind in her education, I offered to help. Not a full curriculum, you understand, but I designed a plan with her. English literature and history, suggested some books and set her some essays.' He felt confident now, kept talking unprompted. 'She really should have been back at school by now. There's a very good facility outside Huntingdon for pupils with challenging conditions. Holly was far too bright to be left atrophying in that house.'

'So why wasn't she going?'

A grimace stretched his face. 'She was embarrassed. I don't think Holly was ever a particularly vain girl but being paralysed seemed to bring it out in her.'

'Nobody could judge her at a place like that, surely?' Ferreira said. 'They'd all be in the same boat.'

'Not really. Some of the children would have behavioural problems or minor disabilities. Holly was very much at the extreme end of the scale. She went for a few days, as a test run, but she refused to go back and Dawn wouldn't force her to do anything she didn't want to.' He shrugged. 'I gather there was some unpleasantness.'

'What kind of unpleasantness?'

He waved a hand. 'Nothing that would lead to murder. Just the usual name calling you get at all schools. But Holly took it much worse than she would have before the accident and Dawn didn't want her going back there to face any more of it.'

‘Was Dawn a good mother?’

‘Of course she was.’ He cocked his head. ‘Anyone who’s told you otherwise can’t have known her very well. Dawn was entirely dedicated to Holly. She fought tooth and nail to make her life as comfortable as possible. Under very difficult circumstances.’

‘Difficult circumstances like Julia not helping out with Holly any more?’ Ferreira asked. The question sent Matthew’s hand to his fatly knotted tie again. ‘Why did Dawn and your wife fall out, Mr Campbell?’

‘They haven’t. They didn’t.’

The classroom door opened and Zigic turned to see a cleaner in a blue tabard and a headscarf. Matthew told her to come back later and she backed out, mumbling an apology.

‘I don’t understand what bearing this could possibly have on their murders,’ he said.

‘We’re just trying to get some background,’ Ferreria told him. ‘From their friends.’

‘Was Dawn worried about anything?’ Zigic asked. ‘Anyone hanging around the house? Hassling her?’

‘There was an incident last year. Someone vandalised her car.’

‘And since then?’

‘She didn’t mention anything. They lived a very insular life. I really can’t imagine anyone having a reason to kill them.’ He glanced away, out of the window to where a group of girls were walking past, their voices high and fast, hyper. ‘People don’t always need a reason, though, do they?’

He said it under his breath, almost to himself.

‘Women are usually murdered by their lovers,’ Ferreira said. ‘Or rejected hopefuls.’

Matthew Campbell turned a hard stare on her. ‘In that case you should be speaking to Warren. They always had a combustible relationship.’

‘Was he violent?’

'He's volatile. Especially after a few drinks.' Matthew flexed his fingers against the arm of his chair. 'I don't think he ever hit her, but they were in the middle of a divorce and that tends to bring out the worst in people.'

'Warren claims it's amicable,' Ferreira said.

'He could hardly say anything else now, could he? She's been murdered.' A thin and humourless smile cut his face. 'He doesn't pay a penny towards Holly's care. Did he tell you that? He let his business go under, he lost their house, gave up on work. All within months of Holly's accident. By the time she was well enough to leave hospital her home was gone and her father was living with another woman. How amicable does that sound to you?'

'Dawn must have been angry,' Zigic said.

Matthew snorted. 'She was a tad miffed, yes.'

'What about Holly?'

'She loved her father.'

'After all that?' Ferreira asked. 'She didn't resent him for leaving?'

Matthew considered it for a moment, staring into the middle distance. 'Dawn said Holly blamed her for driving him away. It's not unusual in separations, I suppose. But it made it difficult for her. Holly couldn't just walk through the village and go to see him.'

'But Warren could go to her,' Ferreira said. 'Or wouldn't Dawn let him?'

'She wasn't using Holly against him,' Matthew said wearily. 'If he tells you that he's lying. Dawn needed him to man up and start acting like a proper father again but he wouldn't or couldn't do it. Maybe Sally had a hand in it. All I know for certain is that Dawn was bearing the full emotional and financial burden of caring for Holly and it was wearing her down to nothing.'

His sympathy for Dawn was clear but Zigic thought his version of Dawn and Warren's relationship was a bit too black and white. Matthew telling him what he believed they wanted to hear. It was easy to be cynical, though, and he knew that if the same information had come from Julia Campbell he wouldn't be questioning it.

They seemed too close, him and Dawn, and he couldn't shake the feeling that emotional intimacy was often accompanied by physical intimacy when a man and woman were friends. Or that at least one of them would want it to be.

Dawn was alone with a disabled child, living in reduced circumstances, struggling and in need of support. Would Matthew have looked like a good bet? Older and steady and caring. It was only a short step from friend to lover.

'Where were you on Thursday evening, Mr Campbell?' Ferreira asked.

'At home with the children. Caitlin can tell you that. Since I evidently need an alibi.' A bitter tone came into his voice, as if the question was a betrayal after the honesty he'd shown. 'Nathan could too if he was here.'

Ferreira didn't pursue it, maybe because Matthew so blatantly wanted them to. She'd asked Caitlin already, knew where he was at the time of the murder and they'd come here to speak to him as a friend of the family rather than a suspect.

The taint of guilt clung to him, though. Not the guilt they were interested in, Zigic thought, but he was hiding something.

19

Nathan could still feel the policewoman's fingernails at the back of his neck, the scratch marks she'd left there stinging. She almost caught him. Grabbed the collar of his hoodie, dragged him away so sharply that he stumbled, dropping the handbag he'd swiped off the back of a cafe chair.

He'd slipped her, though. Pulled his arms out of his top and left her holding it, stupidly, as he bolted for the train station's main doors, heard her shouting, heard her boots striking the tile floor fast and heavy but didn't look back because you should never look back or you'd be caught.

She was too big and too old to catch him, gave up in no time but he kept running, down a side street, then another, turning at random, following an instinct which made him run for longer than he needed to, only stopping finally when he turned his ankle on an uneven concrete slab.

She knew his name. She'd shouted it at him: 'Nathan, stop!'

Rachel knew where he was, so the local police knew to look for him. Maybe she was already here, waiting for him, watching. Ready to snatch him off the street and bundle him into the back of a car.

The thought made his heart race and stomach tumble.

He needed to get away. Fast.

But not the train station. It wasn't safe to go back there.

He went into a supermarket and locked himself in a toilet cubicle to count the money he'd stolen. The policewoman had spotted him as he was about to dump the handbag in a bin, the small pink purse already zipped into the pocket of his shorts. He felt ashamed for what he'd done but he needed money.

The woman was old, tiny and grey haired, too busy reading her newspaper to notice him coming up behind her. She looked like his nan.

Nathan counted the notes. Just over two hundred pounds and some change he'd use to buy food. No more stealing. Not unless he had to. The money would get him a bus ticket and a train ticket after that. He'd seen the bus station in the town centre and knew it would be busy soon with people heading home after work, kids leaving school. There were some in the supermarket already, shopping with their mums.

He squeezed his eyes closed.

His mum dragging him around Lidl, telling him no every time he asked for something. No, we can't afford it. No, it's bad for you. No, they'll rot your teeth. What did I just fucking tell you? No!

His mum crying. Begging. Screaming.

Nathan's hands curled into fists, screwing up the crisp banknotes. He pushed away the memories, tried to breathe around the stone in his throat, blank out the blood and the tears, the way his mother fell, the way Dawn's dead eyes looked through him as he stood over her.

The door of the next cubicle slammed and Nathan snapped out of it. He stayed still, feeling unsafe suddenly, wanting to be alone again.

When the man was gone he separated his money into three small bundles and put them in different pockets, then sat down on the toilet lid and took out his phone. The battery showed sixty-one per cent, enough to get him home.

More messages waiting for him. The same people.

Julia wanting him to call her.

Rachel telling him to go to the train station and wait for her. 'You're safer with me.'

Caitlin had called a few minutes ago, texted before that:

The police are looking for you.

He knew that already. Didn't know how she did.

Nathan deleted every message. It was as if none of them existed any more. Julia, Caitlin, Dawn; that life was gone. No going back. He looked at the last message from Dawn and deleted that too. As soon as he did it he regretted it. As if getting rid of her words made her even deader.

Don't think about it.

A small voice asked him if he could go back. It was a weak voice, childish and scared, and he told it to shut up, snapping at the walls of the cubicle. It kept talking, though.

Couldn't you call Rachel and explain everything? She doesn't care what happened, she only wants one thing and as long as she gets that she can make everything else right again. She'll save you. She wants to. And you want that too. You want to go home to Julia's house. She doesn't need to know about the rest. She'll defend you, she'll understand.

He was supposed to trust Rachel, her and only her, no matter what anyone else threatened or promised. She was the person who kept him safe, changed his name and his hair, took him to the other side of the country and gave him to Julia.

But if he could trust her why did she set the police on him? Why did she tell them who he was?

He wasn't allowed to tell anyone, but she could?

She'd told him the police weren't his friends. As if he was stupid. From the earliest time he could remember he'd known that and nothing in his life made him think differently. She told him not to answer questions, to use the lies she'd given him, and if a policeman ever tried to take him away he should run. Hide. Call her and she would fetch him. Wherever he was, she would come.

No.

Nathan's phone blurred in front of his eyes and he tapped the screen with shaking fingers, pulled up the map to double-check where he was going. Then looked up which train he needed to get home and what the nearest station to get him there was. Doncaster. Fifteen miles. He found the bus timetables so he wouldn't have to ask anyone at the station which one he needed.

The journey scared him and he tried not to think about all the things that could go wrong – getting stopped at the bus, Rachel catching up with him – what would be waiting for him when he arrived in Liverpool. But he'd come this far and he wasn't going to turn around now.

His phone rang. Caitlin.

For a second he thought about answering. He wanted to hear a friendly voice and he wanted to let her know he was safe so she could tell Julia. He knew she'd be upset with him, angry even, and he wanted to ask her about Holly but he didn't too, because he was scared what she'd say.

Thinking about Holly made him feel sick again.

He switched his phone off. No more looking at it. No more messages. Those people had never been his friends. They might have liked the boy Rachel told him to be but they wouldn't like the one he really was.

Nathan left the toilets and went into the supermarket, trying to act like he belonged there, trying to blend in. It was easier now, more kids about. He got some sandwiches from the fridge and a Coke, took some chocolate bars. The security guard by the door was watching him.

He walked further into the shop, heading for the clothes. Picked up a beanie. The guard was following him now and he wanted to drop everything and run but he knew he might not make it to the door.

The man didn't know who he was. He just thought he was a shoplifter.

Nathan walked back to the tills with the man behind him, his radio squawking, and waited in a short queue, holding his things to his chest. When his turn came the woman behind the counter smiled at him and asked him how he was today. He mumbled a reply and she kept the smile in place as she scanned the items, putting them in a bag for him.

'Are you going to wear this now?' she asked. 'It's getting cold out.'

'Yeah. Ta.'

Her smile was gone and she was looking at him funnily as he pulled on the grey beanie.

'Where's your mum, love?'

She's dead. Dead and burnt and scattered.

He swallowed, couldn't meet her eye. 'She's in the car.'

Fumbling, he brought out the money and she frowned at the crumpled purple notes but didn't say anything more and he held his breath all the way out of the shop, expecting the security guard to come after him.

Outside, he walked fast towards the bus station in the town centre, lots of people on the pavements, lots of cars on the road, enough of them to get lost in. He tugged the beanie lower to hide his face, then pulled his hood up over it.

At the bus station he discovered he needed to go in and buy a ticket but he got through that smoothly and followed the man in the booth's directions. The bus was waiting, a few passengers on it already and it seemed too easy, just climb up three steps and take a seat near the back, hunker down low and don't make eye contact with anyone.

Wait.

Wait some more.

It couldn't be this easy.

Then the bus was full and the driver was making his announcement and suddenly they were moving, heading out of the town and onto the motorway, taking him closer to home and all the people who knew who he really was.

He tried not to think about that. Ate his chocolate and his sandwiches, washed them down with the Coke. Right away he felt sick, all that food going into his empty stomach so quickly, feeding the gnawing fear that always lived there.

He wished he still had the knife. Knew he was going to need it when he got home.

20

Ferreira poured a cup of coffee and rolled a cigarette she didn't smoke, but held unlit between her fingertips as she went back to the beginning. Holly's very first blog post, written on 22 March 2014.

The doctors say I'll never walk again. They say I'll never be able to move my arms or feed myself or piss without this stupid catheter.

And I say, 'Fuck you, doctors. You don't know me.'

I've run the half-marathon in one hour, forty. I've pushed my body – this body you tell me is my prison – through fatigue and pain and beyond every boundary set for it.

I will not be trapped by it.

I will not be dictated to by it.

I will recover.

Just you watch me.

That was Holly Prentice six months after she fell from a cliff face thanks to an improperly secured guide rope, and broke her back on the jagged rocks below, wild and defiant, convinced she'd prove everyone wrong. Ferreira felt her eyes sting as she read the words a second time, hearing them in her own voice because she didn't know how Holly sounded beyond a quick 'hello', imagining the immense courage the girl had within her.

She lay in the bed she couldn't get out of and wrote that post, while the friends she'd been climbing with continued living just as before, the same petty concerns and petty hopes dwarfed by what she was dealing with.

Did they keep in touch? she wondered. Did they care at all?

She made a note to check Holly's Facebook page later, see if releasing her name on the local news this evening provoked a response.

Zigic was in his office changing into a suit, while the press officer hovered around the door, eyes averted, telling him what to say. As if he hadn't done it a hundred times before.

Ferreira scrolled up through the next few posts, weeks between them and slowly the defiance was wavering. Holly expected a quick recovery but she soon found out how accurate the doctors' dire prognoses were.

Two months on and there was a photograph of her new electric wheelchair, Holly sitting in it, strapped around the chest to keep her upright, arms secured and only her hand on the joystick control able to move. She was smiling but it looked forced.

Four months and there were no more links to half-marathons she was planning to run the next year or surfing destinations she idly fantasised about going to when she recovered. The reality was sinking in.

There were no negative comments either, Ferreira noticed with a vague sense of irritation. These were the posts she expected to see them on, the ones where Holly looked vulnerable. A sick mind, bent on upsetting her, should have targeted her when she was at her weakest but they hadn't.

Unless Gibson was in charge of her security settings at that point and they'd all got snagged by the filter and deleted. It was better for Holly that way but didn't help her identify a pattern or an aggressor.

Autumn 2014 was very quiet and Ferreira wondered what Holly was doing for the six weeks she ignored her blog. Had she found a better distraction or was she too exhausted by fighting against her disability to bother with it?

Ferreira knew how tiring it was to keep acting strong when all your body wanted was to be perfectly still. She'd given in to it a few times during her recovery, spent a week straight rewatching the old *Buffy* DVDs she'd been addicted to when she was at school, losing herself in the familiar world of Sunnydale High. Wasted days on end lying in bed just staring at the ceiling with the same Mogwai playlist on repeat for hours.

The torpor sucked you down so easily if you let it.

Mid-October the posts started again and the tone was different, less personal and more political. Holly returning with a piece about the government agreeing to give their MPs a free vote on a scheduled assisted-suicide bill. She was in favour of the bill but didn't think it went far enough. She wanted Dignitas-style clinics in the UK where anyone of sound mind could be helped to a civilised and painless death whether they were terminally ill or not.

She didn't mention her own situation in the post but the commentators did.

Somewhere along the way her security settings must have been adjusted and now, mixed in with the relatively even-tempered responses and the voices of outright support, there were curses and threats. People telling her she would go to hell, that she was a traitor to her kind, asking if she was too stupid to realise how the vulnerable would be bullied into committing suicide to save their families the trouble of caring for them.

The anonymous accounts were even worse.

Are you still alive?

People like you are a burden, you should be made to kill yourself.

Just do it already. Stop bitching and DIE.

Ferreira blew out a slow breath, leaned back from the screen to see where Zigic was, wanting him to look at this, but he wasn't in the office. Across the desk Wahlia was deep in thought, brow furrowed, fingertips massaging his neck.

She went back to the blog.

Holly had answered the comments where a reasonable response was possible and ignored the rest, but the anonymous voices carried on their own conversations, escalating and goading her, and Ferreira wondered why she let that happen. It was her blog, her space, she could have shut them down whenever she wanted, so why let it continue?

She scrolled on, found antagonism and vitriol following every post Holly wrote now, obscure profile images, different IDs. But could it all be the same person? she wondered. Some sad, sick bastard talking to himself, spinning a conversation to make her think there was a whole chorus of vicious dissent out there?

I've got a hammer if you want to end it. LOL.
You won't even need to hold her down.:-)
Yeah, no fun is it? Killing some bitch who can't fight back.
Can you talk Hol? Will you scream for me?

'Fucking hell,' Ferreira said, whispered it at the screen, wishing she could get her hands on these people. This person.

She knew they could be anywhere in the country. Christ, anywhere in the world. And the way Holly died made it highly unlikely they were involved, but she wanted them to suffer for the pleasure they'd taken in attacking her. The harassment was illegal, the mechanism for prosecuting them was in place, but she held out little hope for tracking them down.

This was Holly's only window onto the world and the view was bleak. What had that done to her psychologically? What toll did it take, day after day, week after week?

Why didn't she stop them?

A few minutes later Ferreira got an answer of sorts. A short post linking to a piece Holly had written for the Comment is Free section of the *Guardian* about online abuse directed at people with disabilities. She quoted the conversations directly and picked them apart, called it the last acceptable prejudice.

Ferreira pushed away from her desk and went over to the window to light her cigarette, sat down on the sill, staring at the floor between her feet.

Dawn must have known about this.

Long-term harassment, ongoing and getting worse. Holly was trying to turn it into something positive, using it to highlight a problem that was bigger than just her, but it must have been consuming her entire life. She'd been in a national newspaper – or its online version at least – for Christ's sake.

The article was published in December last year, a few days before Ferreira visited her.

She looked up from the floor.

A few days before the car was vandalised.

'Epiphany face,' Wahlia said, grinning at her as he walked over to the counter where the coffee machine needed refilling. 'Come on, then. Let's hear it.'

Ferreira told him.

'So what? We already know what motivated the vandalism. Not exactly subtle, were they? Spraying "Cripple" on the car in big black letters.'

'No, think about it, Bobby. We've got a brutal and sustained online harassment targeting Holly. This is every fucking day for her. And then she publishes a piece in the *Guardian*. Attention, right? Prestige even. Her troll hates that. He wants to see her cut down to size but months of nasty comments haven't made a dent – she's turned them around, benefited from them. So he wants to strike in real life.' Ferreira waited, hands spread wide, inviting him to finish the thought, but he didn't. 'This isn't just some one-off bit of graffiti any more. It's the first physical act in a campaign of harassment that's been going on for months.'

Wahlia considered it for a moment. 'Why didn't Dawn mention any of this?'

'She didn't know.'

'Seriously?'

'Yeah, fucking seriously. Do you think kids tell their parents what they're doing online?'

'It's a massive leap,' Wahlia said. 'Wankers like that, they don't go out and actually do stuff in real life, they just sit on their arses and troll people for cheap entertainment.'

'This is concerted,' Ferreira said firmly. 'And it's personal. Go look at it and tell me I'm wrong.'

She flicked her cigarette out of the window and followed him over to her desk, stood with her hands braced on the back of the chair, watching over his shoulder as he started to read.

'See?'

'What's this?' Zigic asked, pulling at his tie as he walked into the office, free to remove it now the press conference was done with.

Ferreira explained again, getting the same look of guarded interest as before and the same reservations. Wahlia stood up and Zigic replaced him at the desk, scanning through the posts, stopping when she told him to, pointing out the worst comments, the ones she thought went beyond standard-issue insults.

'We can't ignore this.'

Zigic murmured agreement. 'How does it lead to Dawn's murder, though?'

'I don't know yet,' she admitted. 'But I think there's something here. Although maybe the harassment wasn't about Holly's disability, that was just the weak point. This person might have had their own, totally separate, reasons to hate Dawn and they thought hurting Holly would hurt her.'

'Look into it,' Zigic said, rising from her chair. 'Tomorrow, though.'

'I'll give it another hour.'

He pushed her chair under the desk before she could sit down. 'No, it's gone seven, get out of here. Both of you. I want clear heads in the morning.'

Reluctantly Ferreira switched off her computer, closed the window she'd left open and gathered her things into her bag, knowing she could go straight back to the blog when she got home. One night away from the gym wouldn't hurt her recovery.

In the car, bombing along the parkway towards Werrington with the Dead Weather blaring, she thought about the faceless, nameless pieces of shit who'd targeted Holly and wondered if they knew she was dead yet, whether any of them would feel guilty when they found out or just annoyed that one of their toys had been taken away.

TUESDAY

21

Julia watched the small red numbers on the alarm clock blinking: four o'clock becoming half past, becoming five. Kept closing her eyes and willing herself to sleep but her mind was ticking away too insistently, thinking about Nathan, still out there and no news from Rachel since yesterday afternoon. Even though she'd said she knew where he was. Shouldn't she have found him by now? How long could he stay hidden in a town as small as Grantham?

Maybe Rachel had found him. That thought was a persistent one. She'd found him too late and wasn't ready to admit that the worst had happened.

The numbers moved on, blurring as she tried to focus on them.

Next to her Matthew was snoring, big, ugly gulping growls. Grunting and snorting like an animal, the way he always did when he'd had too much to drink.

He'd spent the previous evening holed up in his study. Marking, he claimed, but she didn't believe it. He hardly ever did it at home, preferred to stay and finish it in his classroom, preserve the separation between work time and leisure time. It was almost seven o'clock when he pulled into the drive and if he wasn't marking then what was he doing until so late?

She didn't ask. Didn't want to see him lie.

Matthew let out a protracted groan, turned over and mumbled something into his pillow. She touched her fingertips to his temple, feeling the slackness of his skin, and as she traced the line of his jaw the muscles there tensed.

Even asleep he was withdrawing from her.

In the half-lit room, horribly awake and experiencing the piercing clarity which came with sleepless nights, she realised he'd been like that for months now, reluctant to touch her unless he wanted something doing; a shirt ironing or paperwork finding or just for an uncomfortable conversation to end. They hadn't had sex since she'd fallen pregnant. He claimed he was scared of 'stressing' her body, that after trying for so many years he wouldn't jeopardise the health of their unborn child with his 'demands'. As if she didn't have any of her own.

He'd never been particularly physical, always left it to her to instigate, but when she did he responded with enthusiasm. Not now, though.

A barrier had come up between them and it would be easy to blame it on the baby, but she couldn't make herself believe that deeply enough to stop every loveless peck on the lips feeling like an act of duty.

Most women would think he was having an affair.

And then they would convince themselves he wasn't, because it was easier to keep getting up and going on with your life that way.

They lied to themselves, Julia thought. Every woman did it. Maybe men did too. Built up the rickety lie of mutual fidelity, tended it and shielded it, fixed the fine cracks, plugged the holes when they opened and smoothed over the ragged scars with the same old salves; he loves me, he wouldn't, he trusts me so I trust him.

Carefully she sat up, not wanting to wake Matthew, and slipped her feet into the sheepskin moccasins waiting on the rug at the side of the bed, shivering as the chill air hit her bare arms. She took her dressing gown from the hook on the back of the door and pulled it on as she made her way downstairs to the kitchen.

The room was still and silent and something of last night's awkward dinner seemed to be hanging in the air, a stale undertone like the odour of dirty ashtrays or food beginning to spoil.

Julia switched on all the lights and the television, changed channels away from the news and left some documentary about birds playing as she put away the crockery from the drying rack, thinking about what Caitlin had told her. The policewoman who'd come here, the one Julia took an instant dislike to, had turned up at the school and bullied her way in, demanding to know everything Caitlin knew about Nathan. She said she told her nothing, only that he'd run away, and Julia believed her, because she didn't know any more than that.

Warren wasn't so easily fobbed off. After he'd searched the house, storming through the rooms like a man possessed, he'd returned to the kitchen and interrogated her with a tenacity the police officers might have envied. She'd remained calm, well used to soothing tantrums and that's what it was really, a furious venting of impotence and fear and grief. But knowing that didn't make him any less intimidating. He'd always been volatile, she knew that much from Dawn, who chose to call it passion because that made him a brooding romantic rather than a bully.

As he shouted at her, pushing her about Nathan, she realised she'd never really known Warren, even though they'd been in and out of each other's houses for years, dinner parties and barbecues, pub lunches and theatre trips, shared jokes and confidences. For a while the four of them had been inseparable.

Maybe he was thinking about it too, that closeness, and that was why he suddenly turned his fury towards Matthew.

A small moan escaped her lips.

This wasn't healthy.

She needed to find a way to deal with it or her baby was going to suffer. She knew all the ways a mother could harm her child before it was even born, the obvious vices and what they did to a developing brain, how they could weaken a still-forming body. Any decent women cut out drink and cigarettes, didn't do drugs, didn't use chemical-heavy beauty products. They all thought that was enough of a safeguard.

But it wasn't. Julia knew that all of this stress was flooding her baby with cortisol, making her more likely to suffer from anxiety and attention deficit disorder once she was born. She knew she was lowering her baby's IQ but she couldn't make the stress go away and that made her feel guilty which made her feel even more stressed.

If only she'd been here the night Dawn was killed, there would be no question of alibis for any of them.

Julia made herself a cup of tea and took it into the workshop, feeling the cold coming up through the uninsulated concrete floor, before she went to curl up in the armchair near the window, pulling her dressing gown across her bare legs. She watched the grey dawn recede and the sky lighten in increments, nothing but a few thin, high clouds to mar the blue, listened to the birdsong and the scratching of mice behind her workbench, losing herself in the predictable rhythms, until car engines began to sound on the lane outside, the familiar rattling slam of her neighbour's front door as he left for the train station, then ten minutes later his girlfriend taking their dog for a walk.

The telephone in the kitchen rang.

It wouldn't be good news at this time of morning.

'We've found him,' Rachel said.

'Alive?'

'Yes.'

Relief flooded over her and she smiled into the handset, only dimly registering how serious Rachel sounded.

'What time will you be here?' she asked, already walking to the fridge, taking out butter for a welcome-home cake. 'Is he hungry? I'll make you both breakfast.'

'I'm not bringing him back to yours,' Rachel said flatly. 'Not yet, anyway.'

'Why? Rachel, please, he needs his home now.'

'It's not his home.'

The words hit her like a slap.

'You were supposed to keep him safe and you let him walk out of there. Christ, you didn't even notice he was gone for hours. Anything could have happened to him.'

'Don't you think I know that?' Julia said. 'I've been going out of my mind.'

'Yeah, I'm sure this has been very tough on you,' Rachel sneered. 'You're the real victim in all this, aren't you?'

She wanted to snap back at her but she had no defence against the truth. 'Please, can I talk to him at least?'

'Later,' Rachel said. 'I'll ring you when we're on the road.'

She ended the call before Julia could say any more and she stood for a moment with the phone in her hand, having to remind herself that this was good news because it didn't feel as good as she'd expected, the relief tainted by Rachel's attitude.

The kitchen door opened and she quickly arranged her face into a smile for Caitlin.

'Nathan's coming home. Isn't that brilliant?'

Caitlin's smile was far more genuine than hers and she rushed across the kitchen to hug Julia, throwing her arms around her neck in a rare display of spontaneous emotion. Julia hugged her back, shifting slightly to ease the pressure against her stomach.

'I thought he was dead,' Caitlin said.

Julia smoothed her hand over the girl's hair. 'Nathan must be tougher than he looks.'

'Can I skip school today?' she asked. 'I want to be here when he gets back.'

'Of course you can. We'll say you've got a tummy bug.' Julia checked the wall clock, almost seven. 'Why don't you go back to bed for a little bit?'

'Okay.' Caitlin stopped halfway to the door and Julia saw the tension flex across her shoulders before she turned around. 'What if Nathan did kill Dawn?'

'He didn't,' Julia said firmly.

'The police think he did.'

'And they're wrong. They don't know him like we do.'

Caitlin chewed on her bottom lip, eyes unreadable behind the over-long fringe Julia wished she'd get cut. 'What if they fit him up?'

'Rachel won't let that happen.'

That seemed to satisfy Caitlin and she went up to bed without another word, leaving Julia to wonder if she'd reassured the girl or lied to her.

22

'Please don't tell me you've been here all night,' Zigic said.

Ferreira spun away from her desk, wired looking and fizzing with nervous energy. The computer screen behind her showed a Twitter page, Holly's he guessed. 'No, I just wanted to get an early start.'

'How early?'

'I've been here about an hour. Do you want a doughnut?' She gestured towards the counter where a bright pink bag sat next to the coffee machine. 'First batch, they're always the best ones. I got jam.'

'Not for breakfast.'

She shrugged and it was like an electric shock passing through her body. Full of caffeine and sugar, he thought. Nicotine too, judging by the smoky smell in the office. She smoothed her palm over her hair, pulled back into a low ponytail, and he noticed her hand drop down to her calf, not scratching, just toying at something with her fingertips. She stopped when she realised he was looking and he turned away, biting down – yet again – on the instinct to ask what was wrong, if maybe she was overdoing it.

'Do you want to see what I found on here then?' she asked.

'Anything interesting?'

'Oh, yeah. You might want to get a chair.'

'Coffee first.'

'Thanks.'

'You've had enough.' He went over to the machine, saw that she'd already downed half a pot, and when he poured his own the strength of it was overpowering, bitter and blacker than anyone else in the office brewed it.

The board taunted him as he walked past and he ignored it, knowing he'd have to face it later.

'So, Luke Gibson gave me admin access to the back end of Holly's blog,' she said, as he pulled another chair up to her desk. 'Basically, that means we can see all the posts she didn't finish or the ones she chose not to publish.'

'And that's useful because . . .'

'I know, shouldn't be, right?' She switched tabs and a dashboard came up. More information than Zigic wanted to trawl through at half past seven in the morning. 'I mean, Holly's living very publicly, she's informed, opinionated. So what *wouldn't* she publish?'

Ferreira clicked into the deleted posts, selected one titled 'Cripple'. It opened in a small box, not even large enough to show the entirety of the image that headed it up but Zigic recognised the photograph, the silver paintwork of Dawn's people carrier, the black spray-paint lettering.

'Where did Holly get this photo?' he asked.

'Someone sent her it,' Ferreira said, scrolling down in the draft box. 'Look – "To the person who emailed me this, I hope you die alone, in agony, knowing how much I fucking hate you."'

Zigic blew out a fast, hard breath. 'That doesn't sound like her other posts.'

'No, that's pure, unadulterated fury. Honestly, I'm amazed she had the self-control not to hit Publish and regret it later.'

'She didn't want to give them the satisfaction of knowing they'd got to her.'

'It's not the worst thing anyone's ever said to her.'

'But it's at her house,' Zigic said. 'They were virtually under her bedroom window.'

Ferreira twisted where she sat, a thin smile on her lips. 'I think it's someone in the village.'

'Or local, certainly. We thought that already, though.'

'You don't see this as an escalation?' Ferreira asked. 'All of those threats, then this – actually emailing her evidence of what they've done. They're making damn sure she knows they can get to her whenever they want.'

He sipped his coffee, eyeing her across the rim of the cup, seeing the certainty glowing behind her face. She'd not left this alone last night, he realised, she'd been probing and researching and she'd formulated a motive which made perfect sense to her even if the evidence didn't fit. And she wasn't going to give up until she'd voiced it.

'I'm not arguing with you,' he said. 'It's outright harassment. But how does it lead to Dawn's murder?'

Ferreira went back to the Twitter tab. 'Look, we've got lots of perfectly nice, supportive people, great. Good for her. But we've also got a significant amount of threats and abusive messages.' She pointed to one. '"Who died and made you queen of the cripples?" It's about cutting Holly down to size. All of this is. They want to take the one outlet she's got and cut it off.'

'Where does Dawn's murder come into this?'

'Holly won't interact with them,' Ferreira said, getting exasperated with him. 'Okay, don't think of this as a hate crime for a minute, pretend you got given this when you were in Anti-Stalking. What happens when a stalkee refuses to answer the phone calls and the text messages?'

'The stalker changes tack. Steps up to physical confrontation.'

'Yes, exactly. They want a reaction and they keep doing ever more extreme things until they finally get that reaction. So what's the next logical move after being outside the house?'

'You think they went inside?'

'Say they did. Say there's a confrontation with Dawn. She wants to know what the hell they're doing in her house. She's scared, she reacts. They react.' Ferreira's hands wheeled in the air in front of her, building it up. 'We know this probably wasn't a premeditated killing. The murder weapon's one of her own knives. It's been grabbed out of the block on the spur of the moment.'

'I think they'd be expecting to run into Dawn in her own home, don't you?'

'Maybe we're looking for a complete whack-job.'

'Says the woman with a psychology degree.'

'I'm tailoring this to my audience,' she said, a teasing sting in her voice.

'If they've gone there to get at Holly, why don't they even go in her bedroom?'

'We don't know they didn't go in there,' she said. 'All we know for sure is that they didn't go in there *after* Dawn was murdered. Maybe she caught them as they were leaving. Now that situation has blow-up potential.'

'I don't know.' Zigic scratched his beard. 'You're making a hell of a lot of assumptions, Mel.'

'I think it's a mistake to rule out the possibility,' she said. 'Especially when Riggott's looking to move this back into CID because you can't convince him it's a hate crime.'

She was right.

'Riggott's going to want more than tweets,' he said.

'I'll get more.' Her fingers twitched across the keyboard. 'This bastard's been so active, he'll have made a mistake somewhere.'

'You can't spend too long on this.' Zigic got up and wheeled the chair back around to Wahlia's side of the desk. 'I need you to talk to Holly's doctors today, find out what the situation with her physical therapy was. If there was any hint of neglect from Dawn.'

'Okay. I'll run this lot up to the tech department now. Ethan gets in early, I'll grab him before someone else does.' She fetched the bag of doughnuts and left the office with them, hoping a combination of insistence and bribery would keep him focused on their case for a few hours.

Zigic finished his coffee standing in front of the murder board, seeing how the case had changed since yesterday morning's briefing. The builder – Westman – had been alibied by his wife and the staff at the pub where they'd gone for dinner. His labourer, Dean Carter, was out of the picture now too. They were always unlikely suspects, Zigic told himself, so their loss from the column wasn't quite such a blow.

The lack of a murder weapon was bothering him almost as much as their current lack of credible suspects. The missing second knife was downright weird.

It was possible Dawn had thrown it out months ago for some reason but the block looked very new.

Why had the murderer taken it with them?

Easier to wipe your fingerprints off it and drop it there at the scene. No worries about where to dispose of it. No need to throw it into a river or bury it in the back garden.

He thought of how much effort they'd put into cleaning up after afterwards, the bloody towels they'd left behind in the bathroom and the smears up the banister to wipe away their fingerprints. All of that care but they walked out of the house with a six-inch knife in their hand?

Ferreira came back into the office, still holding her doughnuts.

'No takers?' Zigic asked.

'Ethan's "eating clean" this month. Whatever the hell that means.' She dumped the bag on the counter. 'He's just sent over the info from Dawn's phone. Apparently there's a lot of interesting stuff on there. Sounds like she was heavily into the hook-ups.'

Zigic went to check his emails and found the report from Ethan sitting at the top.

He scanned the attached files, seeing that Ferreira wasn't exaggerating. Ethan had extracted the dating profiles Dawn had set up, two sites, both using the same photograph, a smiling headshot, carefully posed; she looked approachable but not overtly sexual, just a woman looking for fun.

She'd certainly found it.

Her text messages revealed meetings arranged with thirty-nine men during the previous year, mostly at their places, sometimes hotels, lay-bys, car parks, different times of day. A couple of months ago that changed and she started having them over to her house, some in the day but most in the evening; a smaller pool of men, ones she must have trusted to have in her home. Several messages suggested they'd had sex in the unfinished extension or the garden – the men treated it like a kink, obviously didn't realise she was trying to maintain some separation between them and her child. It would have seemed furtive to them, Zigic thought, exciting, but did Dawn spend the whole time stifling her responses, worried about Holly hearing?

Zigic remembered the disgusted way Julia's nose hitched when she discussed Dawn's relationships, and wondered why she'd withdrawn her help so suddenly, forcing Dawn to make a decision that the tone of the messages suggested she wasn't entirely comfortable with. She needed these men but she didn't want them in her home. Not really. When she had an alternative she took it, when it was no longer available she tried to contain them.

It must have gnawed at her. The guilt fighting the need.

He put the thought aside – all parents obsessed about not being good enough and it wasn't what mattered right now – and went back to the paperwork.

There were several men she'd slept with on multiple occasions across an extended period and that was who they would focus on, the ones she'd built relationships with, who might have cause to kill her. It was going to be a mammoth task tracking them all down. The dating sites she'd used could stump up their details but that might take time, the mobile phone numbers would probably be the fastest way to get behind the usernames but there was a high probability that the SIM cards would be pay-as-you-gos, especially if the men were already in relationships.

They'd try those options first and only as a last resort would he have the men cold-called and asked to come into the station. It was never wise to give suspects a head start but sometimes there was no alternative.

Through his office door Zigic saw Parr arrive, followed a few minutes later by Colleen Murray, who was carrying a stainless-steel thermos and the fragile air of someone who'd hit the bottle pretty hard the night before. Wahlia was already at his desk, computer on, Ferreira at his shoulder, and Zigic could hear him protesting as she expounded her theory a second time, trying to drum up support for it because she liked being told she was right even when she already had the necessary go ahead.

If Riggott wasn't on their backs he'd have shut down her line of inquiry, saw nothing at the end of it beyond a particularly vile parade of bullies.

And yet . . . could she be right?

Dawn's murder was frenzied but the clean-up operation afterwards was cool headed and thorough, suggesting a calculating mind, a stalker's mentality. He thought of the stalking cases he'd worked where the victim went unharmed while their friends, lovers and family members bore the brunt of the aggression, and wondered if that's why Dawn was dead. She'd got between Holly and her attacker.

Ferreira had nothing but conjecture, though, and he knew she'd work harder if he didn't openly acknowledge the potential of her theory. She wanted to prove him wrong and he hoped she could.

But today was about these men.

23

It was a journey Ferreira thought she was finished with. Past the reception desk at City Hospital, then follow the lines marked on the floor to the lift which had taken her up to the occupational therapy unit. Twice a week, through the spring and into early summer, she'd struggled on crutches, forcing herself to keep moving while her mother fussed at her elbow, telling her off in Portuguese so colourful that the Brazilian cleaners in the corridors laughed into their chests. And each time she'd felt a little stronger, a little more impatient, until she realised she didn't need it any more and could stop pretending she was comfortable with being coddled and instructed and patronised.

Did Holly feel that way, she wondered, so thoroughly infantilised by the process?

The first entry in her blog was bold and defiant, a girl prepared to fight for her recovery no matter how dire the prognosis was. Something had changed, at some point she'd given up.

Ferreira had seen her medical records, knew who was treating Holly and just how good he was. If anyone could have helped her through to some greater mobility, it was Ray Deacon.

He was tough and honest. *You do the work, you feel the benefit.*

The double doors slid open as Ferreira approached and she hesitated for a brief second, a pinprick tweaking the ligament in her right leg. A remembered pain, she decided, brought on by the specific slant of morning sun across the large, open room and the sounds of exertion which filled it, low encouraging voices and the scuffing of trainers against crash mats as palms slapped down on the parallel bars.

One more step, Mel. Come on. And another, keep going, pet.

She used to hear Ray's voice in her sleep, urging her on as she dreamt her recovery to its ultimate end. Still heard it sometimes when she was on the treadmill, the sessions when each stride burnt.

Across the room he was working with a young man in khakis, all ripped upper body and buzz-cut hair, as he tried to find his balance on a prosthetic leg. This time of morning it was mostly injured servicemen, the ones who wanted an early start. To maintain the hours and the discipline the army had given them before it took their limbs.

There were a couple more with other therapists, a partial amputee lifting light weights and a woman with her left arm gone at the shoulder, the side of her face badly scarred, doing resistance tests. All of them pushing on hard, focused but aware of each other, Ferreira saw, feeding on the competition.

It was the right environment for people who wanted that, but if you needed privacy, if you didn't want your weakness on display, it could be uncomfortably combative, she guessed. And every failure would be magnified by the audience, even a supportive one.

Ray spotted her and made a 'one sec' gesture.

He called another therapist to get the young soldier on his feet and walked over to Ferreira with his usual welcoming smile and his hand held out.

'Alright, stranger. Back for a tune-up?'

She shook his hand, smiling. 'Without an appointment? I wouldn't dare.'

'You're looking strong, pet.'

'I feel strong.'

He folded his arms across his chest. He was a big man and the action made him look even more solid. It wasn't a natural pose, though, he was better trained than that. Always open, always encouraging. He spent half his life with his hands held out to catch you when you stumbled.

'You know why I'm here?' Ferreira asked.

'I've an inkling this is a professional visit.'

'Holly Prentice.'

'I saw the news. Terrible shame.' He looked down at his feet. 'Did it make a difference?'

'What?'

'Her not being able to move, like.' His fists tightened. 'Could she have got away?'

'Maybe,' Ferreira admitted. 'She could have raised the alarm at least, saved herself.'

He nodded. 'Best do this in my office.'

It was a small room, painted lavender and surprisingly cluttered for such a particular man; files on the desk and on the chair he cleared for her, children's drawings taking up most of the wall above his computer, postcards and thank-you notes filling a cork-board propped on top of the filing cabinet.

She should have thanked him properly, she realised. Sent a bottle of something. The relief of being free had overridden her manners, though.

'So, what can I tell you?' Ray asked, lowering himself into the chair.

'Tell me about Holly. How did she get on here?'

'She was impatient. But that's common enough.' He gave her a pointed look and she smiled. 'Sometimes it's a good thing, gets you lot down here, keeps you focused.'

'Sometimes it's not good, though?'

'No. Like I told you when you first came, the body can only do so much and it'll do it at its own pace. With your injuries a bit of impatience never hurt, it just got you fixed quicker. But Holly was never going to be the girl she was before the accident.'

'Surely she realised that,' Ferreira said.

'She was a kid, she didn't want to hear the truth.'

'But you had to tell her?'

'No point promising folk things they'll never achieve.' His gaze drifted away across the desk, following the sweep of his hand as it found a pen to grip. 'She was never going to walk again.'

'Definitely?'

'Never. Her spinal cord was completely severed, vertebrae crushed. It wasn't a clean injury.'

'But Holly was still adamant she'd recover,' Ferreira said.

Ray smiled with half his mouth, nodded. 'Aye, wilful as hell, that one. We made some good progress early on. A sight more than I expected. She got the use of her hands back, started to get a bit more movement in her forearms. And it happened quick.'

'Which only made her more determined to prove you wrong about walking?'

He turned the pen around between his fingers. 'Worst thing that can happen sometimes, fast progress. She started on thinking the doctors had her diagnosis wrong, convinced herself they'd mixed up her records with someone else. She was sure she'd walk again. She told me, "One day I'm going to run out of this hospital."'

'She might've been right,' Ferreira said. 'It happens.'

'What, miracles?'

'Misdiagnoses.'

Ray looked at the thank-you cards tacked up on the board, the thin skin around his eyes pinching.

'How long ago did she stop coming for treatment?'

'Autumn of last year,' he said. 'October time. I thought she'd be back but she'd had enough of it.'

'Are you sure that's why she stopped?' Ferreira asked. 'We've been hearing that there might have been some neglect issues with the mother.'

'Dawn? Never.' He threw the pen down. 'She was a good mother. Trust me, I see a lot of parents coming in here, going through the motions, and I can see in their eyes they're resenting every minute of it.'

'But not Dawn?'

'No. She was having a tough time of it but she was always there for Holly. And she wasn't an easy girl to look after, if you want my honest opinion.'

'Wilful?'

'And vocal.' Ray's cheeks flushed. 'Dawn bore the full brunt of it.'

'Tell me what happened. Exactly.'

'It was mid-September. Holly cried off an appointment and I called to check up on her, reschedule. Dawn said Holly didn't want to come but I convinced Dawn to bring her the next week.' He frowned. 'They turned up as agreed but Holly wouldn't do anything. Refused to do any of the excersies, didn't even want to talk to me. It happens. She'd been putting herself under too much pressure to improve and it wasn't possible, not to the degree she wanted. She was frustrated and angry, anyone could see that. But she needed to stick with it.'

'Did you manage to talk her round?'

His shoulders tensed, then sagged, chin dropping onto his chest. 'No. I tried. She threw an almighty tantrum, screaming and swearing. Laying into Dawn, accusing her of all sorts.'

Ferreira straightened. 'What did she accuse her of?'

'She said Dawn wished she was dead so she wouldn't have to look after her any more.'

'Was she right about that?' Ferreira asked. 'In your opinion.'

'No way. Not a bit of it.' Ray rubbed his hand across the back of his neck. 'Dawn broke down, ran out crying. I went after her.'

'What did she say?'

'She was devastated. There wasn't a word of truth in any of it. She wanted Holly to get better. For herself, yes. A bit. It was a big strain caring for the girl on her own. But she wanted Holly to have a life beyond her bedroom. She knew there'd come a point when she wasn't there any more and Holly would have to be independent.'

'Dawn was only thirty-eight.'

'Time passes quick, Mel. You're young, but you wait.'

He looked away as the sound of a body hitting the crash mats came through the office door, but he didn't move, only sighed. Another moment of failure. Another person to pick up and dust off and encourage to try again.

'What provoked the change of attitude?' Ferreira asked. 'Did Dawn tell you?'

'Yeah, it sounded like something of nothing to me, but Holly had done a couple of days at a new school and it didn't go well. Kids taking the piss on account of her being in the chair.' He rubbed his hand over his head. 'I reckon she'd have been able to put it aside if she was making better progress but she'd hit a wall. Maybe all that was sinking in finally and the school thing was just the last straw.'

The same story they'd heard from Matthew Campbell. Ferreira could imagine the toll it would have taken on Holly, finding herself verbally abused in what should have been a safe, inclusive environment, how she would have felt as if nowhere would ever be welcoming again if a place set up specifically to cater for people like her was so hostile.

'Was that the last time she came?'

'No. Bloody hell, Mel, you can't give up on folks that easy. I gave her a couple of weeks to cool down and we made another appointment.' His bushy grey brows drew in. 'Dawn brought her as usual and I thought it was all over and done with. But she woudn't do anything. She just sat there, wouldn't speak, wouldn't acknowledge any of us. Total passive resistance. There's no dealing with it.'

'You tried, though?'

'Course I did. Her mum too. She was begging her. I mean, literally on her knees begging her not to give up. But Holly had made her decision. She was finished with it.' He shook his head, a bitter look on his face. 'Dawn was crying when they left.'

Ferreira thought of what Luke Gibson had said, Holly's sudden withdrawal at the end of last year; no more trips out, no more parties with family friends in the garden. He'd taken it to be a sign of neglect on Dawn's part, hadn't credited Holly with the stubbornness to refuse or considered that she might have been so crushingly depressed that leaving her bedroom was no longer the positive experience it had been.

'Was that the last contact you had with them?' Ferreira asked.

'Last time I saw either of them, yup.'

'But you spoke to Dawn again?'

'I phoned her up a couple of times. I wanted her to know Holly could come back whenever she was ready.' He scratched his neck, slow fingers, thoughtful expression. 'And I was worried about Dawn, she didn't seem like the toughest woman in the world even when things were going well with Holly. I wanted to check she was coping.'

'Was she?'

'She cried a lot. On the phone, I mean. She told me she wasn't sleeping very well, she kept breaking down over nothing.'

He frowned again. She'd never seen him so downcast before and realised how much of a front he'd put on during her treatement, all of these worries for other people neatly compartmentalised but still deeply felt. It made him good at his job but it also made him vulnerable to suffering the effects of other people's traumas.

'It was breaking her heart,' he said. 'Holly was a strong girl, Dawn thought she'd be able to deal with her disability, overcome it, like. But instead she crumbled. That's a hard thing to deal with as a parent, knowing your child would rather die than fight on.'

'Holly said that?' Ferreira asked. 'She said she'd rather be dead?'

'The last-but-one session, aye. Big no-no, we don't allow that sort of negativity up here.'

She remembered; all those high fives and fist bumps, the smiles and circles of support for each milestone passed.

'I gave Dawn some numbers,' Ray said. 'Support groups, respite care. I don't know if she ever used them but she needed help, something.'

Dawn found it, Ferreira thought. Not the kind of help Ray had in mind but those men she hooked up with must have worked for her, provided distraction if nothing else, some brief moments outside herself.

'Such a waste,' Ray said quietly. 'I really thought I could help her.'

Ferreira reached over and squeezed his arm. 'You did everything you could. If someone doesn't want help, you can't force them to take it.'

He nodded but the words sounded hollow and she knew he'd beat himself up about it for weeks to come, maybe longer.

He walked with her as far as the double doors and she thanked him for his help, shook his hand again, held onto it until he finally met her eyes.

'I should have said this ages ago . . .' Ray waved away her words with his free hand. 'If it wasn't for you I wouldn't be standing here now. I'd be – well – doesn't matter now, does it?'

'You beat it, pet. That's all that matters.'

In the lift back down she turned over what he'd said about Holly and Dawn, her impressions of the pair changing again, their uneasy relationship taking on new dimensions. She wondered how much Warren knew about Holly's refusal to continue her treatment. If he'd tried to change her mind, use his paternal authority.

More questions to ask him.

Zigic called as she was getting into her car. 'Need you back at the office. Holly's nurse is here.'

24

Siona Croft was solidly built, broad across the shoulders and thick-armed, muscular rather than fat, as if she spent a lot of time in a weights room. Exactly the right physique for lifting infirm patients in and out of the beds and baths they couldn't afford to upgrade to suit their new conditions. Young, though, no older than twenty-five, with an open and friendly face.

As he waited for Ferreira to go through the usual formalities of identification for the tape and explanation of the situation for Croft's benefit, Zigic wondered if Dawn had seen her like that – approachable – if she'd confided in her.

'I can't believe this,' Croft said. 'I was only round there last week.'

She toyed with the scalding-hot tea Zigic had brought her from the vending machine, touching the plastic cup with her fingertips until she couldn't stand it any longer.

'You're Holly's home-care nurse, is that right?' Ferreira asked.

'I was.' Croft frowned at her. 'Didn't they tell you at the office?'

'What?'

'Dawn sacked me last week.'

'Which day?' Zigic asked.

'Wednesday.'

If Croft knew how damning that bit of information was she didn't show it, kept looking steadily back at Zigic across the scarred and scratched table, face on the shocked side of neutral. Nurses were used to presenting blank faces, though; couldn't show disgust, couldn't show fear, always had to look unflappable.

'What reason did she give for letting you go?'

'She said I turned up for work drunk. I'd had a couple of pints the night before, I might have been a bit worse for wear, but I definitely wasn't drunk. I wasn't even hungover.'

'And how did you feel about that?'

'I didn't take it personal. It was my own fault.' She shrugged. 'I've been expecting it since my first shift there, to be honest. She's got a right reputation, that one.'

'For what?'

Croft went to sip her tea, stopped. 'Put it this way, I'd been looking after Holly for a month and that's the longest any nurse from the company has lasted with her. The woman before me got sacked for using her mobile in the house. The one before that Dawn didn't like because she talked to Holly about her boyfriend and she said it upset her.'

'Was Holly easily upset?' Ferreira asked.

'No. I mean, she was quite low but even, if that makes sense. I thought she was coping fairly well, considering what had happened to her and all.'

'Do you know why she stopped going for physio?' Ferreira asked.

'I mentioned it to Holly the first time I went there and she said she'd tried it but it didn't help. She said she had better things to do with her time.'

Like blogging, Zigic thought.

'Did you mention any of this to Dawn?'

'Christ, no. I wasn't going to give her any excuse to sack me. I liked Holly, she was a nice girl, easy to get on with. She wasn't self-pitying, you know? A lot of people are, they turn on everyone around them. Nurses worse than anyone, because we have to do so much for them and that's really uncomfortable for most people. Holly was a pleasure to look after.'

'Sounds like she trusted you,' Ferreira said, and got a cautious nod in return. 'Did she tell you why she wasn't going to school?'

'She didn't see the point in that either.'

'But she was a bright girl.'

'Yeah, she was. Bright enough to realise no one was going to employ her in that condition, even if she had the best education in the world.'

'There are discrimination laws,' Ferreira pointed out. 'Holly had options.'

'Look, it's really easy to say that, just like it's really easy for me or you to say, "Do the physio, one day you'll be able to move your arms as well as your hands, won't that be great." But Holly had gone from being incredibly fit and active to a basically inert lump of flesh – that's how she described herself. She hated being like that. School, university, job, it was all theoretically possible but she'd have to go out in the world again to get those things and she didn't want people seeing her how she was.'

Matthew Campbell had suggested as much and Zigic could understand Holly feeling that way. In her position would he have been prepared to open himself up to becoming a spectacle, an object of ridicule and pity?

Siona Croft was staring into her tea, hands clasped under her chin. 'God, I wish I hadn't had those beers.'

Zigic wished it too. He'd seen the time sheets, sent over from the agency; Croft was a daily visitor to the house, she even did the weekend shifts. If Dawn hadn't sacked her she would have arrived there on Friday morning as usual and been unable to get in. Maybe she would have raised the alarm right away. Looking at her Zigic could imagine one of those big shoulders battering through the front door.

'The agency didn't mention that Dawn sacked you,' Zigic said. 'Did you tell them?'

'Of course I did. They needed to find someone else to go in there.'

'They don't have any record of that call.'

'Didn't they send anyone in on Thursday?' Croft asked. 'Holly would have needed bathing and medicating Thursday morning.'

'They claim not to have heard from you,' Zigic told her. 'So they didn't send anyone else.'

Croft took her phone out. 'I emailed Pauline – she runs the office. Well, she's supposed to run it. She spends half her time playing online bingo from what I've heard and she's not the sharpest tool in the box to begin with. Look –' She slid her phone across the table, the screen showing an email sent to the agency's address a few minutes after ten on Wednesday morning:

Mommy dearest strikes again! I'm out. Better see if Fran's available for tomorrow.

'"Mommy dearest?"'

'It was just a joke.' Croft dipped her head, embarrassed now, and Zigic noticed the dark rings around her eyes, incompletely covered by her make-up, and an old bruise on the exposed skin on her shoulder, a distinct grab mark fading to yellow, too old to have happened less than a week ago. 'I didn't mean anything by it.'

'You meant something,' Ferreira said sharply.

Croft sighed, reached for her tea again and this time she found it drinkable or perhaps she was happy enough to take the burn in exchange for a few more seconds of silence. 'It isn't easy being a carer. Doing it for money is challenging enough but in some ways doing it for love is worse, because everyone expects you to be a twenty-four/seven saint. You need to understand that. The demands it makes on you.'

Zigic nodded for her to go on.

'And it makes you demanding on everyone else too. Dawn wanted the best care for Holly and I don't blame her. I'd want that for my daughter. But she was beyond picky. She sacked people for nothing.'

'Turning up hungover isn't nothing,' Ferreira said.

Zigic wondered if she realised how ironic a judgement that was coming from her.

'Did you ever see any sign of Dawn neglecting Holly?' he asked.

Croft looked at him as if it was a stupid question.

'No. Never. Dawn was one hundred per cent dedicated to Holly.' Croft rubbed her arm. 'They had their arguments but that's normal. In each other's faces every day, mother and teenage daughter. It's going to happen.'

'What did they argue about?'

'Petty stuff. Holly couldn't exactly do the full-on rebellious teen thing. Mostly Dawn was annoyed because Holly never wanted to get out of bed. I think she'd accepted her staying at home but she wanted her downstairs with her. Watching TV or whatever. Holly just wanted to do stuff on her laptop.'

It fitted with what Holly's physical therapist had told Ferreira and Zigic didn't doubt Siona Croft's opinion of the situation within the house. It wasn't getting them anywhere, though.

'Did you see anyone hanging around the house on Wednesday morning?'

She thought about it for a moment and Zigic guessed the hang-over she'd had at the time wouldn't have helped.

'No, I don't think so. I'd have noticed anyone weird.'

'Holly's dad,' he said. 'Warren. Did you ever see him there?'

'No. She talked about him a lot. Absolutely idolised him. I don't think Dawn appreciated that. She told me he left her while Holly was still in hospital.' Croft frowned. 'He sounds like a right shit.'

'Was that all she said about him?'

'I didn't want to pry.' Her eyes widened. 'Is that who you think killed them?'

'We're keeping an open mind right now,' Zigic said. 'But Holly died of natural causes.'

'Because nobody was looking after her?'

'I'm afraid so, yes.'

'Poor Holly.' She shook her head, sucked her bottom lip into her mouth and bit down on it. 'This is all that fucking Pauline's fault. If she'd opened her emails and sent someone else around to see to Holly this would have never happened.' She slammed her fist onto the table. 'Useless bitch!'

There was nothing more to say and Zigic motioned for Ferreira to stop the recording equipment, feeling as if Holly's death had become even more tragic than it was half an hour earlier, even more senseless. It pained him to think how easily she could have been saved.

25

At first Nathan thought he was dreaming.

This wasn't his soft, warm bed, that couldn't be his nan sitting on the side of it holding his hand. She looked sad even though she was smiling and he didn't want her to go. He squeezed her fingers, feeling the hardness of the gold rings she wore, the sharp points of the stones biting his skin.

'Do you want something to eat, love?'

He didn't dare answer in case he woke himself up.

'How about boiled eggs and soldiers?'

His eyes were open but that happened in dreams. You thought you were awake and everything was real but it wasn't.

He'd dreamt his mum back to life a thousand times. Hugged her, clutching handfuls of her jumper, the pink one with stars on she was wearing when she died. Felt her kiss the top of his head, smelled her perfume, heard her voice.

None of it real.

And no matter how hard he tried to hold on to her she would always leave him again.

'Natty, come on, love, time to get up now.'

A tear rolled down his cheek and he knew that didn't make it real either.

His nana took a tissue out of her cardigan pocket and dabbed at his face. Then he remembered. She'd done the same thing last night when she found him outside her kitchen door, shivering and sick with nerves, tears streaming down his face because he'd fallen coming over her fence from the alley that ran down the back of the house.

'I'm here,' his nan said. 'You're safe now.'

He hugged her, pressing his face into her shoulder. She smelled just like his mum. The same perfume and cigarettes and hairspray.

'Alright, that's enough crying.' She pushed him away. 'Bring your cover down onto the settee and I'll make you boily eggs.'

Nathan dragged the duvet around his shoulders like a cape and followed her down the stairs. She'd put cartoons on the telly but they were too young for him really. He was old enough now to know that getting hit on the head with a hammer didn't just raise a big pink bump. It killed you.

Don't think about that.

You're safe. She said so.

He wasn't, though.

This was just the beginning and he didn't know how to tell her what he wanted to do. Why he'd come home.

He wanted to tell her about Dawn but he wasn't sure he should.

She came back with his breakfast on a tray.

'There we go. You be a good boy and eat that up.'

There was a glass of milk and two boiled eggs in the cup shaped like a chicken he'd had since he was little. His brother had one as well. Just the same so they wouldn't argue over them. He ate quickly, hungrier than he'd thought he was, dipping the stale soldiers in the runny yolks. She sat in her chair by the electric fire, smoking a cigarette while she watched him.

When he was finished she took the tray back into the kitchen and he followed her.

'I wanna go to the arcade.'

The plate slipped from her hands and soapy water splashed her as it landed in the sink. She swore, reached for a tea towel and patted her face dry.

'You're not going there.'

'I need to talk to him.'

'No.'

'But I need to tell him something.'

She turned away from the sink and he could see how angry she was. For a second he thought she was going to slap him. Prepared himself for it.

'Alright, Natty. We'll go later.'

'No, I've gotta go on me own.'

'Okay. But let me finish this washing-up first. I'll come with you on the bus and you can go in and I'll have a look round the shops. Then we can meet up after.' She smiled. 'Is that a plan?'

He nodded.

'Go up and have a bath first. You can't go out smelling like that.'

Nathan gathered the duvet off the settee and carried it upstairs again, thrown over his shoulder. He wanted to get back in bed, just sleep. Stay there for days or longer, pretend none of this had happened.

Last night, as the train pulled into Lime Street station, he switched on his phone. Shouldn't have, didn't need to, but he did it anyway, wanting to see if Rachel was still after him. If Julia or Caitlin had been in touch.

They hadn't.

In the bedroom he looked for his phone but couldn't find it. Maybe he'd lost it climbing over the fence. It didn't matter. He didn't need it any more.

He knew how to find the arcade and after he'd gone there he wouldn't need Rachel or Julia any more. He could come home with his nan, have his tea, watch some telly and go to bed. He would have his old life again.

A few words. That's all it would take.

You don't need to be scared.

Nathan ran the bath, feeling weird about having one in the morning, but he knew he smelled bad. He squeezed in purple stuff from a bottle on the shelf and it bubbled fast and thick, the steam coating the window and the mirror over the sink. He wiped it clear with his hand.

He'd ask his nan to cut his hair later. Rachel said it had to be long but he didn't care what she said now. He'd get it shaved back to his skull how he liked it. You couldn't walk around this estate with girl's hair. Not unless you were prepared to fight for it and he wasn't.

When he turned the taps off he heard them.

His nan talking downstairs. A woman answering her.

One of her friends.

No. You know that voice.

Rachel.

'. . . won't make any difference.'

'I told him that. But he's only a boy, he doesn't understand the kind of people he's dealing with. He thinks he can talk to them. Thank God he came here first. If he'd gone there—'

Rachel interrupted her, voice too low for him to hear. Nathan crept down the stairs to try and catch what she was saying and realised too late where they were, standing in the living-room doorway, both looking up at him.

'There you are,' Rachel said, smiling her dead smile. 'Well, we've had a fun few days, haven't we?'

He bolted for the front door but she got there first and caught him around the chest, stronger than she looked. Rachel wrestled him to the stairs and sat him down on them.

'I'm not going with you.'

'You have to go with her. You know that.' His nana looked at Rachel and she looked back at her.

'I don't need her. I can fix this.'

'How?' Rachel asked.

'I'm gonna talk to him.'

'Talking to him won't make you safe, Nathan. It'll get you killed. We've been over this before and I'm not going to argue with you about it again.' She folded her arms. 'You know Julia's been worried sick about you.'

'I don't care.'

But he did and he turned away from her so she wouldn't see that.

Rachel squatted down in front of him. 'Look, I know this has been hard for you and I know you're scared, but we're almost through now. You're strong enough to do this and when you've finished there'll be nothing more to worry about.'

She was lying.

Her voice always went like that, soft and girlie, when she was lying.

Or maybe she was doing it so his nan would think she was nice and wouldn't stop her taking him away.

Stupid. She called her to come and get you. She doesn't want you here, causing trouble, bringing it to her door.

No. That wasn't right. She wanted him to be safe. That's why she called Rachel. She was an old woman and she was scared. She didn't get to run away and be looked after by people the way he did. She was left here with his mess.

That's why he ran. He needed to sort everything out so they'd both be safe again.

She didn't know that, though, and that's why she called Rachel. If he'd told her last night . . .

Shit. It wasn't supposed to happen like this.

He could never do anything right.

Stupid. Stupid. Stupid.

'What's he doing?'

'He's switched off.'

'I thought you'd got him on pills for that.'

'He hasn't had them for three days.'

Rachel shook his shoulders and he stared through her. Seeing the door, knowing he should make a run for it, now, while she was squatting down off balance.

'His pills are in the glovebox of my car.' Rachel took a set of keys from her pocket. 'Could you fetch them, please? He should have one as soon as possible.'

His nan hurried out of the front door and the gap was there but too small and Rachel seemed to know what he was thinking because she stood up, blocking his path until the door slammed shut.

'What did you do to Dawn Prentice?'

His eyes snapped back onto her. 'Nothing.'

'The police think you killed her.'

He was going to be sick.

No. Don't. Hold it down.

'I don't care if you killed her, Nathan.'

Nathan closed his eyes.

'Look at me.'

Opened them.

'You know what the police can be like. If they think you murdered Dawn and they can't find anyone else, that's it. You'll be thrown in a young offenders' institution just like your brother was. And we know how that turned out.'

His breakfast came up in a hot rush and she stepped back sharply. He retched and spat and cried but she didn't stop talking.

'You are going to do exactly what I tell you from now on. Right?'

He nodded, spit trailing down his chin, throat burning.

'Good. Then we both know where we stand.'

26

Ferreira drove down the rutted, sun-baked track towards Nene House, trailing a cloud of dust that swirled around her car, feeling every bump rattle up through the steering wheel, the sound of barking dogs audible above the music as she drew closer.

Warren's Range Rover was parked in front of the house but it was the only vehicle there and she was glad Sally wouldn't be around to police their conversation.

She walked down the side of the house, past a recycling box full of wine bottles and a washing line hung with wet laundry. The dogs started barking furiously, whining and yelping, catching a new scent on the air. She caught one herself, marijuana and tobacco, and she followed it to a small paved area hidden behind an old outhouse where Warren was sitting staring across what passed for their garden, a few tangled shrubs dotted around the edge of a lawn which needed mowing, running down to a ranch fence that divided their land from a grass field beyond and after that the river.

His feet were on an upturned milk crate dragged from a pile of others just like it stacked against the crumbling red-brick wall, and he barely stirred as she pulled out a heavy cast-iron chair to sit down on opposite him at the table. He was even more gaunt than when she had seen him two days before at the hospital, greyer looking and smaller and somehow desiccated.

'Is there any news?' he asked, dragging his attention away from the play of the wind across the lawn.

'We're making progress.'

'That's a no, then.'

'It takes time, Warren. I'm sorry I don't have anything to give you just yet.'

He cleared his throat. 'When can we have Holly's body back?'

'Soon, I think.'

He didn't ask about Dawn's and she wondered if that was significant, decided it probably wasn't. They'd separated, why would he expect to be responsible for her burial? Zigic was still trying to get in touch with her parents, retired to Cyprus and facing the worst kind of homecoming now.

'Where's Sally?' Ferreira asked.

'Shopping.' He took a long draw on his joint. 'At least that's where she said she was going.'

'You don't believe her?'

'I'm not easy to be around right now.' He said it as if it was a direct quote. 'I suppose you can't blame her for wanting to get away for a few hours. Holly wasn't her child, what does she care?'

'I'm sure she cares,' Ferreira said.

'That's because you don't know her.' Contempt flared around his nostrils. 'Sally thinks it was a "mercy". Like she went peacefully in her sleep.'

Ferreira said nothing.

'She didn't, did she?' he asked. 'She can't have, not being left alone like that for days.'

'It was a stroke. A pretty massive one, the pathologist said, so Holly would have died quickly, relatively painlessly.'

'And what about before the pretty massive stroke?'

Ferreira looked away from him, knowing how Sally must have felt, why she needed to get away from his boiling fury for a few hours. He needed more green in that joint, or better-quality stuff, if he was maintaining this level of anger on it.

'Well?'

'I need to talk to you about Holly's blog,' she said.

'You haven't answered my question.'

She reminded herself what he was going through. That grief affected people in lots of different ways and that she should be patient with him. Understanding. Indulgent even, because he had lost his only child and that bought you a lot of grace.

But she didn't like his attitude. She'd always believed that extreme situations like this brought out people's true characters and if this was his . . .

'Come on,' he snapped. 'What do you think her death was like? The long, drawn-out bit before she had a stroke?'

'I imagine it was terrifying,' Ferreira said. 'I imagine she felt scared and powerless and she couldn't work out why nobody came to help her for days on end.'

He nodded. 'Because I should have gone to see her, shouldn't I?'

'Only you know the answer to that question, Warren.'

'I should.' His face crumpled but there were no tears, just the dry reflexes that came when a person was all cried out. 'I should have known something was wrong. You hear people say it when their child dies, they all say the same thing – "I could feel it. I knew." – and I thought that's what happened. But they're liars. You don't feel anything. They die and you feel nothing.'

Warren reached for his lighter and tried to get a flame out of it, until, on the sixth or seventh attempt, he shook it and swore and threw it into the long grass.

Ferreira took her own from her pocket and held it steady while he relit the stub of his joint. Up close she could see just how strong he'd made it, hardly any black visible through the thin paper. He inhaled deeply and slumped in the uncomfortable chair, elbow on the table, head in hand.

'What's this about then?' Warren asked. 'Holly's blog?'

'You didn't follow it?'

'Not really. I knew she had one. We didn't talk as often as I would have liked. What with the divorce and all of that mess.'

Suddenly Ferreira wished they were having this conversation on record. She thought of his quick temper and that ferocious attack, the grabbed knife.

Sally would cover for him. She was punching well above her weight looks-wise and his guilt would tie him to her for ever. Of course she wouldn't call the police if he came home covered in blood.

Her gaze drifted across the garden, to a stainless-steel incinerator where he might have burnt his clothes and the gentle slope leading down to the river where he might have thrown the knife.

'Holly's death doesn't rule anyone out', Zigic had said. The nurse was supposed to come the next morning and Warren would have known that.

'I didn't kill Dawn,' he said, as if he'd heard her thoughts. 'We were bickering over money, that's all, nothing serious.'

'Bickering over money motivates the vast majority of crime in the world.'

'Only when people care about it and I don't. Christ, I don't have any to care about. If I did I'd have given her it long ago.'

He started to make another joint and Ferreira took her own tobacco out, got hers rolled and semi-smoked while he was still breaking up a nugget of dark, noxious-smelling skunk into the paper. His fingertips were stained with it, nails rimmed an oily green.

'Why does her blog matter anyway?'

'Along with all the support, Holly was receiving a heavy dose of abusive feedback. Anonymous comments, insults, threats.'

His fingers froze. 'What kind of threats?'

'Every kind,' Ferreira said. 'I think at least one of the people targeting her's local.'

He reached for her lighter and lit up. 'In the village, you mean?'

'Quite possibly. We're working on tracking down IP addresses, that kind of thing, but most online abusers manage to hide where they are with proxy servers.' Ethan had explained it all, didn't hold out much hope of giving her a target. 'The abuse looks personal, though, so what I wanted to ask you was whether Holly had any enemies before her accident?'

'She was fourteen,' he said incredulously.

Sixteen, Ferreira thought. Sixteen when she died but to him she would always be the fourteen-year-old he waved off on her rock-climbing weekend.

'Kids can be vicious, Warren. And Holly doesn't seem to have stayed in touch with any of her old school friends. She hadn't used her Facebook page since the day of the accident – her friends kept trying to contact her for a while but she never answered any of their messages.'

He watched a tattered white butterfly come to land on the tabletop.

'I assumed she was still in touch with them.'

'No. And that can offend people.'

'Her friends were nice girls.'

'What about the girls she wasn't friends with?' Ferreira asked. 'Is there anyone you can think of who might want to upset her?'

He took a hit, held the smoke down in his lungs for a long time before he reluctantly exhaled. 'I was working a lot back then. You have to when it's your own business. I didn't take much of an interest in Holly's school life.'

'But you two went out running together?'

'She never mentioned having problems. She would have if there was something troubling her.' He followed the butterfly with his eyes as it took off, fluttering over to a large shrub with acid-yellow flowers beginning to droop. 'Holly was popular and she was sensible, girls like that don't get in fights.'

'Did she have a boyfriend?'

'No.' He tried to scowl at her but couldn't seem to focus properly, hunched over the table, neck loose, all awkward angles. 'What's it got to do with anything now? Dawn's the person who was murdered. Holly was just . . . unlucky enough to be there.'

'It matters because whoever did it left Holly to die when it would have been the easiest thing in the world to make an anonymous nine-nine-nine call and save her. Whoever killed Dawn didn't care what happened to Holly.'

He winced.

'Won't it be someone she was talking to online? They're all freaks,' he spat.

'It's a possibility. People form very intense friendships. And enmities. She was spending most of her waking hours online. It was her whole life.'

Another wince as he read an accusation into her words.

'Did Holly ever talk to you about why she quit physio?' His head bobbed but he didn't answer. 'And school? Why did she stop caring, Warren?'

'Do you think we were happy about that? Do you think we wanted her to give up? Holly knew her own mind. She was a strong girl. Stronger than either of us.' He took a long pull on his joint. 'You've got to respect your child as an individual, they're not little mini-mes you shape with your own prejudices and beliefs. Holly knew her mind. Dawn wanted to dictate to her, right, she thought she knew what was best for all of us, all of the time. She was a control freak. She got it from her dad. Bastard. It wasn't her fault, not really, she was raised bad. She didn't know how to let Holly be.'

'You two argued about it,' Ferreira said, trying to get him to look at her. 'Holly's right-to-die campaigning?'

He was staring past her, across her left shoulder, lips parted.

'Holly wanted to die, didn't she?'

'She had no future,' he said, the words running together. 'Dawn wouldn't accept it.'

'But you did? You agreed with her?'

Warren blinked, one eye moving slightly slower than the other.

'Is that what you and Dawn were arguing over?'

No answer. No denial.

'Is that why Dawn wouldn't let you see Holly?'

She waited, seeing how he swayed slightly where he sat, free hand hanging limp over the back of the chair, thumb brushing circles across his fingertips as if there was something intriguingly textured on his skin.

He was past the point of talking to, she realised.

She thanked him for his time and walked away feeling as if she'd wasted hours, caught up in the time-bending quality of his self-medicated grief.

As she turned the corner around the house she spotted a T-shirt lying on the ground under the washing line, went to pick it up without thinking, meaning to throw it back over the line just to get it out of the dirt, but as she held it between her hands she saw the decal on the front, a symbol she recognised but wasn't sure where from.

She pegged it out on the line, stretching it taut, and snapped a photograph of it with her phone. Seeing it like that, captured on the screen, she remembered – last night, fatigued and propping herself up with rum-spiked coffee as she sat in bed with her laptop on her knees, going through Holly's Twitter feed, looking for patterns in the chaotic hate.

27

The dating sites Dawn used came through within an hour. Zigic had impressed upon them the benefit of cooperation and the potential harm a negative statement to the press could cause their PR department. Appealing to their public spirit might have yielded a result as quickly but somehow he doubted it.

Dawn had found her lovers through two of the bigger sites and with that came mandatory credit-card registration, which meant real names, mobile numbers and addresses too, cutting out days of work for the team. Handily they also had the men's profile pictures. Everything in neat bundles waiting to be tapped.

But for that they needed resources.

'How many we looking at?' Riggott asked, sitting in Zigic's chair, commanding from it the way he always did when he came up to Hate Crimes.

'Thirty-nine men.'

'I was expecting more the way you were going on about her.'

'These are only from the last twelve months.'

'You get it once a week, I reckon. Why shouldn't she?' Riggott gave him a goatish look. 'Any of these studs got a record of disability-related harassment?'

'A few of them have got violent offences to their names.'

He'd had them checked for that already, Wahlia's first job as soon as morning briefing was over. Two men with histories of domestic abuse, one convicted rapist, one particularly charming individual who'd been fired from his security guard's job for trying to coerce a shoplifter into giving him a blow job in exchange for her freedom.

She knew her rights and was savvy enough to hit the record feature on her phone the second he escorted her off the shop floor.

'This is looking more and more like a CID matter, Ziggy.'

'It's one avenue we're pursuing.'

'Come on, son, I've seen the board. It's your only avenue. Barring that wee boy. And for all you know he's seen something that's shit him up bad enough to leg it.'

Zigic leaned against the glass partition. The rest of the team were out there, waiting for Riggott's verdict, doing the grunt work, checking backgrounds and prioritising the most likely candidates, but what the DCS decided now would dictate whether they had the support to do the job right or not.

'Mel's found something, but we need time to get the relevant information back from the techies,' Zigic said. 'We've got a long-running and escalating campaign of harassment against Holly. Including death threats.'

'Delivered how?'

'Online. Her blog, emails, Twitter.'

'Viable?'

'They vandalised Dawn's car. They know where Holly lives. I think we might be looking at a stalking-type situation that was provoked by Holly's growing prominence as a disability-rights blogger.'

'Suspects?' Riggott asked, posture straightening, interested now.

'No names, not yet. But we're thinking it's someone local. Someone she probably knew, which is a limited group because of her age and situation. The abuse has a personal ring to it.' He sounded so certain he almost convinced himself it was a credible line of inquiry rather than a way of assuaging Riggott. 'We need more time, though. Getting behind online aliases isn't as easy as calling in accounts from dating websites.'

'Sure, it's nigh-on impossible if they know what they're doing,' Riggott said, rising from the chair, going over to the filing cabinet where Zigic's suit was hanging up.

The clear plastic cover was unzipped and he pulled out one sleeve, testing the feel of the wool, seeing how many buttons were on the cuff; so much the peacock that he couldn't resist a quick look at the label inside the jacket. It was from Zara, Anna's choice, nothing like the quality Riggott wore himself but he nodded slightly.

'Nice. Tidy stitching for high street.' He sealed the cover and turned back to Zigic. 'I know what you're trying to do and I don't blame you. If it was my case I'd try and distract my boss with some outlandish bollocks like this to buy time.'

'It's a solid theory.'

'Yes.' Riggott pointed at him. 'A theory. Mel's theory at that. And we both know she's not back up to match fitness. Course she's fastened on this disability-rights stuff as a motive. Look what the girl's been through.'

'I don't think that's had a bearing.'

Didn't think it before but now he was wondering if her sympathies had got the better of her judgement. Had she seen something of herself in Holly and decided to pursue that line of inquiry as a proxy vengeance for the closure she'd never achieved with Christian Palmer?

'This should never have come up to you,' Riggott said. 'One vandalised car and some nasty emails might constitute a hate crime but that isn't what you're investigating now, is it? This is the murder of a woman who was indulging in unsafe sexual practices and just happened to be the mother of a hate-crime victim.'

'Somebody needs to talk to those men.' Zigic positioned himself between Riggott and the office door; he wasn't going to lose this case when they'd worked so hard already. 'It might as well be us. We can do the initial interviews, run down alibis, see who the most likely candidates are.'

'Not with the size of team you've got.'

'So give me some bodies.'

'How does that benefit me?' Riggott asked, amused looking but testy sounding. 'I'll be putting the same arses on different chairs.'

Zigic pressed his hands together. 'We need to talk to these men one way or another. They've been in Dawn's house, they were close to her. Some of them visited her on several occasions which means maybe they witnessed incidents that can help us catch her killer.'

'Oh, aye, I'm sure you'll find they witnessed anything that makes them look innocent.'

'We do the grunt work, you get the credit.' Zigic stepped back, giving him a path to the door again. 'I think that benefits you.'

Riggott smiled thinly, fingers curling around the door handle. 'You're learning.'

Twenty minutes later the list of Dawn's lovers was divided up; Parr, Colleen Murray and a young DC who Riggott had sent, taking thirteen each, more than a day's work to bring them in and question them but they were starting with the ones deemed most capable of violence. Those with criminal records would be brought in first, then the most recent visitors, the ones she'd seen more than once, a couple of them targeted because their messages contained what Colleen termed 'red flags', sadistic suggestions, hints of jealousy, anger at being rescheduled or rebuffed.

It was a guessing game but they needed a system. He would have liked Ferreira to take a look at the messages, knew she had experience Colleen probably didn't, understood the etiquette better, the nuances. She was still out of the office, though, and when he called her she said she had a strong lead to follow up.

By lunchtime they'd interviewed six men, disregarded five who were able to provide solid alibis for the time of Dawn's murder. Their reactions varied from cool indifference to lukewarm regret and Zigic wondered whether Dawn realised how little emotional impact she'd made on them, if she'd even care if she knew. All seemed to regard her as nothing more than a willing body, knew little about her, had never cared to find out more.

Crucially, none of them knew she had a daughter.

Zigic had listened in on the questioning via live feeds from the interview rooms and saw a common theme developing.

Dawn said she was single, they saw no reason to disbelieve her. One man had noticed the photographs of Holly as he followed her through the house but hadn't asked about her, figuring she'd grown up and moved out already. Another recalled making a joke about the stairlift – 'You're gonna need that by the time I'm done with you' – repeated it to Parr expecting him to laugh along. Again he didn't question why it was there, assumed an elderly relative who'd passed.

None of them saw Holly or heard her.

Following their hard-ons, Zigic thought, wanting to get in and out as fast as possible, head home to the wives and girlfriends they all had, the women they'd likely claim weren't as interested in sex as them, but they loved them anyway.

All were unaware that Dawn was being harassed.

The sixth man was yet to be questioned.

Ian Bowe – the security guard with the illegal line in quid pro quo – requested a solicitor the moment he stepped into the station, and was currently waiting for her to arrive.

A guilty man would do that but so would an innocent one, coming in trailing his criminal record and the awareness of police procedure which tended to go along with it. Or maybe he'd spent the fifteen-minute journey to the station thinking back over his text messages to Dawn and realised how they might be interpreted in light of her murder.

DC Wheatley said he got the impression Bowe was expecting them when he and two uniforms turned up at the van showroom where he worked now, valeting the vehicles before they went out. He wasn't shocked by the news, but that was to be expected. Dawn's name was released to the public during yesterday's press conference and her phone records showed that they were in relatively steady contact between meetings.

'Do you want to wait for the solicitor or go and get another one?' Zigic asked.

Wheatley was on his feet immediately, something of the eager puppy dog about him. 'No point me hanging around, is there, sir?'

They were blocking the interview rooms solid and Zigic wasn't sure what they were going to do with the next man Wheatley brought in, but he liked the young DC's enthusiasm and willingness to put the greater good ahead of ego. Too many junior officers tried to guard their suspects, hoping to make the vital breakthrough in a case, take personal credit for the cumulative efforts of the team. His energy was making Zigic feel old, though.

Or maybe it was because he'd spent the morning managing and observing rather than doing something that actually felt constructive. They were making progress but he didn't feel as if he was at the sharp end of it.

He paced around the office, went to the murder board but didn't linger there long, moved to the desk where the files on Dawn's lovers were lined up, twenty-two, ordered by priority. Wahlia was working on the rest, hunched over his computer, furiously chewing on his gum, barely blinking. When he got up to collect a sheaf of papers from the printer he moved with purpose, brisk and efficient as ever.

Zigic picked up one of the files – the next suspect on Parr's list – and flicked through it. Nothing remarkable about the man inside but you never knew what was hiding in between the lines of phone records and bank statements and text messages peppered with emoticons.

'It's Benjamin,' Ferreira said.

She was standing on the other side of the desk looking pleased with herself.

'What?'

'Sally Lange's kid. The online abuse. It's him.' She came around the desk. 'I went to the kennels this morning to talk to Warren—'

'He told you?'

'No. He was stoned out of his head. Totally useless. But as I was leaving I saw this T-shirt, right, and it had this symbol on it I knew I'd seen before and me and Ethan have gone right back through everything.' She rocked on her heels. 'I mean, *everything*. And we've found it. Benjamin used the symbol from this T-shirt as an ID image on one of the accounts he was using to harass Holly.'

Zigic sighed. 'That isn't evidence, Mel. How many people do you think own that T-shirt?'

She smiled. 'Not as many as you'd think. It's a small company, they only make limited runs of each given design, for limited periods, and they only sell through their own website.'

'So, what, thousands?'

'Hundreds. Two hundred and fifty to be precise. I called them.'

'It isn't enough.'

'It's enough for a warrant to seize his laptop,' she said. 'All the proof we need will be on it. I'll lay any money you like it is.'

Wahlia's phone started to ring and he snatched it up fast. A three-second conversation that put theirs on pause, much to Ferreira's evident annoyance.

'Bowe's solicitor just arrived.'

'I need that warrant,' she said.

Zigic found Bowe's file and held it out to her. 'Interview first, then we'll discuss it.'

28

Ian Bowe looked at home in an interview room, no signs of agitation or discomfort; he didn't even straighten up in his seat as they walked in and most people did, an unconscious shiver of movement stiffening their spine, signalling that they were taking this seriously, that they wanted to appear upstanding even whilst sitting down.

His slightly stooped posture might have been a sign of defeat or disrespect. Zigic was leaning towards the latter but hoped he was wrong.

As Ferreira closed the door behind him, slamming it harder than necessary, he realised he shouldn't have brought her in here. He'd seen Bowe's photograph already, but hadn't registered the likeness to Christian Palmer; the same big, no-nonsense physique, same square features and dirty blond hair cut with regimental precision. Now he saw the man through her eyes and he felt the displaced anger bubbling up in her when she took the seat next to him, noticing the jerky way she moved, the bite in her voice as she set up the recording equipment, barking at Bowe to state his name.

That straightened him up and raised an eyebrow from his solicitor, who had looked bored until then, picking bits of fluff off her black pinstripe trousers.

'I didn't kill Dawn,' Bowe said.

'No messing, hey?' Ferreira sneered at him. 'Get your denial in quick. Is that what Ms Quinn there told you to do?'

'I know how you lot work,' he said. 'Dawn dies and you pick me up because I've got a record. It's not fair. I've had treatment for that.'

'Treatment for trying to blackmail women into giving you blow jobs?' Ferreira asked. 'Which church hall do they hold those meetings in?'

Ms Quinn interrupted. 'Sex addiction is no laughing matter, Sergeant.'

'Are you a sex addict, Mr Bowe?'

'I'm learning how to manage my urges.'

'And what about when you can't manage them?' Ferreira asked. 'What do you do when someone says no to you?'

'Dawn didn't say no to me. She couldn't get enough of it. You ask me, she'd got an addiction too. Sometimes I'd hardly get in the door before she had her hand in my trousers.'

'How often did you visit her?' Zigic asked.

'Five, six times. I didn't keep score.'

It tallied with the information pulled off her phone. So did his previous comment. Dawn came across as the instigator, texting him on a whim, at short notice often, telling him she needed him right then. One of the few men she allowed in her house, suggesting that she trusted him.

'When was the last time you saw her?'

'Last week,' he said, squinted as he tried to recall the details and then a smile. 'Tuesday evening. She called when I was in Tesco's. I bought a bottle of wine and went round there.'

'Wine?' Ferreira smiled right back at him. 'You old romantic.'

'I was always told you shouldn't turn up at someone's house empty-handed.'

'You're a gentleman?'

'I try to be.'

'You liked Dawn?' she asked.

He nodded. 'Yeah, liked her enough.'

'Enough for what? To fuck, to date?'

'It was a casual thing,' he said, a hint of wariness creeping into his voice. 'I've got a girlfriend.'

Of course he did, Zigic thought. All these puffed-up, emotionally stunted men, sniffing around the dating sites for some action on the side while their wives and girlfriends were – where? At home with the kids, working late, out doing the exact same thing? He tried to imagine the level of contempt involved, knew he couldn't ever act like that and go home to Anna. Wouldn't want to even if he knew for certain he'd get away with it.

Bowe licked his lips. 'I liked Dawn, but it wasn't serious.'

'To you maybe,' Ferreira said. 'You might have thought it was casual but did she?'

'She knew I've got a girlfriend.'

'Why did you tell her that? Was she getting a bit clingy?'

'I never told her. She guessed. Women just know, they can smell it on you.' He glanced at Zigic. 'She was probably seeing other men.'

'She was. Quite a lot of them.' Ferraira leaned in conspiratorially. 'Dozens.'

'How does that make you feel?' Zigic asked.

Bowe shrugged but there was hurt on his face, an almost imperceptible ripple around his lower lip. 'It's her business what she does with her body.'

'If it makes you feel any better you were her favourite,' Ferreira said. 'Most of them only got the one go, whereas you, well . . . six times in just over a month. You were obviously giving her something the others couldn't.'

This time when he shrugged it was half pride, half faux-humility.

'What did she tell you about her daughter?' Zigic asked.

'Only that she'd had an accident and she couldn't walk any more.' He frowned. 'She stayed with Dawn sometimes, when her ex let her, but she was living with him and his new woman.'

'Did you ever see her?'

'No. Dawn wouldn't have had her in the house when she had dates, would she?'

Neither of them answered him and he seemed to take the lack of reply as agreement with his assessment of Dawn.

'You know Holly's dead too.'

'I saw it on the news.' Bowe clicked his tongue against the roof of his mouth. 'How fucking unlucky was that? Her being there when Dawn died.'

'Not died,' Ferreira said. 'Was murdered.'

'Where were you Thursday night between seven p.m. and midnight?' Zigic asked.

Bowe braced his hands against the table and leaned back in his chair. Another unconscious gesture; creating distance, breathing space.

'I was at home.'

'With your long-suffering, ever-trusting girlfriend?'

'You don't need to talk to her,' he said quickly. 'I'm not giving her as alibi. She doesn't need to be involved in this.'

'Who were you with then?'

'No one. I stayed in, ordered pizza and watched *Breaking Bad*.'

'What series are you on?'

He stumbled. 'What?'

'Series?'

'Um, three.'

'Yeah, what happens in the first episode?'

He looked at Ms Quinn and she sighed. 'Really, I don't think that's relevant.'

'If his alibi is sitting at home watching TV he should be able to tell us what he saw,' Ferreira said. 'It's a pretty spectacular opening, Ian. Not one you'd forget.'

He swore under his breath. 'Alright, I wasn't watching *Breaking Bad*, I was watching porn. Happy now? I ordered a pizza and had a wank.'

'That's a very poor-quality alibi.'

'Talk to the pizza-delivery guy, he'll tell you I was at home.'

'Unless he came in and spent the rest of the evening wanking with you his word doesn't cut it.' Ferreira leaned across the table, fists tucked under her chin. 'I think you went to see Dawn. Your girlfriend's out at work, you're all horned up. So you decided to drop by.'

'No.'

'You knew Dawn would be up for it. She always is.'

'I didn't go there.'

'She wasn't happy to see you. Was she with another man?' Ferreira asked. 'Was that why you lost your temper and stabbed her ten times with her own kitchen knife?'

'I wouldn't hurt her.'

'Not even if she pushed you?'

'No.'

'Not even if she threatened to tell your girlfriend?'

'She wasn't like that.'

'We're all like that, Ian. When we want someone.'

'It was just sex!'

'No. Dawn was looking for love. She wanted someone to take care of her and aren't you the perfect candidate with your wine and your kindness and all the amazing sex?'

Bowe threw his hands up. 'Where is this shit coming from?'

'It's coming from you,' Ferreira said, stabbing her finger at him. 'The kind of man you are. That we know damn well you are.'

'So you don't have any actual evidence against Mr Bowe,' his solicitor said.

'Of course they don't, because I didn't fucking do it.'

He was breathing hard, face flushed puce against the whiteness of his T-shirt, and Zigic could see how hard he was working to stay calm, seem reasonable, in control of himself. Not the kind of man who'd snap and grab the nearest pointed object to end an argument.

'I'd like a moment with my client,' Ms Quinn said.

They stopped the recording and went out into the corridor. Ferreira was pumped up, pacing back and forward, virtually strutting. 'What do you think? He's rattled, right?'

'Yes, Mel, you've done a very good job of winding him up.'

'That's what you brought me along for, isn't it?'

'You went in a bit hard.'

'He's a piece of shit, you've only got to look at him.'

'He looks normal enough to me.'

She dismissed the idea with a wave of her hand and Zigic wondered if she realised why she'd pegged him as a killer. What precisely about his appearance was antagonising her so much. She was always abrasive in interviews but that one had crossed a line and if he took her back in he felt sure her behaviour would worsen.

'This warrant,' he began.

'It can wait. The kid's not going anywhere.' She glanced at her watch. 'He'll be in school for hours. Actually, he'll probably have his laptop with him, won't he? There's no point going now.'

She stalked up the corridor and back again, stopped dead as the door to Interview Room 3 opened and Colleen Murray rushed out.

'We've got another sighting of the man in the burgundy car,' she said. 'Three weeks ago, a Wednesday evening. He was parked on that scrap of land opposite the Prentice house.'

'Westman saw him a couple of weeks ago too. So we've got him returning during the evening now. Twice within a few days.' Zigic turned towards Ferreira. 'Do you think you can go in there and ask Bowe about it without bouncing his head off the table?'

She smiled. 'I make no promises.'

He turned back to Murray. 'Did you get a description? Number plates?'

'He's convinced it's a Passat and he's got one himself so I think we can safely presume he's right. Assuming he isn't lying.'

'Westman thought it was a Passat too.'

Murray nodded. 'He doesn't remember the entire reg number but he gave me a partial. We'll see how accurate that is.'

'What about the man?'

'Late fifties, early sixties, he said, bald, overweight, heavy glasses.'

'Can you send the partial down to Bobby, please?'

'Yes, sir.'

'Anything else from your man in there?'

'Clean,' she said. 'His alibi's sound. He was at a show Thursday evening, the tickets are hologrammed and require photo ID to redeem them, so we can follow it up but I think he's out of the frame, personally.'

Ferreira came back out of the interview room, drew the door closed fast behind her.

'Same story. Burgundy car. Parked opposite Dawn's house.'

'When?'

'Last Tuesday,' she said. 'But he didn't stay in the car this time. He went to the house, knocked on the front door. Dawn ignored it. The bloke kept knocking, she kept ignoring it and Bowe got so pissed off with the interruption he went down to tell him to fuck off.'

'Why didn't he tell us about this before?'

'He said he thought the bloke was a hawker.'

'Did he fuck off?' Zigic asked.

'Yeah. But Bowe followed him down the drive to be on the safe side and saw him get into his car.'

'That sounds excessive for a hawker.'

'Security-guard training. He reckons he could tell there was something amiss about the bloke.' Ferreira shoved her hands in her pockets. 'Bowe's a wannabe copper. But he's got a good eye for detail, I'll give him that. He got the reg number.'

29

'Arnold Fletcher,' Wahlia said. 'Sixty-seven years old, based in Corby, with a . . . colourful history I guess you'd say. Multiple convictions going back to the late seventies.'

Zigic came of out his office, car keys in hand. 'What for?'

'Public-order offences, trespass, intimidation, a couple of instances of actual bodily harm. Threats, harassment, criminal damage. Looks like he was heavily involved in the animal-rights movement up until the early nineties. He's been fairly quiet since then.'

'Age catches up with all of us,' Zigic said.

Over Wahlia's shoulder he could see Fletcher's last mugshot. Twenty years ago but he was already an old man, all jowls and pouches, bloodshot eyes and skin pricked with broken veins across his cheeks, a drinker's florid nose.

'The animal-rights stuff stopped in ninety-four,' Wahlia said. 'But he's been cautioned for harassment since.'

'Who did he harass?' Ferreira asked.

'A hospice in Cambridge. He picketed the entrance for a week.'

'Who pickets a hospice?'

Wahlia rocked back in his chair. 'According to his statement he didn't agree with their line on assisted dying.'

Zigic shifted a few files out of the way, sat down on the edge of the desk.

'Is that what he was doing at Dawn's? Picketing her?'

'Holly was a right-to-die advocate,' Ferreira said. 'It's possible he considered her a legitimate target.'

'He's tied up with a pressure group called Compassion Not Killing,' Wahlia said. 'Their main goal seems to be opposing any changes in the law on assisted suicide.'

'Have they been in touch with Holly?' Zigic asked.

'Via Twitter, yeah, nothing overtly nasty. Lots of links to articles about injured sports people who were living full lives, still competing, that kind of thing. Very passive aggressive.'

'Going to the house was a step up.'

'He wanted something from Dawn,' Ferreira said. 'Three visits we know about now, he's got an agenda.'

Zigic rattled his car keys in his hand.

'Let's ask him about it then.'

Corby was an old steel town that had never managed to find another industry to replace the one now gone, impoverished in comparison to the affluent villages they passed through on the way, all stone and thatch, hamlets with only a few well-spaced houses, horses in paddocks and fields already cut and ploughed.

Quickly the rural idyll gave way to suburbs, low-rise offices and industrial units occupied by companies with an impermanent air suggested by cheap signage and sale banners plastered up in the smoked-glass windows, discount places and hand car washes, boxy retail outlets with filthy corrugated walls and empty car parks, advertising services you wouldn't trust and products you could buy in dozens of other places with more confidence.

On the drive over they'd hardly spoken but as they approached a housing estate Ferreira began to direct him from the map on her phone, stopping when they reached a pebble-dashed semi opposite the train station.

There was a burgundy Passat in the driveway and the toplights in the front windows were open. The patrol car pulled onto the kerb behind them and Zigic gestured for PCs Hale and Bright to wait until he called for them. Fletcher might kick off – he certainly had the form for it – but he was almost seventy and Zigic doubted they'd need back-up to restrain him.

'How do you want to play this?' Ferreira asked.

'Civil until he gives us a reason not to be.'

Zigic peered into the car through its driver's-side window, saw light grey leather seats and grey carpet in the footwell, smudged by dirty feet and littered with fast-food wrappers. A lot of debris but not enough to cover up the fact that the carpet there was markedly lighter than on the passenger's side, its pile scrubbed and tufted.

'Mel, tell me what you see there.'

He stood aside as she shaded her eyes from the sun and looked in.

'Clean-up job,' she said. 'Not a very good one. Whoever did it missed a spot on the underside of the console.'

It was easily done, Zigic thought. He'd not seen it on first inspection and it was only when he looked again that he saw a dark smear where the driver's knees would have touched the moulded plastic under the steering column.

'It might not be blood,' Ferreira said.

The front door opened before they reached it. Fletcher stood in a washed-out cheesecloth shirt and striped pyjama bottoms, looked between the two of them and nodded to himself.

'Best put some proper kecks on, had I?'

'Do you know why we're here, sir?' Zigic asked.

'Haven't got the foggiest but if you've brought the knuckleheads with you I don't reckon you'll be leaving on your own.'

'Can we come in, please?'

'I've got nowt to hide.' He stepped back and let them into a small hallway, cluttered with junk mail and piles of old newspapers. Zigic noticed a stairlift fixed to the wall and wondered if Fletcher was less firm in body than he looked. 'What d'you want then?'

'Dawn Prentice,' Zigic said. 'What's your interest in her?'

'You tell me.'

'It'd be best for you if you cooperate.'

'Oh, yeah, I've heard that one before.' Fletcher crossed his arms. 'Going to knock me about a bit, aye? I'm a pensioner now, you want to think about that before you start getting heavy-handed.'

'You've been harassing Mrs Prentice,' Zigic said.

'Has she made a complaint?'

'Dawn Prentice is dead. She was murdered last week.'

Fletcher's expression didn't change.

'You were hanging around her house last week too,' Zigic said. 'And for a good while before that. So, what was your interest in her?'

Fletcher walked away from them and they followed him into the living room, where the curtains were still drawn against the crisp light. A television in the corner was playing Al Jazeera rolling news but Fletcher's desk was turned away from it, a bulky old desktop computer running noisily.

'I wanted to give her these.' He pulled a couple of leaflets out of his desk drawer.

Ferreira took them from him, made a dumb face. 'Compassion Not Killing?'

'She's got a very ill little girl,' he said. 'We were getting concerned about her welfare.'

'Why?'

'Mrs Prentice was pressurising her into committing suicide.' He dropped heavily into the padded office chair, visibly relieved to be seated again. 'Must have been interfering with her love life having a kid that dependent. That's the usual reason people want to get shot of their sick relatives. Don't want the hassle of caring for them. They make out it's an act of mercy but it's selfishness pure and simple.'

'What makes you think the pressure was coming from Dawn?' Zigic asked. 'Holly was old enough to make her own decisions.'

'No teenage girl knows what's best for her,' Fletcher said, then his face dropped. 'Was? What do you mean "was"? What's happened to her?'

'Holly's dead too.'

His head sagged as if his neck was broken. 'We should have been pushier. We could have saved her.'

'From what, Mr Fletcher?'

'From her bloody parents,' he snapped. 'They were trying to get her over to Dignitas. They had her campaigning for it. Lucky for her even those murdering Swiss bastards won't kill a child.'

Zigic glanced at Ferreira but she looked as confused as he felt by the sudden swerve in Fletcher's rambling.

'They were manipulating everything,' he went on, talking fast. 'I don't even think she wrote half of them blog posts. People like Holly recover, they've got the tenacity. Do you really believe someone like that just gives up? They wake up one morning and decide they want to kill theirselves? Bollocks, do they.'

'We've seen nothing to suggest that Mr and Mrs Prentice were doing that,' Zigic said.

Fletcher snorted. 'Then you've not been looking very hard.'

He spun around in his chair and started clicking through bookmarked links on his computer until a page opened with a video screen set at its center: Holly in her motorised wheelchair, seated in a light-filled conservatory with a sun-baked lawn unfolding beyond the windows. Dawn was sitting on her right, Warren on her left, clutching her hand.

Fletcher hit Play and Holly's voice came out of the speakers, strong and sure, as if she was reading from a script:

'It should be unthinkable in a civilised country that people who are doomed to live limited lives have no option for ending them. Our families have to watch us suffer, they have to do everything for us and I'm grateful –' she strained to turn towards Dawn, who was staring dead ahead – 'I am grateful to my mother for her selfless care. But it's my life and nobody should be able to dictate the length of it. If I was able-bodied and wanted to die I could. As it is I'm reliant on the kindness of my family and the people they pay to care for me. And I have no life. I have no future. Or not the one I wanted before the accident that put me in this chair. I will never walk again. Everything I loved in my life has been taken away from me and I don't want to go on if I can't do the things which defined me.'

Fletcher nodded. 'Look at them.'

Dawn was statue still. Warren watched Holly talk with unmistakable pride, rubbing her hand with his thumb.

'There needs to be a change in law,' she said firmly. 'Tens of thousands of people are forced to endure pain and anguish as incurable illnesses slowly rob them of their mobility and their mental faculties. Their families and friends have to watch this happen, powerless to ease their suffering, and when they do – if they can bring themselves to make that horrific choice and help them end their lives – they face prosecution. A mercy killing is just that. It is a *mercy* I, and thousands of people like me, are begging to be given.'

Warren wiped his eyes.

'We are not asking for anything unreasonable, just the same right to decide the course of our lives and deaths as the able-bodied enjoy.'

The video ended abruptly and Fletcher turned back to them. 'Does that look like a good mother to you?' Fletcher stabbed a finger at the screen. 'She'd have put a pillow over that girl's face in a heartbeat.'

'Why didn't she then?' Ferreira asked.

'I reckon she was scared of getting arrested. That's why the likes of her need Dignitas, it saves them getting their hands dirty. But they're still murderers.'

Zigic looked at the faces, frozen on screen. Dawn's gaze had drifted off camera, Warren's eyes were closed, and only Holly stared back at the viewer, her chin thrown up, all defiance. If Fletcher saw a manipulated victim and a cold-hearted mother it said more about him than any of them. Zigic saw a strong young woman who believed she could change things with determination and debate; an idealist in straitened circumstances.

They couldn't ignore the questions this threw up, though.

Fletcher stroked the grey stubble on his sagging cheeks, deflated now that he'd presented his evidence. Could he have murdered Dawn? Zigic wondered. He was getting on but he was a big man and the offences on his record showed he wasn't shy of using violence to further his cause either. He'd spent thirty years threatening lives and orchestrating campaigns of violence and intimidation for the sake of animals locked in cages behind twelve-foot-high walls and electric gates. Who was to say how far he'd be prepared to go to save a child?

'We should discuss this further at the station, Mr Fletcher.'

The man got to his feet, knees cracking. 'They tell you to be polite now, don't they? But you're not fooling anyone. I can see the psycho in you, son.'

He went upstairs to get dressed and Ferreira called in Hale and Bright to keep an eye on him. When he was changed they took him outside to the car, Bright placing a firm hand on top of his head as he manoeuvred him into the back.

'What do you think?' Ferreira asked. 'Has he got it in him?'

'He's capable,' Zigic said. 'But why kill Dawn and then let Holly die when he claims he wanted to protect her?'

'We can put him in the category of people who knew their routine, wouldn't you say? He was hanging around the house enough to know the nurse should have found her.'

Zigic looked into Fletcher's battered old Passat, the dingy interior and the very clean footwell, eyes automatically going to the console now he knew what was underneath it. Those stains that looked like lots of different fluids but almost always turned out to be blood.

'Call forensics,' he said. 'Let's see what Fletcher was so determined to clean up.'

30

They'd been in the car for hours, no radio, no conversation, just the sound of the engine and a slight squeak whenever Rachel braked.

It was squeaking now, as she slowed down and turned into the car park of a low, brown-brick hotel next to the gutted shell of a fast-food restaurant with grilles over its windows. A man was standing smoking outside the main doors. He threw the cigarette aside as Rachel parked up and went back in.

She twisted in her seat. 'We're staying here tonight, Nathan.'

'Why?'

'So we can talk.'

About Dawn.

Rachel unbuckled his seat belt. 'We're going to walk into this motel and you're going to behave yourself. No acting weird, no talking to anyone. And don't even think about running.'

The roar of the motorway was deafening when he got out of the car and he stood watching the traffic, rocking slightly, feeling the thrum of the wheels under his feet and the tug coming off the road, until Rachel grabbed his hand and pulled him after her, heading for the big reception sign.

She hardly spoke to the man behind the desk and when she did her accent was different, like someone from home.

The man asked if her son was okay and Nathan glared at him.

'Yeah, he's just a bit rough, like. Carsick.'

They went along a corridor and up a stairwell that smelled of lemons, through another corridor to the last doorway on the right which she opened up with a plastic card.

'After you.'

Nathan went in.

It was a big room with two small beds and immediately he knew he wouldn't be able to sleep tonight, couldn't risk it when she would be close enough to hear him talking in his nightmares. He might say something she could use against him. Or she could say he had and he wouldn't know whether it was true or not, wouldn't know which lie to tell to fix the problem.

'Sit down then, we're not going anywhere.'

She unpacked the bags of food, bringing out sandwiches and crisps, opened a bottle of water and drank it down in one go.

'Do you want something to eat?'

'No.'

'You need to eat.'

'I'm not hungry.'

Nathan sat down on the bed under the window, his back against the wall.

The room was getting smaller. He noticed the stains on the carpet and the smudges on the paint, a boot mark on the back of the door as if he wasn't the first person to be locked in here against his will.

Rachel pulled the chair out from under the table where the television was and sat down on it with her feet up on the end of his bed. She looked tired but he knew he still needed to be careful. He couldn't see her gun but it was there, under her shirt, tucked away around the back so the man on the reception desk wouldn't catch sight of it and know what she was.

'Why did you run away, Nathan?'

'I dunno.'

She sighed. 'Look, whatever you tell anyone else, you have to tell me the truth. I'm the only person who cares what happens to you now. So don't make this harder than it needs to be.'

He brought his knees up to his chin, wrapped his arms around his shins, making himself as small as he could.

'The police are going to ask you these questions and we need to sort out what you'll tell them.'

'I don't wanna talk to them.'

'Yeah, well, I don't want that either but we won't be able to avoid it,' she said. 'They know about you. Thanks to Julia.'

What had she told them?

She wouldn't say anything.

Rachel was lying.

'You liked it at Julia's, didn't you?'

He nodded.

'So why would you run away?'

'I was scared.'

'What of?'

He couldn't tell her.

'Your nan told me what you wanted to do,' she said. 'Is that why you went home?'

It was and it wasn't but he nodded because he thought that would be enough.

'Okay. We've talked about this before, haven't we? You know there's no way around the situation. You can't make it go away with talking. I thought you understood that by now.' She brushed her hair out of her eyes. 'Especially after what happened to Tyler.'

Nathan dug his fingertips into his legs until he hit bone.

Nobody fucked with Tyler. Grown men backed down from him when he gave them his hard-eyed stare and the threats they threw about turned into apologies and wary smiles. Tyler smiled along with them but he didn't forget. Always caught up with them in the end.

Then someone caught up with him.

No. Forget about Tyler.

If Tyler was tougher he'd be the one in here with Rachel, but inside wasn't like outside and even when they said you were safe – watched, segregated, protected – you weren't really. You were only as safe as the people guarding you wanted you to be.

At least Rachel wanted him safe.

'Why now?' she asked. 'You could have run off whenever you liked. Julia wasn't strict with you. So why did you run away now?'

He didn't have an answer.

'It's because of Dawn, isn't it?' She stared at him, didn't blink, as if she was boring through his skull, into the place where he kept his darkest secrets. 'Dawn was murdered and then you ran away.'

'I didn't kill her.'

'But you took the knife from her house?'

'Yes.'

'After she was killed?'

He started rocking back and forth, spine hitting the wall but not so much that he couldn't stand the pain.

'Stop that!'

He stopped.

'Did you see her dead?'

Dawn on the kitchen floor, lying in her own blood, soaked in it. Bile in his throat but he wouldn't be sick. Not there. He wouldn't make her even dirtier than she already was.

Don't look at her.

Nathan closed his eyes. Saw the knife in his hand and the blood on his shoes.

'You need to tell me the truth,' Rachel said, voice soft, encouraging, the way she was at the beginning, trying to coax that other, earlier truth out of him.

That was in a hotel room too. Some hotel like this one and just the two of them there, but he knew now she was recording every word he said then and maybe she was doing the same thing here. Trying to make him think this place was safe, telling him only the truth could protect him, but she was lying because it's what she did. Lied to get what she wanted even if it killed someone. It killed Tyler.

But she wouldn't stop asking. Not until he told her what he'd seen.

'The man,' he said.

She cocked her head. She knew that was true.

'What man?'

'At Dawn's. In a car. I saw him. I thought he was coming to get me.'

'Did you recognise him?'

'No.'

'Think, Nathan, I need you to be sure. Did you recognise him from home?'

'I dunno.' That was the truth too. 'Maybe. I never got a good look at him.'

'What did he look like?'

'An old man. In a red car.'

Rachel thought about it for a moment and he kept looking at her, trying to decide what she was thinking.

'Why would he be at Dawn's house if he was looking for you?'

'I dunno. I went round there.'

'You weren't supposed to.'

'Julia said it was okay.'

She reached behind her for another bottle of water. 'Did he kill Dawn?'

He shrugged.

'That's not an answer. Did you see him do something to her?'

'I only saw him outside.'

'Okay, that's good. We'll tell the police that much. You saw someone who might be responsible. That should keep them happy.' She opened the bottle and took a long drink. 'Do you see, Nathan? This is just like before. We need to have a good story. A simple story we can tell them so they leave you alone.'

'I can do that,' he said.

'I know you can. You're a very smart boy.' She smiled at him and for a split second he thought it was a real smile and he found himself matching it. 'And because you're smart you know I know you were in Dawn's kitchen after she was murdered or else you wouldn't have her blood on the shoes you're wearing right now.'

He looked at the dark stains on the white rubber. Dirty enough after the last few days that he thought they could pass for grease or oil. He scrunched his toes away from the blood, skin scraping against the canvas upper.

'So, we'll come up with a nice, logical story for the local police. Just to keep you out of trouble. But before we do, you are going to tell me what really happened. Because I won't help you if you keep lying to me, Nathan.'

31

Zigic went over to the murder board to check what progress had been made while they were out. Saw that Parr and Wheatley had run down another man apiece, meaning they were less than a quarter of the way through Dawn's lovers. Eight of them ruled out, one missing in action but according to his boss he was always unpredictable.

Colleen Murray was in the process of trying to break or establish Ian Bowe's alibi, such as it was.

At this rate, with this size of team, the job was going to take days, and so far they'd been lucky. Or as lucky as they could be without actually identifying Dawn's murderer. The men had come quietly, wary of gossip or repercussions at work, and had provided decent alibis which were swiftly checked with minimal legwork.

The contamination of the crime scene remained the biggest stumbling block and left them with little leverage or direction. No fingerprints, no murder weapon. The only DNA they had was from the bathroom, snagged in a bloodstained towel. Damning to them but not enough for the CPS to build a case on.

Zigic's phone rang and he started at the sight of Rachel's name on the screen, walked into his office before answering.

'Have you found Nathan?' he asked.

'Yeah, I've got him,' she said, her voice echoing slightly.

'When can I talk to him?'

'Tomorrow maybe. It depends on how he's doing. He's exhausted.'

'So why are you telling me this now?' Zigic asked.

‘Professional courtesy.’ He could hear the smile in her voice, more of a sneer. ‘And there’s one thing I thought you should know as soon as possible. Might be important to your case.’

‘What?’

‘Nathan saw a man hanging around Dawn’s house. In a red car.’

Arnold Fletcher. Back again.

‘When was this?’

Rachel let out a small sigh. ‘The thing you have to understand about Nathan is he’s delicate, okay? He’s suffering from PTSD, he’s got anxiety and depression and I’m sure you get how tough that is for a boy his age.’

‘Does he have dissociative episodes?’ Zigic asked.

A beat before she answered, considering the implications. She was smart enough to know it made him potentially unreliable as a witness.

‘Occasionally, yes, he does. But judging by how agitated he was by the sight of this man I’d say it’s fair to assume he saw him quite close to the time he ran away.’

It was too vague to be useful and made Zigic even more determined to talk to the boy properly. He’d thought from the very start that Nathan was an important witness and she was as good as admitting it now.

‘Is this why he ran away? Did he see something bad?’

‘I’m still trying to find that out,’ she said. ‘He needs to be handled carefully. I’ll be in touch if I find out anything more.’

She ended the call.

Now they had a witness of sorts. A little bit of leverage to use on Fletcher.

Ferreira was going through his record, searching for some raw nerve to scratch at during the interview. Without forensic evidence they were left with psychology and outright bluff and he suspected neither would be much use against a seasoned agitator like Fletcher.

It was her style, though, and he'd seen it work often enough in the past to respect the attempt this time.

As Zigic went back into the main office she shot up straight in her chair.

'Fuck. Me.'

'I take a bit more finessing than that,' Wahlia said.

'No, you don't.' She pushed away from her desk. 'Boss, you need to look at this.'

Zigic took her seat, felt her breathing down the back of his neck as he read through the report on screen, seeing that she'd already gone beyond Fletcher's police record, digging for the kind of dirt which didn't get a person arrested but could sometimes tell you more about them than bald facts about time served and sentences suspended.

'Is his solicitor here?'

'He didn't want one,' Ferreira said.

On the way down to the interview room he filled her in on the phone call from Rachel, saw her toying with how to fit that information around what they'd just found out. They decided she'd lead with Fletcher, but play nice. Since he'd already called Zigic a 'psycho'. Best to feed into that perception.

'You took your sweet time,' Fletcher said, when they went in. He was sitting with his arms folded, a picture of belligerent but passive resistance.

Ferreira apologised and placed the file she'd brought with her on the table.

He eyed the camera as she set up the recording equipment, a new development since the last time he'd been in a police station and Zigic wondered what kind of memories the small white room was evoking. He was old enough to have experienced a more brutal form of interrogation than they could use, all the creative and now illegal techniques which a previous generation of officers had employed to get the result they wanted.

'Okay, Mr Fletcher, why don't you tell us how you first came to be interested in Holly Prentice?'

'I found her out through her blog.'

'You weren't just cruising the Internet looking for disabled teenagers?' Zigic said. 'Were you?'

Fletcher gave him a filthy look. 'My organisation is committed to protecting disabled people who are under pressure to end their lives. She seemed to be at risk of coercion.'

'Your organisation is Compassion Not Killing,' Ferreira said. 'How would you describe it?'

'We're a resistance organisation. We're fighting against an ableist establishment that treats people who have been injured or limited through illness as second-class citizens.'

'You mean the right-to-die movement.'

'That's what they call themselves,' he said. 'I'd call them fascists. They think anything less than perfection is worthless. It's eugenics, plain and simple.'

'You honestly don't believe there's such a thing as a mercy killing?' Ferreira asked. 'Not even when somebody is suffering terribly?'

Realisation widened Fletcher's bloodshot brown eyes but he didn't answer her.

'In your sister's case, for example.'

'She was murdered.' He spat out the words. 'And you fucking know that or you wouldn't be bringing it up now.'

'The judge didn't think so,' Ferreira said. 'He found her husband innocent, he even praised him for providing her with such diligent care for so many years.'

'Three years. *Three*. That's all he could stand it for. And she'd waited on him hand and foot for nigh on thirty.' Fletcher jabbed at the table, ramming his point home. 'This is exactly what I've been talking about. As soon as you're not useful any more you become disposable. Just like Jackie was.'

'Maybe he loved her too much to see her like that.'

'When you love someone you take care of them, even when it breaks your fucking heart to see that they're not in there any more. Me and Jackie did it for Dad. I'd have done it for her but that piece of shit wouldn't let me. He just wanted shot of her.'

Fletcher covered his face with his hands, angry rather than sad, angrier than he wanted them to see him. He looked murderous just sitting there remembering it. Abruptly he dropped his fists onto the table.

'Nobody should have the right to do that. Murder someone because they're an inconvenience.'

'That's why you set up Compassion Not Killing?' Ferreira said. 'To save people like Jackie?'

'If I can save one person it'll be worth it.'

'One person like Holly?' Zigic asked.

'Especially someone like her. She still had her faculties. There was loads she could do with her life.'

'But Holly was an active right-to-die blogger. She believed people in her situation should be allowed to end their lives.'

He snorted. 'You don't know what she believed. Who's to say she wrote any of that stuff herself?'

'Why would you think she didn't?'

'She was a child. She wasn't old enough to make that decision.' He leaned forward, big forearms coming down on the table. 'How do you reckon it feels to know you're a burden?'

Ferreira recrossed her legs under the table and Zigic noticed her fingers twitch.

'Do you think Holly would've thought for a second about killing herself if her mother was looking after her right?' Fletcher was swelling with his belief now. 'No. That woman didn't want the hassle. Any idiot could see that. The way she went on, men coming and going all hours. She put Holly in a position where death was better than life.'

'There's nothing in her blog to suggest she felt that way,' Ferreira said.

'If you think that you weren't reading it right.'

'To be fair, we've only just come to this,' Zigic said, drawing Fletcher's attention. 'Whereas you've been spending a fair old chunk of your ample free time sitting around outside Dawn's house.'

Fletcher struck an indignant pose. 'I went there two or three times to try and talk to the woman.'

'And did the woman want to talk to you?'

'She had company,' he said, visibly disgusted. 'You tell me how that's right. Young girl in the house, stuck in her bed, and her mother's got one strange bloke after another coming in to give her a seeing-to. That's child abuse. You should have arrested her.'

'Hanging around her house for hours on end, week in, week out, is technically stalking,' Zigic said. 'Maybe we should arrest you.'

'There's no crime parking your car on public land.'

'It depends on what the purpose is. If it's to harass someone, it's a crime.'

'Did she make a complaint?' Fletcher asked. 'No, she didn't, or you'd have had me in here weeks back.'

'We're not interested in what you did weeks back.'

Zigic opened the file. A photograph of Dawn, lying dead on her kitchen floor, was on the top; her bloated and blistered face, the knife wound at her neck.

'We're interested in what you were doing there on Thursday night.'

Fletcher kept looking at the photograph, repulsed but attracted. 'I wasn't there Thursday night.'

'We have a witness who says otherwise.'

'Then they're mistaken.'

'Not lying?' Zigic asked.

Fletcher finally managed to drag his eyes up. 'I was there in the afternoon. I put some leaflets through her letter box and then I left.'

'Did you see anyone hanging around the house?' Ferreira asked.

'No. I wasn't there two minutes.'

'But you went to talk to Dawn,' Zigic said. 'You must have knocked on the door. That's your usual MO. What happened? She didn't answer? You got annoyed at being ignored – again – so you went around the back, found the door unlocked, let yourself in.'

'No.'

'Come on. She's been ignoring you for weeks. Tell me you weren't angry about that.'

'I wasn't.'

'Even though you thought Holly's life was at stake.' Fletcher was sweating, crescents under his arms, his denim shirt sticking to his chest. 'For the first time you get there and she's home alone. No builders, no boyfriends. You've got Dawn all to yourself.'

Fletcher stared back at him, breathing heavily, trying to hold it together. 'I put the leaflets through her door and I left.'

'And went home?'

'Yes.'

'So you don't have an alibi?'

'I haven't done anything wrong.'

'Maybe you don't think you have. You're a man of convictions, you probably think you're morally in the right.'

'I'm morally and legally in the right, because I didn't kill her.' Fletcher stood up, uncertain on his legs. 'And unless you've got something you can charge me with, I'm going home.'

Zigic stood up as well, towering over the man. 'You're not going anywhere. Not yet.'

32

Everyone was home when Ferreira arrived at the kennels in Elton, a patrol car behind her, two uniforms inside, ready to bring Benjamin in. Sally appeared from around the back of the house and stood shielding her eyes against the afternoon sun, watching them approach, but as they drew up she disappeared down the path, off to warn whoever she thought was most likely to be guilty of what was coming.

Ferreira had brought Green and Jones with her, two capable female officers she trusted to do the job with minimum fuss. She specifically wanted Benjamin taken in by them, aware of his attitude towards women.

They followed her past the side of the house and she heard Jones give an 'aww' when she saw the dogs penned up in the yard.

Warren was in with them, holding up a small grey terrier as he checked one of its back paws, blood on his hands from some wound it had suffered. He put it down and came over to the gate.

'What is it?' he asked, looking at the PCs. 'Why are they here?'

'Inside,' Ferreira told them and they went without a word. She turned back to Warren. 'We've come for Benjamin.'

He barrelled past her, in through the back door, into the kitchen where Sally had abandoned a pile of cooking apples she'd been peeling, one still trailing its skin where she'd left it, next to a small knife with a wicked blade. Ferreira picked it up and tossed it in the sink.

'Benjamin!' Warren hollered his name, headed for the door into the hallway.

'Let them do their job,' Ferreira said.

From above she could hear Sally's voice, shrill and questioning, and Benjamin's rumbling replies. Then there were feet coming down the stairs and Warren backed up into the kitchen again, red faced and raging.

'What have you done?' He glanced at Ferreira. 'Did he kill them?'

'We just need to talk to him,' she said. 'It's to do with the harassment, that's all.'

'That's all?' he snarled. 'Oh, well, okay then. If that's *all* he's done.'

PC Green put her hand in the middle of Warren's chest and walked him away a few steps. He gave the ground easily.

Jones followed her, holding Benjamin by the arm. His hands were cuffed behind his back and he was protesting every step like the petulant child he was, twisting and trying to shake her off, but she held firm. He was a tall, gangly boy, couldn't have weighed more than nine stone, arms pipecleaner thin sticking out of his T-shirt.

'This isn't fair. I haven't done anything.' He looked at Warren and his expression faltered for a second, fear rather than guilt showing around his eyes. 'They're taking my computer. They can't take that.'

'Yes, we can,' Ferreira said. 'You've mounted an eighteen-month-long campaign of harassment against Holly and that's a serious offence. We can do things you won't even believe.'

'I didn't.'

'He didn't,' Sally said, squeezing around Jones, getting herself in front of Benjamin like a human shield. It took Ferreira a second to catch on to what Sally had already seen.

She snatched at Warren's shirt but it was too late. He barged Sally out of the way and threw a wild punch at Benjamin's face. The boy took it full force on the jaw and fell against Jones, who rolled him away from her and sat him on the ground, blood already flowing from his mouth as he screamed and shouted.

Sally was shouting too, telling Warren to stop.

He moved in again and this time Ferreira caught him and managed to pull him off balance, the kick he'd aimed at Benjamin missing by a few inches. She dragged him away, feeling the full weight of his paternal fury pushing against her, and shoved him two handed towards the kitchen table. He hit it hard, sending the apples tumbling onto the flagstone floor.

'That's assault,' Benjamin shouted, triumph lighting his face. 'I want him charging. He hit me. He can't hit me!'

Sally was crying, looking between the men in her life, and her decision took less than two seconds to make. She went to Benjamin, squatted down and cupped his face.

'I'll call Mr Harold, he'll be at the police station when you get there.' She kept hold of his face as Jones dragged him up, moving with him, ignoring how he tried to shake her off. 'Mummy's going to sort this all out.'

'Does Mummy think she can sort murder out?' Warren asked.

Sally glared at him. 'Pack your things and get out of this house. I don't want to see you here when we get back.'

'Maybe he won't be coming back.' Warren looked at Ferreira, a ragged desperation on his face. 'You think he killed them, don't you? This isn't just about some online harassment.'

Sally was looking at her too, holding her breath, one hand at her throat.

'I can't discuss it right now.'

Sally moaned lightly, buried her face in her hands for so long she didn't even see Jones and Green take her son away. Warren did, though, he watched every wobbly step towards the back door with a vicious smile, eyes boring into Benjamin, throwing every last scrap of contempt he could muster at him.

'Proud of him, are you, Sally? Your little prince.'

She snapped into action suddenly and Warren tracked her movements around the kitchen, stayed on her heels as she found her car keys and her handbag.

‘I told you there was something wrong with him, but you wouldn’t listen.’

She unplugged her mobile from where it was charging on the counter and started dialling as she made for the door, stony faced and moving with a new sense of purpose.

‘He is sick in the head,’ Warren shouted after her. ‘You made him like that.’

For a moment Ferreira thought he was going to run after her but he didn’t, only stood in the doorway, breathing heavily; still full of fight and with nobody else to throw it at he turned on her.

‘How long have you known?’ he demanded.

‘We still don’t know for sure,’ Ferreira said. ‘That’s why we need his laptop.’

Warren’s hands hung in loose fists by his sides. ‘If he killed Holly . . .’

‘What? You’ll kill him?’ she asked. ‘Do you really want to say that to me? You’re in enough trouble as it is.’

‘Have you got children?’

‘No.’

‘Then you don’t understand,’ he said. ‘I would happily spend the rest of my life in prison if it meant I could go to sleep every night knowing I’d got justice for her.’

‘It’s not your place to do that.’

He shook his head, gave her a pitying look she wanted to slap right off his face. ‘You wait. One day you’ll get it.’

Ferreira wanted to tell him that being a parent didn’t give him a monopoly on grief or some special right to retribution. She’d had that shit thrown at her so many times since becoming a police officer that she knew the routine down pat.

‘I have to charge you with assault,’ she said.

‘He deserved it.’

‘Don’t make things any worse for yourself, Warren.’

He went along with no more drama, walked quietly to Ferreira's car and paused for a brief moment to take one last look at the house where he was no longer welcome, before getting in. On the drive he tried to roll a joint and she warned him that she'd have to add possession to his offences if he didn't throw the little nugget of weed away. Reluctantly he opened the window and tossed it out onto the verge.

At the station she officially charged him, explained that he'd probably get away with a slap on the wrists but he didn't seem to care what happened to him. She put him in an interview room with a cup of vending-machine coffee to drive any last vestiges of the afternoon's smoking from his brain and went to process Benjamin.

According to PC Jones he'd become even more agitated on the journey, started threatening Green and her with lawsuits and online exposés, called them fascist bitches, but only under his breath. By the time they were out of the village he'd retreated into a sullen quiet, visibly uncomfortable with the temporary confinement and the smell of the patrol car. By the time the custody officer came for him he was fully mute and shivering with nerves, complied with every request like the well-brought-up child he almost was, removed the laces from his trainers and the dog-tag necklace with a name on that wasn't his. When Ferreira asked who Kurt Montana was he blushed and said it was his Call of Duty ID.

It made her wonder how much time he spent in reality. How far he identified with the characters he pretended to be when he was gaming and whether he realised that attacking Holly was a different kind of game altogether.

He never expected it to catch up with him, Ferreira guessed. He was going to say it was all a joke, it didn't mean anything. It wasn't real.

Assuming there was anything on his laptop for him to deny.

33

'Bowe's out of the frame, sir.'

Zigic looked up from his phone, a missed-call alert from Anna showing in the locked screen. There were two messages underneath, sent within a space of twenty minutes, but he'd been too busy to answer them yet and now Colleen Murray was standing over him.

'What? But his alibi was rubbish.'

'I tracked down the CCTV from his building,' she said. 'There's two doors out – the emergency exit's got an alarm on it but that wasn't triggered, which only leaves the main entrance and that's covered by a camera on a week-long loop. He got home just after five on the Thursday and didn't go out again until he left for work the next morning.'

Zigic threw his hands up. 'Okay. Street him them.'

'Yes, sir.'

She closed the office door after her and as it clicked shut he immediately regretted how short he'd been. She'd done well, acting in her usual effective manner, and it wasn't her fault that what she found cleared Bowe rather than implicating him.

Too late to do anything about it now.

He went back to Anna's messages.

Call me please.

Problem at school. Call me NOW.

'Shit.'

His brain ran quickly through all the terrible possibilities as he rang her back: an accident at the gates, a fire in the building, Stefan choking on something or falling over something else, lost eyes and head injuries and predators waiting for an opportunity.

She answered almost instantly.

'Stefan's been suspended.'

'What? Why?'

'He bit someone.'

'Not Mrs Lomax.'

'No, it was Sara and John's little girl – Amelie – he bit her on her arm. Dushan, you should see the mark he left, I felt sick just looking at it.' Her voice was high and quavering, the way it went when she was really angry. 'Sara's absolutely livid, of course. She wants him expelled.'

Zigic rubbed his face. 'She'll calm down.'

'Why should she?' Anna demanded. 'I wouldn't. You wouldn't. She's right, it's completely unacceptable behaviour. I'm so bloody ashamed of him.'

'Hold on a minute, we don't know what happened. Stefan isn't a bully. Did Amelie hit him or something?'

An icy blast of silence came down the line. 'Mrs Lomax saw the whole thing. They were all sitting down in a circle for storytime and Stefan just grabbed her arm and bit her.'

'He's never done that before.'

'Well, he's done it now.'

Zigic looked helplessly around his office. No advice there. 'What are you supposed to do with biters? Do you bite them back?'

'I really don't think that's going to help, do you? Maybe you could go the whole hog and take your belt off to him.'

He sighed. 'I didn't mean to hurt him, as you well know. I thought it was supposed to show them how wrong biting is. That's all. I'm sure I read it in one of your books.'

She groaned. 'I thought you'd know how to handle this.'

'We tell him off. What else can we do?'

'Have you ever known that to work with him?' Anna asked, suddenly tired-sounding, and he realised that she'd already endured one post-mortem of the incident, excused Stefan and apologised for him, been forced to show contrition for both of them.

'How long's he been suspended for?'

'Two days,' she said. 'And I've got a good mind to make him stay in his bedroom on his own the whole time.' She gave a little grunt of annoyance. 'I hate that woman. Of all the kids he could have bitten, why did it have to be her precious Amelie? Christ – I can't even have a glass of wine.'

Zigic smiled despite himself. 'Won't a cup of tea be just as nice?'

'Oh, shut up. Maybe I'll pour your vodka down the sink, then we'll see how calming tea is.'

Ferreira knocked on the glass partition and he held his hand up to keep her on the other side of it for a minute longer.

'Can you send a couple of PCs around?' Anna said. 'They could pretend to arrest Stefan and put him in a cell for a little while. Maybe that would scare him into behaving.'

'Is that a joke?'

'No if you can do it, yes if you won't.'

'I can't,' he said.

'Then you'll have to scare him into behaving on your own.'

'I'll talk to him when I get in, okay? I'm sure he just needs a talking-to.'

They said their goodbyes, the usual 'I love you's and Zigic waved Ferreira in, still thinking about Stefan, trying to picture him snatching up a little girl's arm to bite her for no reason. He was an excitable, often infuriatingly energetic child, but he had never shown signs of aggression like that before. Maybe Anna hadn't heard the full story, too busy minimising the damage and soothing the injured parties.

'I've got Benjamin Lange downstairs,' Ferreira said. 'And I've got Warren in an interview room. It all kicked off when I brought him in. We've got to charge Warren with assault – he punched the kid.'

'The kid is very punchable,' Zigic said, remembering his attitude that first time at the house.

'Ethan's going through his laptop, that'll take a while.'

'Has he found anything that points to him being responsible?'

'Oh, yeah. He was in the process of deleting one of his fake email accounts when Jones slammed the lid of the laptop down. It booted straight up to the page.' She tucked her hands into her pockets. 'Guess Warren told Sally about my visit, Ben got wind and decided he'd better wipe out his tracks before we caught on to him.'

'How much did he wipe?'

His own computer pinged as an email came in and he looked away from her to open it up.

'We don't know yet. It's all recoverable though.' She started going into details and most of it went over his head but he made the right noises while he read the message from Jenkins.

'I think we need—' Ferreira stopped. 'Okay, that's obviously a really fascinating email.'

'It's from Kate. She's found blood in Arnold Fletcher's car.'

'The marks under the console?'

'Consistent with the driver wearing bloodstained trousers,' he said, imagining Fletcher sliding into his seat, knees brushing against the moulded plastic, the blood rubbing into the dimples.

'But we've got evidence of someone cleaning up at the house. He shouldn't have had blood on him to transfer onto the console.'

'The killer cleaned up but unless this was carefully planned he wouldn't have a change of clothes with him and he could hardly walk out onto the street buck naked, could he?' She seemed to be considering the feasibility of it. 'So, he's wiped the worst of it off him, leaving enough on the fabric to smear inside the car. Kate said they're only small deposits. Which makes sense in that scenario.'

'Nothing on the steering wheel?'

'More on the steering wheel, but it's been cleaned. Along with the carpet and the inside of the door. And the gearstick.'

Ferreira smiled. 'They never learn – fire not bleach. Do you want to take another run at him then?'

'No, let's wait until Kate's got something a bit more substantial. A type match would be a good start.' Zigic closed the email. 'We've got Fletcher for at least twenty-four hours yet. Might as well let him suffer.'

'Ageing hard man like that,' Ferreira said. 'A night in the cells won't break him.'

'"Ageing" being the operative word. He'll find them far less comfortable than he remembers.'

'They're not that bad.'

'Yeah? When was the last time you slept in one?'

'Back in uniform,' she said. 'It was fine. Quieter than home too.'

He resisted the urge to ask how things were there, had tried a few times since she came back and received ever more terse replies. He knew her parents had been against her joining the police right from the start and when he met them at the hospital, mere hours after she'd come out of surgery, still unconscious, they'd not held back from blaming him and the job for putting her in that position.

He could only imagine what pressure she'd faced during her recovery and how angry they were at her for returning and placing herself in danger again.

She was looking at him strangely.

'Long day, hey?'

He nodded. 'You were saying – we need something? See, I was listening.'

'I think we need to start taking Warren a bit more seriously as a suspect,' she said. 'The way he lashed out at Benjamin – deserved or not – he's got a temper.'

'We've got no evidence against him.'

'We've got Matthew Campbell mentioning their volatile relationship, we've got a bitter divorce, and when I talked to him the other day he came very close to admitting that they were fighting over Holly's right-to-die campaigning.'

'They were both on that video,' Zigic said.

'Yeah, and didn't Dawn look reluctant? There was something going on between them we still don't know about and he's riled right now. I think we can crack him.'

Zigic's eyes strayed towards the photograph of Milan and Stefan on his desk, big smiles, best behaviour. It didn't make sense, Stefan turning like that, not without provocation, some reason he'd have to get out of him later. Unless Anna managed to first and he hoped she did, that all of this would be somehow sorted before he got home.

Ferreira was waiting for him at the door and he hauled himself up out of the chair.

'Warren then.'

34

Warren was pacing the interview room when they went in, hands hooked around the back of his neck, the muscles in his face drawn tight with stress or anger. The last few days had taken a heavy toll on him, judging by his greasy hair and ragged beard, the persistence of the wrinkles around his mouth.

'You don't need to do this,' he said, pulling out a seat opposite them. 'I'm not going to deny hitting Ben. Just bail me or put me in a cell or whatever it is happens next.'

'All in good time,' Zigic said. 'For now, why don't we start with where you were Thursday evening?'

Warren cocked his head. 'I'm a *suspect*? Are you fucking serious? My daughter is dead.'

'We need to know so we can rule you out,' Ferreira said gently.

'I was at home.'

'Alone?'

'Ben was there.' He twisted in his chair, turned to sit sideways on to them. 'Although he'll probably lie now and say I wasn't.'

'Did either of you go out at all during the evening?'

'I didn't. I don't know about him, he was upstairs in his bedroom, he could have gone out and killed my wife and daughter, I suppose.' The bitterness dripped off his words. 'Have you questioned him yet? He won't admit it. He's a born liar.'

'What about Sally?' Zigic asked.

'She was out. They have their book club the last Thursday of the month.'

'They who?'

'Sally and Julia and . . .' He drifted again. 'Mona, she's in Warmington – it must have been at hers because Sally was annoyed that she wouldn't be able to drink much because she had to drive – and a couple of other women. I don't know.'

Benjamin could have easily slipped out unnoticed. Warren too. It was a big old house with thick walls and heavy doors which would deaden the sound of either leaving and the state of their relationship would have made an evening of separate rooms and no conversation quite likely.

'You didn't take the opportunity to visit Holly then?' Zigic asked.

Warren gave him a cold look. 'No.'

'When was the last time you saw her?'

The question seemed to stump him and for a long moment Zigic wondered if he was preparing to lie or genuinely couldn't remember. Finally Warren shook his head.

'A few weeks ago, something like that. A woman dropped off her schnauzer with us and Holly always wanted one, so I took him around for her to play with.' He bit his lip. 'Not that she could. Not properly. But I thought she might like to see him at least.'

'And did she?'

'Dawn wouldn't let me take him up to her. She said he was dirty and Holly was too vulnerable to infection to have him in her bedroom.' He shrugged. 'I suppose she was right.'

'Did *you* go up, though?'

'For a few minutes, yes.'

'That's all?'

'I had to get back to the kennels.'

It was a pathetic excuse and even Warren seemed to realise that, weak-voiced as he spoke, unable to look at either of them.

'What did you talk about?' Ferreira asked. 'The last time you saw her.'

He closed his eyes. 'I can't remember.'

'Try please, Warren, it might be important.'

'How could it possibly be important?' he snapped, looking at her suddenly. 'Dawn was murdered. Not Holly. She just died because no one was there to stop her dying. This isn't about her.'

'Holly had a life,' Zigic reminded him. 'And she had enemies. There's a fair chance Holly's campaigning is linked to Dawn's murder.'

'It's Ben you should be talking to.' Warren turned to Ferreira. 'You said it – she was being harassed and threatened. If Ben was doing that then he must have killed Dawn. He always hated me, he'd do that to get back at me for breaking up his parents' marriage.'

'Is that what happened? Ferreira asked. 'You broke them up?'

'No, no, it was over long before we met, but he's a child, he wouldn't understand that.'

It was a ridiculous theory, pulled together out of simmering family tensions and the anger he hadn't fully exorcised by punching the boy in the face; maybe a sense of guilt too, for the breaking up of two families, the wreckage he'd left smouldering behind him.

'I'll tell you what we don't understand,' Ferreira said. 'When I spoke to Dawn last year she didn't have a bad word to say about you. Even though you dumped her. When she was at her lowest point—'

'She isn't the only one who suffered.'

'No, but you got to move on with your life. She was left with Holly and she was struggling, Warren. For money and support and then someone starts harassing her.' He was watching Ferreira carefully, waiting for something to deny. 'Dawn had all of that to contend with but she never accused you. And when I suggested it she swore you weren't that type of man. Because you "had a good relationship still." Was that true?'

He nodded warily. 'We did.'

'But you don't now?'

'No.' Almost a sigh.

Within the close and hushed confines of the interview room it had the quality of a confession, carrying more weight than any single syllable should.

'So what changed?'

'I don't know.'

'Is it Sally?' Ferreira asked. 'Was she annoyed with you going around there?'

'No. She didn't mind.'

'She must trust you.'

'I've never given her a reason not to.'

Ferreira tapped her fingers lightly against the table, as though she was thinking, as though she didn't already have this line of inquiry mapped out.

'Was it Holly? Did her attitude change?'

Warren froze, eyes narrowing. 'Me and Holly got on well. We always did.'

'That's what everyone keeps telling us,' Ferreira said. 'But we've seen very little evidence of it. Why weren't you visiting her more often?'

'It was difficult.' His head dipped and he wrapped his hand around the back of his neck. 'She wasn't the same any more. I couldn't – I didn't know how to talk to her, alright? I couldn't even look at her sometimes. Seeing her like that when she used to be so fit and . . . alive. She wasn't my Holly any more.'

'That must have hurt.'

'It was hell. Nobody tells you you're going to feel like that.'

'Hell for her,' Ferreira said and he flinched at the words.

'You don't know anything.'

Warren shoved away from the table and walked into the corner of the room, a dangerous, prowling quality to his movements, the kind of gait you earned by pushing your body in ways most people didn't. Zigic thought of him climbing with Holly, the cross-country running – he did it himself, knew how demanding it was in comparison to hitting a treadmill, jumping ditches and vaulting fences. He thought of the old farm track which ran around the edge of Elton, from the patch of woodland at the bottom of the drove near Dawn's house, out to the western fringe of the village and down to the river which bordered the kennels.

A route only a local would know. One infrequently used and unlikely to bring you in contact with any witnesses should you be running home covered in blood on a twilit summer evening.

'Holly wanted to die,' he said, still facing the wall. 'That's what all the campaigning was about. She wanted to die and nobody would help her do it so she decided she'd get the law changed.'

'What about Dignitas?' Zigic asked.

'She was too young.' Warren turned to face them, but stayed in the corner of the room. 'And she wasn't prepared to wait. She'd had enough. Nothing either of us said or did could convince her that her life was still worth living.'

Zigic felt the emotion register in his own chest, tried not to think about Stefan or Milan in that situation, his unborn daughter growing up and telling him she wanted to die, but he couldn't quite push the image away.

'If you didn't support the idea why did you make that film with her?' Ferreira asked.

Warren's head dropped. 'Initially we both said no and that only upset Holly more. She refused to do anything, wouldn't speak to Dawn, wouldn't go for physio. She started to fade in front of our eyes. So in the end we did it.'

'Holly didn't go back to physio, though,' Ferreira said.

'No. I don't think she was ever going to – she couldn't see the point any more – but she knew we wanted her to so that's what she used.' He returned to the table, slumped in his chair. 'Don't think she was a bad person, she just knew what she wanted. I admired her hugely for that. It broke my fucking heart but still . . . I respected her decision.'

'How did Dawn feel about all this?' Ferreria asked.

'She didn't want to lose Holly. No matter what state she was in, Dawn would have looked after her for the rest of her life. It was killing her, knowing what Holly wanted to do.'

'You agreed with her, though,' Ferreira said.

'I'd support anyone's right to choose the manner of their death,' he said. 'It should be a basic human right. I thought that before Holly was injured and I still think it now.'

'Did Dawn know how you felt?'

'We'd discussed it, yes, years ago. I've always done a lot of stupid, dangerous sports, so I wanted her to know my wishes if anything happened to me.'

'The same stupid, dangerous sports Holly was doing.'

His eyes filled up but he gritted his teeth, said, 'I know it's my fault. I got her into rock climbing. Dawn never wanted her to do it.'

'You understood how Holly felt then?'

'Just because I understood it doesn't mean I wanted her to die.' He tugged at his beard, fingers tight. 'She was so fucking clever, she knew I got it. She knew exactly how I felt.'

He shook his head, tears running down his cheeks, but he didn't blink, just stared through them, lost in some long-gone conversation, and they both waited, seeing the emotion growing, as his hands went back through his hair and a low growl rumbled around his throat.

The seconds stretched on and Zigic could feel Ferreira straining in the chair next to him, wanting to ask but knowing they were close to something that required patience. Warren was almost there, on the edge now, muttering to himself.

And finally, without prompting, he said:

'Holly asked me to do it. She begged me – my baby – she begged me to end it. And I wanted to. God help me, I didn't want to see her suffering like that. I'd done that to her, I might as well have fucked up her rigging myself. It was my responsibility.'

His head tipped back, as if he was looking for her, up there somewhere. Ferreira started to speak and Zigic touched a staying hand to her arm.

'I couldn't go back after that,' Warren said. 'She begged me and I let her down. Again. I couldn't face her.' He gulped back the tears. 'I wish I'd done it now. At least it would have been quick.'

For a few seconds no one spoke. There was just the sound of Warren sniffing and the clock ticking out the last of the afternoon, while Zigic tried to plot a route from that conversation to Dawn's murder but all he could think about was Holly, stuck in her bed, too depressed to fight on any more, begging her father to kill her, and he wondered if he could have done it. In that position, would it be strength or weakness to agree? Your own pain or your child's, which would you rather endure? Every parent thought they'd die to protect their children but very few ever found themselves in the situation and most would never be tested the way Warren had been.

'Did you tell Dawn about this?' he asked.

'I thought she needed to know.' Warren wiped his eyes. 'What if Holly asked one of her carers and they were crazy enough to actually do it? Dawn needed to be aware of that.'

'How did she take it?'

'Worse than I expected,' he said. 'She thought I'd do it. Like eventually I'd grow the balls and do the right thing for Holly. But I'm a fucking coward.'

At that he broke down completely and they sat in silence for a while, the effects of Warren's words settling on them, before Zigic gestured for Ferreira to end the recording, knowing they'd get nothing more from him now.

Ferreira had been right, they'd cracked him; his confession had been made, not what they expected to hear and not what they needed from him. It wasn't a crime for the police, that moment of cowardice, the betrayal of his daughter's faith. Warren had tried himself for it already and Zigic knew he'd mete out his own punishment and that it would be a stiffer sentence than any court would hand down.

35

'We should search the place before Sally goes home,' Ferreira said, as they went back into the office. 'It's only a matter of time before she realises Ben might be guilty and goes looking for incriminating evidence to destroy.'

'She doesn't know we're looking for the knife.'

'No, but if anyone knows where he'd hide bloodstained clothes it's her.'

Zigic called Parr away from his desk and told him to take a full team to the kennels and thoroughly search the place, gave him a photograph of one of the knives from the block in Dawn's kitchen so they'd know what they were looking for.

Benjamin was arrogant enough to hide it at home, Ferreira thought, and Warren and Sally so busy with their own stuff that his movements probably didn't register from one day to the next. She wasn't sure she bought Warren's recollection of that Thursday night, though.

Something about how clipped his speech became and the way he automatically angled his body away as he'd begun to talk bothered her. It was a liar's posture, designed to shield himself, but it said more than staring either of them dead in the eye could have.

She rolled a cigarette, went over to the window to smoke it, already thinking about how best to attack Benjamin, what buttons to push and what response she wanted to elicit from him. It would be easier if they had any kind of physical evidence but in the absence of that she knew they needed to play on his personality.

It hadn't worked with Ian Bowe or Arnold Fletcher, though.

Bowe had looked like a sound bet, now he was out of the running. Fletcher she still liked for it, saw something on him, a crusader's zeal. He had the courage of his convictions and that made him dangerous.

Her phone pinged – Ethan telling her to come up and check out his findings.

She called across the office to Zigic, 'We've got something from the laptop.'

They went up to the tech department, a smell of toasted bread and tomato sauce in the stairwell, lingering in the corridor, and they followed it to Ethan's office; a half-eaten pepperoni pizza sitting on the counter, well away from where he was working. He had a slice in his hand and he threw it down when they walked in, wiped his fingers on a paper napkin, then scrubbed the sauce from his blond goatee, bringing some pink to his milk-white skin.

'Didn't think you'd be straight up,' he said and nodded towards the grease-stained box. 'Help yourself.'

'I thought you were eating clean this month,' Ferreira said.

'I caved.'

'What have you found then?' Zigic asked.

'Right, yeah.' Ethan looked at the laptop, screen showing Benjamin's browser history. 'So, as we thought, he's behind about seventy per cent of the uber-vicious comments Holly was getting, using a series of aliases, loads of different email accounts, none of them properly screened but he's not very tech savvy by the look of this.'

'We can prove all this?'

'No problem.'

Zigic nodded. 'Good, we're getting somewhere then.'

'What else?' Ferreira asked.

'Nothing you can charge him with but I thought you'd want to know, there's a lot of porn on here.'

'He's a fourteen-year-old boy,' Zigic said.

'This isn't run-of-the-mill.' Ethan hopped up onto the counter, feet on the seat of his chair. 'Sure, there's the usual stuff we all watch but the last few months he's been getting into more hard-core material. Rape and torture, a lot of it looks amateur. *Real* amateur, I mean, not staged. There's videos on there he's watched twenty times in a day.'

Zigic brushed his hand back through his hair, swore lightly.

'We already knew he was a piece of shit,' Ferreira said. 'This doesn't change anything.'

'Some of the videos feature disabled women – paralysed women – and I really don't think they were happy to be taking part. We're talking care homes here, hospitals maybe. It looks really real. You can watch if you want, but—'

'We don't want,' Zigic said.

'Understandable.'

Ethan looked queasy although it hadn't been bad enough to put him off his pizza, Ferreira thought.

He took a couple of pieces of paper from the printer tray. 'I've got his browser history for you, the sites we're talking about are starred. I thought it might be useful.'

They took the paperwork, neither speaking until they were in the stairwell again.

'Does this change anything?' Ferreira asked. 'It's showing us his mindset, but does it have any implications for the murder?'

'Probably not,' Zigic said. 'It's fucking terrifying, though, don't you think? The things a teenager gets up to when no one's looking.'

He was genuinely stunned by it, she saw, and she wondered at his naivety. What did he think online porn was? Just a moving version of the wank mags he probably sneaked a look at in the playground when he was a teenager? Didn't he realise how it was out there now? How extreme tastes had become mainstream.

Maybe he was thinking about his own sons and how he would cope with knowing they'd look at stuff like that when the time came.

'Let's get this done then,' he said.

Benjamin Lange had recovered his composure in the hour since Ferreira had last seen him and she put it down to the presence of his solicitor, an old-school operator in pinstripe suit and red silk tie, his thinning grey hair whipped into something approaching a bouffant.

Mr Harold waited until the recording equipment was running to officially complain about the way Benjamin had been brought in, suggested that a polite request would have served everyone involved far better.

'He's from a respectable family, after all. There was no need for such high-handed tactics.'

'We'll bear that in mind next time we need to arrest him,' Ferreira said.

'You might also bear in mind your failure to protect him from violence during the course of his arrest,' Mr Harold said.

Benjamin winced as he spoke, touched a tentative hand to his jaw, which was badly swollen and shining under the strip light. The bruising hadn't started to come out yet but it would be bad when it did.

'Mr Prentice believes Ben killed his estranged wife and is responsible for the death of his daughter,' Ferreira said. 'Tempers were running high.'

'I didn't kill anyone,' Benjamin said, earning a warning look from Harold. 'What? I didn't. Why would I want to kill her?'

'Let's try another question,' Zigic said. 'One Mr Harold won't be so offended by. Why have you spent the last year stalking Holly?'

'I wasn't stalking her.'

'No, Ben, listen – we're not asking *if* you were stalking her. We know you were, we've been through your computer. We want to know *why* you did it.'

'It's not stalking,' he said. 'It's just . . . making comments.'

Mr Harold looked sternly across the top of his glasses. 'There's nothing illegal about that.'

Ferreira opened the file she'd brought in and passed him a sheet of paper. 'These are some of the comments Ben made. You'll notice a bullying tone, I think. Several death threats. Which *are* illegal and we're taking the matter very seriously. This was a concerted campaign of harassment. Motivated by Holly's disability. Which makes it a hate crime.'

Harold glanced at the paper, then at the boy next to him, and put it down again.

'I'm sure you're aware of the heavy tariffs on hate crimes.' Ferreira stared at Benjamin, waiting for him to look at her. 'So, the question still stands, Ben. Why did you do it?'

He shrugged.

'In words, please.'

'I was bored.'

'And the best thing you could think of to do with your time was harass a disabled schoolmate? Your new dad's daughter.'

Benjamin scowled at her, a little boy having a tantrum. 'He's not my dad.'

'Was that why you picked on Holly? To get at him?'

'No.'

'Why her then?'

He didn't answer, sat very upright with his hands in his lap, the way Mr Harold had probably told him to sit, the attention to detail which came with engaging the partner at a Priestgate law firm.

'You liked Holly,' Ferreira said. 'Before the accident. Is that it?'

'No.'

'You liked her but she wasn't interested in you because she was clever and sporty and super-popular, while you –' Ferreira frowned slightly – 'you weren't any of those things, were you? She didn't even know you existed. But then she got hurt and she wasn't sporty and popular any more, she was just a cripple.'

Benjamin's top lip twitched.

'A cripple with a blog and a Twitter account and not much else in her life. You weren't going to let her ignore you any more.' She slapped the table and he flinched. 'But she did. All of those hours you spent setting up fake email accounts and attacking her blog, all those stupid conversations you were having with yourself – like a mad person, Ben – and she still didn't react. Because she didn't care what some loser like you thought. She was out there, people still liked her. They admired her courage and intelligence. Even paralysed she was still a bigger success than you.'

Benjamin opened his mouth but Mr Harold put a hand on his arm and he stopped.

'This is all completely unnecessary, Sergeant. Benjamin doesn't deny commenting on the young woman's blog so please, curtail the pop psychology.' He turned his attention to Zigic. 'If you wish to pursue this as a hate crime that is your right, but he has been quite clear that his actions arose out of youthful naivety and boredom. There really is nothing else for us to discuss here.'

'Murder,' Zigic said. 'We're going to discuss that.'

Harold snorted. 'I sense somebody's clutching at straws.'

Benjamin didn't find it quite so amusing, though, judging by how fast the colour drained from his face.

'You threatened Holly,' Ferreira said. 'You probably don't remember exactly what you said, let me read it to you.' She found the right piece of paper. '"I've got a hammer if you want to end it. LOL. You won't even need to hold her down. Yeah, no fun is it? Killing some bitch who can't fight back. Can you talk Hol? Will you scream for me?"'

He juddered where he sat, eyes flicking to the door and back again. 'It was a joke.'

'You think she found it funny?'

'No.'

'Do you think she was scared by it?'

'No. She would have done something if she was scared,' he said. 'She'd have blocked me from commenting.'

Ferreira rested her chin in her palm, watched him across the table until he started to fidget and look to his solicitor for some cue how to respond. When none came he clamped his mouth tight shut.

'How do you think your mum's going to feel when she finds out you watched a video of a paralysed woman being raped?'

Benjamin twisted in his seat. 'I didn't.'

'You watched it twelve times in a single day,' Ferreira said. 'A woman who was paralysed from the neck down being raped.'

'She didn't mind.'

'Excuse me?'

'It's not *real*.' Benjamin leaned across the table, all elbows and hands too big for his skinny arms. 'Everyone watches them. It's not a crime.'

'Benjamin is quite correct,' Mr Harold said, but he suddenly looked a tad uneasy.

Odd for a man who'd defended more than his fair share of sex offenders and murderers. It was Ben's age, though, Ferreira thought. Just as they all felt a little worse about the young victims they felt a little more disgusted by the young perpetrators. Innocence taken was disturbing enough, but innocence absent challenged the notions of justice and morality which brought them into work every morning.

'In itself, what Benjamin did isn't illegal,' Zigic said. 'But the fact that he watched the video twelve times in one day and on a daily basis from then on, makes us wonder what kept drawing him back to it.'

Benjamin was becoming visibly agitated, leg jiggling under the table, hands clasped tight on top of it. Ferreira could see his pulse beating at his temple, all of the blood rushing fast to his brain. Zigic unnerved him, she realised. Against their expectations he was the one Ben didn't want to deal with. She sat back in her chair, giving him the cue.

'What happened?' he asked. 'You watched that video – dozens of times – and you thought about Holly, in her bed, unable to move. She wouldn't be able to stop you. Just like that woman couldn't stop the man who raped her.'

'I didn't touch her!'

'No, Dawn got in the way, didn't she?'

'I didn't do anything,' Benjamin said, a childish whine that threatened to erupt into a wail. 'I never went anywhere near either of them.'

'You never went to Dawn's house?'

'No.'

Zigic slipped the photograph of Dawn's vandalised car out of the file. 'Then how did you manage to take this photo you sent to Holly?'

He stared at it for a few long seconds. 'I saw it when I was walking past the house, so I took a photo.'

'Where were you walking from?'

'I can't remember.'

'There's nothing at that end of the village. Unless you were planning on walking the five miles into Peterborough. And somehow I doubt that.' Zigic tapped the photo. 'No, I think you sprayed the car and I think you slashed the tyres.'

'Can you prove any of this?' Mr Harold asked.

'We're not interested in charging Ben with a petty act of vandalism,' Zigic told him. 'We want to know when he was last at Dawn's house.'

'I've never been there,' Benjamin said again and caught himself. 'Except that time. When I was walking past and I saw the car.'

'And where were you during the evening of Thursday the tenth of September?'

'Last Thursday?' the boy asked. 'At home. It's a school night. Warren was there too, he'll tell you.'

Zigic smiled. 'We've already had Warren's version of events. If you're looking for an alibi you need to look elsewhere.'

'I'd like some time to speak with my client,' Mr Harold said.

'Certainly. If you think it'll help.'

36

By six the search team was finished at the kennels, no knife found, no bloodstained clothing, and Zigic reluctantly released Benjamin on police bail, into his mother's care. She'd spent the hours he was in custody waiting in reception and when Zigic took Benjamin back to her she looked tired out and disgusted by what she'd seen pass through there during the afternoon.

'I knew this was a mistake,' she said, trying to take her son's hand.

He pulled away from her, not wanting to appear weak in front of the young man being dragged through the main doors by two heavyset uniforms.

'It wasn't a mistake,' Zigic told her. 'Ben has been charged with harassment and he'll be tried for it. How much further he went remains to be seen.'

'He didn't kill anyone.' She hustled him towards the door and he was out and gone when she turned back to Zigic. 'You shouldn't believe anything Warren says. He hated Dawn for the way she was using Holly against him. I've lost count of the number of times he said he wished she was dead.'

She lingered, waiting for him to ask her more, but he didn't.

Whatever she said now would be coloured by the afternoon's violence and her determination to protect Ben. And if they uncovered some solid evidence against Warren within the next couple of days she'd still be there to talk to, desperate to reveal whatever she'd been hiding about him before.

He was down in the cells now, had gone quietly, face still damp with tears after his outburst during the interview, and Zigic saw resignation on him as he walked away, a PC at his elbow. Guilty or not, Warren felt as if he deserved it.

Zigic didn't believe Sally's words but couldn't quite ignore the accusations she'd made.

'I know that look,' Ferreira said, as he walked into the office. 'What did Sally say?'

He told her.

'She's just trying to protect her sicko kid. Forget about it.'

Zigic went to the murder board and eyed the result of a day's furious activity, lots of names written and crossed out, but they were essentially at the same point as they had been this morning. All of those men questioned and the ones still to do, picked up because of their intimacy with Dawn. The most superficial kind, just physical, brief and perfunctory, the kind which led to violence depressingly often, but he still felt there was more to Dawn's death.

'Do you remember what you said? Sunday afternoon in the Black Horse?'

Ferreira rustled around in her desk drawer. 'Which bit?'

'You said it always come down to the ex.'

'Yeah, well, she's got a lot more exes than we expected, right?'

'But only one of them who was in the process of divorcing her,' Zigic said. 'And by his own admission it was a messy split. She wanted money he didn't have. She'd stopped him visiting Holly.'

Ferreira pulled an empty sandwich box out of her drawer and dropped it into the bin, moved on to the next one down.

'It wasn't exactly a Fathers4Justice scenario, though, was it?' She binned an old newspaper. 'Warren didn't trust himself with Holly, and Dawn didn't trust him either. They were in agreement. Basically. A weird agreement, granted, but he didn't seem bitter about it.'

'If we believe his version of events.'

'Don't you believe it?'

‘It was a convincing display,’ Zigic said, remembering how Warren’s helpless anger had punched his own heart. ‘But what was behind it? Was he upset because Holly asked him to end her life and he couldn’t or because he wanted to and Dawn wouldn’t let him close enough again?’

Ferreira kicked the drawer shut. ‘It was a conversation with no witnesses. Why hand us a motive?’

‘Does he seem in full control of himself to you?’ Zigic asked. ‘The whole point of interviewing him when we did was because you thought he was ready to crack. Well, we pushed him and what did we get? A confession that he wanted to end Holly’s life.’

‘Not that he did, though.’

‘We should have kept pushing.’

Ferreira perched on the edge of her desk. ‘Okay, say that’s his motivation – he’s going to kill Holly. He goes to the house planning to do it, runs into Dawn – not a surprise because of course she’s going to be there – so he has to go in fully expecting her to get in the way and fully prepared to kill her. Because he knows she doesn’t approve. He knows she won’t cover for him in a million years and she’s going to try and stop him. If that’s what he’s planning to do why kill Dawn and not Holly? The person he went there to kill. One murder or two, it’s all the same at that point. He’s going to prison whatever.’

Zigic looked at the board, not really seeing any of it, but thinking back to the forensics report, the efforts to clean up and Holly’s closed bedroom door.

‘Assuming he was expecting to get caught.’

‘He’d have to be a complete idiot to think we wouldn’t come for him,’ Ferreira said. ‘The estranged husband? Everyone knows that’s the first port of call.’

‘Maybe he just couldn’t bring himself to do it. He murders Dawn in the heat of the moment. She knows why he’s there. They argue. It escalates. But Holly’s a different matter altogether.’

Ferreira shook her head, giving him a withering look.

'That makes no sense. Why would he have left Holly like that?'

'The nurse was due in – what – twelve hours? Less? It wouldn't have seemed like a big risk.'

Ferreira looked unconvinced. 'Ben's the killer in that house. He's spent a year building up to attacking Holly. Whether he knew it or not he was getting into the right head space for it. You know how this shit works. And he's got no alibi.'

'Neither's Warren.'

'I just don't see the motive,' she said.

Zigic rubbed his face, in no mood for further discussion. It had been a long day of fruitless arguments and endorphin spikes which flattened out hard when the progress they thought they were making turned out to be another dead end. Twenty men still to question tomorrow and a search of the village to be overseen.

Riggott had finally okayed that. Weighed the budgetary issues against the odds of finding the murder weapon somewhere between Dawn's house and the kennels and decided they could have the resources for a fingertip search, bodies and dogs, whatever it took to get in and out in a day.

A day that would start very early, Zigic thought.

Parr and Murray had gone home already, Wheatley was finishing up with one of Dawn's men. This one had a sturdy alibi but his attitude to being cornered at work and brought in was less than cooperative and when Wheatley ran his fingerprints he found they matched those lifted off a broken bottle used in a brawl two years earlier, the case still unsolved, the victim permanently disfigured. Somebody had got justice today at least.

'Alright, let's pick this up tomorrow. No point staying here any longer.'

Neither of them needed telling twice and he walked out to the car park with them, declined the invitation to the pub and climbed into his car before the suggestion got any more tempting than it already was.

37

It was a rare night he wasn't desperate to get home but Anna would be waiting for him to do the stern-father routine and he had no idea how to handle Stefan's behaviour. He'd spent half an hour in his office googling what to do if your child was a biter and found that it was very common, but not at Stefan's age, and very difficult to deal with. Mainly because it was a stage children went through at two or three, when they were too young to express themselves or know right from wrong. At five they should have grown out of it. They definitely shouldn't *start* doing it at that age.

As he pulled into the driveway and climbed out of the car he said a little prayer that Anna had already found a solution and dealt with the issue, but when he let himself in the back door he realised she hadn't. She was sitting at the kitchen table with her chin in her hands, laptop open on one of the sites he'd visited. It advocated firm words and rewards for good behaviour. He hoped that would be enough.

'You're early tonight,' she said.

He kissed her on the top of her head. 'How's he been?'

'Oh, he's been a perfect little angel.'

'Knows he's in trouble then?'

'I told him he would be when Daddy gets home.'

'Yeah, I bet that put the fear of God in him.'

She smiled, tired looking. 'You're the only one he ever listens to.'

Zigic opened the fridge, thought for a moment about the bottle of Żubrówka in the freezer below, but took out a mineral water, not wanting to be the kind of parent who disciplined his son with vodka on his breath.

'I don't understand why he's done it all of a sudden. All the sites I looked at said it's a toddler thing. He didn't do it then, why start now?'

Anna shrugged. 'Starting a new school, not being the centre of attention any more maybe? I think he's probably just acting out but we can't let this turn into a habit. God, Dushan, it was so humiliating, everyone looking at me like I was the worst mother in the world.'

'You can't worry about what other people think of you. Lots of kids do it and every parent feels terrible when they do.'

'Mrs Lomax was very understanding,' she said. 'I suppose that's something. If Sara hadn't been so hysterical I don't think she'd have even suspended him.'

'A couple of days at home won't hurt.' He sat down across the table from her. 'It's probably a better punishment than anything we'd do.'

She murmured agreement.

'What?'

'Do you think he's settling in there? Surely he wouldn't be misbehaving like this if he was happy.'

'It's one incident,' Zigic said. 'Don't read too much into it.'

'But it's not normal,' she said, angrier now. 'Milan didn't do it – even when he was being bullied that time he didn't lash out like this. Where did Stefan learn to behave like that?'

'I'll talk to him, okay? Maybe he thought he had a good reason.'

'There's no good reason for biting a little girl.'

He went upstairs to the boys' room, found Stefan sitting on the floor between their beds, already bathed and in his Batman pyjamas, playing with a pair of plastic dinosaurs. Milan slipped off his bed as Zigic walked in, tactfully withdrawing from what he knew was coming up, and Zigic tousled his hair as he left the room, thinking what a diplomat he was growing into.

Stefan glanced up at him, all big blue eyes and innocently blank expression, the one he'd perfected during the last year and deployed every time a lamp got knocked over or he was caught at the end of a trail of muddy footprints that ran through the house.

Zigic sat down on Milan's bed and Stefan kept playing with his dinosaurs, walking them across the floor and making them climb a set of Lego stairs he'd built, leading up to the shelves of picture books and toys in bright stacking crates.

'Do you want to tell me what happened at school today?'

Stefan ignored him, kept running his triceratops up and down the stairs.

'Stefan, look at me when I'm talking to you, please.'

He made the dinosaur jump off the top step and Zigic snatched it out of his hand.

'Why did you bite Amelie?'

'I didn't.'

'I know you did and I want to know why.'

He shrugged extravagantly and Zigic wondered if they should at least stop him watching so much football.

'I'm not angry with you,' he said, as gently as he could. 'But you need to tell me why you did it.'

Stefan kicked out weakly at the air, his little face a picture of sullen reluctance. 'Amelie's mean.'

'Did she do something to you?' When Stefan didn't answer, Zigic slipped off the bed and crouched down in front of him, ducking into his eye line, seeing the sadness and childish anger bubbling up there. 'It's okay, you can tell me.'

His bottom lip trembled. 'She pinched me.'

Zigic cursed in his head. 'Where did she pinch you?'

Stefan pulled up the sleeve of his pyjamas and held out his arm, the faintest pink mark on his skin. 'It hurt.'

'I know, but you're not supposed to bite people, are you?'

'She started it.'

'It doesn't matter. You tell Mrs Lomax.'

'Amelie's her favourite.'

'We'll get Mummy to talk to Mrs Lomax, okay?' Stefan nodded and roughly pulled his sleeve down again. 'If she does it again you tell your teacher, right?'

He looked dubious about the idea and Zigic could see the budding rebellion in his big blue eyes. Remembered his own sister when they were kids, scrapping with all comers, and wondered if Stefan had inherited this behaviour from his side of the family.

'We don't bite, do we?'

Stefan's eyes narrowed.

'No matter what she does, you don't bite her again.'

'But—'

'No, Stefan. Mummy will talk to Mrs Lomax but you're going to be a good boy. People don't bite.' He held up the triceratops. 'Dinosaurs bite, people don't. And what are you?'

Stefan tucked his elbows into his sides and flapped his shortened arms around like a T. rex, roaring at Zigic and laughing.

'Right. If you're going to be a baby about it . . .' He dragged a box of toys off the shelf and picked up the stegosaurus from the floor. 'This is what happens when you don't behave. If you do it again I'm taking two boxes away.'

Zigic shut the door on Stefan's screaming protests, knowing he'd get bored within a few minutes, and shoved the toys away at the top of his own wardrobe, finding another box of them forgotten up there from the last time Stefan misbehaved.

In the living room Milan was curled up in the corner of the sofa, reading a Roald Dahl book with his brows knitted in concentration. *Charlie and the Chocolate Factory* again, his favourite.

'That went well then,' Anna said, when he returned to the kitchen.

'He told me Amelie pinched him.'

She frowned. 'That doesn't really excuse him biting her, though, does it?'

'It explains it. At least we know he wasn't just . . . attacking her. I said you'd speak to Mrs Lomax about it.'

'Okay.' Anna sighed and looked up to the ceiling, following the sound of Stefan's little feet thumping the floor, muffled by the thick wool rug but still making enough noise to register as an act of protest. 'Why is everything such a production with him?'

'Let him get it out of his system.'

'The neighbours are going to think we're beating him.'

'I'm pretty sure they're used to the sound of his tantrums by now.' Zigic took the iced Żubrówka out of the freezer and poured a shot. 'That was by far the worst interrogation I've carried out all day and one of the blokes was a hardened animal-rights activist.'

'Maybe you should have brought Mel home with you to help,' she said, something arch in her tone.

'I doubt she'd be much use with a kid.'

Anna placed a bowl of salad on the table and went back to the hob where a pan was heating up, waiting for her to fry two fillets of Dover sole. He watched her movements, trying to decide what that slight edge in her voice meant or if he'd just imagined it, decided it was probably him. Long day, combative discussions; of course he was hearing inflections that weren't there.

He picked a chicory leaf out of the bowl and ate it with his vodka, the slight bitterness combining nicely with the herbiness of the bison grass.

'Did you give her that oil I bought her?' Anna asked.

'Yeah, last week. She said to thank you. I forgot, sorry.'

The lavender-scented oil Anna used to ward off stretch marks, diligently applying it after every bath and shower, rubbing it into her skin in slow circles, as if part of its potency lay in her willing it to work. It was good for scars, she'd said, handing him the white-and-orange box one morning before work.

'Good. I hope it helps her.' She flipped the fish over in the pan. 'I wish I'd thought of it sooner, though, you really need to use it as early as possible. For stretch marks anyway. Maybe it's different for scarring.'

It wasn't going to work because he hadn't given it to Ferreira, couldn't imagine handing it over with Anna's best wishes and the implication that they'd discussed the matter and what a mess she must be in under her jeans. He didn't want her to know how much Anna pitied her.

They ate to the muffled sound of Stefan's diminishing temper, talked about finishing painting the nursery at the weekend and whether they should buy something nice for the boys so they wouldn't feel neglected, Zigic trying to put work completely out of his mind but failing, because the day had finished on an unsatisfactory note and he knew they were up against Riggott's ticking clock. Benjamin Lange's arrest had assuaged him but it was only a stopgap and they needed something more promising tomorrow if he was going to keep the investigation in Hate Crimes.

Part of him knew it was a petty concern and he shouldn't care about handing Dawn and Holly over to CID, but he liked to finish what he started.

After dinner they lay on the sofa, watching Anna's latest boxed-set obsession, and he had to keep asking her what was going on because he never could keep his full attention on these things. Secretly he suspected her of skipping on ahead of him during the day.

Long after his bedtime Stefan came down and stood in front of the television to apologise for biting Amelia, hands tucked behind his back, one foot twisting against the carpet as he spoke.

'Next time she does something like that you tell me and I'll deal with it,' Anna said. 'You don't bite anyone. Okay?'

'Okay.'

Zigic lifted him into his lap and fell asleep with his chin on his head.

38

The pub seemed like a good idea until they were at a table. It was full of teenagers who didn't look old enough to qualify for even a fake ID, and proper grown-ups trying to outdo them for noise level and stupidity. After their second round Wahlia suggested going back to his and Ferreira was on her feet immediately, draining the last of her rum as she headed for the doors.

He was renting a place that overlooked the park, six storeys of heavy-duty urban sophistication that was completely out of kilter with the surrounding terraced houses and way beyond Wahlia's budget, but the flat was owned by one of his uncles, an investment purchase he'd rather have in safe hands at below market value than risk it being trashed by some undesirable professional with strange habits and a cavalier attitude towards the high-spec finish.

'No,' Ferreira said, as she walked in. 'I'm still totally jealous. Not getting over it at all.'

Acres of open-plan polished walnut floor and pristine white walls, a large feature window at one end of the space and a glossy black kitchen at the other, complete with monolithic fridge and a swanky oven Wahlia had never turned on. It was sparsely furnished but what was there was good stuff, a huge brown leather sofa facing a flat-screen TV with Wahlia's junk sitting on the floor in piles underneath it, a perspex coffee table that matched the dining table and chairs. A man's idea of interior design, all clean, hard lines and minimal softening embellishments, but she could live with it.

'There's one on the floor below up for rent.'

'Yeah, I saw it. Twelve hundred a month.'

'You're still looking then?'

'I viewed a couple of places.'

'And?' He kicked his trainers off, onto the pile next to the door.

'One possible.'

She followed him into the kitchen area and leaned against the counter as he took a beer and a bottle of rum out of the fridge, handed her a tumbler from one of the shiny cupboards and poured a stiff measure into it.

'You're definitely going then?' he asked.

'I think so.'

'That doesn't sound very definite.'

'I'm going.' She sipped the rum, washing away the reasons she could give him but wouldn't. Knew he already understood how it had been, those months laid up at the pub, comforted and coddled beyond her tolerance, being treated like a child when she'd survived an act of violence she hoped none of them would ever have to go through but which they couldn't see made her stronger. She couldn't tell him about the tears and the arguments, her father telling her to quit her job, insisting nobody and nothing was important enough to risk her life for, or waking up to find her mother wiping her legs with holy water and praying for her scars to heal.

'It feels like the right time.'

He nodded. 'I need a quick shower. Get us cued up and order, will you? The menus are—'

'I know.' She opened the drawer near the sink, dozens of takeout leaflets in there. 'Chinese?'

'Yeah.'

She dialled the number and ordered their regulars, then took her drink over to the window, stood for a few minutes looking out across the park, thinking it was a nice enough view but not twelve-hundred-a-month's worth. Not when you knew the things that had happened there, the grooming of vulnerable children, the rapes. It was a side effect of the job, seeing places tainted by the crimes that occurred around them, never being able to look at them with innocent eyes again.

The place she wanted had been a crime scene. Not the exact flat but another one in the building. She wouldn't let it ruin the place for her, though, everything else about it was too perfect; the size and layout, its position right in the centre of the city, just off Cathedral Square. She imagined herself getting up early to run down along the river before work, buying cushions and pieces of art and fresh flowers from the stall on the square some Saturday morning.

It wouldn't be like that. Obviously. She wasn't undergoing a complete personality transplant. But she liked the sense of potential.

'You were supposed to be getting us set up,' Wahlia said.

'I got distracted by the view.'

He finished drying his hair in the kitchen and threw the towel into the washing machine, came over to switch on the TV and the Xbox. GTA was still in there from last time they played. It was getting to be a regular thing and she couldn't decide if it meant they were getting old or boring or both that they'd rather blast the hell of computer-generated people than go out pulling real ones.

She'd spent hundreds of hours playing on her brothers' machine while she was convalescing, retreating into the kind of adolescence she'd been too studious to enjoy the first time around.

They played for an hour, raced high-performance sports cars and went to shoot up a bunch of rednecks who all reminded her of Christian Palmer, pausing for more drinks and cigarettes, and by the time the delivery guy arrived they were sitting on the floor, hyper with alcohol and adrenalin.

She paused the game while he went for the food, fetched him another beer and finally got around to taking off her Converse.

Her phone pinged as Wahlia was unpacking their order.

'Work?' he asked, sliding her chow mein across the table.

'No.'

She opened the message from Aaron, remembering his stupid smile and gym-hard body and the sad look on his little face when she left him standing in the cafeteria.

A string of emojis she took to be an invitation for a drink.

She texted back, told him she was working late. Another time.

'Who is it then?' Wahlia asked, poking her in the ribs with his chopsticks.

'Some guy.' Her phone pinged again. She opened his message and laughed. 'Jesus Christ.'

Wahlia grabbed her phone, eyes widening at the sight of Aaron's stiff cock and waxed balls filling the screen.

'Classy.'

'Like you've never done it.' She took her phone back, still smiling. 'Actually, I think I need an early night, can you call me a cab?'

Wahlia choked on a mouthful of rice. 'He's got warts.'

'No, he hasn't.'

He reached over and flicked at the screen, expanding the shot. 'Look, warts. Shit, I feel like I need to wash my hands and I've only touched a photo of it.'

'And he seemed like such a nice, clean boy.' She tossed her phone onto the table, ignored the next message that came through as she batted away Wahlia's jokes.

The food was salty and sour, demanded more drinks to wash the taste away; she switched to beers and made Wahlia take a couple of rum chasers to even them up.

After that the game didn't last long, shots went astray and cars crashed in spectacular fireballs and when Wahlia accidentally blew himself up with one of his own grenades she made him take a shot of rum as a punishment for the gross act of incompetence.

'Let's break for a bit,' she said, putting down her controller. 'You need to sober up if you're going to do anyone serious damage.'

'Coffee?'

'No, you're not that drunk.'

She curled up on the sofa, let her head drop onto the arm.

When she opened her eyes again there was a mug on the table in front of her and the television was playing some stupid action film from when Bruce Willis still had hair. No sign of Bobby. She reached for the cup and missed it and flinched when an explosion on screen sent a remembered wave of heat across the backs of her legs.

Not heat, not exactly, it was more localised than that, more distinct.

A tingling sensation.

She rolled over on the sofa, pressed her face against the back cushion and let the wooziness draw her down into another short sleep where the rednecks who looked like Christian Palmer never stopped coming and she never ran out of ammo, just calmly picked them off, one by one, letting their bodies pile up at her feet.

The tingling sensation broke through into her dream and brought her around with a start. Suddenly she was sitting upright, head spinning but she could deal with that, knew to just go with it. She couldn't deal with the gnawing, spiky pain any more though. Not for another day, not an hour, not even a minute.

Bobby had turned off all the lights, except for the discreet spots sunk into the skirting boards in the hallway. They washed milkily across the floor, guiding her into the bathroom with the slick black tile walls and the big white tub, lights hidden behind mirrors and floating shelves full of however many products it took for him to look that good.

She couldn't see what she wanted there though.

The medicine cabinet was full of aftershave and face creams, pills and balms and oils that scattered when she reached in with an unsteady hand. Most of the stuff landed in the sink and the things that hit the floor didn't break. She found what she was looking for, a small plastic packet she held between her teeth while she unpeeled her jeans and climbed into the porcelain bathtub that was so deep she could hardly see over the edge once she was sitting down.

At the back of her right calf the tingling pain had shrunk to one intense spot and her fingers went to it, toying with the hard little something that was pushing its way up through her flesh, close to the surface now. Her thumb brushed over it, felt a wicked point that wasn't there before. It was still moving, turning and cutting through her like it had on the way in. Only slower now and she was sure it hurt more.

She opened the plastic packet and unwrapped one of the razor blades. It looked dull under the subdued lighting but she knew it was sharp enough.

'Come on,' she whispered to herself.

It wasn't the first piece of shrapnel she'd cut out of her legs and she knew there would be more yet. Couldn't see them or feel them as obviously as this one, but she knew there were things in her body that didn't belong.

Gritting her teeth she pulled the skin tight over the lump, seeing its shape more clearly, the colour of it: creamy white.

She took a deep breath and swiped the razor blade across the lump. The blood welled fast and the pain shot straight up her spine, hitting her like a punch to thc back of the neck. She tried to suppress the shocked yelp but it came out anyway and seemed to echo forever in the black-tiled room.

Blood ran down her calf to her ankle and began to pool at her heel.

'Mel, I think you should give me the razor blade, okay?' Bobby was standing over her, staring at the seeping wound. 'Please, before you hurt yourself.'

'I need to get this out.'

She squeezed the hard little lump, working the tip up through the cut, wincing and swearing as it emerged. Bobby was swearing as well, the same two words over and over, but she barely registered his presence, concentrating on holding onto the blood-slick nugget as it popped out of her calf.

'See.' She held it out to him but he wasn't looking at her hand.

'What the fuck are you doing to yourself?' He sat down on the edge of the bathtub and the expression on his face sobered her instantly, the sadness and disbelief. 'You're going to make it worse.'

'I'm only doing what the doctor would do,' she said.

'Your doctor wouldn't operate at three in the morning, drunk, in a bath with an unsterilised razor blade.'

'I've had my tetanus.' The wound was still bleeding. 'Have you got some gauze or something?'

'Hold on.'

He went out and returned a minute later with a first-aid kit, made her dry-swallow two painkillers and climbed into the bath with her. He knelt by her feet as he silently cleaned the blood off with an antiseptic wipe. The sting of it made her wince but she tried to hide it, didn't want to make the situation any worse than it already was by showing how much pain she was in.

Wahlia wrapped sterile gauze around her calf and pinned it up, frowning when pink spots started to show through the pad.

'That's the best I can do. You might need a couple of stitches.'

'It'll be fine,' Ferreira said, feeling very naked, sitting there in her knickers and shirt. Naked and ridiculous because their evening had started normally and ended like this. 'Thanks, Bobby. And sorry, I shouldn't have done this here.'

'You shouldn't be doing it at all.' He pushed his fingers back through his hair, leaving a smear of blood glistening in the black. 'How often are you cutting yourself?'

She glared at him, couldn't believe he thought she going through some stupid, self-harming phase like a depressed teenager. Did he think she was that weak?

'I'm not "cutting" for fun. I've got shrapnel in my legs. You know that. Look.' She straightened her right leg and showed him the dozens of scars, watching him for revulsion that didn't come and pity he wasn't quick enough to smother. 'It migrates to the surface and has to be cut out. Should I have done it myself? Probably not. Was I drunk enough to think it was a good idea? Totally.'

'And that's all it is?'

'Give me your hand.'

Reluctantly he held out his cupped palm and she dropped the piece of creamy shrapnel into it. Five minutes ago she had only suspected what it was but as it slipped out of her leg she knew why the shape felt so familiar.

'Now do you understand?'

It only took Bobby a couple of seconds to realise that what he held in his hand, bloodied and broken as if it had only just been knocked out, was a sharp sliver of one of Christian Palmer's teeth.

WEDNESDAY

39

Zigic wasn't the kind of person who believed in the power of positive thinking, all that New Age claptrap about visualising your wants into reality, but as he stood in front of the murder board, a dozen faces looking back at him, he imagined the day's work closing successfully; a solid name in the Suspects column, an in-situ photograph of the actual knife that killed Dawn Prentice, something to show for what they were all going to spend the next twelve hours doing.

Six a.m now. The sky lightening but the sun not yet properly risen and there was an autumnal chill in the air, mist hanging above the parkway when he glanced through the window, and all the lights switched on to chase away the gloom. They revealed just how unprepared his team were, dark smudges under eyes, sleep-creased faces and hastily pulled-on clothes. Except for Parr, who was hyper-alert and sharply dressed, visibly straining at the leash.

Ferreira and Wahlia looked the worst of the bunch. They'd arrived together carrying large takeaway coffees, Mel still wearing the day before's outfit, her hair pulled back into a tight, high ponytail and her face scrubbed clean, no make-up to hide the effects of last night's drinking. She was walking gingerly too and the obvious assumption was there to be made but he doubted it was the right one. Wahlia kept throwing her concerned looks that she studiously ignored, staring into space with an unlit cigarette between her fingers.

Was she up to directing a search of the village?

He was doubtful about that too but he had a plan of action prepared already and certain bodies allotted to certain tasks and he was just going to have to trust her to pull it together within the next half-hour. Better she was out in the field clearing her head than dealing with any of the remaining men they needed to question.

'Okay, people.' He clapped his hands together, did a fast sweep of the room, making sure he had everyone's attention. 'We've got a lot to do today and time is of the essence. Parr, Wheatley, Murray –'

Three heads nodded at him.

'We pick up from where we left off. Dawn's boyfriends are still the main focus for us and I want to clear this up by end of play one way or another. We've got –' he glanced at the files lined up on the desk nearby – 'sixteen men still to question, so uniform teams out for collection and turn them round fast once you've got them here.'

Colleen Murray stuck her hand up. 'What about Arnold Fletcher? Are we considering him a viable suspect?'

Zigic gestured at the board, Fletcher's name up there but not struck through. 'Blood deposits have been found in his car but we're waiting for more details from forensics before questioning him again. So, yes. Same goes for Warren Prentice and Benjamin Lange. All three have motives and none managed to give us satisfactory alibis, but we have limited lines of attack on Prentice and Lange until we find that murder weapon.' He pointed at the cluster of freshly drafted uniforms. 'Which is where you lot come in.'

As if on cue Kate Jenkins entered the office, dressed in loose clothes and sturdy boots, ready to hit the ground.

'Kate, do you want to take over from here?'

He stepped aside and the focus of the group shifted from the murder board to the map of Elton she'd already marked up; a black dot for the crime scene and a green one for the kennels, the primary search area marked out with a thick red line. They would be in people's front gardens, checking their bins and lifting grilles over the drains, ferreting out any hidey-holes big enough to secrete a six-inch kitchen knife in. A second, smaller team would be deployed to the grass track between Dawn's and the kennels, an unlikely dump site for any killer except Warren, but Zigic wanted it checked while they had the resources. A third group were tasked to concentrate on the locus itself, make another sweep of the gardens and the surrounding scrub, dredge the small pond two fields away they hadn't spotted on the first pass.

It was a mistake Jenkins had highlighted, cursing herself for missing it, knowing how much damage an extra couple of days' submersion in filthy water could do. DNA traces washed away, fingerprints corrupted.

A small, negative voice in Zigic's head said, so what? Nobody would be stupid enough to dump a weapon without wiping it clean first. Especially not a murderer who had gone so far as to clean the banister they'd touched and rub their footprints off the carpet.

Jenkins finished her briefing and he thanked her as she walked away, seeing a sense of anticipation begin to stir through the room, feet shuffling, low murmurs of conversation, a sign that it was time to kick them loose.

'Alright then, let's get to it.'

Half the uniforms cleared out immediately, following Ferreira and Jenkins. The rest remained, divided into pairs centred on three different desks as they were briefed a second time by his remaining DCs, who all looked perfectly controlled and focused as they managed the assigned lists of Dawn's lovers. It was the easiest job really and Zigic wouldn't have minded spending a couple of hours doing that this morning, for the sense of movement if nothing else.

Instead he poured a coffee and took it into his office to catch up on the seemingly endless flow of paperwork that passed across his desk, always behind schedule, always urgent, because he didn't want to see himself as some middle manager – even though he knew he was – and grabbed any excuse to leave it in favour of proper policing.

He was saved by an email from the lab. Opened it to find that the deposits in Fletcher's car didn't match Dawn's blood group.

Zigic swore sharply. Maybe he hadn't pegged Fletcher as a prime suspect but it was another possibility swept off the table, another maddening dead end they'd run straight into. Then again the blood had very likely come from him, being the same type and a rare one at that, and until they could establish why he'd been bleeding there were questions for Fletcher to answer still. Ones best asked direct.

Ten minutes later Zigic was sitting at the table in Interview Room 2, listening to Fletcher complain about the quality of breakfast they served in the station.

'Milk was on the turn,' he said. 'But the beds are more comfortable than in my day. I'll give you that.'

He looked as if he'd slept badly despite the bravado, thinning grey hair mussed up and dark rings around his deep-set eyes, and Zigic had noticed a slight hunch in his posture when he walked in.

'Before we start, I must advise you that you have the right to request a solicitor at any point.'

'And I'll tell you what I told you before, I've not done owt and I don't need one.'

Zigic nodded. 'Alright. Why don't you tell me how your car came to have blood all over the steering wheel and the gearstick?'

Fletcher scratched the dry skin at the side of his mouth. 'I had a nosebleed. Couple of weeks back. Bad one. I got these polyps up my nose.'

'It's a lot of blood for a nosebleed.'

'You're telling me.'

'Why haven't you had them treated?'

Fletcher smirked. 'You been to the doctor's lately? Three-month wait for a consultation and they keep pushing that back. Non-emergency, isn't it? So I get to bleed like a tap every time I sneeze. Bloody David Cameron and his PFI cronies.'

'You sneezed? That's your story for how the blood got all over the inside of your car?'

'It's what happened.'

Zigic leaned back in his chair. 'And how did it get on the underside of the console?'

Fletcher turned a beady eye on him. 'Must have been on my hands.'

'Must have? No, Mr Fletcher, if you'd sneezed we'd see the splatter. But we don't. We see smears and handprints and tracks.'

'I had it valeted,' Fletcher said. 'So don't give me that bollocks.'

'Blood is far more persistent than you'd imagine. Especially in those hard-to-reach spots.'

For a moment Fletcher looked scared, but he was an old hand at interrogation and he quickly cocked his head, seeing an out.

'Doesn't matter how my blood got there. It's *mine*.' His shoulders squared. 'Your bosses might be steering us into a police state but we're not quite there yet and the last I checked it's not illegal to bleed.'

'No, it's not illegal,' Zigic conceded. 'But when a murder suspect shows signs of serious injury we have to consider whether that injury was inflicted by their victim.'

Fletcher scowled at him.

'Did Dawn put up a fight?'

'I didn't touch her.'

Zigic waited for more but Fletcher knew better than to run off at the mouth at a point like this. So he waited too and they stared each other out for a few seconds, Zigic thinking about whether he could divert some of the search team to Fletcher's house, get in there before they'd be forced to release him tomorrow. The seconds drew on into minutes and Zigic realised with a prick of irritation that the man wouldn't give up anything easily. He'd have to work for whatever information there was to be had.

'Let's go through this again,' he said. 'From the start. Last Thursday, tell me your movements.'

Fletcher started to speak, resenting every breath he was using, each word spat out like a bad taste, and Zigic listened, waiting for him to make a slip-up, contradict something he'd said previously, get the sequence of events wrong. Anything to give him an opening.

More unglamorous police work but sometimes it was the only way: grind a suspect down with repetition, bore them into betraying themselves or revealing something new.

And eventually Fletcher did.

'Hold on,' Zigic said. 'You saw a kid coming out of Dawn's house? What kid? What was he doing there?'

'I dunno. Supposed he was one of Holly's friends. He went down the side and came back. Ran off over the road.' Fletcher's hand swept through the air. 'Near got himself knocked over.'

'What did he look like?'

'Just some kid. 'Bout ten or eleven.'

'Why didn't you mention him before?'

Fletcher shrugged. 'Didn't think it was important. He weren't there two minutes.'

Zigic paused the interview to go up to his office, returned with the photograph of Nathan, smiling over his birthday cake.

'Is this the boy?'

'Yeah, that's him.' He handed the photo back. 'We done?'

'For now.'

'I can go, then?'

'I didn't say that.'

40

Wahlia was on his feet when Zigic returned to the office, tapping a pen against his palm, that look he got when something needed dealing with and he couldn't find anyone to do it.

'We've got a problem,' he said. 'I've been checking out the nine-nine-nine calls across the weekend after the murder.'

'Hasn't that been done already?' Zigic asked.

'First pass, yeah.' Wahlia tugged at the gold stud in his left ear. 'Up to the Friday morning, anything associated with the address, but I wanted to be thorough. Saturday evening we've got a call placed from the phone box on the village green at eighteen forty-seven, requesting assistance. The caller reports an incident.'

Zigic swore. 'Details?'

Wahlia turned the screen towards him and Zigic read the highlighted section:

Operator – '*What's your emergency?*'
Caller – '*I need the police. She's hurt.*'
Operator – '*Who's hurt?*'
Caller – '*You have to hurry.*'

The operator repeated the question, didn't get a reply, told the caller they needed more details and was given the address.

After that nothing. The operator left talking to someone who'd rung off, wanting to know who was hurt, was it serious.

'This is two days after the murder,' Zigic said, thinking aloud. 'So we're looking at somebody stumbling across the scene?'

'Who doesn't want to identify themself.' Wahlia took a mouthful of Red Bull from the can on his desk. 'Which means we've got a witness who doesn't want to come forward for some reason.'

'Arnold Fletcher just told me he saw Nathan there on Saturday afternoon.'

Wahlia's eyebrows lifted in surprise. 'That's not in his previous statement.'

'Yeah, I was sceptical but looking at this . . . maybe he's telling the truth. It would make sense – Nathan sees what's happened, freaks out, runs.'

'It's an overreaction, isn't it? What would you have done at that age? I'd have gone home and cried to my mum about it.'

Nathan wasn't Bobby, though. And Julia wasn't Mrs Wahlia.

'There's another possibility,' Zigic said. 'Maybe whoever killed Dawn expected the alarm to be raised on Friday or Saturday when the nurse arrived but when they saw no movement at the house they realised they'd have to do it themselves.'

'Because of Holly?'

'Yeah. Makes sense if it's Fletcher. He doesn't want Holly to die so he calls the police to find her and save her.'

Zigic pictured Arnold Fletcher in the old red phone box on the village green, making the call, saying the minimum, knowing Holly had spent the last two days alone in bed with the smell of her mother's corpse rising through the house, scared and alone and already dying herself. Would he have waited to see the police car arrive? Wouldn't he have needed to see it and know she was going to be okay?

'They must have dispatched a car,' Zigic said.

'Yeah. Looks like they didn't see anything amiss, though.'

'Find out who the responders were and get them up here, right now.'

Zigic stalked away into his office, feeling a ball of rage swelling in his chest, told himself to hold it down. He paced the narrow channel between his desk and the wall, thinking of that patrol car pulling up outside the house on Saturday evening, Holly still alive upstairs, fading fast, the toxins backing up into her bloodstream.

Did they knock? Did she hear them and think she was saved?

She was probably in a coma already, he realised, wouldn't even have known she'd been abandoned, failed again, by people whose sole concern should have been investigating what was happening inside that house.

A couple of minutes later new voices entered the office and he went out to find PCs Jackson and Cooper standing by the door, unwilling to come in any further. Jackson was the older of the two, pushing retirement, old enough to know better, and his seniority put him in the firing line. His posture said he realised that, spine ramrod straight, hands going into the small of his back as Zigic approached.

'Saturday evening,' Zigic said. 'Elton. You two geniuses left a dead woman and a dying child in a house. How the hell did you manage that?'

Cooper inched back a few steps. Jackson swallowed, forced himself to hold Zigic's stare.

'We didn't see any sign of occupation.'

'Her car was on the drive.'

Jackson's Adam's apple bobbed again. 'We knocked on the front door, sir. There was no answer.'

'Because Dawn Prentice was dead inside,' Zigic shouted. 'You get a call reporting an injured woman and you didn't think she might not be a position to answer?'

'We went around back,' Jackson said, voice wavering as if it could be a lie. 'The blinds were down in the kitchen window. There was nothing to see. No signs of disturbance. What were we supposed to do, kick the door in?'

'You didn't need to. The back door was unlocked.'

Cooper's head snapped around, eyes wide, watching Jackson.

One of them would have gone down the side of the garage, to the back of the house, the other would have stayed out front, knocked and waited, looked through the letter box, through the window into the living room. Done that rather than walk a few yards past the skip and check the door cut into the new extension the way he should.

Jackson, he guessed. With age came the privilege of not having to dirty your boots on unpaved ground or risk snagging your arms on overgrown hedges.

'What happened?' Zigic asked. 'You had it down as "just a domestic"? Nothing you needed to take seriously.'

'Sir, with all due –'

'Don't you fucking dare.' Zigic jabbed a finger at him. 'Go over there. Look at the board.'

Reluctantly the pair of them crossed the office to the murder board, a fast glance passing between them.

'Look at her,' Zigic said. 'Holly Prentice. Sixteen years old. That girl was lying in her bed dying and you two walked away, got in your car and left her. If you'd done your job right she'd still be alive now.'

Cooper's head dropped, eyes on his highly polished boots. Next to him Jackson was studying the spread of information tacked up there, probably deciding this dressing-down was buck passing from a DI whose case was hitting the skids. Nothing he hadn't been through before.

Zigic felt the anger thrumming in his chest. Knew Jackson was just waiting for him to finish saying his piece and excuse them. Maybe he truly believed they'd done enough to be spared their share of blame. Maybe he'd manage to sleep soundly tonight without Holly Prentice invading his dreams.

Zigic wanted to grab Jackson by the back of the head and slam his face into the board. Force that photograph into his brain, make sure he never forgot what Holly looked like.

'This bloke,' Jackson said, tapping the board. 'He ran past the house as we were leaving.'

Warren Prentice.

Did he really trust the observational skills of a man so inept he couldn't even be relied upon to turn a door handle?

'That's him, isn't it, Wayne?'

Cooper nodded, croaked out his agreement.

Zigic swallowed the rest of the bollocking he'd been preparing to see them off with.

'You say he was running past the house. Running like exercising or running like getting the hell away from something?'

Jackson considered it. 'Coudn't say. He was wearing trainers and shorts, though.'

'What direction was he going in?'

'Out of the village, towards Alwalton.'

Away from his house, Zigic thought, meaning perhaps he was intending to go to Dawn's and the sight of a police car kept him moving, forced him to act like any other jogger out on a perfectly innocent evening run.

'Why did you notice him?'

Jackson shrugged. 'Didn't like the look of him much. The beard and that.'

Zigic pushed them for more but it was all they had and he dismissed the pair of them back to their duties. He'd have to take it up with their superior, but that could wait.

Warren Prentice just happened to be running past the house after the 999 call was made?

No, he didn't buy the coincidence.

'We've got the recording,' Wahlia said, straightening in his chair, hand going to the mouse. 'Okay, here we go.'

Zigic braced his hand against the desk, waiting, sure he was going to hear Warren, maybe disguising his voice, although he felt confident he'd spent enough time interviewing the man to see through any attempt at misdirection.

A small box appeared on screen, the sound file starting automatically, a woman's voice, calm and even, the standardised first response and then a Liverpudlian accent:

'I need the police. She's hurt.'

'Who's hurt?'

'You have to hurry.' Voice cracking.

The woman pressed him for more details and the sound of breathing filled the long pause before she was answered, gasping breaths and a foot scuffing the ground. Seconds of it, five, six and Zigic saw Nathan standing in the phone box, eyes wide, clutching the receiver. Was it a stunned silence or a moment of realisation? He'd put himself on record, he'd created a trail that led from Dawn's murder back to him and there was no undoing it.

He blurted out the address and put the phone down.

Wahlia swore. 'We've got a new suspect then.'

'A witness at least,' Zigic said, heading into his office to retrieve the photograph propped up on his desk. 'Getting hold of him's going to be the problem.'

He stuck Nathan's photo to the board and took out his mobile, scrolled down to Rachel's number, looking at the boy's smiling face as he waited for her to answer.

41

The first hour of the search went smoothly enough, no traffic to speak of, only a few early-morning runners and dog walkers out in Elton to witness the figures in white plastic bodysuits combing Dawn Prentice's garden and the ragged line of uniforms stretched out along the footpath which looped around the northern edge of the village, swiping at the undergrowth, occasionally stooping when they saw some silvery glint which might have been the handle of a stainless-steel kitchen knife but so far wasn't.

By half past seven the commuters were stirring, emerging from their houses suited and fully caffeinated, only to find that the lane from the main road down to the kennels was sealed off and they couldn't get out of their driveways to make the ten-minute journey to the train station.

Most people were understanding, irritated but accepting of the necessity when a murderer was on the loose in their safe little village.

Things got dicey again when the school run kicked in, leading to a hastily convened meeting near the village shop and some creative car pooling. Ferreira apologised to them too, noticing that Sally and Benjamin Lange hadn't appeared; he wouldn't be going in today, though, not with what he had hanging over his head.

A short while later it was the primary-school crowd, but they were within walking distance and didn't prove as problematic. The odd, ever-so polite enquiry into what was going on, some expressions of regret and sympathy, and an ear-splitting scream when a man in a bodysuit suddenly emerged from a narrow stone cut, startling a small girl in an all-terrain buggy.

After that the village retreated into a quiet spell again and the search team worked on in peace, steadily progressing up the slight rise of Church Lane from the kennels, heading towards the main road. Slow but thorough, eerily quiet as they moved, the whole scene slightly surreal, even to Ferreira who'd done this countless times before. Maybe it was the lack of civilians, combined with the closed blinds and empty front gardens. It felt as if a bigger tragedy had happened, something which had wiped out everyone but them.

Watching them work she felt surplus to requirements, so she moved between the sites, trying to drive out the last dregs of her hangover and walk off the stinging pain in her calf that was worse this morning than it had been last night. It didn't bother her as much now, though. It was a good pain, bright and clean, her body healing finally.

Still, some ibuprofen wouldn't go amiss.

The village shop was open but doing very little business, thanks to its position inside the search perimeter. If the owner was annoyed he didn't show it. He made her for a copper right away, asked if there were any developments, if he should be worried for his family's safety. She gave him the standard replies, a politer version of 'no comment' and 'no need', then asked her own questions.

The man knew Dawn, liked her, kept a particular brand of boxed pink wine in stock just for her. He hadn't seen Holly since the accident, remembered her coming in for sweets when she was still at the village primary.

'Lovely young girl, very clever.'

But he didn't know anything useful.

Her mobile rang as she walked out, down the concave stone steps.

'Mel, I need you to go to Julia Campbell's house.' There was excitement in Zigic's voice, more energy than he'd mustered at the morning briefing. 'We've got a nine-nine-nine call from the Saturday night, someone reported an incident at Dawn's.'

'What?' Ferreira stopped dead; she knew they'd been hiding something. 'Was it Julia?'

'No, it's almost certainly Nathan who made the call. It's definitely a boy rather than a man. Liverpudlian accent. And it ties in with when he ran off.'

'Then we need to bring him in.'

'First we need to positively identify his voice,' Zigic said. 'And Julia's our best bet.'

'What about Rachel?'

'She isn't picking up. Unsurprisingly.' He was running up the stairwell, footfalls echoing against the glass-block walls. 'If we can ID Nathan on the call she'll have to cooperate.'

'Okay, send me it over.'

'It should be in your inbox,' he said. 'Go gentle, Mel. You'll get more out of her.'

He ended the call and she stood for a moment, looking at the screen, wondering why he felt the need to give her direction like that. Would he have done it a year ago? Didn't he trust her to handle someone as uncomplicated as Julia Campbell?

On the way down the lane she listened to the recording, heard a boy's wavering voice, choked with emotion, barely able to form the few words he said.

Did he sound guilty? Or just scared?

The sun was shining on the front of Julia Campbell's house, showing up the dirt on the small mullioned windows and the hint of scorching on the flowers in their wooden planters. A wasp was buzzing around them and it darted at her as she knocked on the door. She swatted it away, stepping back as it went in for another attack, and she saw Julia's face retreat quickly from an upstairs window as she moved.

She knocked again, the wasp bored with her now, and tried to remember which bedroom that was. Nathan's she thought, the cold blue walls and the single bed.

Julia opened the door, holding a defensive hand over the curve of her stomach. She looked better today, skin glowing, a slick of red lipstick brightening her face, all traces of worry wiped away now that Nathan was safe.

'What do you want?'

Ferreira held her phone up, hit Play on the recording and watched Julia's reaction as Nathan's voice said:

'She's hurt.'

Her hand went to her mouth and stayed there as he gave the operator Dawn's address, eyes on the phone which Ferreira had angled away from her, not wanting her to see any of the information attached to the sound file.

When the clip finished playing Julia turned back into the house and Ferreira followed her through the hallway and the kitchen, where something sweet and chocolatey was baking in the oven, through another door that stood open, into what looked like a converted garage, full of painted furniture and chairs that needed throwing out. It smelled fusty and slightly mouldy, with a chemical undertone from the bottles and tins lined up on sturdy pine shelves. The late-summer sun left the room untouched and Julia had lit a wood burner to raise the temperature.

At least, Ferreira hoped that was why it was lit.

Julia went to a long workbench set under a window that looked out across the back garden, her seat placed in front of a sewing machine where two pieces of gingham fabric had been left mid-seam, the needle pinning them in place. She turned something on the side of the machine and the needle lifted, allowing her to remove the fabric. She held it on her lap, staring out of the window.

Ferreira moved closer, saw that her eyes were damp.

Julia's initial reaction was as good as an admission but Ferreira needed to hear the words.

She bit down on the urge to prompt her and waited out the silence, hearing the gentle tick of the logs in the burner and the hum of the oven in the next room, watching the passing seconds and minutes wearing down Julia's resolve more effectively than anything she would say.

'It doesn't mean he killed her,' she said.

Ferreira didn't reply.

'You don't know Nathan's history. Seeing her like that . . . all he did was call for help. How can you think that makes him a murderer? He did what any decent person would have done.' She tugged at the stiff cotton fabric. 'He's a good boy.'

She lapsed into silence again and Ferreira went back into the kitchen, watched her through the open door as she dialled Zigic's number; Julia didn't move, barely seemed to be breathing.

He answered quickly.

'Is it him?'

'Yes.'

'She said that?'

'Yes.' Julia cocked her head slightly, not quite as deep in thought as she appeared and Ferreira decided she'd been guarded long enough. 'Can you send a warrant over? We need to toss this place.'

42

'Okay, this is what's going to happen.' Riggott took a puff of his e-cigarette. 'She'll bring the boy in but she'll only let him talk to you. No one else can be in there, not even Mel. And you can't hold a formal interview. No camera, no recording. Best thing would be to use the family suite. It's out of the way, you can contain him there.'

'That's unacceptable,' Zigic said. 'We need his statement on the record, you know that. If he's just a witness we're going to need whatever he tells us to be handed over to the CPS.'

'Reckon you're getting a touch ahead of yourself there, Ziggy. We don't know what he knows.'

Zigic paced a few steps, trying to walk away the frustration at Riggott's attitude, the sensation that this was moving out of his control even further, just at the point when the case seemed to be cracking finally.

'He was at the murder scene. For all we know he might actually be the killer.'

Riggott made a tamping gesture with his hand. 'One step at a time.'

'What? You'd stand for this if you were me?'

'I don't think you realise what's going on here.'

'We're being fucked about, that's what's happening.' Zigic felt a knot of stress tighten across the back of his neck. He'd spoken to Rachel already, got her usual attitude. Riggott was supposed to fix it, speak to her boss, make clear how unreasonable they were being in refusing to turn Nathan over for questioning.

Instead he'd let himself get fobbed off.

He was going soft, too many hours in this swanky office filling out forms and liaising with other agencies, too many good lunches and fact-finding missions. The old Riggott, the raging gobshite Zigic had come up under, wouldn't have accepted these ridiculous terms and he didn't see why he should either.

'What happens if he confesses?'

Riggott shifted his weight in the soft leather chair and for once in his life didn't seem to have an answer.

'You must have thought about it. Can I charge him?' Zigic asked. 'If Rachel tries to intervene – say she tries to take him out of the station – can I stop her?'

'Look, I don't like this fucking situation any more than you do, but I'm not calling the shots here.' The colour had risen in Riggott's face. 'You can accept it or you can try and pursue this case without the kid, because them's your options.'

'This isn't going to end easy, not if we keep letting them push us around.'

'I've told your woman she can have what she wants,' Riggott said. 'Now, if you're not prepared to play ball that's it. She won't let anyone else talk to the boy. So you lose your case and whoever I put on it loses a vital witness.'

'Fine then.'

'You bet your bollocks it's fine then.'

An hour later he got a call from reception and went down to find Rachel standing with her arm around a slightly built boy in baggy shorts and a sweatshirt too warm for the weather, his hood up, hiding his face. Her hand was on the side of his head, the posture forced and awkward looking until Zigic realised she was keeping him turned away from the desk sergeant and the CCTV camera above him.

'Thanks for coming,' Zigic said coldly.

'Let's make this quick.'

He led them upstairs, taking the stairwell, past CID and Hate Crimes, up to the Domestic Violence unit with its well-insulated walls and the soft carpets that swallowed up their footsteps. There were three lounges, each almost perfectly soundproof, with heavy doors that couldn't be slammed and curtained observation windows.

Two were in use but you couldn't tell from the hallway. The third one had been kept empty for him. Zigic gestured towards it and Rachel ushered Nathan inside, told him they'd just be a minute before closing the door again.

'You know the deal,' Rachel said.

'I just want him to tell me what he saw,' Zigic said, ignoring her attitude because he had to, even though it was already grating on him. 'Surely you don't have a problem with that?'

'I'm happy to help you however I can.'

She gave him a thin-lipped smile and he followed her into the lounge, swallowing the annoyance her sarcastic tone had provoked in him.

The room was cramped and overlit, a too-bright bulb burning through a paper shade, showing up every smudge on the pale green walls, the dinginess of the carpet and well-worn upholstery. A two-seater sofa was pushed against one wall, an armchair opposite it, separated by a low table with a box of tissues on it.

'Nathan, this is the man I told you about.'

He looked up at Zigic, pale face, watchful eyes. Just a child.

Seeing him like that Zigic wondered how he'd ever imagined he could be capable of murdering Dawn. He was tiny, physically weak and completely passive. Boys of eleven could and did kill, but he didn't think this one had it in him.

'Hi Nathan, I'm Dushan.'

He nodded slightly and glanced at Rachel, who slipped the hood off his head as she sat down next to him on the sofa. Zigic took the chair, perched on the edge, elbows on his knees.

'You don't need to be scared,' she said. 'You're perfectly safe here. Dushan is just going to ask you some questions.'

'About Dawn?' he asked, accent not as thick as it had sounded on the 999 call.

'That's right. You tried to help her, didn't you?'

Nathan glanced at Rachel again, as if he needed her approval before answering, and Zigic though of all the children who'd been in this room before him, reluctant to tell what they'd seen, not entirely understanding the significance or fearing the repercussions, looking to their mothers or fathers or the social workers who were often their only comfort for some cue of how to behave.

'You called nine-nine-nine,' Zigic said, drawing his attention again. 'You said she was hurt.'

'Yeah.' Nathan shivered despite the warmth of the room.

'Did you see her?'

'Yeah.'

'You went inside the house, is that right?'

Nathan nodded, queasy looking, and Zigic imagined this child walking into the kitchen of Dawn's house, a scene which had shocked him, hardened detective that he was. All of that blood, the ferocity of the attack on her openly displayed.

'Was the door open when you got there?'

'It were unlocked.'

'Was that usual?'

He shook his head.

'How often did you go around there?'

A shrug. 'Sometimes. In the day and that, I went round with Julia.'

'To see Holly?'

'Yeah.'

'Were you friends?'

'She were nice. We watched stuff on YouTube. Music and stuff.' He frowned, a deep trench appearing between his eyebrows, suggesting more stress and worry than any eleven-year-old should have experienced. 'She's dead, isn't she?'

'I'm afraid so,' Zigic said. 'Maybe you can help us catch whoever killed her, though. They shouldn't be able to get away with it.'

Nathan looked at Rachel again and she placed her hand on his back, gave him a smile that might have been genuine, an encouraging nod of the head.

'I want to help,' he said.

'Can you tell me what you saw? When you went inside the house – as much as you can remember.'

'Dawn were dead. She were on the floor and there were all this blood.' His eyes darted across the table as if he was seeing it all over again. 'She were looking at me.'

Rachel rubbed his back. 'It's okay, Nathan, you're doing really well.'

'I wanted to go and see Holly,' he said, tears welling. 'I couldn't – I – I didn't wanna walk over Dawn and I couldn't get to Holly if I didn't walk over her.'

He started to cry, big sobs, and Rachel drew him close to her, watching Zigic over his head, giving him a 'happy now?' look. The expression of an angry mother protecting her distraught child. She turned away, whispered something in Nathan's ear that only seemed to upset him more.

'It's my fault,' Nathan said, words muffled against her shoulder.

Rachel's soothing hand gripped his arm. 'No, it wasn't.'

'It was!'

'Nathan, we've been through this.'

'But—'

'No.'

'What did you do?' Zigic asked, trying to catch his eye. 'Nathan, look at me, what did you do to Dawn?'

'He were looking for me,' Nathan said. 'It's my fault he were there. He found me.'

'Who?'

'He's killed everyone.'

Rachel cupped his face in her hands. 'Nobody knew you were there, Nathan. How many times do I have to tell you that? It wasn't about you. You're safe. Okay? I said I'd keep you safe, didn't I?'

'I saw him.' Nathan's hands closed around the sofa cushion's frayed edge, nervous fingers digging in, his knuckles going white.

'Who did you see?' Zigic asked.

'The man. He were there.'

Zigic inched forwards on the chair. 'What man?'

'In the car,' Rachel said. 'I told you already.'

'Is that right, Nathan?'

His cheeks were shining wet under the forensic light boiling through the lampshade. 'In the red car.'

Arnold Fletcher. He'd admitted to being there, placed Nathan there too. But why go back to the house if he'd murdered Dawn two days earlier? Unless it was to check whether Holly had been found, look for the telltale police tape strung over the doors. He'd want to know she was safe.

Zigic took out a photograph of Fletcher.

'Is this the man you saw?'

Nathan nodded.

'He wasn't looking for you. We know who he is.'

'See,' Rachel said. 'It's not your fault.'

It took her a couple of minutes longer to calm him down and Zigic was surprised how gentle she was with him, a different woman from the one he'd met at the old knothole on the side of London Road. Eventually she coaxed him round, handed him some tissues to dry his eyes.

'Did you take a knife from Dawn's kitchen?' Zigic asked.

Nathan hunched over, feet hitting the bottom of the sofa as he drew away from the question. Zigic fought the urge to move forward, into his personal space, reminding himself that he had to tread carefully with the boy. This could be it, though, the murder weapon they'd been searching for. The vital missing link.

'Answer Dushan,' Rachel said, her voice hardening for the first time since they'd entered the room.

'I were scared.' Nathan's freckled hands kneaded at the edge of the sofa cushion again. 'I thought the man were gonna get me. I needed it.'

'Where did you take the knife from?' Zigic asked, willing him to look up from the worn chenille fabric he was fretting at. 'Nathan, this is very important. The knife you took, where was it when you picked it up?'

'On the table.'

'And where is it now?'

'I lost it.'

Zigic's hands clenched into fists between his knees. The murder weapon; gone, lost, along with all the forensic evidence laid on it. He stood up, Rachel's eyes following him and he saw fear in them. Until now Zigic had believed Nathan to be an important witness, an unfortunate stumbling across the scene, but not a credible suspect. This changed everything and she knew that the balance had shifted.

He started for the door.

'Wait,' Rachel said, urgency in her voice. 'Nathan, was there blood on the knife?'

'No.' He inched away from her. 'No, it was on the table.'

The second knife, missing from the scene, the one they thought Dawn might have thrown out for some reason, accidentally or on purpose. Could it be that one he'd taken? A brief hope stirred in Zigic again.

'What did this knife look like?' he asked.

'It were the same—' Nathan gulped. 'It looked like the one in Dawn's chest.'

Zigic blinked at him, processing this new information. One knife taken by Nathan, one remaining at the scene.

'The knife was still there when you saw her?'

He nodded and started crying again.

The killer went back to retrieve it.

Some time between Nathan seeing it on the Saturday afternoon and the emergency services going in during the early hours of Sunday morning the killer returned and took the murder weapon.

43

The search warrant arrived within the hour, along with two uniforms who Ferreira dispatched to the first floor of the cottage, telling them to start in the small blue bedroom. Jenkins headed straight for a corroded-metal incinerator in the far corner of the garden while her assistant went out to check the ground around an apple tree where Ferreira had spotted a heavy coating of ash. She'd nipped out for a quick smoke and lingered on the patio area to keep an eye on Julia through the workroom window, noticed it then and thought it seemed odd.

A third person made a beeline for the garden shed, a rickety structure lilting slightly, but freshly painted and bearing a garland of fairy lights.

Was there nothing this woman didn't feel the need to prettify?

Julia had barely stirred, just moved from the uncomfortable wooden stool to a half-rotten-looking armchair, and she made no effort to protest against the search, as most householders would. She seemed to accept it as an inevitability, too middle class to challenge a police officer or so certain they wouldn't find anything that she was content to wait it out and demand an apology when they walked out empty-handed.

That wouldn't be happening, Ferreira thought.

Jenkins's assistant was kneeling down sifting through the ash, face covered as it blew back up at him.

'Can you tell what it was?' Ferreira asked.

'Not yet, we'll need to run some tests. There are small fragments of wood, though, so it might just be off a log fire.'

'In September?'

'Those old houses get cold easily,' he said. 'I grew up in a place like this. It was always freezing, even in summer. We had to wear our coats indoors during the winter.'

It hadn't felt cold in there to her, especially not the workshop where the wood burner was still chugging away, pumping thin smoke out into the clear blue sky.

She swore at herself, rushed back inside and searched the kitchen cupboards until she found a jug, filled it with cold water and went into the workshop.

'What are you doing?' Julia asked.

Ferreira opened the door of the wood burner and threw the water onto the surging flames. They died down in a fizz and a puff of ash she managed to mostly escape, only the slightest dusting hitting her knees, speckling the grey fabric.

Julia shook her head sadly. 'That wasn't necessary. We've got nothing to hide.'

'You might not have,' Ferreira said. 'But you're not the only person who lives in this house.' She nodded towards the kitchen, the burnt smell from there mingling with the smoke from the just-extinguished fire. 'I think your cake needs to come out, by the way.'

Slowly she rose from the chair, moving so awkwardly that Ferreira put a hand out to help. Julia ignored it and finally got to her feet, went through to the kitchen, shuffling in her fur-lined boots.

Ferreira turned her attention to the chair, slipped on a pair of latex gloves from her pocket and patted the mismatched seat cushion, checking for knife-shaped bulges, turned it over and patted it again before throwing it aside. She worked her hands down the inner crease of the chair, hating the smell of it, repulsed by the prickling sensation coming through the worn fabric. What the hell was this thing stuffed with? Around the back she found a long, narrow gash, and got her answer. Some kind of hair. She prodded around with her fingertips, nothing in there either.

There had to be some reason Julia was reluctant to abandon this room.

In the kitchen she was standing over the ruined chocolate cake, shoulders slumped, head hanging, so thoroughly defeated that Ferreira wasn't sure how much longer she'd manage to hold herself upright, clinging onto the worktop like that.

'Maybe you should sit down,' she said. 'Minimise the stress on your baby and all that.'

'As if you care,' Julia snapped.

'I appreciate what a difficult thing this is to go through.'

'Oh, you do, do you? How many times have you been subjected to this kind of – of – violation?'

'We have to follow the evidence, Mrs Campbell,' Ferreira said wearily, sick of being the bad guy when she was just doing her job.

'Nathan tried to help. Calling the police makes him less likely to be guilty if anything. But you refuse to see that.'

'He ran,' Ferreira said.

'He was scared.'

Julia gasped, doubled up, her hand going to her stomach. Ferreira took her by the shoulders and guided her over to the table, lowered her into a chair.

'Are you okay?'

'Leave me alone,' Julia said, through gritted teeth. Her face was flushed, perspiration rising on her forehead.

'You're not going into labour, are you?'

'Just get out.'

'Maybe you should call your husband,' Ferreira said, lifting the phone from its dock. 'This is a big thing to go through without support.'

The colour drained instantly from her cheeks. 'I don't need support, I just need you all to get out of my home.'

'It takes as long as it takes, Mrs Campbell.'

Ferreira's mobile started ringing and she went outside to answer, not wanting to talk to Zigic in front of Julia. The plastic-suited man under the apple tree was bagging up scoops of ash; Jenkins was at the far end of the garden, moving towards her colleague who waved her over from the doorway of the fairy-tale shed.

'Anything?' he asked.

'Not yet, but I'm pretty sure we're in the right place.' She glanced back in through the kitchen window, saw Julia stroking her stomach, talking to it. 'What about you?'

'Rachel brought Nathan in,' he said. 'The knife was still in Dawn's body when he went into the house on Saturday night – the killer must have gone back and removed it later on.'

Ferreira put her hand to her head. 'Hang on, are you sure he's telling the truth? Because that doesn't make any sense.'

'He could be lying, but why?'

'Because he killed her.'

'I don't think he's intelligent enough to come up with that kind of lie.'

'No, but Rachel is.'

'It wouldn't help her. It doesn't change anything. He's admitted to being at the scene. If she was trying to keep him out of trouble she'd have told him to lie about that.'

'You know what this means then,' Ferreira said. 'Whoever killed Dawn knew the alarm hadn't been raised and they knew Holly hadn't been found, but they still walked in there and took the knife. They didn't care what happened to her.'

'That rules Warren and Fletcher out but everyone else is still in play.'

'It's more than that, surely. Killing Dawn and walking away is one thing, going back into the house and doing nothing to help Holly, it's beyond callous. They must have been happy for her to die too. That's pure hatred.'

'I don't know,' Zigic said. 'All the men we spoke to had no idea Holly was even in the house.'

'That's what they said anyway.'

'It was the same story from all of them, meaning it's most likely true.'

A shout went up from the shed and she started across the lawn.

'Hold on, I think we've got something,' she said, holding the phone to her ear as she ran.

Jenkins was inside now, her assistant standing near the door, looking mildly perturbed at how she'd taken over. Behind her Ferreira could see a mess of gardening equipment, two lawnmowers, shelves stacked with paint tins and boxes of fertiliser and weedkiller, rags and plastic pots and lengths of knotted rope, everything thrown in at random, covered in cobwebs and dust.

'What is it?'

'Your knife,' she said, stepping back to let Ferreira see what they'd found.

The perforated silver handle and the six-inch blade, both covered in dried blood, scraps of flesh on the blade where it had been pulled out of Dawn's two-day-dead body. It was wrapped in grey fleece fabric, a strand of grosgrain with a toggle on the end lying across it.

'Gotcha,' Ferreira said, smiling slightly. She'd felt sure that something was amiss in this house from the moment Julia invited them inside, read lies behind her strained good manners and secrets in the locks on the bedroom windows, and now here they were holding concrete evidence that her instinct had been well founded. 'Is that a hoodie it's wrapped in?'

'Looks like it.' Jenkins squatted down and plucked at something with a pair of tweezers, dropped it into an evidence bag and brought it out into the sunlight, held it up for Ferreira to see: a single strand of brown hair with a complete root. 'We'll get DNA off that, no problem.'

Ferreira took it from her and squinted at it, turning the bag until she found the right angle. 'Is it just me or does it look ginger towards the root?'

Jenkins checked. 'No, it's not just you. That's a natural redhead's hair.'

'Are you hearing this?' she asked Zigic.

He swore. 'She's taking him out of the station.'

The phone went dead in Ferreira's hand.

44

Zigic bolted down the stairs, taking them two at a time, slammed through the stairwell and shouted for a couple of uniforms to follow him as he made for the reception area, the men at his heels. They burst out through the main doors, onto the brown brick steps.

'Rachel, wait!'

She glanced across her shoulder and pushed Nathan on towards her car. The remote locks popped. She told him to get in the car; a firm, low voice which sent him running.

'I need to talk to him,' Zigic said.

Nathan scrambled across the driver's seat and hit the locks, looked out with an expression of absolute terror as one of the pursuing constables skidded to a halt at the door.

Rachel kept walking. 'We're done.'

'No, we're not.'

'He's answered your questions.'

Zigic caught up to her, spun her around by her arm. 'I've got more questions for him. And you're going to bring him back inside so I can ask them on record.'

'Get your fucking hand off me,' she growled, and when he did she stepped closer, into his face. 'I didn't have to bring him here and I don't have to take him back in.'

'You seriously want this kicking up to your boss?' Zigic asked. 'You're obstructing a murder investigation.'

'My boss doesn't give a shit about your investigation.'

'We've found the knife,' Zigic said. 'At Julia's house, wrapped up in one of Nathan's hoodies. So you are going to let me question him.'

A flicker of panic punched through her resolve and she looked away at the uniforms, one standing by the car, the other at her back now, ready to grab her if she made a move.

'You're not going anywhere, Rachel. Neither of you are leaving this station until I'm satisfied that Nathan didn't murder Dawn Prentice.'

'He didn't,' she said. 'Jesus Christ, does he look like a murderer to you?'

'No, he looks like a witness but your attitude is making me wonder about that.' Zigic lowered his voice, aware that they were drawing attention from a couple of civilians waiting around on the steps. 'What are you scared of, Rachel? If he's innocent there's no problem, is there?'

Her jaw clenched.

'He saw more than he's saying. Just let me talk to him again, okay? I know he can help us.'

She shook her head and started towards the car but found herself blocked off by PC Hale, standing with his hands spread wide. It was supposed to be a calming gesture but she was angry beyond the soothing nuances of body language.

'Shift it.'

He held firm. Feet planted wide. A foot taller than her, six stone heavier.

Rachel turned back to Zigic.

'Tell him to move or I'll move him myself.'

'If you take another step he'll be forced to restrain you.'

'You'll regret trying it,' she said and Zigic wasn't sure which of them she was talking to.

She turned a slow circle, assessing the situation.

'If you want to force your way out of here you can. But I promise the first thing I'll do is release Nathan's photo to the press. He's going to be everywhere. Local news, national news, social media – his face will be seen across the whole country.'

Rachel stared at him, eyes blazing, small body stiff with rage and still he wasn't sure whether he had her, not until she thumbed the key fob, unlocking the car doors, and gestured for Nathan to get out.

'I hope you're happy being a DI,' she said. 'Because this is *it* for you.'

They went back inside, up through the grey-washed stairwell with its smell of sweat and aftershave and bitter coffee, up to the Domestic Violence unit's insulated silence. Rachel walked into the lounge with Nathan, who sat down obediently, didn't look at her, just stared into space, shivering slightly even though it was a steady seventy degrees in there.

Zigic called Riggott and debriefed him quickly, watching Rachel through the observation window as they talked, seeing her making an urgent phone call he guessed was to her own boss – trying to drum up some more weight to drop on their shoulders. From the expression on her face Zigic doubted she was getting it.

The lift doors opened and Riggott stepped off into the thickly carpeted hallway, hard faced and determined looking. He rapped on the observation window and waved Rachel out.

'Quite the little scene youse two made out there,' he said. 'Thought you were after keeping a low profile, DI Baxter.'

'If you trained your officers better it wouldn't be an issue.'

Riggott drew himself up to his full height. 'We've been very indulgent with you. Now would be a good time to stop fucking us about and explain exactly what your boy there's been on with.'

She shook her head. 'I can't.'

'We've got enough to charge him with murder,' Zigic said. He'd bluffed her once before, out at the knothole, but this time he felt more certain about the threat. 'We've found the murder weapon wrapped in his clothing, he's admitted being at the scene.'

'You'll be making a mistake.' Rachel looked between the two of them, lips pursed, the skin around her eyes tight. 'If you charge him and he goes into a young offenders' institution he's as good as dead. He isn't even safe here.'

'What on earth do you think's going to happen to him in a police station?' Zigic asked.

A man's voice came out of her phone, surprisingly high and light with a cultured Liverpudlian twang, and he realised she'd had it on speaker the whole time. 'Tell them, Baxter.'

'ACC Fallon?' Riggott asked.

'This information goes no further than you and DI Zigic,' Fallon said. 'Any breach will result in disciplinary action and criminal charges. Needless to say your careers will be over and I'll make sure neither of you see a penny of your pensions.'

He put the phone down at his end but Rachel held onto her mobile, pressed it to her bottom lip as she met Zigic's expectant stare. Part of her still didn't want to talk, not after so long, not after all the evasions and lies, but her boss had given the order.

'Come on, Baxter,' Riggott said, saccharine sweet. 'You're among friends now.'

She steeled herself. 'Nathan's a protected witness.'

'A witness to what?' Zigic asked.

'In May this year his mother was murdered by her boyfriend. Beaten to death with a hammer in her living room. Nathan saw everything, so did his brother Tyler.'

That explained a lot, Zigic thought. The boy's reticence and twitchiness, the sense of emptiness in his dark green eyes when he talked about seeing Dawn's body.

'The boyfriend is Sean McCarthy.' Rachel said it as if it was significant but the name meant nothing to Zigic. 'Okay. He's the cousin of Cain McCarthy, drug dealer, gun runner. Merseyside's gangster number three by our reckoning. We've been after the family for a long time.' She frowned but it seemed forced. 'Sadly for the boys their mother's murder provided us with leverage to bring Sean over.'

'This bloke isn't going to sell out his entire family to avoid a short stretch,' Riggott said incredulously. 'What's he looking at for murdering his girlfriend? Ten years, five served. Any hard man worth his salt can do that.'

'Ordinarily, yes.' She smiled with genuine pleasure. 'But our Sean is looking at a five-to-ten-year stretch in a prison controlled by a rival family. The McCarthys are up-and-comers and they're smart. Their boys don't get caught. Consequently, no protection for Sean when he's banged up. He'll be lucky to last a week. If he wants to survive he has to give us what we want.'

Across her shoulder Zigic could see Nathan sitting perfectly still on the sofa. He didn't look comfortable, more as if he'd been frozen to the spot where Rachel had told him to sit, as if her orders had to be followed to the letter even when she wasn't there to watch over him.

'What happened to Nathan's brother?' Zigic asked. 'Wouldn't he be a better witness?'

Her face darkened. 'We didn't want it to come to this. The plan was always to use Tyler. We put him in a secure facility for his own safety – there was a price on his head, he couldn't stay outside.'

'And?'

'And they got to him,' she said. 'We're not sure how exactly but ten weeks ago Tyler was found dead in his room. Someone gave him a massive shot of heroin. He wasn't a user so we have to assume it was administered to silence him. Nathan's all we've got now.'

'Which is why he's here with Julia?'

'He was supposed to be safe with the Campbells. Who'd think of looking for him out here in the arse end of nowhere?' She glanced back through the window into the lounge. 'That's why Nathan ran. He saw some bloke in a car outside Dawn's house, found her dead inside, and thought they'd tracked him down.'

'Shouldn't he have called you, rather than running?'

'He should, yeah. But he's a child. A scared, not very bright child, who thinks he can go to the McCarthys and promise them he won't give evidence. He was trying to protect his nan from reprisals. She's the only close family he's got left now.'

'So why did you take him away from her?' Zigic asked. 'You should have put them both in protective custody.'

'And then what?' Rachel demanded. 'We take his nan in, what about his aunts and uncles? His cousins? You think the budget's there to hide thirty-odd people?' She shook her head. 'We did what we had to.'

Zigic folded his arms, feeling disgusted by her and Fallon's power-playing, their utter disregard for Nathan and his brother and nan, who were just pieces of varying value they were moving around a game board. Tyler had been lost through poor judgement, the grandmother could be sacrificed, but Nathan had to be protected at all costs.

'What makes you think you can get him to give evidence?' Riggott took his e-cigarette out of his shirt pocket. 'He's run away to avoid doing it. He's terrified what's going to happen to his nan. Sounds like he's sharp enough to keep shtum.'

'I can convince him,' Rachel said, a hint of threat in her tone.

'By protecting him from a murder charge?' Zigic asked.

'He doesn't need protecting because he didn't do it.' She stepped away from the window and lowered her voice. 'But if he did I'm happy to turn him over. Once he's done what I need him to, of course.'

'That isn't how it works,' Zigic said.

'You don't want to go against Fallon,' Rachel told him. 'Believe me, that man will destroy you if you cross him. He's got political aspirations that are way bigger than this case and he won't stand for you two scuppering him.' She turned towards Riggott. 'Nathan gives evidence next week. After that, he's all yours. I'll deliver him back here personally.'

Zigic gave a disgusted snort but neither of them was paying any attention to him. The decision had been made, a deal cut, and now it would fall to Riggott to smooth out the details with her.

He half listened as they talked logistics and safe houses, watching Nathan through the glass, wondering what was going on inside his head, memories of Dawn mixed up with ones of his mother, dead on her living-room floor, beaten to death with a hammer. He'd seen and heard enough to be a compelling witness and that was all that mattered to Rachel, but did it make him more or less likely to commit a terrible act of violence himself?

The question of why he ran had been cleared up, the question of why he was being so fiercely shielded too, everything explained away except for the knife and that was all they needed to charge him. It was a result. A solid one.

But still some nebulous doubt stirred at the back of his mind, little things which didn't quite make sense, illogical actions and unexplained absences.

The copper in him said to ignore them, but the father, looking at Nathan sitting small and cowed on that sofa, wouldn't be satisfied while the questions remained unanswered.

45

In his office Zigic made a list, wrote down every element of the case against Nathan which didn't sit right, spidered each doubt out across the page with queries and notes until the sheet of lined A4 was thick with question marks.

He now knew that Dawn's love life had been a distraction and he realised how eager they'd been to fasten on it because women were usually murdered by current boyfriends or exes. He'd considered the overwhelming odds and gone with them, spending valuable man hours tracking down every one-night stand and semi-casual fuck buddy she'd been with, certain that her killer would be among them.

Holly's online existence had been another compelling possibility, inflated in importance by Ferreira's certainty and the frustrating, petty need to satisfy Riggott that this was a potential hate crime and keep the case under his control. That problem, at least, was solved, thanks to Baxter and Fallon's insistence on absolute discretion.

Zigic knew it was normal to go down these blind alleys, that it happened in the vast majority of cases, and that you only kicked yourself afterwards, with the benefit of hindsight to illuminate every overlooked lead and the gaps in knowledge which arose from focusing on the wrong people.

Now the gaps were where he'd find Dawn's killer.

An hour ago he was prepared to put his career on the line to bring Nathan in, defy Rachel Baxter and her politically inclined boss, but looking at all of those questions he was increasingly convinced that Nathan was innocent.

He pulled up the forensics reports from the house and pored over them once again, while that vague sense of having missed something tickled away at him, sure that there was something hiding between the lines.

He found the details of the post-mortem, knew what he was looking for there and concentrated on the specifics of the stab wounds which had killed Dawn Prentice, the angles of entry and the implications drawn from them. Only one blow had been landed while she was upright – the slash across her throat which would have robbed her of air – and the rest had been delivered as she lay dying, the killer kneeling astride her hips, driving the knife down into her chest and stomach, over and again. Nine more stab wounds, plunged in deep, the final blow the hardest; it had gone clean through her left lung and pierced the muscles around her shoulder blade.

It took strength to inflict multiple injuries like that, he knew. Brute physical strength or intense emotional strength. He didn't think Nathan was capable of the former and he strongly suspected that the angle of the initial strike was inconsistent with somebody so short.

He called the pathologist and left a message.

The moment he put the phone down he realised there was more the doctor could tell him and he called back, asked his second question, the more important one, said it was urgent.

Jenkins did answer when he phoned her, slightly breathless.

'I've only just got back, Ziggy,' she said. 'You're going to have to give me a chance to do the actual work before you can have the report.'

'It's not about what you found at the Campbells'. Well, it sort of is.'

'This sounds like a poorly thought-out theory you're formulating.'

'The hair you found, it was dyed, right?'

She sighed. 'On casual first inspection with the naked eye, yes, it appears to be a ginger hair that has been dyed brown. Mel tells me the boy you're looking at has dyed hair.'

'He does, but the ones you found in Dawn Prentice's bathroom weren't coloured, were they?'

A drawer opened at her end. 'No, they weren't. Is that all? You've got the report, everything's in there.'

'Can you do a comparison for me, please, Kate? First job, okay? It's urgent.'

'Alright, bear with me a couple of minutes and I'll get on it.'

'And Kate . . .'

She sighed. 'Yes?'

'This is the murder weapon, right?'

'It's the right size, right kind of blade, and it matches the marks found on Dawn Prentice's ribs, so I think you're safe to assume it is, yes.'

She put the phone down and Zigic went out into the office. Wheatley was back in CID, still pursuing the attacker he'd fortuitously discovered while questioning Dawn's lovers, and Zigic realised he might have to drag him up to Hate Crimes again if his theory – not as poorly thought out as Jenkins assumed but still sketchy – turned out to have legs. Parr and Murray were eating lunch at their desks, waiting to have new tasks assigned now the discovery of the knife had rendered their day's work pointless.

Wahlia's desk was empty and when Zigic crossed the office floor he saw him out in the hallway with Ferreira, the pair of them standing by the vending machine caught up in a low but intense-looking conversation.

'You need to get it checked out,' Wahlia said.

'It's fine. It doesn't even hurt.'

'Just let the doctor take a look.'

Ferreira snatched her drink out of the tray and straightened up into Wahlia's face. 'For Christ's sake, Bobby! Would you stop going on about it.'

She walked away from him, meeting Zigic's gaze as she returned to the office. He saw the split second of rage before she made her face blank.

'You don't look very happy for a man who's just closed his case.'

'It isn't closed,' Zigic told her.

'We've got the knife. It was wrapped up in Nathan's clothing. What else do you want?' She dropped into her chair and put her feet up on the corner of the desk. There was a speck of dried blood on the calf of her jeans, rusty looking against the grey. 'Except for a confession. You always want one of them.'

'What have you done to your leg?'

'Shaving cut.'

She stared back at him, waiting for him to push her about it, but now wasn't the time or place.

He waited until Wahlia was back at his desk and everyone was paying attention before starting the debrief. It was a severely edited one, because most of what he'd learned about Nathan this morning couldn't be shared with them and maybe that was why he received so many dubious looks and outright bemusement when he suggested Nathan might not be the guilty party.

'But he still ran,' Parr said.

'He was scared. I can't go into details but I'm telling you he had a very good reason that was in no way linked to Dawn being murdered.'

'So why run so close to her death?' Parr threw his hands up. 'If he was scared why not go a week before or today? There has to be some significance.'

'He believed her murder was related to him and that's all you're getting,' Zigic said firmly. 'We will no longer be considering it a sign of potential guilt.'

'What about the knife?' Ferreira asked. 'Isn't that enough to charge him?'

'I want to be sure we're charging the right person.' Zigic sat on the edge of an empty desk, the murder board in his eye line, full of ruled-out suspects. 'And the problem we have is the gap between Dawn being murdered and Nathan calling the police. Anyone got an explanation for that?'

'He was worried about Holly, obviously,' Ferreira said. 'His issue was with Dawn, he realised Holly hadn't been found, so he makes an anonymous call to get the police there and save her.'

'Possibly, but if he was worried about her wouldn't he have called the police sooner?'

'Not necessarily,' she said. 'Heat of the moment, he wants to get out, maybe he didn't even consider Holly until the next day.'

'Then he should have called the next day. Why wait until two days had passed? And then go to recover the knife? Why do that at all?'

Zigic looked around the room, settling on each of their faces for a second before moving on, everyone at a loss to explain it.

'Are we sure that was when the knife was taken?' Wahlia asked. 'We've only got Nathan's word for it.'

'The post-mortem results show tearing around one of the chest wounds,' Zigic said, touching two fingers to his breastbone. 'I'm still waiting for clarification but even I know that's consistent with the knife being removed some time after death.'

'Maybe he wanted a trophy,' Parr suggested.

'That he then went and wrapped up in his own clothing and hid at the house?'

'He's a kid.' Parr gave a slight shrug. 'Most killers do something stupid eventually.'

'Not the kind who carefully destroys almost every piece of physical evidence they've left behind at the murder scene,' Zigic said. 'Dawn's murderer wiped down surfaces, including the carpet in the hallway and up the stairs, so we wouldn't even be able to lift a footprint. That takes intelligence and it takes time, suggesting our killer wasn't panicking. Nathan is a nervy kid. He's traumatised and easily confused. That kind of behaviour doesn't fit with his personality.'

'Whose version of his personality?' Ferreira asked. 'Rachel's? Because we know she's come in her with her own agenda.'

‘I’ve spoken to him,’ Zigic said. ‘He isn’t a cold-blooded killer and that’s what we’re looking for here. Someone who lost it, then quickly changed gear and managed to clean up after themselves very effectively. Then went home without raising any suspicions and spent two days going about their business before returning to take the knife and hide it in the Campbells’ shed. This is an adult’s crime.’

‘We’re thinking it’s someone in that house then?’ Wahlia asked.

Zigic’s eye snagged on Benjamin Lange’s name in the Suspects column, Warren Prentice above it. He thought of PC Jackson’s report of seeing Warren running past the house when they were there. Maybe he was just out for a jog; maybe not.

‘Not necessarily. The knife was found in the garden shed. There’s an alley down the back of the chapel that would give easy access to the Campbells’ garden – anyone could have got access through it.’

‘And access to Nathan’s clothing to wrap it in?’

He turned back to Ferreira, saw the annoyance beginning to harden her jaw.

‘That could easily have been taken from the washing line.’

Zigic stood up, democratic interlude over.

‘We have an awful lot of questions that lack satisfactory answers and I want those answers before charging an eleven-year-old boy with murder.’ He gave Ferreira a pointed look. ‘As of right now Nathan has no motive, an alibi we haven’t even looked into and potential forensic evidence which undermines his guilt. These things need clearing up one way or the other.’

He moved over to the board, heads turning to follow, and picked up a red pen.

‘Our main focus is going to be on the night Dawn was murdered.’ He ringed a point on the timeline. ‘So we’re going back through her phone logs and internet history and we’re going to piece together what exactly she was doing in the hours leading up to her murder. Parr, Murray – that’s you two.’

Half-hearted 'yes, sir's from that side of the office.

He pointed at Wahlia. 'Bobby, I want you to dig up absolutely everything you can on the Campbells. We're going to be speaking to them very soon and it would be good to have something useful to hit them with.'

'Apart from the knife?' Ferreira asked.

'You were there for the search,' Zigic said. 'What kind of vibe did you get off Julia?'

'Defiant, angry, a bit scared. She didn't want Matthew there, for some reason.'

'Okay, bring her in. Let's see what she's got to say for herself.'

Ferreira grabbed her bag and strode out of the office.

'Alright then, everyone knows what they're doing.' And none of them looked particularly inspired by it. 'Crack on, folks.'

He left them to it, returned to his desk and the page full of questions.

An email was waiting for him, flagged as urgent, from the pathologist. Brief and concise the way the man always was.

Yes, one of the wounds to Dawn's chest showed signs of tearing consistent with the knife being removed at some point after death. At least twenty-four hours later.

Yes, the downward angle of the slash across her throat suggested an attacker slightly taller than Dawn. He gave the details in metric and imperial – used to dealing with older coppers who hadn't adapted to the conversion yet. Dawn was five foot six, her killer somewhere between five seven and five nine.

Nathan was far shorter, incapable of landing that precise blow.

Zigic rocked back in his chair, seeing one theory unspool and another begin to knit together. Somebody in the Campbell household had hidden that knife in the shed.

One of them had murdered Dawn and left Holly to die.

Then they'd set Nathan up to take the fall.

46

For a long time after the police left Julia couldn't move. She listened to them pack their things away, doors slamming in the lane outside, brash voices and laughter which stabbed at her, as she imagined what about the disintegration of her life they found so damn amusing.

She'd seen them bagging up the contents of the rusted old incinerator and she knew they'd found the knife which killed Dawn hidden in the shed.

Bile rose in her throat and she lunged for the kitchen sink, but nothing came out. She stared at the bright white porcelain, a few tea leaves dotting it from the pot she'd made after Matthew and Caitlin left the house, and wondered how long she had before there was another knock on the front door and someone came to take her away.

Part of her knew she should sit down and think through what she would tell them, but she couldn't bring herself to admit that her innocence was in doubt.

She turned on the tap and watched the water swill away the tea leaves, leaving the big butler's sink perfectly clean.

It would take more effort to tidy the rest of the house.

Nothing was broken but everywhere she looked she saw things moved from their proper positions and left slightly askew. In her workshop each and every drawer had been opened, contents rifled, shoved back clumsily. There was water on the floor around the wood burner and a scattering of ash where the forensics officer had emptied it, more charred remains to be checked through. She let out a small gasp of horror when she saw the ripped back of her club chair, horsehair stuffing hanging in clumps. But her eye strayed away from the chair, up to the shelves behind it which showed gaps now where bottles had been removed. Not all of them, not even most, but when she worked out which ones were missing she realised they had taken anything which might have been used to start a fire.

Julia went back into the kitchen and called Matthew's mobile again. Lunchtime now and there was no reason for him to have his phone switched off. Still he didn't answer and she didn't bother to leave a message because he had ignored the earlier ones and would ignore this one too.

He was avoiding her. He'd barely spoken this morning, only the briefest answers given when she asked if he wanted breakfast, if that shirt could do with ironing, and his impatience with Caitlin was so marked that she turned to Julia behind his back and made a face of pure incomprehension.

They'd argued last night, about whether Nathan should return to the house now that Rachel had found him. Julia wanted him to come home, Matthew refused, no negotiation, no softening his position even when she begged. It would only be for a few days, she pointed out, and they did need the money. At that he snapped, shouted things she couldn't bring herself to think of again, and stormed upstairs to bed.

It wasn't the argument they needed to have, the one they'd started and aborted months ago. Maybe if they'd finished it then none of this would have happened, but they were both avoiders. She backed down from him, he ran away from her, and the problem festered between them.

She went through into the hallway and busied herself tidying the mess the police had left behind, realigning the coats on the rack and the shoes underneath it, making the drawers in the console sit straight and true again.

In the living room the sofa and armchairs had been pulled about and she took her time straightening them and refolding the throws she draped over the arms, ready for the coming autumn when they'd sit under them watching TV. Just her and Matthew because the children would be gone.

She punched her fist into a tweed cushion, ostensibly plumping it up, but she threw a second shot it didn't need and a third which made her feel petty and stupid.

A thought was sneaking up on her and she kept moving, walking away from it, leaving it sitting in his usual chair by the fireplace only to find it waiting for her at the top of the stairs where a rag rug sat wrinkled across the floorboards.

The thought tracked her through the children's bedrooms, hovering at her shoulder as she made everything nice and tidy for Caitlin when she came home. It was a sly, stealthy thought, which somehow hung around the smug look that policewoman gave her as she left.

What did she know?

The master bedroom showed less overt disturbance than the rest of the house and she cursed herself for not making the bed as soon as Matthew left this morning. A keen-eyed officer would have noticed that only one side had been slept on, and she didn't doubt that such small insights could be blown up into questions of fidelity and guilt, that even now the state of her marriage bed was being discussed.

Did she suspect him? Did he suspect her?

Julia knew she wouldn't hold up well under interrogation. She'd never been a good liar.

Not like Matthew.

She smoothed down the duvet cover and puffed up his pillow, thinking of him tossing and turning there last night, replaying the argument just as she had done in Nathan's narrow pine bed, picking apart the long run-up to it and everything they hadn't said but would eventually have to.

Things the police might already know about him and her and Dawn.

She'd made a mistake confiding in Sally. She was a terrible gossip and that was fun when Julia wasn't the subject of it, but what if she'd already told the police? She would say anything to move their attention away from Warren.

Downstairs again she went into Matthew's study, found the books he kept lined up so precisely sitting messily on the shelves, spines all higgledy-piggledy, box files out of order. He'd taken his laptop to work with him so they'd been denied the chance to go through that, and she wondered what they would find when they finally seized it. She'd never been the kind of woman to snoop but now she wished she had. So that at least it wouldn't be a surprise when they told her he had a gambling problem or a fetish for Asian women who looked like children.

She drew the curtains back at the small, leaded-glass window although very little light ever made it into this room. She'd painted it dark blue, almost black, at his request, and it resembled a teenage boy's room, albeit a very pretentious teenage boy, with the French film posters framed on the walls and the collection of prog rock on vinyl he never played because he'd broken his turntable years ago and hadn't replaced it.

There was nothing but a notepad of ideas for his lesson plans on his desk, and she sat down in the leather chair, taking in the smell of his secretly smoked cigarettes, touched her fingers to a watermark on the walnut veneer; not water, but whisky, another pleasure he took when the door was locked.

He was in here Thursday night when she left the house.

She'd made him a coffee after dinner and he said he had marking to do – that lazy lie of his – didn't answer her when she shouted a goodbye, leaving for her book club.

She'd expected to find him still locked away when she returned. Had been mildly surprised to discover him in the back garden, changed into stained cords and his wash-faded gardening shirt, with the incinerator glowing nearby, thin branches sticking out of the top, licked by the flames.

There it was again; the doubt she couldn't shake off, the sergeant's triumphant air.

Had the police talked to their neighbours already? They were overlooked on all sides and a fire burning on a pleasant, late-summer evening wouldn't have gone unnoticed, smoking out people's al-fresco suppers and polluting their washing.

Had they arrested him?

Was that why he wasn't answering his phone?

A car pulled up outside the house, music blaring for a second after the engine stopped turning and she felt her stomach plunge, knew they were coming here even before the door knocker sounded three hard cracks.

Julia opened the door to the dark-haired sergeant, whose name her brain refused to remember.

'We need you to come into the station, Mrs Campbell.'

Her hand went to her chest. 'Is it Matthew?'

'Should it be?'

'Why do you need me to come with you?'

'Just to make a statement,' the woman said, the hard lines of her face at odds with the simplicity of the request. 'It shouldn't take long.'

Something had changed, that was the only explanation. Something significant had been unearthed since the police had left this morning and deep in her gut Julia knew what it was.

They must have spoken to Matthew. He was a good liar with her but not to them, perhaps. She couldn't imagine him keeping it together under police questioning.

He'd told them everything and now they knew that the only person in the house with a reason to murder Dawn was her.

47

Rachel was in the corridor when Zigic went up to the Domestic Violence unit, holding a one-sided phone conversation, shoulders hunched, frown deeply set. Whoever was on the other end was doing all the talking. Nearby, in one of the lounges, a woman was crying, the sound muted by a heavy door but the helplessness clear from the pitch of her unbroken wails. Rachel pocketed her phone and looked towards the noise.

'This isn't the ideal place for Nathan to be right now.'

'A few more questions, then we're done,' Zigic said. 'I've brought him some lunch.'

She eyed the sandwiches he held and the bottle of juice. 'Nothing for me?'

'Do you want me to go down to the canteen again?'

'Forget it,' she said wearily. Her initial bullishness had worn off and now she looked so tired and deflated that he actually felt sorry for her.

Nathan was still sitting on the edge of the sofa, a well-read comic discarded on the table in front of him. There was nothing in the room for a boy his age, the facilities set up for younger children who could be distracted from the horrors these four walls bore constant witness to by stuffed bears and toy cars and dolls with unconvincing smiles painted on their faces.

'I thought you might be hungry.'

Zigic set the food down and Rachel told Nathan to say thank you as he began to fiddle with the plastic packaging around his ham sandwich.

'I need to ask you about the evening Dawn died,' Zigic said.

Nathan dropped the packet, apologised even though he didn't need to, and picked it up again.

'I dunno what happened.'

'That's okay.' Rachel opened the package and handed it back to him. 'Just tell Dushan as much as you can remember.'

'It was a Thursday,' Zigic said.

Nathan looked at him blankly, as if the word meant nothing, and he realised that the days of the week were likely all the same to the boy. He wasn't going to school, he stayed in most of the time. You could lose weeks like that, no routine to differentiate a Thursday from a Monday.

'Julia goes out on Thursdays,' Rachel said. 'To her book club. Remember?'

He nodded.

'Did she go out last week?' Zigic asked.

'Yeah.'

He made a mental note to follow up on that. Nail down the exact time she left the house and when she returned. She'd neglected to mention it when they spoke previously and that bothered him. Most people were quick to supply their alibis in murder cases, whether they were asked to or not.

'So Matthew looks after you both that night,' he said. 'Can you remember what he was doing?'

'He don't do anything,' Nathan said. 'He goes in his office and listens to music.'

'What were you doing?'

'Watching a film. *Spiderman*. Julia got me them on DVD.'

Zigic smiled. 'They're good films. My boys love them.'

It didn't elicit any reaction from Nathan. He was tired, Zigic realised, from being here and from the days spent on the run, alone and scared. All of the weeks before that, knowing what lay ahead of him, fearing the process of giving evidence and what came afterwards. Did he know what would happen to him once Rachel had what she needed? Was he scared of that too?

And all the time, in the background, his mother's murder, images no child should ever have to see imprinted forever on his young mind.

There was a limit to what he could tell them and Zigic wasn't sure he knew how to get the information out of him. He needed a child psychologist, someone versed in post-traumatic stress, but he knew Rachel wouldn't allow it.

'Do you like Matthew?' he asked.

'He's alright.'

'Does he watch films with you?'

Nathan shook his head.

'What kind of man is he?' No answer. 'Nice?'

'I s'pose.'

Rachel brought a packet of gum out of her handbag. 'I had him checked out. He's clean.'

'Everyone's clean until they're not,' Zigic said.

She folded a stick of gum into her mouth. 'Granted. But he's your standard-issue frustrated intellectual. Teaching thick posh kids about the Tudors when he'd rather be lecturing wide-eyed undergrads. Boring, stable. Not the best fostering material in the world but okay.'

'He were in the garden,' Nathan said suddenly, his open mouth full of claggy white bread. 'I went to get a drink and he were setting fire to things in the garden.'

Zigic thought of the ash Jenkins's team had recovered from the incinerator, more of it from the garden. Several burn sites, Ferreira had told him, and it hadn't seemed particularly strange then, because there were a dozen innocent reasons to use your incinerator, but now the timing sent a jolt of energy up his spine.

'What was he burning?'

'Garden stuff.'

'What time was it?'

Nathan looked to Rachel for help.

'Was it dark?' she asked.

He nodded.

'After nine then,' she said.

They would need to speak to the neighbours again. Uniforms had already performed a first round of door-to-door and found every house that bordered the Campbells' garden empty. A second round after six thirty would be necessary if they were going to find witnesses who might have seen Matthew stripping off bloodstained clothing and stuffing it into the incinerator.

'Did Matthew ever take you to Dawn's house?'

'No.'

'Never?'

'We went with Julia.'

'Or on your own,' Rachel said, the disapproval clear in her voice.

'She never minded. She liked having us round.'

'I'm sure she did, but you weren't supposed to go out on your own, were you?'

Zigic shot her a look and she shook her head slightly. She was just as tired as Nathan, the stress of his disappearance lingering around her, compounded by the change in plans it had necessitated. A safe house organised by Riggott that he just knew she wouldn't trust. The ramifications when she finally reported back to her boss. This was a career-changing case for her and Fallon, he guessed, and it wasn't playing out how either would have wished.

'Did Dawn ever come to your house when Julia was out?' he asked.

'She never came to the house,' Nathan said. 'She couldn't leave Holly, could she?'

'Okay, so, going back to Thursday night – you were watching a film and Matthew was in the garden. What about Caitlin? What was she doing?'

'She were in her bedroom,' Nathan said.

'All evening?'

'I think so. She has a lot of homework.' He looked at Rachel. 'She's clever. Like you.'

Rachel bristled at the compliment and Zigic couldn't understand why.

'Was Caitlin friends with Dawn?' Zigic asked.

'She went round there with Julia a lot. Dawn used to paint her nails.' He put down the rest of his sandwich. 'Holly never liked her.'

'Why not?'

'She said she were thick.'

'But she isn't?'

'No. It was just what Holly said.' He wiped his nose across the back of his hand. 'Holly were dead clever.'

Rachel patted him on the back and stood up. 'I need a coffee. Can you show me where the machine is, Dushan?'

He followed her out into the corridor, pointed towards the stairwell. 'The machine's along there but the coffee's dire. If you go down to Hate Crimes, there's a pot on.'

'God almighty, are you serious?' She sighed. 'I don't want a fucking coffee, I need to talk to you without Nathan listening.'

'You're all charm, aren't you,' Zigic said.

She bowed her head for a second, came up serious faced. 'Have you spoken to Caitlin yet?'

'My sergeant has. She's the one who gave us the photograph of Nathan.'

Rachel smiled thinly. 'Of course she did. She wanted you to find him.'

'The impression I got was that Caitlin was worried about him and she wanted him bringing home safely. Nothing more to it than that.'

'So you've not looked into her background yet?'

'I imagine it's fairly innocuous or you wouldn't have placed Nathan there. You seem to have done your homework on Matthew.'

'I made a judgement call,' Rachel said. 'I'd heard good things about Julia and I thought she was the best option. The rest of them passed my lowest bar, just about. Caitlin Johnson almost changed my mind.'

'Why?'

Rachel reached into her roomy leather shoulder bag and came up with a grey cardboard file, half an inch of paperwork inside it.

'This did not come from me.'

She handed it over and Zigic only needed to look at the top page to know what he was holding: Caitlin Johnson's juvenile record.

'How did you get this?' 'I've got clout,' she said. 'And a thank you would be nice.'

'Why are you giving me it now?'

'Because you obviously need some help and there's no way you'd manage to get a copy on your own.'

'There's a good reason for that,' Zigic said. 'This is supposed to be a sealed record.'

She held her hand out. 'Give me it back then.'

'You brought this with you to take the heat off Nathan.'

'Yes, I did, but that doesn't matter now, does it?' Her brow furrowed. 'Whatever you might think of me, I'm a good copper, and I don't want two people's deaths going unpunished.'

Zigic tapped the file against his knuckles, feeling the weight of the paper inside, all of that ink detailing the parts of Caitlin's life they knew nothing about and would never uncover any other way. Not just secrets but offences. Criminal offences which had led to prosecution and punishment.

No amount of moral unease on his part could outweigh the detective's instinct to know what the file held.

Rachel smiled, deeper this time, as if she knew she'd corrupted him.

'Just read it, Dushan.' She paused at the lounge door. 'Then you can thank me.'

48

Caitlin Johnson had a history of violence.

That was the simplistic way to interpret the file Rachel had given him. A serious offence committed when she was just eleven years old. The judge who presided over the case had taken a lenient view and sentenced her to twelve months in a young offenders' institution, suggested intensive psychological treatment to address the underlying cause and went so far as to state that her actions were understandable even as he refused to accept her solicitor's claim of self-defence.

After reading all the details Zigic came to the same conclusion.

He guessed Rachel had too or she wouldn't have put Nathan in the same house as the girl.

The mugshot showed a sullen child with long brown hair hanging limp either side of a slim, almost malnourished face, eyes pink from crying when it had been taken, black smudges on her skin.

According to the police report she hadn't tried to run, just waited on a bench opposite the house she'd set fire to, and handed herself in when the first patrol car arrived. Along with a laptop she was clutching to her chest. The occupants of the house, her foster parents, were screaming from an upstairs window, glass smashed, smoke pouring out into the night.

Caitlin never explained why she did it, refused to talk at all, but when the investigating officers finally got around to examining the computer she'd saved from the fire they got their answer. Tens of thousands of images of child abuse, many of them filmed in the destroyed house, some of them featuring her. The husband and wife both involved.

Zigic closed the file, sickened and angry at Rachel for thinking she could use this to move their suspicions away from Nathan and onto a child who had suffered so much.

Nothing he'd read suggested Caitlin was a murderer. She'd committed an act of violence but when he imagined himself in her position – scared, damaged, hopeless – he could fully understand why she'd acted as she had.

Knuckles rapped on the office door and snapped him out of his thoughts.

He called Ferreira in.

'I've got Julia downstairs,' she said. 'She's really pissed off.'

'She'll have to wait. Come in and shut the door.'

Ferreira took the seat opposite him. 'What's up?'

'Caitlin's got a criminal record.' He pushed it across the desk. 'A pretty serious one.'

'Where did you get this?' she asked as she opened it.

'Rachel.'

'She wants to serve Caitlin up as a suspect so we ignore Nathan?'

'That's about the size of it, yeah.'

Ferreira wrinkled her nose but didn't reply, reading already. Fast. Turning through the arrest sheets and witness statements, the photographs of Caitlin's crime, which made her shake her head and let out low curses under her breath.

Zigic waited, looking at the photographs of his boys, thinking that he should have called Anna to check how Stefan was behaving himself. He'd got up this morning and dressed himself for school, came into the bedroom trailing his bag while they were still asleep. Zigic explained why he was staying at home and got treated to an epic tantrum, the night before's apology forgotten in a hail of shouting and stamping and red-faced bag throwing. They tried to draw a positive from it; at least he was enjoying school enough that being kept home registered as a punishment. He would phone Anna later, once he was finished with Julia Campbell.

A minute later Ferreira closed the file, placed it on his desk and sat back in her chair.

'I'd have done the same thing,' she said. 'Wouldn't you, if you were Caitlin?'

'That's not the issue. She's shown a propensity for violence.'

'Against her abusers. Do you think Dawn was abusing her?'

'I'd say it's highly unlikely but we need to bear in mind what she's capable of.'

Ferreira sighed. 'It's so not the same thing, though. She acted in self-defence.'

'It's a short step from self-defence to actual offence once you've crossed that line,' Zigic said. 'And we don't have any idea what the relationship between her and Dawn was like.'

'I bet Julia knows.'

As they were heading down the stairwell an email pinged into both their phones at the same time – forensics coming back on the ash samples from the incinerator. Early testing showed fabric present, along with an as yet unidentified accelerant. More to follow.

'Still think someone else planted the knife in their shed?' Ferreira asked.

'The incinerator's out in the open, I assume. The same person who hid the knife could have used it.'

'What?' she asked, stopping dead. 'The same time they planted the knife? Or do you think they jumped over the garden fence on Thursday to burn their clothes, then went back on Saturday some time to break into the shed? Come on.'

There was no more space for doubt, he realised. Someone in the Campbell household was responsible for Dawn and Holly's deaths.

Ferreira had put Julia in the most comfortable room they had access to, the one usually reserved for witnesses rather than suspects. Its walls were painted cream, the chairs padded and the table unscarred. People they spoke to here didn't scratch their name into any available surface, they were friends or family members dealing with grief and worry, the secondary victims in any given crime.

As he sat down opposite Julia Campbell, Zigic wondered if they had her in the right place.

She was angry, and struggling to hide it, sitting stiffly, hands making tight fists in her lap until she realised he'd noticed, then she placed her palm on her swollen stomach, took a couple of deep breaths, in through her nose, out through her mouth, as if it was a tried and tested technique she used when she felt herself about to snap.

Once Ferreira had the recording equipment set up he took over, explained the situation so she couldn't later say that she didn't understand.

'This is only a chat, Mrs Campbell. You haven't been cautioned or charged with anything. We simply want to ask you a few questions.'

'Please don't insult my intelligence.' Her voice was low, thick with emotion. 'Your people have ripped my house apart this morning.'

'And they found the murder weapon,' Ferreira said.

'Anyone could have gained access to our garden. It doesn't mean anything.'

'Thursday evening,' Zigic said, drawing her attention back to him. 'Can you tell us where you were, please?'

'I went to my book club,' she said, eyes still fixed on the curve of her stomach, fingers twitching there. 'In Warmington.'

'What time did you leave?'

'About seven.'

'And when did you get home?'

'Just after ten.'

Zigic asked her for the names of the other people who were there, contact details so they could follow up her alibi and she provided them from memory, Sally Lange among them, two other women. He expected Sally to be the most forthcoming, though.

'What was Matthew doing when you got home?'

'Some gardening.'

'At ten o'clock at night?'

She nodded.

'Was that usual for him? Gardening in the dark?'

'We have halogen lights.'

'He was burning something,' Zigic said. 'Do you know what?'

'Some branches from one of the apple trees. He'd cut them at the weekend but hadn't got around to clearing them away yet.' She sounded uncertain. 'I suppose he didn't know what to do with himself since I wasn't at home.'

'The children were there. He could have spent some time with them,' Zigic suggested. 'But he didn't. In fact, Nathan tells us he didn't see Matthew all evening. Not until he went to get a drink and noticed him in the garden. Burning something, he said. But we know now it was clothing.'

Julia's eyes widened. 'You've spoken to Nathan?'

'We're no longer considering him a suspect.'

The relief bloomed briefly across her face, replaced within seconds by a realisation that made her glance at the interview-room door.

'So you see our problem,' Ferreira said. 'Matthew's burning clothes late at night, very soon after Dawn was killed. The murder weapon is found in his shed. Wrapped in clothing which can only have come from inside the house.'

'We've ruled Nathan out,' Zigic said. 'Which leaves you and Caitlin and Matthew.'

'How did Matthew get on with Dawn?' Ferreira asked.

Julia pressed her lips together, a millisecond of forced composure to cover a reaction she didn't want them to see.

'Matthew's not particularly sociable,' she said. 'He's a thinker, not really one for small talk, so they didn't have much in common.'

'Opposites attract,' Ferreira said.

Zigic didn't need to look at her to know she was smiling.

'If you're suggesting that something was going on between Matthew and Dawn . . .'

'Yes, Mrs Campbell?' The smile left Ferreira's voice, ice in its place. 'If we are . . . then what?'

She huffed. 'Well, it's ridiculous. Dawn wouldn't be interested in him for one thing.'

'I think we've already established that Dawn was interested in anything with a dick and a pulse,' Ferreira said.

'There was nothing going on between them.'

'We've spoken to dozens of men who were sleeping with Dawn and none of their wives or girlfriends knew there was anything going on between them either.' Zigic watched her make another pursed-lip face. 'It would have been easy for him to slip out while you were at your book club, wouldn't it?'

'I trust my husband.'

'He wouldn't be the first to man to stray while his wife's pregnant,' Ferreira said.

The barest flicker of pain tightened Julia's eyes, fine lines springing up, melting away slowly.

'He was a frequent visitor until quite recently,' Zigic said. 'Isn't that right? Helping with Holly's education until they could sort out something more structured.'

Relief on Julia's face but Zigic wasn't sure why. Could she really rule out an affair that easily?

'He was helping her, yes.'

'But that all stopped a few months ago. Why?'

She hesitated. 'Holly suffered something of a downturn in her condition. Depression, I think. She wasn't up to it.'

'Really?' Ferreira asked. 'That's not what Matthew told us.'

'What did he tell you?' Julia demanded.

'I don't think you were happy with him spending so much time there. Dropping in after work for an hour. Once or twice a week?

That's a lot of time to give Holly her assignments and a reading list. Maybe he was giving Dawn something too.'

'Matthew was not sleeping with Dawn.'

Ferreira planted her elbow on the table, chin in her palm. 'Funny that Matthew stopped going around about the same time you stopped minding Holly. Why was that?'

'I don't know what you're talking about.'

'No? You don't remember telling us that you used to go and look after Holly so Dawn could have her dates?' Julia's eyes narrowed; caught in the lie and she knew it. 'What was it, Julia? You thought maybe it was Matthew she was meeting?'

'No!'

'Would have been a good system for them. Gets you out of the way, frees up Matthew to meet Dawn.'

'You're wrong. That's ridiculous.' A flush coloured her cheeks. 'I've told you there was nothing between Dawn and Matthew.'

Neither of them challenged her about it, left the words hanging there, let them play on Julia's mind for a few seconds, let her realise how firm they'd sounded. Too firm. Spoken with the full force of hopeful denial rather than absolute truth. Because she couldn't know, not for sure, and the longer she sat there, hearing those words echoing in her head, the more she would question them and every tiny glitch in their relationship would silt up around them; Matthew's hand lingering on Dawn's shoulder, some shared joke, some intercepted look that might suggest an inappropriate level of intimacy. Things she'd chosen to brush off now taking on new significance.

It would take time for her to turn on him, though, longer than they could keep her sitting in this interview room.

'What about Caitlin?' Zigic asked. 'Were she and Dawn close?'

'Dawn was very kind to her,' Julia said, looking perplexed by the change in tack. 'You're surely not suggesting that she's a suspect now? My God, you people are disgusting. Caitlin adored her.

If you knew the life that poor girl's had you wouldn't even consider suggesting something so . . . so . . . horrific.'

Zigic wanted to tell her that he knew exactly what kind of life Caitlin had had. Knew it better than her probably, but her juvenile record was sealed and he couldn't admit to having seen it, not without compromising the entire case.

'How often did Caitlin visit Dawn?' he asked.

'I took her around there with me occasionally.'

'And how often did she go on her own?'

'A few times,' Julia said. 'Dawn's been a very good influence on her. Caitlin has had a tough time of it and most people can't see past the way she looks, but Dawn did. She drew her out of herself. It's absolutely unthinkable that Caitlin would hurt her.'

Zigic listened while Ferreira pressed her further, wanting to know more about their friendship, challenging everything she said, trying to find some inconsistency or weakness, but Julia mounted an impassioned defence of the girl, even more convinced of her innocence than she had been of Nathan's. Zigic thought of what he'd said, about Holly hating Caitlin, and realised she was likely to have been jealous of the time and attention her mother lavished on this interloper, a part-time daughter who fulfilled her need for gossip and nail painting in a way Holly couldn't and maybe wouldn't have even if she'd never been injured.

Why would Caitlin turn on her? This woman Julia portrayed as the cool aunt figure, who bought her clothes and sat for hours watching films with her, invited her to barbecues and made her feel as if she was part of a stable and happy group of people living the kind of contented life she hadn't known before, a world away from the households where she was at best grudgingly tolerated and at worst horribly abused. It made no sense.

He wanted to talk to the girl, though. Suspected she was paying more attention to what was happening in the Campbell household that Thursday night, maybe all the other nights too. Teenage girls were born snoopers he suspected and ones who'd been shunted from pillar to post like Caitlin would be even more sensitive to the currents shifting within a family, needing to be aware of who their allies and enemies were.

'Will this take much longer?' Julia asked. 'I really do need to go and collect Caitlin from school.'

'No, that'll be all for now,' Zigic said.

He thanked her and left Ferreira to see her down to reception, find a car to take her home.

Back in Hate Crimes he passed the details of Julia's alibi to Colleen Murray, told her to get onto it right away, still not entirely convinced of the woman's innocence. There was something in her vehement denials that smacked of self-delusion.

His gut had been towards an ex-lover right from the start and with three suspects to pick from his money was on Matthew.

49

Twenty-five minutes after she put Julia in the back of a patrol car Ferreira was in reception again, called down to deal with Matthew Campbell who had arrived after going home to find his house turned inside out and his wife missing.

'Mrs Campbell left a little while ago,' Ferreira said. 'She should be home now.'

'Thank you.'

He turned to leave and she called him back.

'We do have a few questions for you, sir.' She smiled. 'Since you're already here.'

She took him up to the same interview room his wife had recently vacated and he sat down in the same chair, looked around himself as if these surroundings were a source more of curiosity than anxiety.

It was an odd attitude to strike, she thought, as she went up to Hate Crimes, taking the stairs two at a time, just to see if she could. The small wound in her calf complained about the movement and she decided not to do that again today, paused at the doorway to check that no fresh blood had welled up.

Zigic was standing over Wahlia, listening as he ran through the Campbells' financial records.

'Anything in there we can use against the husband?' Ferreira asked.

Wahlia shook his head. 'Mortgage, car payments, pension plan. No expensive vices. No cheap ones either from the looks of this.'

'Affairs can be cheap,' she said. 'As long as you don't need hotels.'

Zigic flicked an eyebrow up. 'Our resident expert.'

'Stands to reason, doesn't it? If he's screwing Dawn she's right there in the village and she didn't seem like the high-maintenance type. No paper trail doesn't mean no affair.'

'You like him for it?' Zigic asked.

'More than Julia or Caitlin, yeah.' She took a mouthful of water from the bottle she'd left on her desk. 'Has Jenkins got anything off the knife yet?'

'No fingerprints,' Zigic said. 'It's been wiped clean. Predictably. Hairs in the clothing are a type match for Nathan but not for the ones she recovered from Dawn's bathroom so we'd better get a DNA sample off Matthew Campbell.'

'Incidental, do you think? Or was someone trying to frame Nathan?'

Zigic shrugged. 'Could be either but since the knife was taken *after* he ran off there's a possibility that whoever killed Dawn saw him as a good scapegoat.'

'Any signs of phone contact between Matthew and Dawn?'

'Nothing,' Wahlia said.

'How far back have you gone?'

'Eight weeks.'

'How pregnant do you reckon Julia is?' she asked Zigic.

'Twenty-eight weeks.'

'Our resident expert,' Ferreira said, with a smile he returned slightly goofily. 'You think we should look back some more?'

He nodded, told Wahlia to get the relevant paperwork as a priority.

'You want to wait for that to come in?' she asked. 'Or take a run at Matthew now?'

'Might as well soften him up.'

Matthew Campbell stood as they entered the room, held a hand out for Zigic to shake; reflexive good manners or an attempt to lift himself above the situation? Ferreira wasn't sure, but she watched him as she set up the recording equipment, saw him compose himself, spine straightening, shoulders back, hands clasped loosely on the tabletop.

She saw through it, though, in how he touched a fingertip to his glasses, then his earlobe, heard his feet dragging against the floor as he tucked them under the chair, leaning forward slightly to state his name for the recording.

'You're aware that we recovered a knife from your garden shed this morning, Mr Campbell?' Zigic said. 'The knife that we believe killed Dawn Prentice.'

'Julia texted me, yes.'

'The night Dawn was murdered – Thursday the tenth – where were you?'

'At home. With the children.'

'And what were you doing?'

'Marking.' He gave them a weak smile. 'Unfortunately a teacher's working day doesn't end at three o'clock like most people assume.'

'But you have enough free time to do some late-night gardening,' Zigic said. 'What were you burning?'

'Branches, brambles. That kind of thing.'

'Clothing?'

His fingers knitted tighter together. 'No.'

'Could you explain why we found traces of burnt clothing in your incinerator then?' Zigic asked.

'I suppose somebody else put the clothes in there once the fire was burning. Or before I lit it perhaps. It was already full of branches.' His hands broke apart. 'I wish I could explain it.'

He was too calm, Ferreira thought. The implications were clear, he was obviously a suspect. So why persist in acting as if it hadn't occurred to him?

'That's your alibi?' she asked. 'You were burning stuff.'

Matthew blinked slowly. 'No, the children would be my alibi. If I need one.'

'You need one, Mr Campbell.'

'I didn't kill Dawn.'

'We wouldn't expect you to say anything else.'

He brushed his hand back over his hair. 'I don't know what else to say. I was at home with the children. Isn't that good enough for you?'

'Nathan didn't see you all evening,' Zigic said. 'That's half your alibi shot.'

Matthew glared at him across the table. 'Maybe you should be asking where Nathan was when Dawn was killed. He was always going around there, just wandered over whenever he felt like it.'

'We know all about Nathan,' Zigic said, a hint of warning in his tone. 'And he's no longer being considered a suspect. You very much are.'

'Ask Caitlin then, she saw me.' Matthew looked between them, the way every suspect did, trying to decide who would be more receptive, and settled on Ferreira. 'I had a long talk with her before I went out into the garden.'

'About what?'

'She was upset. She hardly ate anything at dinner, then Julia went out and she went up to sulk in her bedroom. I heard her crying a while later and thought I should check on her.'

Zigic tensed slightly next to her. 'What was she crying about?'

'Leaving us. She's going in a few weeks. On to another family.'

'Why? Has she been causing trouble?'

'No, she's been perfectly well behaved. But with the baby coming . . . we discussed it and Julia feels it's better if we don't take any more children in for a while.' He opened his hands up. 'She wants some time to enjoying being a real mother. Those first months are so important for bonding. She doesn't want any distractions.'

'Julia didn't mention that,' Zigic said. 'Why do you think that is?'

Matthew's face twisted. 'I honestly couldn't say. I suppose she doesn't think it has any bearing on the situation.'

Because Julia didn't want to look like a bitch, Ferreira thought. That was the only explanantion. She'd come in playing the maternal saint, wanting to look too fundamentally good to be guilty, and admitting to kicking out a troubled young girl would undermine that version of herself.

'It seems very harsh on Caitlin,' Zigic said, clearly troubled by the idea.

He frowned. 'It is slightly, yes. But it was never a permanent arrangement. We were only fostering her.'

Ferreira's phone vibrated in her pocket and she took it out, checked the display and turned it towards Zigic, who motioned for her to go, recording the time as she left the interview room.

Outside in the corridor Wahlia was waiting for her.

'Are we sure about this?' she asked.

'Murray called it in about twenty minutes ago,' he said. 'It was gossip at that point.'

'From who?'

'Sally Lange. But it suits her, doesn't it? So I wanted to wait until I could back it up.' He handed her a few sheets of paper, phone logs covered in yellow highlighter. 'It backs up big.'

She scanned the times and dates, saw that her thinking about the pregnancy had been right and smiled; she hadn't completely lost her touch then.

'Thanks, Bobby.'

She went back in, Zigic announcing her arrival for the recording. Matthew stopped talking while he did so but then went straight back into his flow.

'It's why she's taken Dawn's death so badly. She was part of a unit here. She'd known her for almost two years, they'd become very close.' He eyed Ferreira as she sat down. 'Dawn was a proper friend to her, she hadn't had many of those.'

'How about you and Dawn?' Ferreira asked, hands on the file. 'Proper friends?'

He looked perturbed by the interruption. 'She was Julia's friend more than mine but we got on well enough. As I think I told you before.'

Ferreira took a sheet of paper out of the file and pushed it across the table.

'That is your mobile phone number highlighted, isn't it?'

He stared at it but the number refused to change.

'Yes.'

'Long phone calls,' she said. 'Twenty minutes, thirty. An hour some of them. How did Julia feel about that?'

'It isn't what you think,' he said.

'An affair? Looks like one to me.'

He took off his glasses and rubbed his eyes. 'There was nothing physical between me and Dawn, we just talked.'

'Emotional infidelity,' Ferreira said. 'Some women think that's worse. Much more intimate, pouring out your soul to a woman who isn't your wife.'

'I needed to talk to someone who wasn't going to judge me.'

'About what?' Zigic asked.

Matthew slipped his glasses back on but didn't look at either of them. 'I'm forty-seven years old and I'm about to become a father. I was planning on retiring at fifty, now I'll have to work until I drop. I'll be pushing seventy when it's leaving university. How could I talk to Julia about that? She thought she couldn't have children, then suddenly she's pregnant. I couldn't say anything. All she's ever wanted was a child of her own.'

He sagged in the chair, drained but relieved, Ferreira thought, as if it had been weighing impossibly heavy on him. The room doing its work; dragging out a confession but, just like Warren Prentice's yesterday, not the one they wanted.

'How did Julia react?' she asked. 'When she found out about Dawn and you?'

'She was livid.'

'Can you blame her?'

'Yes, I bloody well can,' he snapped. 'We were friends. Why shouldn't I confide in my friend? She wouldn't have reacted like that if it was another man.'

'It isn't the same and you know it,' Ferreira said. 'Which is why you had to be careful. No more phone calls.'

'I haven't spoken to Dawn since Julia found out.' Matthew cocked his head. 'Do you think I'd jeopardise my marriage for the sake of conversation?'

'You've made it clear you don't want to have a baby. Maybe you want out of your marriage altogether.'

'I love my wife,' he said. 'Dawn was a friend. The decision wasn't difficult.'

'You weren't allowed to have any contact with her?' Ferreira asked, checking the story that had come from Sally Lange.

'Not alone, no.'

'How did Dawn feel about that? Losing you?'

'I have no idea,' he said sharply. 'I didn't speak to her again.'

Zigic rapped his fingertips against the tabletop. 'If Julia was so livid about it why didn't she cut Dawn off completely?'

Matthew smiled, lopsided and vicious.

'You really don't understand women, do you, Inspector? Julia won. She wanted to rub it in. So she can be friends with Dawn and I can't. But really she wanted to see Dawn suffering and you can't do that from a distance.'

Ferreira thought of the woman she'd first encountered when they went to look for Nathan, all sickly grin and saccharine manners, playing the perfect host while she lied and evaded, covering for Nathan when he could well have been a murderer.

She knew how to keep secrets.

She'd done the same thing not more than ninety minutes ago, sat across the table where her husband was now listening as Zigic explained the next part of the process, the statement to be signed and the DNA sample they could compel him to provide. She'd sat there and vehemently denied that Matthew and Dawn were sleeping together; not lying but not quite telling the truth either.

An affair without sex. Physical sex anyway.

Ferreira eyed the list of late-evening calls, wondering how often the soulful outpourings became more bodily, fingers straying, breaths quickening. It's what Julia would have suspected. Any woman would.

Zigic handed Matthew Campbell over to a uniform, had him taken away so a DNA sample could be collected. No resistance from Matthew, which meant he was innocent enough to willingly submit or so confident in his cleaning up that he didn't think they'd have anything to test it against.

Back in the office she went to the murder board, looked at the timeline with its yawning four-hour space; the exact point of Dawn's death impossible to plot with any accuracy. Her phone logs gave them her last definite contact, a call to check her bank balance at 8.20; the system was automated but the details required to clear security suggested it was her.

After that, nothing.

Three suspects with incomplete or unsatisfactory alibis. Caitlin and Matthew could vouch for each other, but only within a limited time frame. Nathan told the same story but his recollection of the night was imprecise.

Julia's alibi was similarly open to interpretation. The women from the book club all agreed she was there and that they broke up at ten o'clock on the dot, but without a concrete time for her arrival home she could easily have dropped by Dawn's house.

Premeditated murders didn't require a lengthy build-up.

'Could Julia have killed her?' she asked.

'She's heavily pregnant,' Zigic said, heading for the coffee machine.

'But it isn't impossible.'

'You've seen her – does she look nimble?'

'Do you need to be to cut someone's throat?'

He poured himself a drink and she shook her head when he offered her one.

'I'm not sure Julia would be capable of squatting over Dawn's body and repeatedly stabbing her,' he said. 'There was so much blood, she's already unsteady on her feet. It's the kind of risk pregnant women would avoid taking. Like walking on an icy pavement.'

'If she was thinking logically, yeah. But she what if she just totally lost her shit with Dawn?'

'Why?'

Ferreira started to roll a cigarette. 'Because she found out Matthew and Dawn were still in contact. We keep hearing all this about the kids going round – wandering over whenever they felt like it – what about if Nathan or Caitlin caught them at it and reported back to Julia?'

'Nathan didn't mention that.'

'Well, say he saw them talking then, he wouldn't know it was significant.' She sealed her roll-up. 'And she's the one who's out of the house. We've got her going to the book club but what was she doing before and after?'

Zigic dropped into a seat at one of the free desks. No sign of Murray and Parr.

'Maybe we just have to wait for the DNA results to come back.'

Ferreira shoved the window open and lit her cigarette. 'I didn't become a copper to sit around waiting for DNA matches, did you?'

'Sometimes you have to let the science do the work.' His phone pinged and he smiled as he looked at the display. 'It's like Jenkins can hear us.'

'Anything useful?'

'They've recovered a care label from the incinerator.' Read on, eyes narrowing. 'She's traced the product code. Christ, there's only one person that can be.'

Ferreira tossed her cigarette out of the window. He held his phone out to her and she scanned down the information Jenkins had sent over.

'Shit.'

'Yeah.'

'I'll drive.'

50

The traffic was rammed bumper to bumper on the Oundle Road, as it always was at that time of day, slowed by the speed cameras and the interminable roadworks on the parkway that backed up cars along the flyover exit, making everyone fractious. Julia felt their nerves playing on her, adding to the tension tightening the muscles in her shoulders, small stabbing pains going into her lower back.

The baby kicked so hard she thought she was going to be sick. No sense of wonder in it now, just another disturbance in her system, another discomfort to add to all the others. It had kicked in the interview room, at the exact moment she denied that Matthew was sleeping with Dawn, and she felt as if her unborn daughter was exposing her, betraying her just like her father had.

They hadn't asked the questions she feared they would, the ones she had no good answer for, and that was a relief. She knew they would find out eventually, though, and when they did this mess was only going to get worse.

Caitlin was waiting for her in the bus shelter at the entrance to Ferry Meadows, alone and downcast looking, holding onto the strap of her bag with both hands. When she got into the car she clutched it on her lap as if it contained something more precious than books and pens.

'How was school?'

'Fine.'

Julia wanted to fake some brightness for her but found she couldn't. There were no more words in her, everything used up in that interview room, and she was grateful Caitlin didn't want to talk either, happy enough to spend the ten-minute drive home in a passable approximation of contented silence.

Her mind was whirring, though, hands tightening around the steering wheel as she tried and failed to push away thoughts of Dawn and Matthew, his voice – damn him – that soft, caressing voice he never used with her any more, coming through the study door when he thought she was asleep, the words so low she had to strain to hear them, his directions and encouragement, then that last strangled gasp as he came.

No.

This wasn't about her.

She needed to think of Caitlin.

The police didn't seem to consider her a serious suspect but she could see that their options were limited and they'd had no compunctions about aggressively pursuing Nathan, damaged boy that he was. Caitlin had no Rachel to protect her, though. She only had Julia and she wasn't going to let whatever fragile recovery she'd made be smashed apart for the sake of Dawn fucking Prentice.

By the time she pulled into the driveway Julia knew what she needed to do.

'Go and get changed and I'll make you a sandwich,' she said, forcing a smile for Caitlin.

She watched her trudge up the stairs, then went into the kitchen, found the number for Susan Russell, Caitlin's social worker, and called it, got one of the other women in the department and left a message, said it was important and she needed to speak to her immediately.

Julia switched the lights on and the radio, trying to conjure some sense of normality into the kitchen, chase out the ghosts of this morning's occupation, but as she began to make a snack for Caitlin the tears welled in her eyes and she remembered the conversation with Matthew. Months ago now but it didn't feel that long, the pain he'd caused her made fresh again; how he'd stammered and denied and finally lost his temper, raised a fist he didn't use but there had been a split second when she shrank back, sure he would.

What would happen if she told the police about that?

Would it be enough to damn him?

The phone bleated at her and she took a couple of deep breaths before she answered it.

'Julia, what's happened?' Susan asked. 'Is Caitlin okay?'

'I think you should come and collect her,' Julia said.

'Is she being difficult?'

'No, God, no, it's not that.' Julia looked out across the garden; the shed door had been left open and it swung slightly on the breeze. 'I'm so sorry to have to ask this, but things are . . . escalating here.'

There was a pause at Susan's end. 'Because of your friend's murder?'

'Yes.' She felt her cheeks flushing. 'The police have been here, they've searched the house. I don't know where Matthew is, he's not answering his phone. I think they might have arrested him.'

'I see.'

A couple of tears ran down her cheeks. Everything was ending. So suddenly that it felt unreal to her, this room that she knew so well made alien and insubstantial, pieces of it spinning away from her, losing their meaning and the memories attached to them. She felt her heart pounding against her ribcage and the baby shifted, an elbow or a foot poking her sharply.

'Caitlin shouldn't have to see us like this,' she said. 'I want her to remember this as a happy home, Susan. Do you understand? She was so close to Dawn, I can't even begin to imagine how hard it's going to hit her when she knows.'

Another moment of charged silence from Susan, phones ringing at her end, voices chattering, dealing with their own emergencies but nothing as big as this.

'I know she isn't due to leave for a few weeks but can't you speed things up?'

'Yes, I think that would be best,' Susan said, brisk now, businesslike.

'Today? Could you arrange that?'

'Hold on a moment, please.'

'I'm not going.'

Julia turned to see Caitlin standing in the kitchen door, eyes red behind the dark wedge of her fringe.

'Sweetheart, I'm only thinking of what's best for you.'

'You don't care what's best for me,' she said. 'You just want shot of me because you've got your own baby coming.'

'It isn't like that,' Julia said. 'This is for your own good, believe me.'

'My own good?' Caitlin came around the table, shoving aside a pink-painted chair. 'Where am I going? D'you know? Have you asked them?'

'Susan's sorting –'

'You don't know and you don't care. Doesn't matter as long as I'm gone.' Caitlin let out a wordless cry, animal in its intensity, all pain and frustration. 'I did as I was told. I've been *good*. You can't make me go for no reason. It's not fair.'

The doorbell rang and Julia imagined one of the neighbours coming around to interrogate her about the police activity this morning. Couldn't face them. Not after everything else today had thrown at her.

'You can't stay here, lovey. I'm sorry, honestly I am.' Julia went over to her, placed a hand on her arm. 'This isn't the right home for you any more. We can't give you what you need.'

'You said you'd look after me. You promised!'

'We have, haven't we?'

Caitlin shrugged her off. 'You hate me.'

'No—'

'You only wanted me here for the money, didn't you?'

Susan's voice was bleeding out of the phone, urgent and high-pitched, and Caitlin snatched it out of Julia's hand.

'I'm not going,' she shouted into the phone.

Julia didn't hear Susan's reply but whatever she said she misjudged it and Caitlin threw the handset across the room. It hit the fridge and broke apart, leaving a dent in the enamel.

'Please, Caitlin, sweetheart, just calm down.'

'Why should I?' she snarled. 'Say it. Say you hate me.'

'Why would I hate you? You're a lovely girl.'

Julia heard the fear in her own voice, began to back away, but Caitlin followed each faltering step, growing larger and angrier.

The doorbell rang again and Julia glanced towards the door, praying it was Matthew, key forgotten, about to come around into the back garden.

'Nobody cares what I want.'

She was crying and Julia was crying too.

'Nobody cares about me.'

'That's not true,' Julia said, pleading with her, willing her to believe it. 'We do care, we're trying to do what's best for you.'

'Stop lying to me!' Caitlin's hand lashed out and swept the drying rack off the draining board, glasses smashing around their feet. 'You think I'm shit. You all do.'

Julia could feel pieces of broken glass through the thin soles of her ballet pumps as she backed away, heard them crunching but only distantly, her pulse thundering in her head as Caitlin swore at her.

She curled her arms around her stomach, a tiny foot kicking out as if her baby knew it was in danger, some defensive urge rushing along the umbilical cord, screaming *fight*.

51

Ferreira rang the doorbell. Again. Held it down for a few seconds this time, unignorable.

The sound of smashing glass answered it.

'Round the back,' Zigic said, already moving, heading for the tight channel between the Campbells' house and the rear wall of the neighbouring chapel, a swirl of dead leaves trapped there, bits of rubbish blown in off the lane.

Behind him Ferreira was calling to the uniforms, telling them to stay out front in case she made a run for it.

He heard raised voices inside the house as he rushed along the narrow alleyway, Caitlin shouting, screaming, more smashing sounds that spurred him on and over the hip-high stone wall which bordered the garden, foot landing in a flower bed, something spiking his ankle but he could see them now through the kitchen window, Caitlin yelling in Julia's face, backing her up against the worktop, Julia crying, shaking her head.

The back door was locked when he rattled the handle.

'Kick the fucker in,' Ferreira said.

He struck out at it, felt it wobble but hold, an old door on flimsy hinges, the woodwork softened by damp. The second kick opened it and they were in.

Julia looked up, straight into Zigic's eyes and he saw the terror there, but Caitlin didn't turn, kept shouting.

'You're a liar!'

She grabbed a handful of Julia's hair, twisted it in her fingers.

'Caitlin, that's enough,' Zigic shouted.

Julia was trying to pull free, dipping and squirming, but Caitlin moved with her, chunks of glass squeaking and crunching under her feet.

'Don't make this worse than it already is,' Zigic said, taking a couple of steps closer. 'I know you don't want to hurt Julia.'

A low growl rumbled around the kitchen, a formless, furious despair from Caitlin, and Julia was pleading with the girl in a desperate whisper, both arms hugging her swollen stomach.

Zigic glanced at Ferreira, saw his own discomfort reflected back at him. She had a baton in her hand, already extended, and she nodded towards Caitlin, inviting him to give her the word so she could move in and restrain her.

But she was a child, for all her aggression, and he didn't want to have to justify the use of force later, in some bland, safe room where this atmosphere couldn't be recreated as explanation.

'Caitlin, you need to step away from Julia now.'

The growl became a snarl and he saw the movement she was going to make ripple across Caitlin's back a split second before she twisted and lunged, shoving Julia away from her with every ounce of strength her stocky figure held.

Then it was chaos.

Caitlin bolted for the door, slamming into his shoulder as she went, Ferreira diving after her. He tried to reach Julia but there was so much space between them suddenly, too much for him to cross, as she struggled to regain her balance, stumbling, feet tangling, one gold pump finding solid ground, the other a shard of glass that sent her skidding across the tiled floor.

And she was falling.

Her hands flew out but it wasn't enough. The chair she grabbed at tipped and she hit the floor in stages, stomach striking the edge of the table, knees buckling, and he went down at the same time. Too late to do anything but soften the drop.

Julia screamed, a long piercing wail as she rolled into a ball, arms around herself, legs kicking weakly at the air.

'You're going to be okay,' he said, fumbling his phone out of his pocket.

He found her hand and gripped it tight, told the dispatcher he needed an ambulance, urgently, gave them his name, the address. The voice on the other end wanted to know what the problem was and he couldn't bring himself to say it.

'It's a fucking emergency, just get someone here now.'

Julia tried to sit up. A small spot of blood appeared at the groin of her lemon-yellow jeans, began to spread faster than he'd have thought possible.

'No, don't move, okay. You need to stay as still as you can.'

'It's too late,' she groaned.

'The ambulance is on its way, they'll be able to fix this.'

'This won't get *fixed*.' She gasped as she moved, sat up, groaned at the sight of the blood. 'Oh my God, what have I done?'

'It isn't your fault.'

The tears were flowing freely down her face, hair stuck to her flushed and damp cheeks. Zigic put his arm around her and she slumped against him, wept quietly, muttering to herself, words that sounded like a prayer.

He stroked her shoulder and strained for the sound of a siren, heard only shouts in the street and an engine revving before pulling away.

A minute later Ferreira was standing at the back door, eyes magnetised to the blood for a second before she gathered herself.

'We got her.'

'Go and make sure the ambulance can find us.'

Julia's shoulders shook under his hand and he felt the weight of this like a stone in his chest; wanted to apologise, wanted to reassure her, but the blood was spreading and he was sure she was losing the baby. He tried not to think of Anna, stared at the smashed tumblers and crockery which had done this to Julia, the pieces blurring under his gaze, but all he could think of was what a fragile state pregnancy was and what small things could end it. There had been violence here but it was painfully easy to imagine Anna tripping over a dropped toy or that stupid tufted rug in their living room. He knew that even if he was mere feet away from her he wouldn't be able to stop it happening.

Then he hated himself for laying his own fears over Julia's tragedy.

'I can't feel her moving,' she said, in a thin voice. 'Why isn't she moving?'

Zigic squeezed her hand. 'Come on, Julia. She needs you to stay strong.'

'It's too late.'

'No, it's not. Babies are tougher than you think.' He willed some certainty into his voice even though it was cracking. 'She's going to be fine, she's a fighter. You're going to get through this. Both of you.'

In the distance he heard sirens, drawing closer very fast, until the blare of them filled the lane. Ferreira came back through the kitchen door and went to let them in at the front, two women with hard faces and soft voices who swept in with a confidence which inspired a moment of bright hope to flood across Julia's face.

They eased him out of the way and he stood by uselessly while they performed the most perfunctory of examinations, before lifting Julia to her feet, one either side of her, strong hands under her arms, encouraging her in sweet but determined tones.

'There we go.'

'Well done, Julia.'

'Let's get you outside, shall we?'

'There's a good girl.'

Zigic couldn't tell from their attitude whether the baby was okay or not. They were too practised at controlling people's fears and the potentially violent reactions which could follow the realisation of them. The bleeding seemed to have slowed but maybe that wasn't a good sign. Twenty-eight weeks gone, she'd told him the first time he'd come here. Six and a half months. Babies were born that premature all the time, he thought, were born and survived if their care was good enough.

Assuming that sickening impact wasn't as fierce as it looked.

He walked outside behind them and numbly watched them guide her into the back of the ambulance, one painful step at a time, the younger of the two women climbing in after her and slamming the door.

'Are you okay?' Ferreira asked, touching his arm lightly.

'Yeah.' He went to wipe his eyes and saw the blood on his hands, no idea how it got there. 'I – uh – I think I need to go home. Change out of these . . .' He looked down at the blood on his jeans: too much of it, too bright. Fresh tears welled and he turned away from Ferreira to deal with them, hoping she hadn't noticed how his fingers trembled. 'I need to wash up. I can't go back in like this. I really should go home and change.'

She frowned. 'You couldn't have stopped that.'

'We could. If she'd already been in custody it would never have happened.'

'This job—' she bit her lip. 'You can't spend your life blaming yourself for not stopping shitty people doing fucked-up things. This isn't on you.'

He nodded, feeling his throat tightening.

'Here, take my car.' She held her keys out. 'I'll call for a ride.'

'Sure?'

'Yeah, go.'

A couple of minutes out of the village, driving along a winding back road towards Ailsworth with his eyes prickling and his jaw clenched tight, he forced the swell of sadness away, toed the accelerator and concentrated as he swung the unfamiliar car into a sharp bend.

You couldn't let these things touch you.

For your own sanity, they had to be boxed up securely and pushed to the back of your mind.

It was stupid. All the murder victims, the rape victims, the men and women beaten half to death; their names and faces would be with him for a few days or a few weeks, as long as it took to find the person responsible for their suffering. But quickly they'd fade, to be replaced by the next tragic case that landed on his desk. Forgotten to the point where he'd sometimes see one of them in a shop or a cafe and start towards them as if he knew them, only to realise, usually quickly enough, why he recognised them and that the smile on his face, the warm greeting on his tongue, would not be welcome.

This was going to stay with him, though.

When he got home the boys were playing in the garden. He heard them laughing and screaming as he climbed out of the car, the thwack of the tethered tennis ball he thought they were too young for, and he went through the side gate, found Anna picking over the wilting herbs in the wooden planter alongside the fence. She straightened at the sound of the gate opening and smiled at him, squinting into the sun.

'Home in the afternoon,' she said, walking over to him. 'Either you've got a press conference or you're—'

She'd caught sight of the dried blood on his hands, the faint traces which he hadn't managed to wipe off onto his jeans before he got in the car.

'Is that yours?'

It all came out in a rush, even though he didn't mean to tell her, and her hand went to her stomach as he described the moment Julia hit the table and how close he'd been to catching her but not close enough, Anna's face paling as he spoke. The boys had fallen silent, both standing with their plastic rackets dangling at their sides while the tennis ball continued to swing around its post.

He shouldn't have brought this home with him.

'Is she going to be okay?' Anna asked.

'I don't know.'

She slipped her arms around his neck, up on tiptoes, and kissed him, whispered in his ear that it wasn't his fault, he shouldn't blame himself. He hugged her as tightly as he dared, aware of that delicate little body inside her, cocooned between them.

52

Ferreira glanced at her watch for the umpteenth time, wondering what was keeping Zigic. She'd been back at the station almost an hour, gathered together everything they would need during Caitlin Johnson's questioning, had her fingerprinted and swabbed and sent down to the cells. Only a short stay because her social worker had arrived within fifteen minutes of being called, bringing a solicitor with her, and now they were both talking with the girl in an interview room. Straightening out her story and deciding upon the best way to proceed.

She wondered if Caitlin would be honest with them, hoped she wouldn't, giving them an excuse to lay it all out on the table: crime-scene photos for shock value and forensics reports which put Caitlin's clothing in the Campbells' incinerator – along with the brambles and twigs Matthew really had been burning – her fingerprints on the bottle of white spirit which had been used to feed the fire, those short, dark brown hairs removed from the bloodstained towels in Dawn's bathroom showing a type match. The DNA would have to wait but it felt like more than enough.

The only question that remained now was why she had murdered Dawn Prentice; her friend, her cool aunt, the woman who had coaxed her out of her shell.

That and why she'd gone back to retrieve the knife, leaving Holly to die when she could have saved her.

Ferreira walked over to the window and waited for her car to pull into the station, thinking of how easily Caitlin came along when she caught up with her in the lane next to the house. The uniforms were blocking her path but she might have made some attempt to slip them. Instead she just stopped and waited for the cuffs to go on her wrists.

Didn't say anything. No explanations, no apology. Didn't ask if Julia was alright.

She looked dead behind the eyes. Absolutely empty.

Three storeys below, Ferreira saw her Golf enter into the car park and she watched Zigic back it into a space, climb out and head for the steps at a pace which suggested he wasn't relishing the afternoon's work. She couldn't remember ever seeing him as emotional as he'd been with Julia Campbell, stunned and tearful, his usual professionalism shot to hell.

It was his wife, she guessed. Impossible to see a woman lose her baby and not think about his own.

At least he'd been spared the job of passing the bad news on to Matthew Campbell. She shirked that job herself too, delegated it to Colleen Murray, who went down and released him from custody, drove him over to the hospital rather than sending him in a patrol car. She wrote a quick note and stuck it to Murray's computer, asking her to release Arnold Fletcher when she got back, no time to deal with him now.

Zigic trudged into the office, sombre in black jeans and a dark grey shirt.

'Come on then,' he said. 'Let's get it over with.'

On the way down they decided who should take the lead and Ferreira was relieved he wanted her to do it, citing Caitlin's history of abuse and probable mistrust of men. She suspected it was about him, though, that he was self-aware enough to realise he couldn't approach her calmly after what she'd done.

They went in.

Five chairs around the table, three occupied; Caitlin in the middle, flanked by two middle-aged women, and she was the only person to stay seated as they entered the room, didn't even look up at them.

Ferreira made the introductions.

Susan Russell, the social worker, a twitchy woman in a brown linen trouser suit and a necklace made of buttons, who mumbled a 'hello' and, when she sat again, took the opportunity to draw her chair a few inches further away from Caitlin.

The solicitor – Ms Kelso – reminded Zigic that he was dealing with a minor. Made her demands clear regarding meals and comfort breaks and suggested he didn't try 'any funny business'.

He sat down opposite her and stared intently at Caitlin as Ferreira started the recording, rattling through the necessities, eager to get down to it.

'You understand why you're here, Caitlin?'

She nodded. 'Because of Dawn.'

'You've been charged with her murder.'

'I didn't kill her.' Caitlin looked up. 'Nathan did, that's why he ran away. Dawn saw him touching up Holly. She was going to tell Julia. He told me so.' She frowned. 'He didn't mean to do it. He was just scared of getting in trouble.'

Ferreira shook her head. 'No, he didn't. That's quite some story, though. And you did a fairly good job of implicating him for a while. Was that always your plan or did you only decide to do it after he ran off?'

'I didn't.' Caitlin glared at her.

'You were thinking on your feet, I reckon,' Ferreira said. 'That's why you went back and got the knife. You saw the opportunity to tie Nathan to Dawn's murder and you took it. Seriously, wrapping the murder weapon up in one of his jumpers . . . that was inspired.' A glimmer of pride sparked briefly in her eyes, a physical admission if not a verbal one. 'He was right about you, Caitlin. You're very clever.'

'Can you actually prove she did that?' Ms Kelso said.

'We have ample evidence of Caitlin's guilt,' Ferreira told her, keeping her gaze on the girl. 'More than enough to secure a conviction.'

No sign of fear.

She looked indifferent to the situation, almost bored, and Ferreira realised it was perhaps resignation, the same as she'd seen when the uniforms handcuffed her and put her into the back of the patrol car. All her anger had been spent on Julia.

'More than enough evidence to charge her with the assault on Julia Campbell too,' Ferreira said. 'And her unborn baby.'

'What?' Caitlin's hands went to her mouth. 'I never—'

'Oh, yes you did,' Ferreira told her. 'You attacked her and now she's going to lose the baby.'

Caitlin turned to her solicitor. 'But I never meant to hurt her.'

'We were there,' Zigic said darkly. 'You were furious with her and you lashed out. You didn't care what happened to her or the baby.'

Ms Kelso tapped the table lightly. 'For now let's stick to the matter in hand, shall we?'

'You lost it. Didn't you, Caitlin?'

'Inspector—'

'You lost your temper with Julia and now her baby's going to die.'

Under the table Ferreira nudged his leg, reminding him of their plan, but his full attention was fixed on Caitlin as she muttered denials, saying she hardly touched her, that it was an accident, she didn't mean to hurt her, she wouldn't hurt the baby.

'Is that what happened with Dawn?' he asked. 'An accident?'

She went on as if she hadn't heard him, talking in an unbroken stream, looking through the tabletop. 'Julia was pushing me around. You never saw that. She started the whole thing. It's not my fault she fell over, is it? You can't make out I did something I never. She's old, that's why she lost the baby. Old women shouldn't get pregnant. That's her fault. Not mine. I can't—'

'We know you killed Dawn,' Zigic said. 'You're going to be prosecuted and you'll be found guilty because there's no room for interpretation in the evidence.' His voice was pitched low and Ferreira knew he was struggling to keep that steady tone. 'We don't even need to question you, this is a courtesy, it's your chance to explain why you did it.'

Caitlin was shivering inside the baggy cardigan she'd drawn around herself, the reality of the situation hitting her all at once.

'I don't think you meant to hurt Dawn,' Zigic said, opening the file and extracting the post-mortem photos. He spread them across the table as he found the one he wanted, a headless shot, Dawn's bloated and degraded torso captured under the bright lights of the morgue, hyper-real and saturated with colours that didn't belong on human skin, every stab wound clear and distinct. 'These weren't the actions of a rational person. You were furious with her.'

A small murmur escaped Caitlin's lips as she stared at the image.

'What did she do to you?'

No answer.

'Did she start the argument?'

Susan Russell leaned forwards, staring at Caitlin, desperate for some reason, anything to explain the photographs she was studiously avoiding looking at.

'She was your friend, wasn't she?'

Caitlin blinked rapidly through her fringe.

'Dawn welcomed you into her home, treated you like family . . .'

Her fingers dug into her sides, handfuls of thick cotton cable-knit bunching into her hands.

'Families aren't always happy though, are they, Caitlin?' Still no answer. 'They have their ups and downs. They argue. Fight.'

The social worker's mouth opened, but she closed it again fast. A woman used to voicing whatever came into her head, Ferreira thought. She knew something but she couldn't say it here, not when she was serving as Caitlin's 'responsible adult'. There to look out for her interests.

'The night you murdered Dawn you'd argued with Julia, hadn't you?'

Caitlin glared at him but wouldn't answer.

'Matthew told us all about it,' Zigic said. 'You were happy living with them. They're good people. But then Julia falls pregnant and just like that, you're out.'

She pressed her mouth into a hard line.

'You were angry with them.'

'Julia promised me,' Caitlin said, voice quiet but thick with emotion as she spoke Julia's name.

'Promised what?'

'First day I got there she promised they'd look after me as long as I needed them. She's a liar.' Her nostrils flared. 'They're all the same. Say they care but they don't. It's all about the money. That's why they do it.'

'I can see why you'd be angry,' Zigic said, returning to his usual role, the sympathetic ear. 'You were upset but Julia wouldn't listen. She was more interested in going out to her book club. What about Matthew?'

'He does what she tells him.'

'So you went to Dawn for sympathy?'

Caitlin's fingertips pushed holes through the fabric of her cardigan.

'Wasn't she interested?' Ferreira asked.

The colour rose in Caitlin's ashen cheeks.

'No, Dawn cared about you, didn't she?' Zigic said. 'All that time you spent together . . . she liked you. More than she liked Holly, maybe.'

'Who told you she said that?'

'It's obvious, the way she was with you. You two were really close, weren't you?'

'She should have been my mum.' A brief tremble rippled her bottom lip. 'I wanted her to be.'

'Because you were going to have to leave Julia and Matthew's?'

'Yeah.'

'Did you tell Dawn how upset you were about that?'

'She didn't think it was right. I told her what was going to happen to me. *She* was going to dump me in a home.' Caitlin turned on Susan Russell. 'Then you were going to send me to live with some other family who wouldn't want me either. You don't care where I end up, do you?'

Susan Russell stammered out a few low words, about the people who were set to take her in and how nice they were, how many other children they'd looked after, but Caitlin wasn't paying any attention. Her eyes were focused on the space above the table, teeth worrying at her bottom lip.

'It would've been perfect. Me and Dawn.' She smiled but it didn't last. 'She was always saying how great it'd be if I lived there with her. I was the kind of daughter she always wanted. Not Holly. They never liked each other – even before Holly got hurt, they weren't close like we were.'

Caitlin sounded like a spurned lover, building up Dawn's throw-away comments and basic kindnesses into a closeness Ferreira doubted the woman had ever truly felt. But she'd said those things to the wrong person, a desperately lonely girl, about to be turned out from the only security she'd known for years; toyed with her emotions without even realising she was doing it.

'Dawn should have been my mum.'

'Did you ask her to take you in?' Zigic asked.

'I told her social services would pay,' Caitlin said, voice trembling, edged with desperation. 'She's got money problems, like big money problems. Her husband weren't paying for Holly and she weren't getting enough benefits. It would've worked out perfect for all of us.' She huffed out a fast breath through her nose, frustrated, indignant. 'I don't know why she couldn't get that. I told her how it works but she wouldn't do it.'

'Maybe she didn't feel up to looking after you as well as Holly?'

'I'm not a kid,' Caitlin snapped. 'I don't need *looking after*. I told her I'd help with Holly. She'd have been like my sister, right? Course I'd help.'

There was an air of desperation around Caitlin now and Ferreira imagined this was how it must have gone with Dawn. Every gentle let-down she used meeting another layer of resistance, Caitlin prepared to say anything and promise anything to try and convince her that this brilliant idea she had could work. Zigic was playing her perfectly.

'I begged her to let me move in, I swore I wouldn't be any trouble.' She looked down at the photograph, the stabs wounds cut into rotting flesh, blinked once, very slowly, and shook her head. 'She knew I didn't have anywhere else to go. She knew what they'd – what happened to me – and she didn't care. All she cared about was Holly.'

'Surely you understood that,' Zigic said. 'She had to put her daughter first.'

'Holly didn't love her. She didn't even *like* her.' Caitlin glared at him. 'Holly wanted to die. I told her, how long do you think she'll be around for? She don't even love you enough to want to stay alive. She'd rather be *dead* than keep putting up with you.'

The vehemence of her words sat him back in his chair.

She touched two fingertips to the edge of the glossy paper. 'Dawn totally lost it. She started screaming at me to get out, shoving me about. There was a knife on the side and I picked it up and just, kind of, I dunno – cut her. She grabbed me and pulled me down with her and I just wanted her to let go so I stabbed her.' Her fingers slipped away from the photo. 'I didn't know I'd fucked her up that much.'

Susan Russell's hand was at her throat, body rigid with the horror of it all. On the other side of Caitlin Ms Kelso had leaned back in her chair, nothing to do now the confession was in place.

'What about Holly?' Zigic asked. 'You knew what would happen to her without Dawn to take care of her. Why didn't you call an ambulance?'

'I thought she'd be okay,' Caitlin said. 'She had a nurse go and clean her up every morning. It's not my fault she didn't turn up, is it? She's the one you should be blaming for that.'

The statement fell like a chill across the room and Ferreira saw that she felt no guilt, not a shred of it showing on her face, nothing in her eyes but a hint of challenge. Zigic wasn't finished with her, though.

'No, Caitlin, this is on you. You went back to the house on Saturday. You knew the nurse hadn't been or Dawn wouldn't still be lying dead on the floor for you to remove the knife you left in her chest.' He snapped out the words, fury on full display now he had the confession they wanted. No reason to play the nice guy any longer. 'Did you go to check on Holly?'

'No,' she said.

'How long did you think she'd last without medical attention?'

One corner of her mouth flicked up into a contemptuous half-smile. 'Dawn always said she were stronger than she looked. Guess she were wrong.'

'You could have saved her,' he said, hand jabbing the air in front of her face. 'But you didn't. You murdered Holly just as sure as you murdered Dawn.'

Caitlin shrugged, unmoved by his anger and the accusation he spat across the table. 'Holly wanted to die. What's the problem?'

Epilogue

Now that the nursery's final coat of paint was on Zigic had to admit the pink *was* rather strong. More Pepto-Bismol than sugared almond, but he blamed it on the afternoon sun streaming in, a blazing autumn sunset which lit the walls and burnished the coppery tops of the beech trees he could see through the window as he sat on the newly laid carpet, inhaling the faint fumes coming off it. Or maybe it was what the fitters used to stick it down.

This whole DIY, building, fitting, handyman thing was beyond him.

There were services you could call, men in white vans and tool belts who came around and whistled between their teeth as they looked at your botched efforts and discreetly assayed the contents of the house, deciding how much they could charge. He would have happily turned over a week's pay to escape the boxes of flat pack and the challenge they presented, outdated concepts of machismo and threats to his manual prowess be damned.

Anna would never let him hear the end of it, though. She'd joke about how her clever detective husband who spent his days taking apart murders and putting them back together had been defeated by the instructions for a cot.

She'd been subtly pushing him towards the job for weeks, accepting his excuses with an ever-decreasing amount of grace. He couldn't tell her why he didn't want to do it – the real reason, not this boring frustration with nuts and bolts. The truth was that he didn't want to be here, among things for the baby, while the thought of Julia Campbell's daughter still guilted him.

It felt wrong even considering the preparations for the arrival of his little girl while hers was in an incubator at City Hospital, twelve weeks premature and fighting against the injuries her impossibly small and vulnerable body had sustained when Julia's belly struck the kitchen table. She went into labour in the ambulance as it whisked her away from her house, delivered the baby shortly after arriving at the hospital, and nobody expected her to survive.

Zigic had called at regular intervals for updates, ostensibly in an official capacity; the officer in charge of her assault was CID but nobody on the special-care ward questioned his interest and they informed him of each incremental improvement as the days and weeks passed, the setbacks and recoveries, told him Julia was there every day, waiting and praying from a chair next to the incubator, suggested he stop by and see her.

He couldn't bring himself to go and intrude on her vigil, but the longer it went on the more the nurses pushed and when he mentioned it to Anna she told him to go, his feelings weren't the important ones, he should go and show support.

Yesterday he went. Took flowers a nurse relieved him of as he entered the ward, explaining that it was unwise to have them in the room, a teddy bear with a pink bow around its neck and a tin of apple cinnamon muffins Anna had baked.

Julia was dozing in the chair when he walked in and for a second he considered backing away, sure she wouldn't want to be reminded of the violence which had placed her baby in that plastic box, but she heard him put the tin down and opened her eyes. He didn't expect a warm reception, didn't think he deserved one. But she was too tired for rage or recriminations, stood up and stretched, then asked what he'd brought her.

She'd lost weight in her face, looked gaunt and unkempt, and he wondered how often she was going home, if she was managing to eat anything more substantial than whatever she was buying from the hospital cafeteria. In her situation he wouldn't want to leave, not for more than a few minutes at a time.

Their conversation was stilted; he asked how the baby was and heaved a silent sigh of relief when she told him Esme – one of the names Anna was considering too – would hopefully be going home in a couple of weeks. When he enquired after Matthew she told Zigic he would be there be later, had just gone home for a few hours' sleep. He couldn't help but wonder if Matthew's resentment towards the baby, his annoyance at how it would change his life, had been forgotten in the stress and upset, hoped the man saw what a gift he'd been given in this little girl.

He had no intention of mentioning Caitlin but Julia wanted to know what had happened.

Zigic explained it all in a quiet voice, kept it as simple and bland as he could. He told her why she'd killed Dawn and how she'd been in court this week, pleaded guilty with the minimum of fuss. She would go to prison, likely be given a life sentence, and that seemed to satisfy Julia.

Nathan was where her real interest lay, though.

Those questions he couldn't answer and he was surprised that Rachel Baxter hadn't done Julia the courtesy of calling. Like her, he'd tried to make contact, and got an automated message telling him Rachel's mobile number was no longer in service. He could have tried to track her down at whatever station she was serving out of, took a big breath and approached her boss, ACC Fallon, but he wanted done with the whole sorry business and decided to let it lie.

Julia wasn't quite so resigned. She'd lost one foster child to prison, she didn't want to lose Nathan too.

As he left Zigic promised her he'd try to find out how the boy was doing now.

In the car park he made some calls, got a number for Fallon and tapped it in before he could think better of it. Saturday morning, he didn't expect an answer and was predictably put straight through to voicemail. He left an apologetic message, hated the wheedling sound of his voice and quickly deleted it. Tried again. Asked for an update on Nathan, explained that his foster mother was unwell and it would be beneficial to her recovery to know how he was faring.

It would be Monday at the earliest he'd hear back. If Fallon bothered at all. Big man like that, political beast, Zigic could see him ignoring it.

People like Rachel and Fallon made him question if he was cut out for policing. Could he have made the decisions they had? he wondered, as he tried to sort the parts of the cot into some sensible order, leaned the bars against the wall, put the screws and dowels into piles; the pieces of the main frame all in front of him now and he could see how they should fit together at least.

Not bad, it had only taken him half an hour.

He looked over the instructions, an exploded diagram that was somehow sinister; he didn't want to think of a cot exploding. He took a mouthful of beer from the bottle of Peroni Anna had brought up, still cold but almost empty; he knew he shouldn't have another when there was machinery to operate, a wasp-coloured electric drill his father-in-law had bought him last Christmas for some reason known only to himself.

How tough could this be? People put cots together every day.

He'd put together the first one they bought, the one Milan and then Stefan slept in, but he'd blotted out the memory of constructing it. Too many beers that time, perhaps, or maybe it was such a total nightmare his brain had insulated him against it.

The music coming out of the dock on the windowsill paused as his phone rang and he climbed to his feet to answer it, an unfamiliar mobile number on the screen.

'Zigic.'

'It's Rachel. You shouldn't be hassling Fallon.'

A Sunday afternoon and still she managed to sound as if the entire world was lined up against her. Was she calling from home, her kids in another room, partner crashed out on the sofa watching the football?

'I'm just trying to find out what's happened to Nathan,' he said. 'Julia's got enough problems right now without having to worry about him too.'

'Caitlin, yeah? I saw that.' A sliding door opened at her end, then there was lawnmower noise. 'You never did thank me for her file.'

'Thank you.'

'Least I could do,' she said. 'Hit Julia pretty hard, I take it?'

Her turn of phrase made him wince. He explained what had happened and Rachel swore vehemently. Hastily she covered the microphone and he half-heard her apologising to someone at the other end, using an altogether sweeter voice.

'So it would be nice to give her some good news about Nathan,' he said, when he had her full attention again.

'He was very brave,' Rachel said. 'Make sure you tell her that.'

Zigic groaned. 'They got to him?'

'No, no, he's fine. He's back with his nan now – he's doing good, all things considered.'

'Did he give evidence?'

'Yeah, last week. Stellar performance, even from behind a screen. I could see the jury turning one by one, it was perfect. Ninety-minute deliberation and bang, guilty verdict.'

Zigic snatched up his beer from the floor. 'Big pat on the back for you then.'

'Don't come the sanctimony with me,' she snapped. 'His mother deserved justice and she got it.'

'And you got your conviction and your informer-in-waiting right where you want him.'

'It's what I do,' she said.

'Meanwhile Nathan's back at his nan's house, waiting for the reprisals to start. Totally unprotected.'

'There won't be any reprisals.'

'You wouldn't care if there were.'

'You don't fucking know me.' Lowered voice now, harder tone. 'Someone has to make the tough decisions.'

'Leaving people like Nathan to live with the consequences.'

'What do you suggest?' she asked.

'Witness protection.'

'Wow, I hadn't thought of that.' She swore again. 'We offered, okay? In fact we strongly advised it, but his nan won't move. She's lived on the estate all her life and she won't be forced out of her home. Frankly I think she's being stupid and selfish but she's his legal guardian.'

Rachel sounded genuinely frustrated but he wasn't sure he believed her.

'What about Nathan, what does he want?'

She sighed. 'He's not going to leave her and go to some strange family, Dushan. She's all he's got now.'

There was nothing more to say, so he thanked her and ended the call, slotted the phone back onto the dock and let the music wash over him for a few seconds, draining the rest of his beer. He thought of Nathan growing up on some dangerous and dismal housing estate, all unlit alleyways and busted CCTV cameras, the kind of place it was easy to kill someone and get away with it, where witnesses knew better than to come forward. Especially if you'd given evidence against a high-ranking member of a local crime family.

Nathan didn't stand a chance.

He took his phone up again.

Get it over and done with. Waiting wouldn't make it any easier.

Julia answered on the third ring.

'Have you got news? Is he okay?'

'Yes, he's fine. I've just spoken to Rachel. She said to tell you he's been really brave. In court, he gave evidence. It's over now.'

'Oh, thank God,' she said, and he could hear the smile in her voice as it brightened with relief. 'Where is he? Will I be able to visit him? Or maybe he'd like to come down here for a few days. I'd love for him to meet Esme, he was so excited about her.'

Zigic closed his eyes. 'I don't think that'll be possible. Sorry. Rachel's arranged for him and his grandmother to go into witness protection, she's sorting out new identities for them, a new home. After he gave evidence it was really the only way to keep them both safe.'

'Oh.'

'You understand, don't you? It had to be done.'

'Yes, I see. I knew it was a possibility,' she said. 'At least he's safe. That's all that matters.'

They said their goodbyes and he hoped that she believed him enough to put the fear and stress aside and concentrate on her own child now.

Through the nursery window he could see Milan and Stefan running around in the garden, chasing through the bedding Anna had hung out to dry in the last of the afternoon sun, shouting and laughing as they slipped in and out of the sheets, trying to make each other jump. Stefan crept along to the end of the line, stealthy as a cat, and came up inside a white duvet cover, believing he was hidden with just his legs sticking out. Milan shook his head at the childish naivety and Zigic couldn't help but smile.

Anna appeared at the door.

'I'm going to have to call Dad to do this, aren't I?'

Zigic gave her a wounded look. 'That is low. Really.'

'Aw, he'd love to come and help you.' She grinned, an evil twinkle in her eye. 'Share some male-bonding time.'

'I'll do it. Even if I have to stay up all night and call in sick tomorrow. This cot is getting built.'

'Do you want me to assist?'

'Definitely.'

Acknowledgements

Huge thanks, as always, to my marvellous editor Alison Hennessey for her patience, guidance and unwavering positivity. Thanks also to the whole team at Harvill Secker and Vintage who have tirelessly worked to bring my books onto the shelves and into the hands of readers. Áine, Bethan, Vicki, Maria – you ladies are the best! Special mention as well to Fiona Murphy for her expert shepherding into the author-life.

Thanks to my agent, Stan, for doing all that stuff that agents do and writers try not to think about.

The crime-writing scene contains some of the warmest, loveliest people you could ever hope to meet and has been a huge source of support and advice throughout the writing of this, and earlier, books, as well as being fabulous company anywhere you'll find a bar. Particular thanks this time around to Col Bury, K.A. Richardson and Emma Kavanagh, who saved me from some potentially embarrassing procedural slip ups. Any mistakes made are, of course, my own. And to Luca Veste and Nick Quantrill for always talking sense.

Thanks also to all the reviewers and bloggers who have supported the series as it's grown and to the festival organisers who have let me loose on their stages. Far too many to mention by name but gushing appreciation especially to Crime Fiction Lover, Crime Squad and the team at Dead Good Books, as well as the lovely folks at Bloody Scotland and Newcastle Noir. Writing can be a hard graft and you provide much needed spots of brightness.

Finally, eternal gratitude to my family for going above and beyond the call of duty. Boozy lunches, NSFW inspirational posters, emergency cake, non-emergency cake, some genius suggestions and more than a few outlandish ones; they do it all. I love you guys.